Bloodlust

Book 2 of The Blood of the Fae

Abby Moore

Trigger Warnings

This book is an action-packed romantic fantasy novel. Some scenes in this story are dark and could cause distress. There are mentions of miscarriage, blood, death, and gore. There are sexual situations as well as dark scenes that describe torture. Please read with care, and do not pass over the trigger warnings. This is a dark romantasy.

<u>**The Blood of the Fae Series**</u>

Bloodworthy

Bloodlust

<u>**The Dance of Serpents and Men Series**</u>

Vipers Den

Contents

Trals
Clove
Palace
Garden
Hollow
Clem
Croke
Rawgabbit
Snolly
Middle
Brabble
Town
Darnish
Langford
Serena
Saxton
Grove
Earsgorg

I have never believed in myself; I have never felt like I was good enough. Here is to everybody who feels the same. Do not allow those untrue feelings to halt your dreams. You can do whatever you set your mind to.

Thank you, Mom and Dad. I couldn't have done this without you. I love you.

Chapter 1

It has been six long weeks without my powers. It has been six weeks in a world where my father no longer breathes, the man who taught me everything about life. The man who wasn't really my father, but in every way that mattered...was. He taught me control, he taught me patience, he taught me how to live in a kingdom that hated me. He was there for me when I had nobody else. It has also been six weeks without my Sailor. Life keeps going, but I feel as if I have stopped living. I feel as though breathing isn't enough to keep me alive any longer. I may as well be dead.

I no longer feel like myself. I do not understand how I have gotten myself into this situation. Once upon a time, I was a little girl who only wanted a cabin next door to her father. I was a little girl who wanted nothing more than a life where I didn't have to hide who and what I was. I wanted to be accepted, loved, and seen for who I am. I never wanted *this*.

I am no longer a little girl; I am a queen in my own birthright. I am mated to the king, a male whom I have sworn to one day kill. A male who has forced me into a marriage I do not want. A marriage that got me a second kingdom, one I will gladly steal from him. But I no longer have the man I truly desire. I am utterly alone in this gilded cage. I have nothing to show for my time in the palace these last few weeks. I have become a hollow version of myself, and I do not wish to be weak any longer. I do not want to sit here in self-pity; I just hadn't anticipated my heart to break like it did. I didn't think watching my only two family members sail off with the love of my life would kill me, but somewhere on that hilltop, my soul lies waiting. Waiting for them to come home to a safe kingdom in which King Alwin is dead, and I am the only ruler. A kingdom where we are rebuilding everything for the people who have suffered for far too long.

My thumb runs softly over my wrist, just once. A small comfort. The only comfort I have allowed myself to have. I now have two kingdoms resting on my shoulders, and I have only just begun my life.

"Majesty?"

I swallow down my fears of failure and blink several times before running my fingers through my unbrushed hair. "Yes, Millie?" I look at my friend. Her new leg looks as good as her real one once did.

"The girl who was your brother's future wife has not been found yet. What do you wish to do?"

I wipe the sleep from my eyes; it seems all I do now is sleep. I wake up from my sleep with nightmares, only to realize I have woken into another darker nightmare—my life.

I am now the king's weapon; the one thing I never wanted to happen has happened. My father died, I lost Sailor, Wolf isn't himself, and the king won. He held trials, and in winning I failed miserably. I fell into the trap he laid for me.

Millie snaps her fingers in my face. "Highness?"

I huff out a long, tired breath. "We have talked about this, Millie. You do not call me that. My name is Serena." I sigh tirelessly and look into the tempered glass, staring back at a girl who once was me.

"I'm sorry, Serena. It's just..." She shakes her head, as if reliving her own nightmares. "I owe you my life," Millie finishes quickly.

I look away from the fae staring back at me in the mirror, remembering the life I lost, the human part of me. I killed my mother and sister because of my power. I clench my fist tightly and I grind my teeth, pulling myself up from where I had been lying. It's time to embrace the future I must claim as my own. "You owe me nothing; I did nothing more than any decent person would. Not yet have I made the difference I need to." I run my fingers over the necklace that took everything from me.

I am no longer a little girl who fears the king. The fae prince who has promised to return us to our homeland, where there is war on the very land that gives power and life. The land in which my true mother wanted me to rule. She just didn't know I would stand next to her killer, the prince who had followed her here, to the land where the Gods favored humans. The prince whose parents overran mine. They will die for the lives they have taken. I must first save the humans from my husband, then find my way home. I have to stop a war that changed my life before I was even born. "Should be easy," I mumble with a laugh.

"Huh?" Millie asks, confusion written all over her pretty face.

"Nothing, I'm sorry. What were you saying?" I may not have powers right now, but I can feel how annoyed she is with me.

"I was telling you that you should stop in Darnish during the tour. You could find the girl yourself, for your brother." Her tone is laced with annoyance and I wince, as if she has struck me.

"I haven't been back there since..." I trail off. The memories are more painful now than they were when it first happened.

"I know, I'm sorry. You'll have to go there no matter what. May as well make the trip worth it," she chirps. Her face crunches with concern for me when she notices I do not share her hopefulness.

I no longer have Sailor. He has pieces of me, my entire heart, even. He always will. Sailor James. The blond-haired commander who is no longer a commander. His blue eyes once sparkled with unbridled amusement, but the last time I saw him, he wasn't the commander I had fallen for. He wasn't himself at all; he, too, died when I lost the trials. At least now that he is in Clove, he has a chance to start anew. He could live on, find somebody else.

I grip my chest, and I know my heart is bleeding out. I lost everything because of the male who thinks I am falling in love with him. I lost my other half, my family, my life. Everything is in shreds because of *him*.

"Tell the king I would like to see him." My tone has a bite to it.

Millie stands tall then. I see the reluctance in her gaze, but she does as I ask her. She always does, the ever-giving friend I do not deserve. I watch her throat bob as she swallows. "Alright, anything I should tell him you need?" Her voice is laced with concern. She doesn't ever pry outright, but I can sense her panic. I never ask to see *him*.

"Nope. Thank you," I state plainly. She reads her clear dismissal.

"I will let him know," Millie replies curtly. I simply nod, unable to form any type of response.

When she leaves, I spend my time awake looking at my wrist, to where I know my heart is inked onto my skin forever. My Sailor, and the stars that guide him back to my heart. One for each of my family members, and the waves that soothe me until our reunion. I half expect the need to go over the tattoo again, because I rub it endlessly.

Chapter 2

"Wife."

My feet don't slow down as they hit the dark marble floors that house more blood than I care to ever think about again.

"King." My voice is filled with venom.

Wolf and Magnolia stand side by side. My eyes don't travel to Wolf's, even when he begs me to. I won't listen. He is weak-minded, and I hate him for it. I had once valued him, even thought of him as my friend. He is a pawn in this game of life that the king is spinning. I won't play along with his toys.

"I told you to not call me that." His black hair is cropped shorter now; it was shoulder-length, but it isn't even past his pointed ears now.

"You are a king, are you not?" I retort.

"I am." He agrees with me more often than not; one might think he is scared of me. "I *am* scared of you, Serena," he says, plucking the thought right out of my mind with his power, responding to something that no one else heard. He takes a step towards me, and his black combat boots squeak on the polished marble floors. "I am scared *for* you, because I am scared you could end everything I have worked for."

All eyes wander to him. A king who admits he is scared of his queen? Not a smart male. He takes another step towards me, and I step back. This is our game, and he enjoys forcing me to play along.

His height is so staggering that the human men look like tiny boys next to him. His tanned hands grip my chin and force my eyes to stare into his black-and-blue swirls. They seem to whisper promises to me that I know he cannot ever deliver. I hear them sometimes in my sleep, as if he watches me and mumbles into my mind. I know a snake in the grass when I see one. He is watching for my guard to be down, but I won't let it fall.

"I am not a smart male," he says, reading my thoughts again. "Because if I were, I would've killed your two lovers, and used brute force to overrun all the villages that dare go against me." I try to look away, but his fingers tighten their grip on my face. "I would start a war with Clove, in which I know I would win with you by my side. Then I would take us home and stake our claim against our parents." The lies start to spew out now—the same story he has been telling me for weeks—so my ears turn off, and I start to daydream.

"Serena?"

I blink several times. "What, *King*?" I ask defiantly.

He clicks his tongue in irritation. "You are not listening to me. Again." His tone is reprimanding. He is right. More often than not, he is. The king reads me like the romance books I used to believe in. The books I thought my life would look like. I had no idea mine would turn into a dark romance. "I need you to listen to me for once. I am telling you important details about our trip. Could you act like you care for the people you claim to want to save?"

Sometimes, I imagine him as Aldrich again, the man he pretended to be before the trials. I can actually stand that sight. I know it sounds crazy, but with Aldrich, there was kindness. Aldrich cared about me. He liked me, even. Irritation draws my attention to the male who thinks he has claimed me.

"I do care about my people. I want them all safe from *you*," I say with a growl, and the guards take a step towards me. Not for the first time. My eyes never leave the king. He is the only threat I see.

"She is fine," the king assures his men.

I strike him, a move that I have mastered without my powers. "I want my power back," I yell, as I hit him again.

"I know." His eyes melt into navy blue, and I hit him again. His chest is solid rock. That makes me even more mad.

"I want Sailor." I throw insult after insult his way, but he never strikes me back.

"King?" one of the guards asks when I land a slap to my husband's face. My hand leaves a burning red mark against his perfectly smooth, tan cheek.

"I am fine," he hisses. The red handprint causes a smile to light my face, the first one in a long while. He smiles back at me then.

"What?" I ask, unsure why he is smiling at me while I am trying to kill him.

"You will not kill me by slapping me, wife."

I roll my eyes. "Why are you smiling at me like that?" My anger is boiling over again. I had a plan during the trials. He ruined it. He ruined my life; he is supposed to be dead.

"Because, when you smile at me like that, you look beyond this world, beyond my grasp. You, Serena darling, are everything I have ever wanted."

I punch him, a dark chuckle rolling from my lips when his lip splits. "I may be your wife, your mate, whatever you want to claim, but my heart does not, and *will not*, ever belong to you, *King*." I spit the last word with as much hate as I can muster Then, I turn on my heels to get away from the vile creature I have attached myself to.

My strides from the throne room are sure and strong. Even without my power, I am a force to be reckoned with. I am powerful without the gifts from the land or the Gods, The Gods who have abandoned us. But I will not abandon my people. The powers they had once gifted us with are waning. More and more people are born without any at all. The Gods have forsaken us. Whoever thinks they can decide my future is wrong. I do not answer to the Gods, I do not belong to lands, and I, Serena Bloodworthy, will not be held down by a male who thinks I am his.

"You lasted way longer this time with him," Barnett says in a cheerful voice, his golden ginger hair shining. I kick some dirt that the gardeners will have to fix.

"How long?" I ask without really caring.

"Ten minutes. It's a record." He gives me a sad excuse for a smile.

I grab a pink flower from the bush, the thorns poking my fingers and causing blood to pool. "Are you alright?" Barnett rushes over.

"Yes, of course. It's a minor scratch. I want the information I asked you for." Barnett knows me now; he understands that I don't beat around the bush.

"I haven't found any evidence of them being alive."

My heart pounds, I need good news. I need good news more than I need oxygen. "Does that mean they are dead?" I suck the blood into my mouth, trying to stop it.

He chews on his lip, obviously not wanting to give me any bad news. I haven't handled it well in the recent past. "I have no idea, but I will continue to investigate it. I promise if I hear anything, I will tell you."

"Thank you," I respond simply. Barnett is a good friend. The best. He helped me during the days I didn't feel like I was worth saving. The weeks after I sent my family away were a dark place for me. I had every intention of being brave, strong, and fierce. That didn't happen, though.

"Have you and him..." He asks shyly.

I know what he's asking before he can even voice the rest. "No." My response is immediate and sharp. I don't mean for it to be, but this topic is a sensitive one for me. "We have not," I say to make certain Barnett knows.

The sunlight dwindles, causing the sky to melt into rays of pinks and yellows. The colors blend so beautifully, I can't help but wonder if my father is looking down on me in his afterlife.

"I'm glad." Barnett's voice startles me from my thoughts.

"Me too... He had said it would be a nightly thing." I grimace thinking of our *time* together. "But after dinner, he usually makes an excuse to go elsewhere."

I can't blame him. The first day after my family left, the Fae priest sat us down and told us what we needed to do in order to secure our homelands. I wasn't responsive. Even still, I don't like to think of having to earn my land from the thieves who stole it in the night. My fists clench, my knuckles turning white.

"You good?" Barnett's voice is wary; he knows not to bother me when I get into these moods.

"Yes." I chew on my lower lip, deciding I need a change of scenery. I steer us towards the cabin I go to daily.

"The King won't like this," Barnett says warily from behind me.

"I don't care. I *haven't* cared. And even if I did, it wouldn't stop me." I march my way towards the last reminder of who I was before, who I became this monster for—my kingdom. Not just one but both of them. I must become stronger than ever, for my people and my other half—Sailor James.

Chapter 3

I fall asleep in the comforting, warm quilts Sailor left behind. His scent is embedded within the very fabric, weaving the thread together. As he has done for me, he wove me into the female I am, and I will rule my people the way he would want me to.

A push to my side causes my hands to flex, as if flames would come to them. My embers are gone, in more ways than just my power, something I still struggle to believe. My heart feels desolate and cracked wide open.

"Serena." A deep growl echoes in my ears, one that my body responds to before my mind does. My legs kick out at him, but he doesn't stumble. "You cannot harm me, darling." The king holds tight around my ankle.

"Let me go." I twist my leg from his tight grip.

"If you beg me," he taunts in a playful voice.

I try to kick against his firm chest. He still does not move, and my foot meets solid muscle. "I will never beg you for anything," I declare, even though I can taste the lie for what it is. I *would* beg him, I *need* him even. He may have taken everything from me, but he is also my only way to everything else I want. Minus Sailor James.

"Coming to bed, wife?" Black swirls are alive in his navy-blue eyes. The color causes shivers to skate down my spine, his eyes change often and I still haven't gotten used to it.

"I *am* in bed." I stand up, needing to pee.

"Not in mine, where you belong." He follows me to the doorframe of the bathing chamber in Sailor's old cottage.

"I don't belong anywhere with you, least of all your bed," I say as I slam the door in his face.

"You missed dinner again." The second I've reopened the door, I am immediately faced with the male who claims to be my mate.

"Give a girl some space, will ya?" I hold my hand up in his face. His eyes turn pure black right before me. The change would make others back down, but I puff my chest right into his.

"Will this become our new foreplay then? You challenge me, I fight back?" he dares me. Mischief dances in his eyes, as if saying he doesn't mind that challenge. Maybe he enjoys the fight. "Is this the marriage—the bond—you wish for?" he asks me.

Yes, I think to myself, as I walk away from the male who tests my patience every day.

"No. I do not wish for a lifetime of fighting with you. I do not want a lifetime with you at all." The Gods are sick bastards, I think to myself as I walk away from him.

"Well, the Fates would say something different, my *mate*."

The Gods or Fates have a say over everything in my life, it would seem. "I think the Gods are wrong," I say bluntly.

The king rushes to me in half a second. His quickness still startles me; even when I had power, I was never that fast. His fingers grip both sides of my face, firm, but somehow also tender.

"They are not wrong," he sneers. His eyes look right into my very soul. "You are mine. Can you really not feel it?" He shakes his head in disbelief. "Is that...*fear* I smell?" His nostrils flare as the words leave his mouth. I keep my mouth shut. "Do you worry that the Gods did in fact pair us as one because we are meant for one another?"

I haven't thought of that. I *don't* think that. My heart is Sailor's. It will always belong to him. "Never has that thought crossed my mind." My voice doesn't waver.

He swallows whatever else he was going to say to me. "Let's go eat. I didn't eat when everybody else did, I was worried about you. We need to discuss our plans for the villages. Can you sit through a meal with me?" he calls over his shoulder as he exits the cabin, descending the stairs. I follow him, even though I wish I didn't have to. Unfortunately, my life will forever be intertwined with his.

"I will sit through anything for my people." My voice is more hushed than I would have liked.

That statement couldn't be truer than it is right in this moment. I sit at a long, white oak table, opposite the king. Magnolia sits next to Wolf, alongside several royal advisors who I have never seen before, as well as a priest for the humans, and the fae one who bonded me and the king.

"My King, I think going to Saxton is okay, but the uprisings in Mickle are getting out of hand. The commanders are out of their depths," the advisor I have nicknamed *Crook* says. He talks fast and often spits his food out when he speaks.

"I can help." Wolf's voice causes my eyes to scan him, the shell of a man I once knew.

"How could you help them, Wolf?" I ask sarcastically, rolling my eyes.

Magnolia slams her hands on the table. "Serena." Her voice is reprimanding.

"'Queen' to you, actually," I say on a giggle. My eyes never leave Wolf's. I play this game with him; it is a game wolves play. Who is the alpha here?

"Or maybe, 'Majesty, Queen Serena Henry,'" the king corrects.

I should be happy he stands up for me every time Magnolia speaks against me or challenges me. I am not, though. I hate him more for it.

"I can speak for myself, and my last name is Bloodworthy." I blink several times at Wolf. "I am your queen, and I expect a response, Sylas Wolfgang. What would you do exactly?" My voice isn't my own. I don't recognize myself most days.

"I am still a commander."

His weak defense causes me to laugh, and all eyes at the table slither my way. Every person sitting here is a viper; they don't care about me. They care about the heirs I will not produce for them or their king.

"Do you disagree, Serena?" Wolf asks me, seeming unsure if he should address me.

"I don't know...Am I speaking to Commander Wolf or brainwashed Sylas?" I slam my hands on the table, standing while clearing the spit from my throat. "I do not see my friend— the man Sailor once called brother—or a man worthy of that title. If I am wrong, can anybody correct me?" I hum to myself, knowing damn well that none of them will challenge me with the fire dancing in the king's eyes.

I am the only one foolish enough to not fear him. I know deep down he will not ever truly harm me. That thought causes my feet to move away from the table and out of the room, because I hate myself for feeling that small comfort. For feeling as if I am safe with him. I shouldn't—I *know* I shouldn't—feel that way.

He lies to me, he tells me stories while I sleep. Stories of a tyrant queen his family had to overthrow. A king and queen who killed for more power, a queen who wanted more than she could have. I know he lies to me because the female who gave me my birthright has come to me as well. Anytime my blood father could hold the gates open, she came. She whispered things to me; everybody whispers things to me. The smart girl my father raised knows that a ruler will listen before speaking, so I do. I listen to everything and anybody. I hear gossip of rulers and leaders, of rivals and treaties. The one thing I actually want to hear about? That news never comes. No, the leaders of Clove have shut me out. I am completely torn from my Sailor. Still, I gather information, storing it for the right time.

I still do not understand the role I play in the Gods' game, but I know that queens do not bow to any. I know that I will shake the very heavens the Gods sit in for thinking they can play with what's mine. I know that when I finally stand up, I may not be the Darnish Serena, but I will fight for my people. And I know death will follow. Lives are expendable to the Gods, but in my kingdom, each and every one is worth its weight in coin.

I will fight for every Mrs. Benson, every Blossom, every life that has been stolen from this world. I will stand up taller than ever. Just as the thought hits me, and ruins the pep talk I give myself every day, I hear it. The footsteps I have learned deep in my soul. The hum of home, just not one I want to ever go to.

"King?" I can't keep this up, I must start playing politics. I am a queen, rightfully so, to two different kingdoms. They deserve the best version of me.

"Serena." His casual use of my name causes my fingers to flex. More this week than ever before, I have been itching to touch him. Since that afternoon he pretended to be Sailor, we have not once touched in an intimate way. I feel starved for attention now. I didn't ever need it before...but now? It feels like I need it to live. I find myself wanting him. I hate myself for the burning desire I feel for him. My inner feelings need to burn alongside him.

His black eyes turn navy. I haven't yet asked him why they so often change. I can't find it in me to voice my curiosity.

"Are you all right?" he asks, his eyes softer than they have been in a while. I hate it.

"Yes. Why are you out here?"

His stone-hard face gives way to a smirk. "Because, darling wife, you need to rest." He says this as if it explains why he is standing in the hallway instead of back with the others.

"And?" I bite my cheek, unsure of why he continues to be nice to me. I know someday soon the male I married will show me his true self.

"And you don't walk alone. Would you rather I get somebody else?" He looks around the empty hallways, making a show of it.

"I am more than capable of walking the stairs to my rooms."

His hands grace my neck with their touch, but I don't lean into him. "But then you will get lonely, My Queen."

I smirk at him out of habit, then wipe my face clean of any amusement. I know he saw it, though, judging by his own responding smile. He smiles often; I cannot stand it.

"I enjoy my own company more than any others. I entertain myself just fine."

His hand travels from my necklace to the back of my neck. I suck in a breath when his warm hand moves my hair to the side.

His mouth is so close to my ear, I swear he may bite it. "And do tell me. What kind of entertainment do you offer yourself?"

Lust spears into my body. I know he is sending the emotions my way, so I shove him hard, pushing my hair back to my shoulder.

"None of your business, King." I turn away from him, ready for this day to be over.

"I will see you for lunch tomorrow. Oh, and Serena?" I

I roll my eyes when I realize he will not stop until I have heard what he wants me to hear. I look back at him, once more. "Yes?" I ask, before turning on my heels to fully face him. Looking into his handsome face, I can't believe he is so evil. My head is completely craning due to his height.

"Tomorrow, no fits. We plan to discuss our wedding tour for the villages. We need to cement our reign here in order to have a firm grip in Mirahalm. We will need soldiers, so we will establish stability for our people before claiming our homeland. Together we can do it, but we must be truly together, Serena."

I know what he is saying—he wants babies. Not going to happen. Ever. Not with him, at least, maybe never with anyone. I have no idea of the future, I just know his evil genes will not be passed on through me.

"When will we leave?" I ask. Hollow will be the first village we see. I know that without having to speak to anybody tomorrow. They love Hollow; that village will offer up anybody to fight for the fae lands. Would the fae do the same for them? Clove sure hasn't.

"A week. We will discuss plans tomorrow."

I nod my head, but before I can turn around to head to my rooms, he stops me. His grip is gentle but controlling, a touch he must have practiced. He is not my friend, I must remind myself.

"Good night." His eyes are soft now, despite the color. I used to think that black was just one color, until I looked into the king's eyes. Now I realize that black is every color, yet still its own. Sometimes I wonder if that is how he is, maybe a little bit of everything—evil, good, strong, weak, powerful. He is an enigma; I do not like him. Yet, when his hand falls from my body, I mourn the loss of him.

Footsteps follow me to my room. I know without even looking that there is a guard behind me. There always is.

"Even without my powers, I know how to kill you in more ways than you could even dream of." I spin around to face my least favorite guard. "That is not what I would do, though, is it?" I taunt him. He pisses his brown pants. "No, I would disable you by paralyzing you from the waist down with a tonic. Then I would chop your dick off and feed it to the beasts of Brabble, even though they deserve a better meal than that."

I chuckle while he runs away. I should feel guilty, but I don't. He helped cause this mess, the least I can do is have some fun.

Chapter 4

"You had to threaten his balls?"

I groan, throwing a pillow at the king. "Yes, go away."

He chuckles while opening up my windows.

"*Don't...*" I moan. Mornings are awful for me. I very seldom sleep well anymore.

"It is time for lunch, and you would sleep better if you slept with me." He jerks the thick blanket from my body, and I immediately miss its warmth and yank it back.

"I wouldn't sleep with you if I were dead and there was only one grave to bury us both."

"Well, lucky for you, fae spirits can only be returned to our land once their bodies pass over."

I ignore his comment. I don't ever listen when he talks about "our land."

"Get up, we have much to do today. I do not want to drag you from your bed, but I will, princess."

Ouch. That nickname is for when he is mad at me but won't tell me as much.

"Upset, King?" I scoff before finally tossing the thick blanket from my suddenly all-too-aware body. Warm, tender feelings cascade into me, followed by disgust when I realize he is trying to make me happy. "I don't need you warming me up. I can be civil." I march my way to the armoire, grabbing an outfit my sister once made me wear—tight black pants, and a cream sweater that will cover my neck.

"It's hot out," the king deadpans.

"I feel chilly. Are you going to dictate what I wear now?"

I make my way to the bathing chamber, where the white stone tub calls to me. I don't answer the call. I no longer have time with the king standing guard outside my room. "Coming in or just creeping about?" I ask, more as a jab than a real question.

"No, I must get to the throne room. We have some issues to soothe over before our plans are cemented. Can you handle getting ready by yourself and meeting me in the war room in, say, an hour?"

I groan. "Yes, I can handle myself, Ald——I clear my throat. "King," I correct myself, hoping he didn't hear my mistake. Of course, he did hear it.

The smirk on his face could light up a dark cave. I want it off his handsome face. The dark chiseled scruff is now clean-shaven, maybe for our wedding tour. His navy-blue outfit looks fit for royalty, the gold accents making him look even more regal. I swear, if he weren't Fae, he would glow anyway. Our King was born to be a king. A tyrant, sure, but royal nonetheless.

"You may call me anything, so long as you are calling me something, Serena. I cannot go through your silence again."

That silence went on for all of two days; he has no idea how stubborn I can truly be.

"You need to get stronger skin if you are going to be married to me," I say curtly.

The king wears a smirk on his face every second we are together, as if it's his own gold-plated armor. "My skin is plenty thick, wife. I have lived through many lives to get to the one I will claim as mine." He says stuff like this often. He doesn't directly say it, but I get the feeling his parents made him into the monster he is today. It doesn't change my feelings for him, but it does make me realize I am losing time to work on strengthening my own powers for when I'll inevitably go up against them.

"I want my powers back," I mumble, more to myself than the king. I throw my sweater over my head, chasing him to the doorway that opens to his room.

"Not yet." His smile is strained, sad almost. It's forced and practiced.

"It's unnatural what you're doing to me," I say, and the dark swirls start up in his eyes again. Only black and white right now.

"I know." True sadness crosses his face before he makes his way into his own room.

My steps are rushed. I play this game every day.

"Slow down, Majesty."

Two steps at a time, three even. A giggle falls from my mouth; this is my fun, and I look forward to it daily.

"Can't keep up, Roman?"

The king has given me guards that I know, mostly; never Wolf, though. Thank the Blessed.

"I can, I just—" He takes flight and lands right in front of me, and I step backwards, backing myself into the last step I just jumped from.

"You cheated," I claim.

He shrugs his thick shoulders. "I don't want you getting hurt. You don't have your power to help you right now."

I flinch as if he has just struck me. He might as well have. "Yeah, thanks for the reminder, bud." My temper is rising to another level.

"I didn't mean you would never have them again—" I push right past him. "Serena. You can't go in there mad. We need to figure out what's going on in the villages." He owes me nothing, but I am still curious.

"Did you know?" To his credit, he doesn't back away from me. His hazel eyes flash with an emotion I cannot read, before somebody touches my shoulder.

Not *somebody*...Wolf.

"He did not know. It was kept from him. If you have questions, you may ask me."

I grab onto Wolf's hand, which still lies on my shoulder, take a deep breath, and then do what I have been wanting to do for over a month. I throw his entire body over my head, right into Roman.

"Majesty!"

I dust my hands off, then turn away from the men, who shouldn't be called men at all.

"I thought we agreed you wouldn't be mad today," Roman says from the ground.

"I am not angry. That was fun, Roman," I say over my shoulder, briefly hearing Wolf mumble something that sounds like, "I'm okay, don't worry."

My voice is cool and casual as I respond, "I didn't ask."

Roman makes it to my side before my hand lands on the large iron door handle. "I'm okay, Roman. I just don't like *him*." He puckers his lips, clearly wanting to say something, but doesn't have a chance before Wolf reaches between us and opens the door. "I was going to do that." I look right into his valley-green eyes. The color is startling now that it doesn't feel like home anymore. Unnatural, evil, and everything I want to burn down.

"You were just standing there, Serena. Let's go in so we can actually have a conversation. Think you can manage?"

I walk in without giving him an answer. Any answer that comes from me will be violence.

Chapter 5

"Majesty, if I may?" Magnolia stands, walking with a sway in her hips, red silk clinging to her curves. "I would stay away from here..." She approaches the map and points to the road that goes right by the sea. The pebbled pathway would be easiest if it weren't for Clove being right across the waters. "I think you should go inland as much as possible. I also believe Earsgorg would do well to see you two unified." There have been more uprisings in the last few weeks than ever.

"The journey, in total, should be about four weeks once you all start," the human priest says. "I would like to go with you. I think they need to see us all. We should also bring extra coin to give them." All heads nod when he says that. *Yeah, that should have happened long ago, Councilors.* "What do you think, Queen?" the priest asks, clearly noticing my irritation.

I purse my lips, standing and making a show of my slow walk. I am the only one not in formal wear. "I think the people deserve more than just seeing us and being handed coin." I run my fingers over the map of our home. The lands my mother thought would be safe.

"What would you suggest, then, Majesty?" the advisor who usually ogles my body speaks up.

"I would suggest spending more time actually getting to know their issues. Lower taxes while they adjust to life, help them rebuild after the uprisings."

Magnolia scoffs at my suggestions, but the king nods.

"Give them a reward for their outburst?" she says, shaking her head.

But the king replies, "We will look into it. Thank you, Serena, for the idea." He always listens to me; I grind my teeth.

"Of course. It really is a simple idea: Help them survive and they may actually like you...may even *follow* you." I don't pretend not to notice the way their eyes scan me over; they still view me as the Darnish scum they believe I once was.

"When will you leave for Hollow?" the Fae priest asks.

I am grateful he is here; he feels slightly like a piece of home, even if it is a home I have never been to. Although he won't answer any of my questions, he voices his desire for me to be pregnant. He pushes this on me every day, claiming that if I am not with child soon, another could rise above me and take my place in Mirahalm as next in line.

"I think we could be ready the day after next," the king says.

His voice is always regal. The thought causes anger to bubble to the surface. His black eyes slowly meet mine, and I can't help but think about how everybody has starved for years, how we were taxed more than we could ever pay, how people died because he treated Hollow and his castle like they deserved everything, while everybody else was left to their own devices.

"A problem, mate?"

He knows I don't like it when he uses the bond to speak into my head. I don't like the intrusion. I bite down hard on my lip before taking a slow bite from the muffin in front of me. Without my powers, I don't need to eat as much as I used to, but that doesn't stop me from trying every treat they bring me.

"None."

"How will you handle Brabble?" Wolf asks, obviously remembering what happened to us on our way here.

"We will not be traveling into Brabble," the king says quickly.

My mind goes right back to the girls I know I left there to die. They haven't shown up here yet, so I can only assume they are no longer with us but instead with the Fates.

"And will you be going to Darnish?" Magnolia asks, her devil eyes staring right into my soul.

"Of course, we will. Your queen is from there." The king stares right at her, daring her to challenge me again.

There is something odd in the way she looks at him. "Yes, Majesty." She bows her head, a show of respect that she does not have—or do—for me.

"Is there anything else we need to discuss?" the advisor asks from beside me. I am more than ready to be done with this and head to Sailor's cottage.

"Yes. I will be traveling with you."

Wolf's voice pierces through my calm. I can handle the king; I can handle one enemy. Not Wolf, too. He may be killed in his sleep if he attempts to come along.

"Oh, you will be, will you?" I ask, daring him. What does he think will happen?

"I will, yes."

I look to the king for help on this, but he doesn't look me in the eyes. Instead, he is looking at Magnolia. I often wonder how she is still alive. What hold does she have over him? Maybe they are having their own sort of affair. She's made comments about him before.

"Wolf is traveling on my behalf; I will not be making the journey with you, sadly," Magnolia chirps.

Oh no, I am just so sad.

The king chuckles from across the table, and my eyes dance with amusement. Sometimes I forget how easily he can creep into my thoughts. Even without using his power, he is inside of me. We are one, even though I hate him. I want nothing more than to be separated from him, but even just thinking that causes my body to become cold. He is a part of me in ways I can feel deep in the very marrow of my bones.

"I will allow this," the king says, his posture rigid with something I can't read.

I stand, realizing there isn't a reason Wolf shouldn't be able to come. I can handle a little trouble, and that's all he is...trouble.

"What would you like to pack?" Millie asks while folding up some of my dresses.

I shake my head. "Not those." I make my way over to my trunk, the very same one I once packed to come here, when I thought I would still go home. I reach in, feeling for the blanket I know I need while on the road. I haven't needed this damn blanket for a week, but I know going back to Darnish will haunt me. "This. This is the only thing I need you to make certain is on the carriage. Please, Mil." She doesn't know the importance of the blanket, but she knows I like it enough.

"Alright, this old thing. Anything else, Majesty?" she taunts me, knowing I hate it when she calls me anything but my name.

"No, but I do wish to hear more about the wedding plans you have so far."

Arlo proposed to her the day after my wedding. He said he felt like life was too precious to wait any longer.

I could have taken that as an insult; my wedding, after all, was a bloodbath. Exactly ninety-eight people died. I will never forget what the king and his priest forced me to do that day. I was selfish, really. I chose my family, my lover, over those in attendance. I didn't have to kill the others, but if I hadn't, I would've still been married but lost everybody I have ever loved. Then what would life be? Worthless. Although, I guess if anything good came out of that horrible day, it was Arlo realizing that forever is never promised. He had felt like it was a calling from the Blessed to not wait any longer.

"I want it to be a small affair. Simple, just like us." She shrugs as if this isn't a conversation about her wedding.

"Millie, weddings are a big deal. Why do you act as if it isn't?"

Her eyes flash with hurt from whatever I said. "Because I feel bad for you."

Ouch. I hate being pitied, but if anything is worse than pity, it is being feared by the people I thought would love me, the people I swore to protect. I did everything to help them. They still see me as the heartless killer I was made into.

"I just mean...I hate that your wedding day wasn't what you wanted, or even who you wanted it to be with." She grabs my hand, a small touch I relish in.

"I know what you mean, Mil. I appreciate it. Really, I do. Thank you." Millie knows I love Sailor; she doesn't know everything, but most things.

The weeks after I made him leave were dark days for me. I wasn't myself. The fae darkness my mother had said she saw in me reared its ugly head. I couldn't get away from it. The nightmares were so suffocating, I believe I had to be drugged during them. I cannot remember. That's the funny thing about trauma—it takes some memories while forcing you to relive others. It isn't fair, but the Gods play games better than I do. That's all this is to them...a big game. We are their toys.

"Have you spoken to him?" Millie's voice pierces through the silence.

"Which one?" My answer is more than likely the same either way, but still, clarification would be nice.

Millie grabs a book to put into my bag, alongside another pair of socks and boots.

"Sailor, Wolf...hell, has the king said anything to you?"

I purse my lips, unsure what I want to say about any of them. "Um..." I pause for a moment before sitting down on my soft, fluffy bed. Millie sits, too, crossing her ankles. "Well, the easiest one is that I have not heard anything from Clove regarding Sailor. I don't even know if they made it there or not." The thought that they may have died traveling across the sea makes my stomach feel uneasy. I can't think that way, though. I have to think positive thoughts. My glass will be half full in that regard, today and always.

"And Wolf hasn't tried to speak to me since the last...incident." He had grabbed onto my shoulder, trying to explain why he did what he did. I beat him as good as I could before I was flung over the king's shoulder and brought to my room like a child in time-out.

"As for the king, we talk nightly about trivial things mostly. Whenever he brings up homelands and babies, that's when I space out and start to daydream." I cock my head and give her a sarcastic closed-mouth smile.

Millie chuckles as she motions for me to turn around so she can redo my hair that is currently in a rat's nest on the top of my head. "He is your husband, and if you believe...then he's your *mate*, Serena." She says this slowly, as if I wasn't totally sure.

"I am aware," I claim, although some clearly believe I am not.

"He is a king, he will need babies. And if you are to even think about claiming your homelands—you know, the ones your mother told you need saving..." Her voice is soft as it trails off.

She isn't what I thought she would be when I first met her, back in the trials. "I know, I just am not ready to have any babies. I don't know if I ever will be with him. I also have trouble believing I must have an heir to claim a land that calls to me. I feel it, Millie."

The brush pulls my head from side to side, in a similar way Evie used to do. "I hear what you're saying, I just know that you want to help both lands...just...never mind." She shakes her head and sighs. "Let's focus on your trip. Are you excited to visit everywhere?"

No.

"I guess I am ready to be out of the palace," I answer, as honestly as I can.

Her eyes soften, and I don't like it. I see what she won't say. "Things will get better, Serena. It can't always be this hard."

Can't it, though?

"I know you're right. The Gods have got to see I have passed their tests."

She nods in agreement, even though I am not sure she *is* right. I think the Gods have just begun their wrath on us.

Chapter 6

My heart hammers in my chest when I walk up to the carriages that brought me here all those months ago. I don't know why I feel so anxious, but I do. I look at the three carriages instead of the many we rode here with last time; somehow, that makes it worse. Less carriages to hide in, I guess.

"Majesty?" One of the guards comes up with my trunk and bags. I point him to the one I will be riding in mostly. I don't have the choice of flying or riding this time.

"Thank you," I mumble, unsure if he hears my voice. I feel numb in a way. I never thought going home would feel like death. We won't make it to Darnish for a week, and even still, I don't know how I feel about the entire trip.

Wolf walks up, a small bag in hand. His black hair is tousled in a way that would once make me want to run my fingers through it. His bright green eyes used to call me home, but now I couldn't think of a worse place to be than trapped in them. His black riding boots look freshly cleaned. I roll my eyes.

"Are we going to have a problem, or are we able to travel together without a fight?" His eyes darken to forest green, and even without my power, I do not step back when he strides into my space.

"I don't know, are you going to tell me why you betrayed Sailor?" I ask icily. Wolf stands toe to toe with me, and I almost wonder if he thinks he has an advantage over me now that my powers are muted. He would be wrong.

"I tried explaining to you, Serena. Come on, I thought we were better than this." He reaches out and puts a loose strand of hair behind my ear. Before he can pull his hand away, his body is being tossed backwards.

"Oh, my Blessed!" My eyes widen slightly, even though I should have seen it coming.

I whirl around to see the king snarling on top of Wolf. "You will *never* lay hands on her again!" he roars.

I once had thought they looked similar. They both have tanned skin and dark waves of cropped hair. Now, seeing them right in front of me, the king holding Wolf down, they couldn't look more different. The king is huge in a way that no human could ever be; he looks more like a God than Fae. Although, I have never seen any other fae, outside of my dream walking. Wolf's green eyes are in total contrast to the king's black ones. The king is a grown male, whereas Wolf looks like a boy.

"I was putting her hair behind her ear...nothing else, Majesty," Wolf says more calmly than I would have thought one could with a fae king planted on him.

"You will not lay any part of yourself on her *ever*. I don't care what you thought you were doing; it won't happen again," the king threatens through clenched teeth, his canines on full display.

"Fine, I won't. But if she is in trouble—"

I take a step then, wondering if the king is going to kill the commander. I hope he does.

"Then *I will save her*. You are nothing to her, nothing to me. I need to be clear about one thing." I hold my breath, unsure where this is going, but knowing this trip will not be like the last one I went on. "You are here because of Magnolia. I do not want you here. You will do and say nothing, am I clear?" Wolf gives a curt nod, and the king pushes off the ground to stride towards me.

"Do you have everything?" The change in subject and demeanor is jarring, and my eyes widen in shock for half a second before I slip the mask on. Millie had told me the palace is about politics. In order to earn the trust back from my people, help Mirahalm and my family, I must play this game.

"I do." I give him a kind smile, one he doesn't deserve.

"Are you okay?" This voice isn't one the king shows many people—it's kind in a way I wish he *would* show his people.

"I am."

He leans into my ear, so much so that his puffy lips wet the tip of my ear. "Why do I sense so many negative emotions wafting from you then?"

I try to throw up an emotional and mental shield, but I fear the damage is already done. I had forgotten, and that is a mistake I cannot keep making. I shrug my shoulders, not bothering to voice any sort of response.

"Are you riding with me?" I ask while we walk side by side.

"I will." *Ugh.*

He chuckles. Darkness seems to follow him around, but not the same that called to me on our wedding day, though. It's almost something that feels like a comfort shadow, an ever-growing presence that feels warmer than my darkness feels. "Do you not want me to ride with you?" he asks, while his eyes burn my flesh every place they search.

I inhale deeply, as he watches my chest rise and fall. "I would think you would be in the front, leading everybody." My anxiety over this trip isn't going to go down anytime soon, at least not until I face my fears in going back to Darnish. I accept the fact that my mother was a fae queen who left me in the body of a human, but I refuse to think that she might have known it would kill my father's wife and their own baby.

"The only being I would like to be in front of is you."

I roll my eyes dramatically. "In front of me?" I ask sarcastically.

"In front of, on my knees for...however you'll take me, really."

I shake my head and step into the next few weeks of my life...torture. "That makes me want to gag." I jab my finger into his ribs, which just makes him chuckle deeply.

"I do have a body part that would make you enjoy gagging... Would you like to test it out?"

He tilts his head, and I grind my teeth to avoid answering him. But I can't help myself. "The only reason you'll be on your knees for me is when you pray for me to spare you."

He licks his lips before whispering. "I would do anything if only you were to look at me with as much passion as I can feel from you right now, forever."

I feel bile rising up, so I walk as fast as I can. Leaving behind more trouble than it's worth.

"I will take that as a maybe, Serena," he says just loud enough for me to hear.

I flip him off over my head, and in response, I get several glances from the guards. I ignore them all.

Chapter 7

We make it to Hollow in less than an hour. As I suspected, Hollow is more than welcoming to us. Children run out in front of our carriages, and mothers bring their babies to us to kiss and hold. Some even ask us to pray to the Gods for their children's lives.

"Smile," the king requests through his lips, which are in a flat smile.

"I am." I don't even look at him. I know he doesn't have to look at me to know I am not, in fact, smiling.

"You need to look approachable to every village, not just the ones you think are mistreated," he whispers to me, which I appreciate, since the alternative is him barging into my head.

I know I have been queen for several weeks now, but coming to the villages and seeing them all—and them seeing me with a black crown atop my head—makes it real to me.

"Why didn't you do this with her?"

I don't even know her name; I haven't asked yet. I think I should, but I just can't find it in me to even think about it. Some deep, dark part of me knows I shouldn't care, but for some odd reason, I hate that he was married before. I hate knowing that I am second. My entire life I have felt like hiding, and when I finally don't want to hide anymore, I feel inferior. I chuckle to myself thinking about it.

The king's chest rises and falls before he responds. "I didn't do this last time because it wasn't a true marriage." His tone is clipped, the same way it gets when he talks about things he doesn't like to talk about.

"Oh?" I ask, mostly because I am confused. But also, I need a distraction. There is a reason I didn't go into the main square of Darnish often. I wasn't wanted there, and I am not wanted here either.

"I wasn't truly married," he says again after waving to some children.

"My King."

A man comes to up to us, bowing before taking my hand in his and looking to the king. The king gives a curt shake of his head before the man withdraws.

"I wasn't mated before you, obviously, as the Gods only give one mate."

My eyes meet his, the man in front of us watching us carefully with furrowed brows.

Before finding out about the fae, I hadn't had any idea, outside of maybe a pack, that mates were a thing. After further research, I have concluded that in fae culture, mates are rare. In fact, they are so uncommon that most fae never find theirs, or don't have one at all.

"So, because you weren't mated, it wasn't real to you?" I think into my head, knowing he has his connection to my mind open, always. He never leaves my headspace. Since I still don't have power, I can't open or close our connection; only he can. I can attempt to keep him out, but never fully. I finally feel what it is like to not have mental abilities. I hate it, and I hate him for making me weak.

"It just wasn't. Being mated to you, meeting you even, is just different. You are second to our kingdom, but in my eyes, you are my first and only. You are mine."

Even in my head, I hear the definitive tone he uses. He means what he says to me; he believes I belong to him.

"Caleb, it is nice to see you again," the king drawls. The man, apparently named Caleb, smiles widely. He isn't a tall man, especially not next to the king.

"You seem so sure that I am your only. You are royal... maybe the Gods gave you more, as they did with your powers," I challenge him back. I am getting used to doing that.

"Dinner will be held to celebrate your strong union. We are glad those trials are over." Caleb wipes a bead of sweat from his brow. It's hot right by the sea, always. I hadn't believed it until now; I thought the books were lying. Father and I used to joke about how miserable it would be to be hot all the time. Now look at me.

"Much appreciated, we will meet you there."

Caleb notices he is being dismissed and turns to leave, but before he can, I stop him.

"*What are you doing?*" the king whispers into my head, and I am trying my best to keep him out. My hand burns on Caleb's pale skin; his wrist almost swallows my fingers up.

"Caleb?" I ask in a sweet voice.

"Yes?" His eyes dart between me and his king.

"*Serena darling?*"

I shut my eyes and count to five. Sure, I might look crazy, but I don't care. Anything to keep him out of my mind.

"Are there any poor folk who live here?" I open my eyes, looking directly into Caleb's nervous ones. His large cheeks blush under my attention.

"Excuse me, Majesty?" He gulps so much, I think he must have been holding in his saliva.

"You heard me. Sadly, I do not know enough about Hollow to know if they have a variety of folks here. I don't want to seem rude, I just would like to know if there are any who might need help?"

The king relaxes a bit, clearly realizing what I am about to do. Caleb, though, seems even more confused.

"There is a small family; they moved here with permission, of course. They aren't as well off as most here, Majesty. Would you like me to move them back to Glen"

I give him a clipped smile, a practiced one. and turn to leave, but only halfway.

"Where do they live, Caleb?"

He again looks to the king for permission.

I huff a sigh. "I am queen, am I not?" I ask, feeling irritated that he keeps looking to *him* for answers. I am powerful in my own right.

"Y-yes," he stutters out. Even without magic, I can feel his anxiety rolling from his body. "They live at the end of the street...small blue home," he informs me.

My steps are filled with purpose; nothing could slow me down. Dinner starts soon, and I would like to do something for this family, even though they live here in Hollow.

"*I will meet you outside the town hall. You have twenty minutes,*" the king informs me. I don't know if that's enough time or not, but I will make whatever I have work. I nod towards him, not giving him any response. I don't need his permission. I am Serena Bloodworthy, heir to Mirahalm and Queen of Nymphamera.

When I walk up the beaten pathway that leads to the small home, my heart starts to hammer in my chest. I wish Sailor were here with me, I wish he wasn't in Clove. I regret sending him there. I knock once, then twice, on the arched door. The overgrown greenery on their house tells me all I am at the right cottage.

The home in and of itself isn't huge, but once the tiny girl opens the door, I know that this is all this family needs.

"Hi." I smile down at the little girl. "Where is your mommy?"

She looks around, then shrugs. Her eyes dart to the black glittering crown on my head, and they widen slightly. I am in a simple gown, yet her eyes sparkle the same as the other kids' had. "I dunno." Her tiny voice seems nervous. I hear a rustling in the back of the house, right as a middle-aged woman walks through the small hallway.

"Lillie, who is this?" The woman's eyes are frantic as she speaks to her daughter. The small child shrugs again; that seems to be the only way she likes to communicate.

"Uh...h-hi," she stutters as I hold out my hand, noticing her gray eyes going right to the dark crown atop my head.

"Hello, there. I am Serena."

The mother pushes the tiny girl behind her body, causing a protectiveness to hang in the air. "You are the new queen." It's a statement, not a question.

"I am." Her gaze goes behind me, and I know who is standing there. My new bodyguard for my honeymoon trip. Wolf's scent has changed, but I can still tell it's him. Cinnamon and oak.

"Have I done something wrong?" the woman gets out after staring at the commander at my back.

"No. In fact, the opposite." I reach into one of the pockets that I demanded all my gowns have. Today I am wearing a forest-green gown, and the gold lace accents the colors well. It wasn't in my color wheel, but I convinced the three lunatics to pack it anyway. "You and your family are invited to the royal dinner. I personally wanted to give you this." I hand her the bag of gold coins I kept from my travels. "You can come wearing whatever you want, or I have sent word to the shopkeeper to give you each an outfit. Use the coins however you would like."

She keeps her hand up, as if frozen in place. The sack of golden coins weighs her hand down slightly. "Why would you do this?" She narrows her eyes in suspicion.

The little girl pops her head out, then says, "Can Bubba come?" The mother shushes her daughter, but I giggle and bend to be at eye level with her.

"Your brother is more than welcome. I encourage it even." I smile as sweetly as I can. I have a feeling my overly-sweet smile scares the child. "I will see you there, then," I say, once I realize she won't be responding to me. I stand up, running my hand over the skirts of my gown. I catch the eyes of a boy, probably teenage years. I might not be much older than him, but his mouth hangs open before he ducks into another room. The mother grabs my wrist, and when Wolf tries to step in, I give him a glare that dares him to intervene.

"Thank you." Her voice is hushed and I give her a small nod.

"Of course." My face doesn't have any signs of fake politics; I give her my most genuine smile.

Chapter 8

"Why did you do that?" Wolf steps in time with me.

"I've been asking you the same question for weeks," I respond. His body is muscular but almost rigid in a way it wasn't before.

"Serena, I have tried to speak with you, but you won't listen to me." His tone has some sort of edge to it. The once-sure Wolf now seems uncertain of himself. I'm not as tall as he is, but our steps are the same length.

"I have listened to you. I hear how you lust after Magnolia. I hear you, Wolf. I also hear a lack of words from you; explain why you betrayed Sailor. Do you remember him?"

I sound bitter, angry even. Because I am. I want to burn the world down. I turn down a pathway. I have no idea where I am going, but I know I need to get away from him. My arms swing at my side, and the faster I walk, the more they swing.

Wolf tries to keep up with me, but I can't stop, I won't. "I don't want excuses from you, Wolfie boy. I want action or nothing," I say over my shoulder.

He reaches me in a matter of seconds. His hands grip my arm tighter than I would have thought he would dare. "You are a married woman now; you don't want action from *me*."

I roll my eyes. As if I would fuck him after *she* has. Even if I wasn't in love with Sailor, Wolf would never look appealing to me ever again. "I—"

He interrupts me. "Ah, I will speak now. You have ignored me for long enough, My Queen." His voice is liquid lust. I swear, if I didn't already want to kill him, I would now for trying to flirt with me. "I have not abandoned Sailor. I do have to think about my family, too, though."

Finally, the anger boils over, seeping from my body as if I had a burning point that I have surpassed.

"*I have family, too, you know?*" I think so loud, I hope it hurts him. I hold nothing back.

"Yeah, I know all about your family," he says so smugly that I almost slap him. My fist clenches. I find myself doing that more often than not.

"I dare you to," I say, challenging him to touch me as I watch his hand slowly raise towards my face. I growl through my teeth, the sharp points of my new canines biting into my lower lip.

"I would love to." He takes a breath, then lowers his hand. "Just your touch would feel great. Your passion, though, Queen?" He bites his lip before smirking brightly at me. "That would be unbelievable." I shake my head in disgust.

"Gross." I yank out of his grasp. "What do you mean you know all about my family?" I don't want this boy knowing *anything* about my family.

"I know more than you would think, Serena. If you would stop hating me so much, I could help you." His dragon-green eyes twinkle in the sunlight. I hope he's burning hot in the tight pants and long gray tunic he's wearing.

"You know nothing about us; I don't need any help from you." I shove past him, needing space. All he ever gives me are half-truths or flat-out lies. I don't know why they keep offering me help; I can handle myself. And that is exactly what I am going to do.

I make it to a building I hadn't seen the last time we were here, when Wolf brought me to buy a gown for the ball. The building has white crown molding on the outside, and I can tell it cost a fortune. I see the king inside speaking with a pretty woman, her chest pressed against his arm. Before I can step inside the building, though, an aggravating voice booms through my mind.

"*Wrong family, darling.*"

I turn around but see no sign of Wolf. Figures. He would say something like that without facing me.

"*I am not your darling. I never was!*" I scream into my mind, not caring if other mind readers hear my fight with him.

"*Really? Then why did I feel like your home, Serena?*" Even in my head, his voice sounds desperate.

"Because I didn't know any better." It's a poor excuse, so I add on for good measure, *"I also wasn't exposed to many men. You are handsome, sure, but the inside of you? Ugly as can be."* Before he can respond, I shut down any pathway I can. I just hope my practice will pay off.

I walk right on into the already-full room, knowing exactly where I am heading. I have no reason to feel the way I am right now, but I do. I blame it on my fae nature. My emotions are still leveling out. Fae are different from humans—in more ways than I even know yet—and I still have no answers for anything in regard to who I truly am.

"Hello." I smile with my eyes, while my lips barely move at the ends.

"Wife," the king says from beside me. I may hate him, but the protectiveness I feel is unmatched. As much as I hate to admit it, I can feel the bond growing tighter and tighter between us. I feel things for him I wish I didn't.

"Who is this?" I ask, not looking at the woman who has now taken several steps away from me.

"Serena, this is the daughter of one of the commanders here in Hollow," Alwin informs me.

I look between the two of them, unsure how I should be feeling. I hate this male in front of me. He lied to me. He hurt me and made me harm others. He took Sailor... Even after all of that, the more time I spend with him, the more I start to understand him. A new view of the male he is. He isn't just the king; he can still be Aldrich in some ways... Like in the way Aldrich cared for me, protected me even. I began liking Aldrich, even seeing him as an ally. If I had met him before Sailor, I may have even loved him.

"And her name is?" I cut through those scary thoughts, realizing he is acting strangely.

"Her name is Tiana."

My eyes stick to his black swirls. There is no sign of blue in them. I don't know what to make of that.

"Oh?" I bite my lower lip, attempting to swallow the sickening feeling of jealousy. "Why can't she speak?" My jaw clenches so tight I swear my teeth might break. I realize the girl has not said one word since I walked up.

"She can," he answers for her again, and for some reason, I feel as though we are in a battle of some sort. All I know is that games are my thing. I do not lose.

Granted, the last thing I won, I would like to return. Especially when he looks at me like he might love me, like he might destroy me. He may have already destroyed me. When

I look at my reflection, I don't see myself anymore. I see a version of me, yes. But the Serena Bloodworthy that my father would be proud of? She is dead and gone. I think she died that night in the clearing, with her one and only father.

"I am Tiana. Nice to meet you, My Queen," the girl with the warm brown skin says. But her eyes don't meet mine. My brows rise when she looks to the king for further instructions. He gives her a slight nod; his jaw is so defined, he makes Wolf look like a baby. She bows, and right as I am about to ask what the hell is going on, Caleb walks towards us with two glasses of a sparkling liquid.

"My King." He bows his head. "My Queen."

The king steps closer towards me, until his arm brushes against mine. The electric shock that goes through me from our point of contact is so strong that it makes it hard to know if the king didn't just send lightning through my body. His eyes meet mine, and the navy-blue swirls I had been looking for are back. When he looks at me, his eyes change; they soften in a way I doubt many others see. Too fast, though, his hard demeanor is set firmly in place. The switch between Aldrich to king kills me every single time.

"Follow me, please." Caleb hands us the glasses, and we walk away from the woman, whom I don't think I like very much. "We have only invited the commanders and noble families tonight. Only the very best to celebrate our new queen," he chimes happily.

Please, Blessed, kill me now.

"I don't want the very best," I say firmly, hoping Caleb will understand that I am not here for the nobles. I am here to make big changes, starting now.

The king hands me a different glass, snatching mine from my hand. "Drink only what I give you." He dumps the sparkling liquid out into a random plant.

I raise a brow. "Worried about me, King?" I taunt him because it's easy to do so.

"Always. You may not see it, Serena, but I care for you. I didn't ever want to hurt you, but there are things you don't know yet."

I huff out a loud breath while we walk side by side to the head of the table. "Because you haven't told me." I sigh the words. He doesn't look my way, but I can feel the heat of his mental attention all the way down my spine. The warm feeling he floods my body with eases me enough that I actually listen to him.

"I haven't had the time or place to tell you the things you need to know. You won't give me any of your time," he grumbles out.

"I am upset with you. I don't trust you." I look at his profile, studying him. I hate how handsome he is; his light stubble lines his jawline so well, and he seems to grow it quickly. I want to see how it would feel on my hands. Is it soft? Would it scrap against my th—

"Majesties, I hope you find your first tour stop pleasing. The dinner will begin shortly." Caleb motions for us to sit. I see only one problem, though.

"Where am I to sit?" I ask softly.

"Next to me, right there." The king places my drink in front of the seat near his, but along the side of the table. I blow out a breath before moving my drink to the head of the table instead. I hear somebody gasp quietly, right before I move my chair right next to the king's. I will not be treated as less than him. We are on all levels equal.

"Uh, My Queen, what are you doing?" Caleb rushes over to me, panic-stricken.

I'd almost laugh if I didn't know he was being serious. "Am I not the queen?" I ask, playing coy. I blink my thick, dark lashes softly and slowly. I purse my lips evenly, playing this game as well as I can.

"You are," he agrees before quickly finishing, "but the queen does not sit at the head of the table." I see the king stiffen beside me, but he doesn't say a word. He does grind his jaw, and the motion makes him look more like a God than the human form he's in.

"Why not?" I watch the short man carefully, sizing him up, as if I am in a wolf pack and hunting for my next kill.

"Well...because he is *the king*." Caleb tilts his head.

I look at the male we are speaking about. "Do you have any issues with me scooting you over some?"

The king smiles slightly at me. "Absolutely none. I would prefer it even. The closer I am to you, the more I can whisper into your pretty ears."

I feel my face heat.

Caleb blanches, unsure what he should do or say. "That isn't what is proper, though, miss—"

The king is in front of him faster than I have ever seen anybody move. He might *be* the God I have been picturing him to be in my head.

The king's hands are wrapped tightly around Caleb's throat, his sharp, pointed teeth on full display, and my body doesn't seem to care that I hate this male in front of us. It craves him now more than ever. Some primal need to devour him whole overtakes me.

"She is your queen. You will address her as such," the king snarls. I gently grab his wrist, which is firmly latched onto Caleb's throat.

"It's okay, I can handle him on my own." I don't know why I am trying to calm him. The need to help him settle down takes me by surprise. I can feel his grip on Caleb's throat lighten slightly.

"I don't doubt you *can*. I *know* you can. I have seen it with my own two eyes. But you don't have to any longer." Our eyes connect for the most tense seconds we have ever shared.

"I'm sorry, My Queen, I meant no disrespect. Truly," Caleb says hurriedly.

The king shoves the man away with more force than necessary, and Caleb runs into somebody walking past.

I shake my head. "It's alright, I am fine. You may leave." I dismiss Caleb before our king kills him. He scurries away, slipping on his feet as he hurries towards a door. I cover my mouth to hide my giggles, and the king watches me intently. His eyes are glowing with need for me, so I turn away before I act on any confusing feelings and take a seat in the blue velvet armchair, the larger of the two seats.

"You invited them." The king sits next to me in the red velvet chair, and I look over to see that he's watching the family from the blue home enter the room.

"I did."

He chuckles. "I have a feeling you are going to change many things."

I chew on my nail, feeling nervous for my first appearance as the people's queen. "Such as?" I smile and wave at them, but carry on our conversation.

"My heart, my purpose...me." He says it so calmly and softly I almost miss his words entirely.

"Anything not to do with you?" I ask, while watching the family I invited walk around nervously.

"The world." He shrugs.

I scoff in response. "Anything else, Majesty?"

He looks at me then, his thick lips look far too inviting. "Hopefully, my sex life."

I turn to him fully now, my mouth hanging agape. "Already working on the last thing?" He smirks at me, the look on his face promising trouble. I slam my mouth shut. "No, never," I swear, not knowing if I can actually keep the promise to never sleep with him again.

"That's not what your thoughts say, *mate*." He says the last word so playfully, I can't help but half smirk.

I run a hand over my face, trying to hide my embarrassment.

"No need to feel ashamed. I am your husband and mate."

I shake my head in disbelief. "And a pain in my ass," I mumble.

"No, not that...*yet*, darling."

"Oh my Gods. You are unbelievable."

Some whimsical music starts up behind me, and I turn to find a woman playing an instrument. Before I can give her my full attention, though, the king leans right into my space. His mouth brushes my ear and causes shivers to run down my spine. His nose is pressed into my hair, and I swear he inhales my scent as if I were the very oxygen keeping him alive. Goose bumps erupt all over my arms; the way he can cause such a physical reaction should scare me.

"I am no God, but I appreciate the compliment. I really should thank them for the amount of time they spent on you, though."

I open my mouth to say something, anything to derail his advances, but before I can, I see a commotion to the side that requires my attention, and I swiftly vacate my seat.

Chapter 9

"Is there a problem here?" I ask the guard who is currently trying to pull the woman I invited away from the party. The small girl has tearstains on her pink cheeks, and the slightly older boy looks embarrassed, but without my empath abilities, I cannot tell for sure.

"Majesty, I'm sorry. This family was just leaving. I don't know who invited *them* here." I can sense his disgust for the family. Our interaction is gaining attention, which I do not want.

"I did," I say calmly, even though I do not feel calm. "I invited them. I was told this is my party, and I am able to invite whomever I please. Is that not true?"

His eyes widen some, enough to show me he's startled. "Uh...yes, Majesty, you can. I-I'm very sorry," he stammers while backing up.

I want this night to be over. We will make it to Rawgabbit tomorrow and I'm more than ready for a break from this torture.

"We just left the palace," the king says softly into my head. The ease he can get into my mind should startle me. I know that it isn't just his power causing it, because I am starting to feel as if I can hear his thoughts, too. Which I know is not true; I have no magic right now. *Dear Gods, help me.* His pathway is open for me.

"I don't like social events like this. I would rather be out there doing something good with our time."

There is a silence for so long that I almost think the king has been distracted, but then, *"I think you do rather well in these types of events. People always seem...interested in you."* I look at the family, realizing I have been standing here without speaking to them.

"You can all follow me. I'm glad you came," I say with a slightly awkward smile on my face. *"Are you referring to when I was poisoned or kidnapped?"*

Having two completely separate conversations isn't easy. I move through the masses of people with ease; I have done this part my entire life. I have been invisible in crowds where I was not wanted.

"Thank you, Majesty," the mother says, rushed and hushed.

"Thank you for allowing us to come," the little girl says softly.

I lead them towards my seat. I want to chat with them, I want to know my people.

"Where are we sitting?" the little girl asks.

At the same moment, the king speaks in my head and I lock eyes with him. *"I seem to remember you saving yourself. I also heard a little rumor you have already started saving your people."*

The little girl keeps pace with me. "You will be sitting by me," I tell her.

Her mother hisses out, "Oh no. We don't need to do that," right as the little girl claps her hands loudly and cheers with her tiny voice.

I chuckle softly. "Come now. Tell me about how you ended up in Hollow." I place my hand on the back of the girl's dress. It looks new. "I love your dress," I tell her, right as I tell the king, *"I will save our people, from Magnolia, from you, or whoever else they need to be saved from."* I do not directly approach the subject of Magnolia's underground chambers.

"What if I told you I am with you? I don't want to harm them either. What if I told you that I am as much a pawn in this cruel game as you?"

I scoff, right as the woman pulls her daughter to her side. I realize she is scared of me. Not the child, no...the mother. Anger blossoms in my belly. *"I would say you are a trained liar, and I would be a fool to believe you,"* I reply to him.

We make it to the end of the table, where the king stands, his dark eyes meeting mine for a split second. He holds up his glass before saying, "Here is a toast to our queen, may the Gods bless our marriage and bring power to the lands." He sips from his glass; I grab my glass and do the same.

"To the king and queen," the people all cheer.

At one point in my life, I had thought it was crazy that people could cheer and pray for royalty, whom they do not know. It still creeps me out. These people are cheering for me, even though they don't know really who I am.

"You will trust me one day; your heart is already telling you to. I can feel it." His words send a shiver down my spine. "Cold?" the king asks me aloud.

"No, actually, I am warm. Some male just creeped me out." I smirk at him, unable to help myself.

"Ah, I see." He leans in closer to me, biting the tip of his finger. "I guess I should threaten him, huh?"

I shrug my shoulders. "Only if you swear to kill him."

He laughs, startling the boy sitting next to his sister.

"Serena." Wolf interrupts our conversation as he sits across from the woman.

"Hello, Wolf," I say, noticing the king stiffening.

"You look lovely tonight," he says.

I don't look different from any other time, but I will play along with his politeness. But only because the tiny girl watches me closely. "Thank you, as do you." I turn my charm up. His eyes widen slightly, and he seems surprised. I am getting decent at reading others now that I don't have power.

"Appreciated." He dips his chin when he responds.

All conversations stop when the large plates of steaming food come out. But no matter how delicious it looks, it all tastes like ash on my tongue. I have found that anything I eat tastes horrid in my mouth. I haven't been able to find enjoyment in anything since Sailor left me, all those weeks ago. I do smile when the two kids dig into their food, though. Their mother watches me carefully; her eyes never drift to the king.

"Mommy, I am still hungry," the little girl whines after the plates are taken away.

The dinner went as smoothly as it could. There was no fighting or yelling; it was as if each and every person here was happy to see their king. They all seem fond of him in a way that tells me he must come here sometimes. Some even call him by his name. Some laugh and clap his back, as if they have inside jokes with him.

"Honey, you can eat more at home," the mother says in a hushed voice.

"But, Mommy, there isn't any food there." The small girl's eyes are pleading with her mother, and my heart drops at her words. I know Hollow is wealthy, but this family right here? They are not from Hollow. My every instinct is to pry into their minds and get the details from them myself. I don't want to embarrass her more than I can see she already is. People talk around them; eyes linger for far too long.

"Majesty, we need you for a moment."

The king stands and holds his hand out to me. I shake my head. "Could I stay here?"

He looks at Wolf like he thinks there is anything left between us. "Of course." He doesn't comment on my wanting to stay, and I also do not clarify that I am not staying for Wolf. I don't need to. "I'll be right back." He leans down as if going to kiss my head, but then he stops himself halfway.

"Okay," I say, noticing the looks we are garnering. I hold my own hands, feeling lonely without Sailor here. He waits for another moment before nodding to himself. I watch him leave, my eyes dragging down his body, and not for the first time do they linger on his tight leather pants.

Chapter 10

<u>SERENA</u>

"How long have you lived here?" I ask the small child.

"We just moved here, Majesty," the mother answers for her quickly. I wave over a server and grab the plate of desserts.

"Thank you," I mumble swiftly. "Here you are." I place the plate in front of the kids while the mother eyes me warily. "I am not going to kill you or your family," I say without hesitation.

Wolf spits his drink out. "Serena." His brows furrow, and he wipes at his mouth. "I apologize for her," he says without my permission. I bite down my response to him before focusing on what I need to.

The woman looks half a second away from bolting, so I add, "I was doing what needed to be done for my union. I do not ever need to kill again, unless I need to protect somebody. Then I will kill, and *only* then. I am no threat to your family." I make certain she understands I want to help them.

"I'm sorry, I didn't mean any disrespect—" She looks between Wolf and me as if trying to get out of trouble.

I place my palm on her forearm. "I understand. I may not have a child yet, but I have family still. Just know, you are welcome here, and I want to help my people. It's the reason I wanted to win the trials," I admit.

She grabs my hand; her own are ice-cold. I can only assume her power is elemental. Most people have elemental magic anymore, elemental is the most common magic the Gods give out to humans.

"How long have you lived in Hollow?" I ask again.

"We moved here right when the new commanders were dispatched." Her voice is small, and the boy stiffens.

"Okay." I nod my head, urging her to continue.

"My husband was killed."

The little girl shoves her food into her small mouth quickly, none the wiser to our conversation. The boy? He listens.

"Who killed him?" I know already, but I still ask.

"The commanders," the mother answers.

"What was their reason?" And I wish I hadn't asked. I feel guilty for prying.

"Me," the boy speaks and, as I guessed, he sounds like a younger teen. His voice cracks.

"Surely not," I say, but that fills his eyes with hurt.

"My son is able to see recent memories. He had accidentally gotten into the commander's head and saw him cheating on his wife. The commander felt it and tried to arrest him. My husband stepped in, and well, long story short, he was killed right then and there."

I don't dare speak; I know she has more to say.

"They paid us for his death; I used the coin to start new here."

"They let the commander get away?" I wonder out loud.

Wolf chimes in with, "I'm glad you were able to relocate your family."

I roll my eyes. He notices, but he doesn't say anything.

"As am I. We enjoy it here." The boy nods.

"How much did they give you?" I know it is rude, but I need to know.

"Twenty coins." My brows raise at her soft words. I'm shocked they gave so little.

"I'm sorry." And then I find myself saying something I wouldn't have ever thought I would be sharing with a stranger. "I lost my father not long ago. I can't imagine how it feels for a person to put a value on the life of your loved one."

She nods her head once, and suddenly, the air feels too heavy. "Excuse me for a moment." I clear my throat and step away from the table.

My breathing starts coming and going quickly; I know this feeling. The problem is that I don't have my sister to help me anymore. I don't have Sailor to assure me that I will, in fact, be okay. I don't know if I *will* be okay anymore. My pace quickens to a steady race, and I rush to the door I know leads outside. I hear *his* voice calling to me, but it doesn't stop me from rushing away. Someone who once gave me such comfort, now sucks it away. I make it to a darkened pathway, my hands meet my knees, and I inhale like it might kill me if I don't. It might. I am alone, and I have no idea how I am going to survive this.

"Serena!" Wolf booms from the entrance of the path. I don't look up at him; I can hear his fury. "What are you—" His words stop when he sees that I am trying hard not to completely come apart. I feel like I can't inhale. My chest feels tight, as if something or somebody is sitting on me. "Are you okay?" He hurries over to where I am hunched over. Right as his hands hit my back, I recoil.

"Don't touch me," I yell, and shove him back. "Do not touch me. I don't trust you!" I shove again, then again. He lets me, I'm sure of it. He holds his hands up in surrender. That only stokes the flames in my heart further.

My chest is heaving, up and down, up and down, in rapid succession. I can't stop it. "You did this!" I scream. "You didn't help him." He nods his head, trying to calm me, I'm sure. Then I feel a tickling sensation that I know well. I know it from when I have used it. Wolf is trying to get through my shields. "Stop it," I spit out at him. "You do not belong inside of my head." I lose all control now, punching, kicking, clawing at him in any way, shape, or form that I can.

"Okay, I was just trying to help you," he says between getting hit and kicked. He doesn't block me; he doesn't keep me from altering his face, one I used to like very much.

What hurts most is that I am not actually upset with Wolf in this moment. No, this fit is about my father. The sadness I've felt being completely alone in the palace. The hollow feeling that I have is eating away at my soul. I have always lived to help my father, my best friend. I lost him and Sailor in such a short time period, as if it all happened at once. My fae emotions are stirring; I don't doubt that it has something to do with my sudden switch in mood.

"What's going on here?" a deep, gruff voice asks loudly. "Serena." Large hands grip my arm as I'm about to hit the commander standing in front of me. "What is going on? Did you hurt her?" the king asks, his eyes lit with fury. There's a wildness about his tone that makes me wonder if he might kill Wolf right here. That would make the trip easier, but it could hurt Sailor. I clench my eyes shut. *Sailor.*

"He didn't hurt me just now; he hurt me when he hurt *him*," I hiss out, and I finally chance a look to see the king's reaction.

"That boy left you, darling," the king says snidely.

I almost explode. But I have two kingdoms riding on my back, or else I would have.

"You need to calm down and breathe."

I can't, I feel like I can't.

"Serena."

The king grabs onto my face, shoving Wolf away from me with whatever power he uses. "You are dismissed," he scolds Wolf. It only takes Wolf one glance between the king and me before he backs up slowly.

"I just want to say, I care for you, Serena. I love my brother, and I wish things were different," Wolf says as he turns the corner. I had once thought Wolf was my comfort, my home. Now he is my nightmare. When I look at that commander, I see the life I could have had.

"Let's get one thing clear, *wife*." The king's tone leaves no room for argument. Still, I jerk out of his grasp, and I back up into the stone wall. He takes up the space around me, eating the distance I created in one stride. His hands go to either side of my head, his scent assaulting me. "You are mine. I am yours. Anything before *us*...?" He leans into me now, and I could tilt my mouth slightly and be kissing him. His tone is deep and low. "Died the day I claimed you as my mate," he finishes. His nose touches mine, almost in the comforting way Evie used to do. This touch, though? It isn't sweet, it isn't comforting. No, it is *consuming*. It sends fire through my body. This slight sensation should scare me, and it does. This means I am moving on from Sailor. I push on his chest, but unlike Wolf, the king gives me no room.

"That *boy* left you with a real male," he growls, and I show my teeth in return. "There is my fae queen popping out." He bites his lip, releasing a cold breath that I feel everywhere. The black swirls in his eyes are going crazy; the white in them is in such contrast that it hurts my eyes to look into them. "You may not have your ears out or your powers, but make no mistake, you will be their queen." His promise makes me realize what he is also not saying: I will have his children.

"I will," I agree with him, nodding my head. "I could bring my fangs out if you would just cut this pretty necklace from my neck."

His eyes roam to where I know the necklace sits. Instead of answering me, he grabs my wrist, the one I look at more times than I take breaths in a day. "He will be a blip on our radar one day, Serena. If you would just give us a chance and stop daydreaming of a future you will not have." I try to yank my wrist from him, but then he does something I would've never thought he would do. He kisses my wrist, right on the sailboat. "Will you try for your people?" he asks me, and I gulp down the guilt I feel when I answer.

"Yes." I realize, being queen, I can't be selfish anymore. I can't pick myself over two kingdoms any longer. I have held out hope for a future I cannot have with Sailor for far too long. I lick my teeth, noticing we have gained a crowd.

"I silenced our fight, but I'm sure some have the ability to hear it," the king says before pushing from the wall and flattening his now wrinkled shirt.

"Okay." I wipe my face, knowing I have messed up my makeup. My panic attack caused sweat to bead along my brows.

"We are starting anew, Serena. Without one another, we will never save the fae you were told you needed to save." His voice is level, calm, and collected.

I know he is right, even if I don't like it. I can't make it without him, but I hate needing his help. I will take it, though. Once I make it to Mirahalm? I will kill the male I am married to. I will avenge my family, Sailor, and every other who has died because of him. I will make my father proud of me. Most of all, I will force the Gods to see me for who I am.

Their one mistake.

Chapter 11

When we get to the carriage, the same woman from earlier comes right on up, Tiana. She hugs the king with such familiarity that I can only assume they *know* each other. I growl low, which earns me several looks from the villagers.

"I had something in my throat," I say with a cough.

I watch the king with this woman, whom I know nothing about, and the strangest thing happens—my belly heats, and my vision gets these black dots. Before I know it, I am rushing over to them.

"Hello. They are ready for us," I say, only looking at the king.

His black eyes look directly into my blue ones. "I will be there shortly. They can wait," he answers.

I finally chance a look at the woman standing with her arms crossed against her busty chest and grind my teeth. "Alright then." I don't make a move. Clearly uncomfortable, the woman sighs.

"I will get going, then. Serena, it was wonderful to meet you." She smiles a flat smile and walks away.

My eyes are glued to the male standing right in front of me. "You ready?" I ask, harsher than intended.

He smirks at me before placing a sturdy hand on my lower back. "I thought you would never ask."

He opens the door for me, but before I step in, I ask, "Who is she to you?" I don't know if he will tell me the truth. I know that our bond is supposed to make it to where we must be honest with one another, but I just don't know if he is strong enough to trick it. I still haven't figured out our bond, how it works, or even how I am supposed to feel about being attached to somebody who I didn't choose for myself.

"She is an ex," he answers, as if it's as simple as that. I don't say anything as I step into the compartment.

I sit on the same red velvet seat I had on the way to the palace, the difference being that I have won the king's heart. I no longer have any choice in who I want to be with. I can't pick Sailor even if he were here; I couldn't be with him.

"I see," I say softly, while stabilizing myself in the tilting carriage. The king sits with crossed legs across from me.

"Are you jealous, My Queen?" His eyes dance with amusement that I want to squash.

"In order to be jealous, I would have to care about you." I lean forward, my elbows digging into my knees. "And I do *not* care about you," I lie through my teeth. I know he knows it, too.

He nods his head slowly. "I see." He, too, leans forward, and our faces are so close to touching again that if I wanted him to kiss me, I could easily get it. "So, if I went and fucked her right now, before we left, you would not care?" His fingers dust his jawline, roaming and teasing me.

A growing green monster bubbles over in my belly. Lo and behold...I *would* care. I just refuse to admit it out loud. "Go ahead. I just won't wait the entire minute for it to end. I'll meet you wherever I end up," I respond more casually than I thought I would be able to.

He chuckles darkly, the sound causing lava to explode in the gap between my thighs. "I thought my cock satisfied you the last time." He shrugs his shoulders.

"Oh, the time you tricked me. That time?"

His eyes turn murderous. "The time you claimed my huge cock was better than before, yes."

I slap his face so hard I can see my handprint. As I pull my hand away, he grabs onto my wrist and pulls me right into him so that I'm on my knees on the ground before him.

He grabs my face between his thumb and forefinger. "Don't tease me, *wife*. If you want to touch me, do it," he drawls. I lean in more, and he bends down into my space. But before our lips meet, he grabs onto my shoulders to stabilize me while the carriage takes off. I pull my body from his grip, and he seems to withdraw from the moment as well.

"Sit, rest; we can chat tomorrow after we have made the journey." He tilts his head to the bench across from him.

"You think I trust you to watch me sleep?" I ask in disbelief. I scramble onto the bench to create distance between us.

"I don't see why you wouldn't trust me."

I roll my eyes and cross my arms over my chest at his words. "You don't see how pretending to be somebody else could be troublesome for our relationship?"

He rolls his eyes now, and the very motion is so attractive it's stupid. "You were falling for Aldrich...can we pretend that he is me, and I him?" he responds.

I shake my head violently. "No, I cannot," I declare.

"Why not?" the king volleys right back. He leans his head back against the wall.

"Because you lied to me and slept with me knowing I wouldn't have slept with you!" I roar, then add on for good measure. "And you took my powers as if I am a child who can't handle myself."

He scratches his chin for a moment. "I didn't take your powers from your body, they still lay dormant. No being can take the power running through your blood, other than the Gods. I am no God, even if you believe me to look like one." My face heats from embarrassment. I want him out of my head. "I have already explained to you why I took your powers, but I could explain further if you don't understand?"

I bite down on my cheek, feeling angry with him for putting me in this situation. "I don't need you to explain anything to me. I am rather intelligent," I inform him. He doesn't say anything, so I add, "You made Sailor leave."

His eyes turn grayish. "I didn't take your *plaything* away. I told you my stance, and *you* sent him away. I thought we were moving on from him, though? Do I need to show you what real fucking is to prove to you that you are better off with your *mate*?" His brows reach his hairline.

Sudden heat floods into my body, and I know he is pushing his temper into me. "Calm down," I say, standing up. I can't seem to relax.

"Why are you standing up?" His eyes roam my body in the most obvious way.

"Why are you checking me out?" I volley back immediately.

"Because you are mine. Again, why are you standing up?" He places his dark crown on the seat beside him.

"That's going to fall," I point out.

"Yeah, maybe if the carriage tilts over, and in that case, I would fall, too," he responds sarcastically.

I sit back down. "Then I would, too," I say to myself. I kick my shoes off my feet, trying to settle in for the long night.

"No, you wouldn't." His tone is harsh, but I don't think it's directed towards me. My ankles cross involuntarily as I make myself comfortable in the cramped space.

"Well, if you fall, then I would fall, too," I say, for no real reason other than just being difficult.

The king closes his eyes before responding. "No, because I won't allow you to be harmed, ever." His voice is stone-hard.

"You can't promise that. And not to point out the obvious, but I *have* been harmed in your care before."

He yawns, the most human thing I have ever seen him do. "That was before. It won't happen again. I can promise you that if you fall, I will catch you. In any situation, Serena, I will always catch you." His words feel like a threat.

Chapter 12

When my eyes spring open, I realize three things—that we are in Rawgabbit, that it is warm in the carriage but not outside, and that the king made me fall asleep.

I remember talking with him about what he remembers of the fae lands. He left them when he was sent to follow my mother. I was finally making progress with him, then darkness took me.

I quickly dress in pants and a blouse; I leave the crown. I do not want it, nor do I think it will be welcomed here. I open the door and notice Barnett and Roman standing guard. "Are you two on *Serena duty* today?" I ask before hugging Barnett.

"We are on *Queen* duty today, yes," he corrects me, and I playfully hit his shoulder.

"Whatever you say, BB." I look around, not knowing where to start.

Rawgabbit is wealthy, but not because of the royal family. They have always had their own trade routes, and they pay for that. There has never been an outright rebellion here, but I can sense tension. Almost all of the villages know there is unfairness in the kingdom. If I hadn't won the trials, I can't imagine what would have happened. Or if the other girl would have tried to save the rest of the villages. Like I want to do.

"Let's start in the market and go from there." I smile up at my friend, who seems to be scared of what I might be doing.

When we make it to their village square, the looks I get show me they know who I am. Even without the crown on my head, they do not care for me.

"Stay close," Barnett says as Roman goes above to scout it out. I still can't for the life of me figure out why the Gods would give such a large man the ability to fly. Roman, throughout our travel, will mostly be watching from above.

"You can't be that nervous for me, can you?" I taunt him. I enjoy Barnett. I knew I would since the river. He is mine; I have claimed him as my friend.

"Things in the villages aren't great; I am hoping things will get better with them seeing you and the king."

I sigh and gesture for him to lead the way. "Let's go, then. Sounds like we have a long day ahead of us."

I follow Barnett, acutely aware of every pair of eyes that follows us. I make my way around the village; some houses are worn down, but not most. Each of them reminds me of the makeshift cottages they made for us during the trials. Most have green gardens, open windows, and are painted bright pastel colors.

Most of this village is market. Unlike Darnish, which has many buildings, Rawgabbit has booths of a sort. Also unlike Darnish, it reeks of coin here. Everywhere you look, somebody wants you to spend your coin. Just walking on the cobblestone streets, people rush you, trying to sell you things. This village lacks a kinship—a feeling of family—that I know Darnish has.

"Would you want a sweater?" an older lady asks me.

And I say exactly what I have said to every other person: "I do not, but I would like to pay you whatever you want for it. You sell it and save the coin." Like everyone else, she takes my coin and bows to me.

"Thank you, My Queen."

I know it is little compared to what I could do, but this is a start.

"Serena, are you hungry? We have been at it all day," Barnett says after putting down a ring. I hadn't noticed the rising moon and falling sun.

"Are we leaving tonight or tomorrow?" I ask while blindly following Barnett.

"Would that change your answer in food choice?" He looks back at me, a worry in his eyes that I don't like seeing.

"Well, no, I guess not. I was just asking." Roman and a few others decided to camp out.

He pretends to wipe sweat from his brow; Barnett clearly likes being dramatic. "Good, because I am starving and ready to get some drinks in." He walks towards a tavern-looking building. The outside looks decent enough, though.

"So?" I probe while following him into the building.

"So, what?" He sits at a table, and I silently beg nobody to notice me.

I didn't wear my crown for a reason; I don't want attention for being queen. I want to help these people's lives but not get attention from it.

"You will gain attention whether you like it or not, mate." The king's voice frightens me enough that I spill some water.

"Stay out of my head," I hiss back.

"You okay?" Barnett and the barkeep look at me, each looking worried.

"Yes, I thought I saw somebody I know," I lie too easily. It seems like my lies are coming easier with time. I guess being royal will do that to you.

"I couldn't stay out of your mind if I wanted to," the king responds lightly.

I place my order quickly. "Do you come here often?" I ask Barnett, since he seems to know so much about the local shops and even a few owners.

"Well, I have come here a few times. There is a shop here that sells magic potions." He fiddles with his fingers, seemingly nervous. "I have bought a few," he admits, and I eye him warily.

"What do you mean 'magic potions'? Like...from witches?" I chuckle at him.

"No, I am serious, Serena." His tone is harsh, unlike the silly Barnett that I am used to. "They work, truly. Obviously, you must buy from a real vendor, but they are real," he swears.

I smirk at him even bigger now. I'm curious if he will tell me what kind he has bought of his own volition. I doubt it. Barnett is openly private. If you don't ask, he won't tell you.

"I have never heard of magic potions. What kind of magic?" I ask before sipping on my water. He looks guilty now, and my eyes narrow. *"Barnett...?"* I pry, not directly asking what I want to know.

"You know, some powers can be replicated," he says slowly. I nod my head, trying to get him to continue. "There are plants that, when mixed together properly, could change things or give people abilities they may not have without it."

The barkeep brings out two ales. I didn't order one; they are both for the guard in front of me. "Such as?" I ask. I can't help the suspicion creeping inside of me.

"Well, an empath is easy enough. Mix a few plants together, and you can change a person's emotions. Give them emotions for a time."

Or poison them...

I shiver remembering what that was like. "So, like what Nova did to me." She made me vomit my guts up; she could have killed me, had *he* not noticed.

Barnett gulps down his first mug in one swig. "Yes, exactly. Or even taking magic away or giving it."

My eyes widen. "Could it help get my powers back?"

He places his cup down on the table. "Maybe. We could go look after this?" he says breathlessly.

I smirk. "I think that sounds amazing."

Chapter 13

SERENA

The cool breeze hits my face in the most brutal ways, causing my hair to billow around me. The feeling of my nipples hardening causes me to cross my arms over my chest. Rawgabbit is colder than I would have thought it would be. The market street is still filled with people, though none of them seem bothered by the chilly breeze. The moon's eating away any daylight left.

"Why are you not wearing your crown?" Barnett's voice pierces through my thoughts. I pry my eyes from the ongoing traffic of the village. Rawgabbit is busy. I don't know where all these people live, but they most definitely live differently from anybody in Darnish.

"I don't want the attention from it," I admit, knowing he won't like that. We pass another tavern, and the crowd there is wilder as the night sets in full.

"Isn't that the point of you becoming queen, Serena?" He glares at me in a way that tells me I have irked him.

I spot the white tent-like booths ahead of us, and my pace quickens. "Yes, but I am doing exactly what you said you wanted me to. I just don't want to wear the crown. They know who I am, Barnett." I don't slow when he stares at me; I can feel my body thrumming with unspent energy for the possibility of magic. My powers. Anything to give my body the power reprieve it desires.

"Fine, don't wear the crown. You need to at least gain supporters. Right now, you have an advantage, and you need to use it," he scolds me. I make my way through the heavy crowd. I see all sorts of things—books with images of crazed monsters, sweaters, and paintings. There is also debauchery in plain sight, which is something I have never seen before. Even in the palace, Magnolia kept her parties private. Women here walk around scantily-clad trying to sell themselves. I have already given several of them coin so they didn't have to work for the next month or so. They then went and gave the coin to a man who stood watch over them.

"There is nothing you can do about that," Barnett says softly.

"Hmm?" I hum, clearly irritated.

"Even if you went and took all the coin to give back to them, he would punish them whenever we leave." *I could always kill him.* The dark thought frightens me enough that I drop the painting I'm holding.

"Oh, Gods," I hiss. Barnett rushes over to where I am, picking up the painting I've just ruined. The lady who works the booth scurries over to me.

"Don't worry about it, Majesty. I will clean it up." Her withered eyes are glued to mine. They are a deep gray, the color I picture storm clouds to be.

"I will take it. I think I might like it better this way." I stand up tall, straightening my shirt, and I notice the tent I have been looking for. "Barnett, can you handle this for me?" I ask while absentmindedly walking away from my friend.

"Uh...yeah, sure, but don't go far, Serena," he says, but I barely register it. I wave over my head, though, just to keep him happy.

"Hi," I say absentmindedly to the man in the tent, running my fingers over the tiny vials on the counter. There are bubbling liquids everywhere, pink, purple, and even green. All sorts of potions sit in front of me, and I'm still unsure how they can bottle powers, especially considering the Gods give us our powers for a reason.

"Looking for anything in particular?" the old man asks from behind a small bench. I eye the vial labels: *Strength, Health, Immunity, Masking, Illusion, Invisibility,* and so on.

"I haven't heard of anybody being able to replicate powers before. I am just admiring." I give him a soft smile that barely raises the ends of my lips.

"I see." He stands up. The short, wrinkled man grabs a red sparkly vial. The shimmery particles are glittering and floating about. It's mesmerizing. I hadn't seen anything like this while looking through all of the other vials.

"I would like to gift you something, My Queen." He places the vial in my hands, and I feel unsure about taking it from him...

"What does it do?" I scan the vial closer now, realizing there isn't any label on it.

"It will bring the life you want; it is luck in a bottle." He shoves the vial into my chest, and he must have the power of strength because, for such an old, withered man, he is *strong*. If I had my power, I would try to scan his brain for more information, but I don't.

So, I shrug and do something I know I shouldn't...I gulp down the bottle that the strange old man just gave me in one swig. I have been poisoned before, and my blood has reacted poorly to muting potions, but sure, why not drink some random liquid?

I quickly grab a few more bottles. "And these, please."

He eyes me warily before nodding. "If you are sure."

The liquid is fizzling in my belly, and my throat feels like it is burning with hot rocks. Sweat beads on my brow. "I am sure." I place far more coin on his bench than I owe him and leave the booth.

"Where did you go?" Barnett asks me when we meet in the middle of the pathway.

"I found something that intrigued me." I cringe a little when the bottles clank in my deep pockets.

"Are you ready to go to the inn?" Barnett asks, and I nod, suddenly feeling unlike myself. I imagine the flush I feel is turning my face bright red. I don't know if this is what luck feels like, but I think I like it.

When the fabric of my blouse glides over my already hard nipples, I release a soft moan. Barnett eyes me before averting his gaze.

"You good?" He clears his throat.

I run my sweaty palms over my pants. "Yes; how far are we from the inn?" I need to get to my room right now. I have no idea what is going on, but the hot rocks in my throat have traveled down to my belly and into the apex of my thighs.

"Almost there," he says while looking at anything but me. "Are you sure you're okay?"

"Yes, why?" I don't see an inn nearby, but I know I am about to explode if my skin doesn't rub against *something...anything*.

He clears his throat, "I just think you seem off. Did something happen?" His voice sounds awkward. I continue my search for the inn, ignoring him completely.

"I need to pee; I am going to run ahead. Where do I need to go?" I finally see an inn. I don't have any clue if it is where we are staying, but I don't care.

"Oh, uh... Okay, well, up ahead and a street over," he stammers out. "You don't look alright, I'll just follo—"

I cut him off abruptly. "I am going to go alone. Understand?" I snap. "I need to be alone. Thanks." Without any further explanation, I sprint towards the inn.

Chapter 14

My body is on fire with a need I haven't felt since Sailor. I feel like I could die if I don't explode from this scorching desire first. I haven't felt a need this primal, *ever*. Even with Sailor, it wasn't this consuming. My body feels fervent, and I sprint to the arched door of the inn, not noticing the large, dark and gloomy male standing outside until he grabs both my shoulders, attempting to halt me from getting to my room to alleviate this urge.

The king tilts his head in a way that has his dark hair falling slightly in his face. He blows his hair out of the way, and the move is undoubtedly attractive. I don't know why I do it, but I raise my hand to his face, closing my eyes when my fingers graze his hot skin. I slowly move my fingers into his shiny black hair, running them through the thick waves. I had never noticed that his hair is soft, and it smells like sage and green tea.

My head feels fuzzy and confused. When my eyes finally open, I suck in a breath when I see his onyx eyes begin swirling with navy-blue and white. He shudders when my fingers run through his locks to the back of his head, my nails scraping against his scalp.

"Is somebody chasing you, My Queen?"

I realize my chest is heaving, and he has just caught me running to the inn. My fingers smooth around to his jaw, just barely touching him. He leans into the touch more than he had before, as if he desires being touched as much as I do. I blink several times before realizing he is talking to me. "Nobody is chasing me," I assure him quickly. Only my own guilt over the feelings and urges I have right now.

"If I were a better male, I would ignore the fact that the arousal from you is so potent I could smell you from a mile away."

I should feel ashamed, I should care that this male in front of me is causing my body to come alive in ways I had thought could only happen for one person. The person who made me a whole Sailor James taught me how to live without hiding myself from our kingdom.

My finger slowly runs over his swollen lips. "Is that a bad thing, King?" I taunt while clenching my thighs together. I am unsure how much more I can take without touching myself right here and now.

"You will do no such thing," he growls at me through clenched teeth.

"Is that so?" I narrow my eyes and pout my lips. I am begging him to take me upstairs and take this pain away from me.

"Did you take something?" His tone is concrete; he is angry, I realize. His brows are furrowed, his eyes narrowed on me.

"I went to the market, and a man gave me a luck potion," I admit. My tone is flirtatious and flippant. "I don't feel very lucky, I just feel *on fire*," I add for good measure. He makes a low grumble before picking me up and kicking the inn door off the hinges. My eyes widen dramatically.

"What are you doing?" I ask right as he walks up to the person manning the inn.

"I am about to kill your guards for letting somebody give you anything to drink from the potions master, then I am getting you a room to cool off in."

The girl at the desk stands at attention; she seems to be shaking. "Majesty." Her voice is little, frightened even.

I don't listen after she speaks, I am too distracted by rubbing my face and body against his. I release a moan when I scratch my breast against his chest.

"Damn it, Serena, I am trying to get a room. Stop grinding yourself on me like a cat," he chastises me, but I don't stop. The sparking sensation in my body when his boiling-hot skin touches mine is causing me to want him even more. I look into his dark features, as if this is the very first time I'm actually seeing *him*. I never realized how breathtaking he is. I was so stuck on Sailor that every time I looked at the king, I looked away without truly taking him in.

The king is so deeply tanned that his skin is like sun-kissed silk. His skin is smooth and glows in a way that only confirms my suspicions. He *has* to be a God. I do not believe that any normal human or fae could look like him. His canines are sharpened to points; he doesn't always have his fae teeth on display, but I am glad he does now. Although his ears are still rounded, he looks every bit the king he is.

"What do you mean? My guards reserved two rooms," he snaps at the girl, slamming his palm down on the counter, which causes me to almost fall out of his tight grip. He bounces me up into a higher hold, and my arms squeeze around him, smiling into the crook of his neck. I lift my hand to run my fingers over his light stubble, the dark hairs prickling my fingers sending jolts of hot pleasure to my core. My eyes are zoned in on him and only him. We could be at war right now, and I wouldn't notice a damned other thing.

"Stop touching me like that unless you want me to bend you over right here on this poor woman's desk and fuck you like the crazed fae you are."

My eyes light up with challenge in them. *"I dare you to."*

His eyes narrow to slits. *"You want that, do you, wife?"* His taunting has distracted me to the point that I hadn't even realized he has walked us upstairs. He sets me down in front of a door and my knees almost give out from the sudden loss of contact. I clutch onto the doorframe.

"What are you doing?" I ask when he walks into the room, leaving me behind.

"Waiting for my mate to follow me inside," he drawls.

I look around, and the hallway is empty. The fuzziness is easing slightly, and I can see and feel more clearly. The scary part? I still want him inside of me.

He stands there, a ripe apple perfect for the picking. He slowly reaches up to take his dark, glittering, jeweled crown from his head. My eyes track each and every move he makes. The king places his crown on the nightstand, then stands to his full height. When his eyes meet mine, I am already staring right at him. His jaw clenches so hard I swear I hear his teeth crack. His throat bobs as we stand here, in a duel almost. Both of us are watching the other, just waiting to see who will make the first move.

I take a step through the doorway, then another. Right into the arms of the awaiting demon.

"Are you staying in my room?" I ask softly, not taking my eyes from the danger in front of me. The male I swore to destroy may end up destroying us both.

My body feels so hot that it leaves me with the urge to undress.

"I am." He nods his head, not making any other move. I reach for the hem of my shirt, hoping he doesn't hear the glass bottles in my pockets clink together. His eyes never leave mine, the heat in them almost searing me. "There was only one room left; she wouldn't kick the others out." He grabs my hand that's trying to rid my body of clothes.

"What are you doing?" My eyes dart between his, trying to gauge him. I miss my powers; I want so badly to pry into his head. I want to see what drives this male, what secrets he's hiding from me.

"I don't want you to make a decision while on Marigold." I lift a brow, urging him to explain. "Marigold is a potent aphrodisiac. It is a lust potion, Serena." His voice sounds strained.

I grin. "If you think I only want you because of a potion, you are wrong," I say in a voice that isn't mine. My lust-filled tone should embarrass me, but for some reason, I cannot for the life of me find any shame.

"I don't know what to think with you, Serena. I wish I could unjumble your feelings for you, but I cannot." He takes a step towards me, reaching out to touch me. I find I want nothing more than endless touches from him. He runs his hand down the side of my face and I moan. "Stop making those sounds or else I won't be able to hold myself back."

I lean into him, pressing my chest right into his. My head is completely craned to look into his luminous eyes. "I don't want you to hold yourself back." I bite down on my lip, wishing he would just give in and kiss me.

"I have already made mistakes with you, I will not have any more regrets when it comes to you." He sounds sincere and a little broken.

I push him backwards, and he allows it. The back of his legs hit the chair in the corner of the room. "You have already fucked me, why wouldn't you want to now?" I groan.

"Because I shouldn't have done it." Hurt flashes in his eyes.

"You regret it?" My brows rise. The heat doesn't dissolve, but I wish it would. The contact is about to send me overboard, just from my palms being on his chest. I need him to touch me so badly that I would do almost anything for him to take the pain away from me.

"I could never regret you, Serena. I have searched for you for as long as I can remember. I remember the exact moment I felt the mating bond start to fall into place..." His eyes seem to wander back to whatever moment he is thinking of. "You were falling head over heels for your commander while I sat back and watched. The jealousy alone almost turned me into the monster you all believe me to be."

I grab onto his face. "I was upset with you, but now, in this moment...?" I need him, I need his touch more than I need to breathe right now. "I *need* you. Right now."

He shakes his head, pain lacing his face. "I want nothing more than to have you in every way possible, but not like this. Not again. You deserve more than this." He motions to the inn room. "You deserve more than to be drugged up. I want to be truly yours the next time you feel me."

In the back of my mind, I want that, too, I realize. Lust-filled Serena, though? She wants anything to be moving inside her. "Okay, well, I am giving you first dibs." I shrug and his dark chuckle causes me to back up while still pushing on his chest to remain standing there.

"Dibs on what?" He licks his canines in a way that is so primal, I have the largest desire to run my own tongue over them.

"On me. I am offering myself to you first. I am getting fucked tonight. I was hoping it would be by you, but—" I throw my hands up in surrender.

My legs hit the light wooden bed frame when he rushes to me. "There he is." I smirk.

His hands come to life with flames sparking in them, and he quickly puts the fire out. "You will do no such thing; any man who touches you will be dead by morning," he roars, and I raise my brows.

"Then you better do something," I challenge, knowing I won't make it without some sort of release.

His chest heaves up and down; he is clearly battling with himself internally. "Sit down," he commands, leaving little to no room for argument. I do as he says. I sit on the very end of the bed, where he kneels in front of me.

"Have you ever touched yourself?" he asks me while slowly taking my boots from my feet.

"Once," I answer honestly, the potion causing me to be more honest than I normally would be about my sexual history.

"I see." His eyes lock onto mine as if I am a Goddess he is praying to. He places the boots on the side of the bed, and then my socks come off. "We're going to do something." He runs his hands along my legs, slowly moving up higher to my upper thighs. He grabs on to the waistband of my pants, at the same time pushing me down onto the bed with his other hand.

The king rips my pants down, glass breaks, and I know my vials are ruined, but he doesn't stop to look. I lie on my back in the small, creaky bed. My panties come off next.

"I know you enjoy games, Serena. Would you like to play one?" he asks me from near my core.

I love a challenge, so I nod eagerly.

"Good." He smirks at me. His soft, wet lips graze my hip bone. A small prickle of pain cuts into my skin right where his mouth was.

"Ah." I grab onto his thick, onyx locks right as he licks the dripping blood with his hot and slick tongue. I remove my blouse and throw it into a forgotten corner of the tiny room.

I look at the male I know I will have to kill...but not tonight. Not soon, even. I can have moments with him, can't I? I should enjoy this; the haze is lifting some, but not enough to cause me to stop.

"What are the rules for this game?" I ask while he rips my lace undergarments from under my body.

"It's easy. Neither of us touches the other."

I open my mouth to protest, but he doesn't allow me to. He shoves my undergarments in my mouth. I taste myself on them.

I groan and he clicks his tongue at me. "Do you want to come or not?" He stands up tall, his eyes scanning my body in a shameless way that makes him more sexy in this moment than ever. His fingers go to his own waistband, and I sit up quickly, swatting his hand away.

"Mine," I growl out in a primal way I didn't know I possessed. He turns to stone but I don't slow down, even knowing that this is the first time I have claimed him as *mine*.

Instead of addressing what just came out of my mouth, I reach for his waistband. He holds no weapons; granted, he himself *is* a weapon. He is more powerful than even I was before he took my power away. He yanks his top from his body with the force of a beast; I reciprocate the eagerness by yanking his pants down. The absolute lust and sin in his dreamy eyes tell me that even though he doesn't have a potion urging him on, he wants this as badly as I do.

His massive cock springs free, ready for me. But he takes a step back, then another, and another.

"What are you doing?" I climb over to the edge of the bed, knowing full well I am completely naked and bared to him.

"Sit down." He pushes a gust of wind towards me, causing me to fall onto my back. He doesn't even *try* to be powerful, he just ripples with it. The room warms in a way that tells me he has something to do with it.

"I need you," I plead, trying but failing to push against the air that's shoving me down onto the mattress.

"I already told you...I refuse to touch you while you're under the influence. This is the best I can offer you tonight."

I sigh, knowing that I won't touch anybody else. I lean onto my elbows and look right into his soulless eyes.

"It's hard to have a soul when my eyes have only ever seen destruction. I want to live for you, though. For us." There is a desperation in his voice that hits me right in the chest. What little amount my heart can feel right now pangs with sadness for him.

"Now what?" I need direction.

"Touch yourself." He tilts his head to me. His hand fists his thick shaft, and the clear bead of cum spreads down with the movement.

I follow his lead, our eyes never leaving one another. My hand slowly moves down my stomach, reaching my apex right in time for his eyes to turn hot navy-blue. It would look black to anybody else, but to me? I can see the brightest flames of life springing inside the king I had once thought of as cruel. The king I had once thought of as a killer, a tyrant, somebody who I would love to kill. But tonight? I am seeking whatever pleasure and reprieve he can offer me.

I rub the sensitive bead at my core; my fingers are slick with my need. "I want you to touch me, it isn't the potion. Please, I *need* you." I beg and plead, but he won't. His legs are spread wide open, his glorious muscles and cock on full display while he strokes himself to me. To my body.

"I won't, not until you beg me for it...*sober*, Serena." His eyes track my fingers. "I want you fully. My mate will be mine in every way before I have her." His tone is stern. Understanding dawns on me in a way that should sober me right up. *Sailor.* He wants my heart fully. That is something I don't think I can ever give him. Surely that isn't what he means; he must want children before he dies.

I ignore my thoughts; clearly, the potion gives me more strength than I would have thought possible. The only thought I have in my head is finishing what we have started.

When his fist starts pumping harder, my fingers slip into my core. A breathy moan escapes my throat; he groans out in pleasure. *"I want you to be mine completely,"* he says again, but when his thoughts meet my mind, I explode. *"That's it, baby, cum for me. Cum on those pretty little fingers while you picture me."* His encouraging words spark something in me, the electric feelings pulsing through my body cause my back to arch. His own hand moves faster until he is coming apart on himself. I watch in awe at the monster sitting across from me. The Gods may have paired us together, we may be bonded, but that doesn't mean I can ever be truly his.

As the waves of pleasure subside, the feeling of guilt I assumed to come never does. My chest heaves up and down while the king hurriedly grabs a rag to wipe me off, then himself. He stands in front of me, completely naked and still half hard. I arch a brow.

"Hmm?" he hums while I eye his throbbing cock. "Can you blame me when you look like that?" he says in defense, and I chuckle. "Put this on." He bends down to grab a loose shirt off the ground. I place the white shirt over my head, suddenly becoming engulfed in him. *Sage and green tea.* His scent overwhelms me in a way that almost has tears springing to my eyes. I still have feelings for this man. Even though he tricked me, even though he hurt me in ways I have never been hurt before. I may love Sailor, but something else is happening with the king that I cannot stop.

Chapter 15

<u>SERENA</u>

"Where will you be sleeping?" I find myself asking while the effects of the potion leave my body.

I want a bath, I want to soak the shame away...but there isn't any shame. I wish there were—I wish I felt badly about this—but I do not. My mind wanders to Sailor now that the moment is over, and I just hope he is living the life I wanted for him when I sent him away.

The king arches a brow at me. "I will be sleeping right there." He points to the bed right next to me.

"Oh?" I am already lying in the middle of the itchy bed, and I refuse to move an inch.

"There is room for us both, isn't there?" he taunts.

"You could sleep on the floor."

"I don't sleep on *floors*, and it isn't like we haven't shared a bed one or two times before."

I scoff. "Because you are a mighty *king*?" I roll my eyes and shake my head against the pillow.

"No, because I am old and simply do not wish to sleep on the hard floor."

I bite back a giggle; I do not want him to think he is funny. "You're old?" I ask instead of flirting.

He moves to the edge of the bed, and sits down. I scoot over when his head meets the pillow right next to my face. An hour ago, I would have attacked his face with anything—my fingers, lips...Blessed, even my teeth.

"I am older than I look. Fae age differently, Serena. When I was sent to find you by my parents, I was only seventy-eight. That is young by fae standards, but living in the human lands has taken a toll on my body. I need home to thrive; we must go back. And not just because the people need our rule. Our bodies aren't made for this land," he tells me. And before I can even process that, he continues, "Many years ago, a Goddess moved the fae to a land that was created for our kind."

I should focus on this information about our homelands considering the fact that I need to steal them from him and his family for my own family. But instead, I say something so unimportant that Juniper would probably burn me alive.

"So, you're ninety-one?" I ask, feeling so confused.

He laughs before rolling over to fully face me. This version of him looks so innocent and human. I almost forget everything that has happened. I could envision a life where we live happily. If things were different, I could love him for *him*, and not Aldrich.

"You are bad at math, darling."

I cross my arms over my chest. "I didn't go to primary school, so be glad I got as close as I did." If I even did get close, it was by pure luck.

The king slowly reaches his hand towards my face, and when his knuckles brush across my cheekbone, I shudder.

"What are you doing?" I whisper.

"Touching my wife." His voice is just as soft as mine, which surprises me because he isn't the type to soften himself for others. He has killed and tortured, yet he sounds genuine when he speaks to me. How can he sound this nice?

"Why didn't you help the villages before?" I finally ask the question that has been burning in the back and front of my mind. He pushes a lock of hair behind my ears, leaving his hand on my head. The gentleness in which he touches me is so soft that it makes me question everything I know about him. His hand is almost as big as my entire head; he holds my face up while I lean into him more than I should.

"I couldn't. There are other forces and beings at play here. Even though I have been crowned king over the humans, I still answer to somebody."

I roll onto my side, fully facing him. Our knees brush, and even though the potion has long since worn off, the touch causes electric shocks throughout my body.

My body forgets that he is our enemy. My body burns with desire for the male who took everything from me. My traitorous body doesn't realize we are in bed with the enemy. I want to remind it, to yell at myself. But I won't. I have deprived myself of happiness my entire life. I have lived with the fear of being found out and killed, or worse...used. Now I can use him at least.

"Who do you answer to?" I ask, almost scared to know who is more powerful than he is.

"My parents, for one." He shrugs, and my body tenses. I don't know if I am ready for this conversation.

"But you want to dethrone them," I state as plainly as I can muster in the moment, just praying to the Blessed that he will tell me more. The hatred I feel for them could boil my body to nothing but liquid.

"They will step down when we ascend the throne."

I bite my retort down. Now is not the time to fight. "I see."

His thumb moves in slow circles on the side of my face. If I didn't know any better, I would say he is trying to calm himself down.

"Anyway, I think it's time to go to bed. We have an early day tomorrow and a long one at that." His face crumbles slightly. He gulps before adding on, "Change in route plans." His voice is gruff.

Brabble.

The last time I was there, I left the girls who got my father killed to rot. I wish I had done more to them. "We have to go through Brabble?" I ask with thinly veiled panic. I'm not scared for myself, even though I don't have power. I still know nothing will happen to me.

"We do... A road gave out. I have tried to find a way around, but there isn't one that makes sense." He pauses for a moment before continuing. "We have shifters and blinks who will help when they can, but nobody wants to burn out. We will get through quickly and strategically. Nothing will hurt you, I promise."

I wish he wouldn't. It feels too soon to say nothing will happen in Brabble when I still have images of the bodies thrown in every direction.

"Are you nervous?" His voice is so soothing that I close my eyes, closer to sleep than I have been in weeks.

"Yes," I answer honestly.

"Not because of Brabble, though." Not a question but a statement. I shake my head. "What worries your pretty little mind, mate?" I sneak a peek at him, squinting one eye slightly open. His eyes are fully trained on me.

Instead of answering, I ask him something that has burned in the back of my mind. "Do you sleep?" I know full well that if he wants to see what is worrying me, he can and will look. His powers are so strong that he can probably look into several minds at a time, if not dozens. His strength is unmatched since we mated. I don't know what causes this bond to strengthen our powers, but whichever God did it is watching us closely. They are cheering us on. I know this because I have snuck into his training rooms to watch him, and the way his body moves isn't like a king. He moves like a warrior preparing for a battle. His powers are stronger than ever; I can taste them. I want my own powers back to train myself against him. It will take years to beat him, but I will do it.

He interrupts my thoughts. "I do...just not in the same way that you do." He smirks at me.

"And why is that?" I wonder, more to myself.

"Because even in Mirahalm, nobody sleeps like you, other than some monsters in the wintertime." I playfully hit his shoulder, and he pretends to be harmed. "Hey! It's not my fault you sleep more than a bear in hibernation."

I roll over to face the wall, pretending to be hurt. He moves immediately, his chest against my back. I can feel the barest hint of his lips moving near my neck, but not touching. Just teasing me, and I love it. His hips move forward, pressing into me. I move my head a little because it tickles my neck when he breathes out, and his stubble scratches against my skin in the most delicious way.

"Don't move away from me," he demands.

"You want me to sleep with a hot box right on top of me?" I ask over my shoulder.

"I'm too hot for you?" He smiles into my neck; goose bumps rise over my arms.

I look over my shoulder at him. "Your body temperature is warmer than I like. If I had my powers, I would just cool myself off, but since I don't..." I let the rest of the statement fall off.

Suddenly, the windows gain some frost on them, my breath is foggy, and I shiver. "Better for you, hellcat?" he drawls.

"Much." My eyelids are heavy, and I struggle to keep them open any longer.

"Serena?" His voice pierces my almost sleep-filled mind.

"Huh?" I barely get out.

"Will you ever give in fully to me...to *us*?"

I almost second-guess that he has actually asked me that. Alwin, our king, is asking me about my feelings for him?

I start to answer but stop, knowing the words will just come out jumbled and wrong, because I know, deep down, I *will* love him one day. I feel it in my heart, my core, my body. My mind is shifting to only see him. Tears threaten to spill over, because even though I feel like Alwin might be my future. I can't see past the fog of Sailor. I don't have it in me to clear him from the forefront of my mind.

"Sailor once told me his power is a part of him." I breathe out, my shaky breath making it hard to finish, but I know I have to. I must put distance between me and the king. He may be my husband, my mate even, but he will never be my sailboat in the storm. He will never be Sailor. I rub my thumb over the place on my wrist where I know I'll find comfort. "That if he lost his power, he would die. The Gods made power within us, so deeply rooted it would kill us to lose them completely." Unlike what I have been going through, I feel more dead inside about Sailor than not being able to heat my body. "I feel the same...but about Sailor. I may die without him in my life, however that looks." I swallow, unsure if I should look behind me and gauge his reaction. A single tear falls onto the arm that lies underneath me. "I need him, even as a friend or guard, I don't care. I just lost far too much in such a short time."

Judging by the room suddenly heating up to almost burning, I decide not to look at the king. I close my eyes and whisper, "Good night, King."

He nods his head, his arms snaking around my body. "Night, Serena," he says gruffly. I nuzzle into his arm under my head.

Darkness encircles me; shadows dance across my skin. I feel them everywhere. The light from the moon outside is completely gone. I fall asleep with a king to my back. Someone who, at one point in my life, I would have turned around to and slit his throat. Tonight? I suck in as much of his scent as I possibly can, and I memorize him completely. The way his body morphs into mine, the way we fit perfectly. The way my fingers fit around his forearm.

When I wake, he is gone. Long since, considering his side of the bed is made neatly and stone-cold. The room is an icebox box, though; something I am grateful for.

I make my way into the bathing chambers; a warm, steaming bath awaits me, along with a note.

Serena,

I had important business to attend to this morning. I will meet you at the carriage whenever you wake. I want you to know, I will give you the time you require. I have infinite years to wait for you to be ready for us. Take all the time you need to figure it out. I am yours always.

Yours truly AAH

He may have time to wait, but our people don't. Neither kingdom is in great shape from what I hear of the fae lands, and the human ones are about as close to war as they can be. The people are done waiting for him to step up and help; there are more and more wrongdoings in their eyes. People are dying for food, coin, or even just shelter. Some are born without any power at all. It seems as if even the Gods are forsaking humankind. We need to take bigger risks to save those who look up to us for guidance. We must take the brunt of the imposing war.

I may be new to being a queen, but I am not new to helping people. My father always gave more than he had; I will do the same. I will make him proud in whatever realm he is in. I hope he looks down to see me following in his footsteps.

Chapter 16

Barnett waits for me right outside my room, his face sullen.

"What's wrong with you?" I ask him right as his steps match with mine. The sun is already rising in the morning sky, and the brisk air opens my lungs. I love the chill, I need it to thrive.

"His Majesty wasn't thrilled about you being drugged," Barnett says sorrowfully. I hadn't even thought about what might happen to Barnett after last night.

"Did he do something to you?" I ask, making my way to the bakery I know is somewhere around the tavern. I had seen it yesterday, and I need something sweet, and I need it to taste normal.

"Not to *me*, no," he deadpans. I furrow my brows, about to ask him what he means, but I don't need to.

When we hit the center of the village, I see what I have done. Well, what the king has ordered to be done. But since I am queen, they will all suspect me of being in on it.

I don't dare show a reaction when I see the elderly man strung up on the rafters; I show absolutely no emotion when his lifeless eyes meet mine. I quicken my steps, my heartbeat racing. I just hope nobody is able to hear my heart break; I doubt they can. I realize how many abilities I am around and just hope none of the gathering crowd are his loved ones. I hope I don't have to kill anybody in my defense.

Barnett protectively grabs onto my hand. "Just stay close. Let's get your breakfast and hurry on up." His grip is firm. Sometimes I forget his power is the strength of the Gods.

"Ouch," I hiss when he pulls a little too hard.

"I'm sorry. I just don't want a fight to occur this morning," he explains as he pulls me around the village. He scans the crowd, doing exactly what he should as my guard. I just can't help but feel guilty. I don't like him thinking my life is more important than his.

The bakery comes into view, and I step into the small bake shop without hesitation.

"Majesty," the owner addresses me while wiping her flour-covered hands on her bright pink apron. I look around at the choices, which are different than back in Darnish. The food here is brightly colored, but there aren't cute little decorations on the cupcakes. The tarts don't have sweet designs depicting woodland creatures. It lacks a sense of home.

"Hello. You've got yourself a cute little bakery," I say, sensing her eyes roaming over me.

"You lie, but I will thank you nonetheless."

I don't know what to say. Living in a cottage in the woods my entire life didn't prepare me for hostile people. There is a reason I never went into Darnish.

"Could I get a few chocolate chip muffins, a scone or two, and some crumbles, please?" I order enough for most of the group. I do realize some of the guards with us will need more food, but between Barnett and me, we won't be able to carry it all.

An ice-cold sensation skirts into my head. "Are you—" I narrow my eyes right as blinding pain erupts behind my eyes. "Ah!" I scream.

Barnett rushes over to her. "What are you doing to her?" he says, grabbing her by the throat.

"She killed them. All of them. She deserves to die." She hisses out the venomous words. *I did kill them.* Maybe I *should* die. I cover my ears as blood trickles down the sides of my face, and I think I'm still screaming.

Then it all stops, the blinding pain, the blood, *her.* I realize Barnett has killed her; the moment I lock eyes with her lifeless form, I choke. It isn't even noon yet, and so far, two people have died for me.

The king rushes in a moment later. "What happened?" he roars. "I was gone for less than a few hours." His strong hands grip my shoulders tightly. "Serena, are you okay?"

Barnett clears his throat. When the king's attention turns to him, I crumple to the ground. "She must have had family at your wedding." Barnett sucks his cheeks in. "She tried to cook the queen's brain from the inside out," he says before shuffling over to me.

I rock back and forth, trying to get rid of the pain in my body. "Are you alright?" The king's eyes blaze with fury as he kneels in front of me. I nod my head, then wince, realizing it hurts to move. Wolf makes it to the door of the bakery a moment later, and his bright green eyes scan my body.

"Are you okay?" Wolf's voice is tender, unlike his rigid form. I lean into the king when his warm hands meet my body.

I cough before answering, "I am fine." The words come out clipped.

The soothing warmth of the king's healing power bleeds into my body in a way that makes me feel safe. I groan when I stand, even with help from Barnett and the king.

"Where were you?" I ask through my teeth, grinding them together.

"I left you a note. As it said, I had business to attend to," the king answers without any hesitation.

"The old man?" I ask lazily as I pull out of their tight grip and make my way behind the countertop and gather more food than I can carry. He grabs some of the tumbling pastries from my hands.

"Among other things, yes." He follows right behind me. I don't miss the fact that Wolf tracks our every move.

"What were these other things?" Feeling anxious, I grab other food from behind the counter, muffins of sorts, anything I can get my grubby hands on.

"Why are you so suddenly curious about my comings and goings?" he asks suspiciously.

"Do you love him?"

The question startles me so much I almost stop mid-bite into a warm muffin. I don't, but it was close enough. I look Wolf right in the eyes. The king looks between us, as if knowing he is not a part of something.

"I don't know," I answer honestly, knowing he doesn't deserve my truth, but I'll give it to him anyway. Wolf turns to leave the bakery, anger rippling from him. Barnett is right on his heels, leaving me and the king alone with the dead body.

"I thought you could fight," he comments, taking the muffin from my hands.

"Hey, that's mine." I try to grab it back, but he takes a large bite out of the steaming muffin. A few crumbs tumble from his mouth. "I *can* fight," I say defensively. I reach for the muffin once more, but before I can grab it, he places a piece right in front of my mouth. I open right up for him.

"Good girl," he coos. I swallow the chunk of muffin, and he watches as my throat bobs up and down. "*I can fight*," I say more aggressively.

"I believe from the stories you told me, you would force yourself to go without powers, and you would try to live and survive without them. Where are those skills now?" He sounds angry with me. His deep tan skin flushes red under his cheeks.

"Gone. With my father, with Sailor, with everybody I have killed. Did you know that I was the one who killed those people in Magnolia's sick club?" My eyes look downwards in shame.

"I had my suspicions, yes." He nods his head, right as his fingers grip my chin. He forces me to look into his eyes. "There she is." He gives me a tilted half-smile.

My eyes look down towards my feet again, and shame burns through my body. The people I have killed, or been the cause of their deaths, are piling up around me.

"Look at me, Serena." My eyes listen before my head can. They meet his, and in this moment, the dead body next to me is gone. The bodies I have piled up are gone. It is me and the king. Just us.

"You are not at fault for her death. She *attacked* you."

A lone tear streaks down my face, and I nod, which causes the tear to fall to the ground. "What about the man?" I ask so softly that he shouldn't have been able to hear me.

"What about him?"

"You killed him because of me, didn't you?" I ask him, unsure of how to feel in this moment.

"I ordered his death because he attacked his queen. I cannot and will not allow anybody to make moves against you." His fingers start to move in a soothing pace.

"There is death everywhere I look. I don't know how to live with it," I say, admitting my weakness.

"You don't. You learn from it, learn from your mistakes, and from others. That is what I have to offer you for advice." His hand releases my face, and he gestures to the door.

"Serena, I don't have all the answers for you. But I do know that with or without your power, you are a force to be reckoned with. You are strong and passionate; you are the queen who two kingdoms have waited for. You do not deserve death. You deserve for every being in the realms to bow at your feet."

I open the door, pastries in hand. I look over my shoulder, and the king is standing so close that if I were to get onto my tiptoes, our lips would touch.

"Including you?" I smirk back at him.

"I would give up my crown to follow your lead. I would gladly kiss your feet if you only asked." His face is so serious, I believe him. That is the scary thing, I am believing him more and more. Trusting my enemy when I know at any moment he could rip the rug from under my feet.

Chapter 17

The bridge into Brabble is worse than I realized. The king is sitting across from me, reading a book on the history of firebending. Elemental magic seems to be his favorite; he uses it more than any other power he has. He speaks to me often in my mind, but at this point, I don't know if that is our mating bond falling into place or his mental abilities.

The bridge creaks as our carriage goes across it. While there aren't as many carriages with us as there were last time, I still have a sinking feeling that the bridge will collapse at any moment. The darkness seems thicker this time, more daunting than when we traveled to the palace. The whispers seem stronger now, too, as if daring to drag us over the edge and into oblivion.

"It will not break. The Gods have magic woven throughout the very essence of the wood." I look out the window, unable to see the bottom of the ravine. "I won't let you fall," he assures me.

I look at him; his eyes have not left his book. "It is rude of you to read my thoughts." My sharp words finally get his attention.

"It is rude to call your mate '*the king*,'" he volleys right back at me. I run my fingers through my hair, feeling nervous now.

"You *are* the king," I say sternly.

"Yes, I am. But to you, I am much more." He goes back to reading as if we weren't just talking. I have never seen somebody read so fast in my life. His eyes scan the pages so quickly, I have trouble believing he actually read a single word on that page.

"You can't possibly be reading that fast," I comment in disbelief, and he looks up again, seemingly annoyed.

"I can, and I do." He smirks. "Does that impress you, darling?" Then a single dimple appears. His smile is so big...I don't think I've seen him this happy before.

"No, a child could read. I think you are skimming," I accuse, and I regret it before I even finish the words. I should have known the Gods would give me somebody as competitive as I am. He hands me the book, and I take it without second-guessing myself.

"Ask me anything from pages one to five hundred."

My eyes widen in surprise before I look at how thick the book is. "Seriously?"

He shrugs. "Yes, seriously," he says sarcastically. His black outfit today fits his body in ways I shouldn't notice, but now that there isn't a massive book covering him, I quickly peruse. His thighs are so strong they look like stone; his arms are bulging in his shirt. I shake my head to focus on the task in front of me.

"How common is it that somebody will have all four elements?" I ask quickly, while flipping through the book.

"About eleven percent of humans were gifted all four elements," he says fast and sure. I suddenly find myself more interested in this book.

"What is the most uncommon power?"

His answer comes right away. "Cloning." I didn't even know they let clones live among others.

"What power comes mostly from your emotions?" I ask in rapid spitfire.

"Healing."

"Why are you reading this?"

"I am seeking to learn more than I know now. Don't you want to learn something every day?" He tilts his head towards the book.

"Aren't you a hundred years old? Don't you already know all of this?"

His dark chuckle sends shivers down my spine, right to my thighs. "I am not a hundred, Serena. You need to know how old your husband is. I am ninety-seven by the way."

He isn't wrong. "Alright then, so you are old," I concede. I decide to switch up my questions. "What's your favorite color?"

"Blue."

Like my eyes, but I don't say that. Surely it isn't because of my eyes.

"Do you have siblings?"

"Three."

Interesting. I will need to dig into that further at a later date.

"Are you close to your parents?" I watch his reaction closely.

"I was." His Adam's apple bobs, but he doesn't show any other sign of discomfort.

"Why did you come here?" I try to keep my tone level.

"To Brabble?" He lifts his brow, crossing his ankles and leaning back into the velvet seat. His hands rest in his lap, fingers intertwined with themselves.

"No, to Nymphamera."

"You."

I suck in a hard breath. "Why?"

"I was sent to follow the queen. She was pregnant with you when she left Mirahalm, but when I found her, she wasn't."

Yeah, because she had teleported me into another. It killed my siblings' mother and the daughter she was pregnant with. Guilt almost constricts my throat for a moment.

"What happened when you found her?" Right as I ask the question, I hear a roar outside the carriage. We are well into Brabble now, I notice.

"I didn't even realize we were here," I whisper while looking out into the foggy unknown, I chance a glance at the king.

"Having too much fun with your questions?" the king taunts, a full-blown smile on his face. I look away immediately, knowing I won't be able to not smile while looking at his smile. I don't dare take my eyes from the thick-misted tree line.

"I don't like it here," I admit. "It feels all wrong." I chew on the side of my cheek.

"Because it is wrong." He doesn't take his eyes off me.

"Then who is letting them out?" I wonder out loud. If it isn't the king, then who? He doesn't answer me, though. His jaw clenches hard; clearly he heard me, but he ignores the question.

The large trees go by in a blur; rocks that are bigger than any home I have ever seen pass by the windows. I watch as small monsters graze in the clearing. They seem totally unfazed by us. They must be eating well enough, since they don't feel the need to chase our carriages. Some of them have sharp, jagged teeth coming out of their mouths. I watch them carefully to make certain they don't follow behind us.

As soon as I think we're going to get through this unscathed, a huge monster with green fur rushes our carriage, and the guards outside kill it without a thought. I gasp as the beast dies in a mist of blue mush. The slimy liquid burns into the ground, causing a massive crater to form.

"Yuck," I say, faking vomiting. That earns me a laugh, a real one, from the king. His smile lights up the entire carriage, and I smile back, teeth and all. I completely forget to watch outside, at the hell we are trapped in.

We are making good progress through the monster-filled lands. The horses haven't had to stop once. They may know what sort of danger awaits us if we do. When I feel a warm liquid trickle down my thighs, I swear I might have peed myself. The king's nostrils flare in a way that causes me to blush. His senses are so homed in on me, I fear he might know I accidentally just wet myself. I don't know how that happened. I haven't peed myself in a long time. Since I was a toddler, actually. I must have drunk too much water trying to distract myself from where we are.

"We're stopping," the king announces abruptly.

"Why?" Concern hits me like a bag of stones.

"Because" is his only explanation. The carriages slow down to a stop. I push to stand up, feeling more warm liquid seeping from my body. My face turns bright red and I gulp down my saliva before I finally stand up completely. I now realize what has happened and I know I have made a mess. Something I don't want him to see, but I need to move.

"Wait here for a few moments, please," he says, standing up as much as he can before ducking out of the carriage.

"Okay then." I don't dare look down at my pants, unsure if I want to see the evidence of what I know is true.

Mother Nature is a bitch, and she has a sick sense of humor. I run my hand over my face, and I can feel just how flushed I am. I know I must look like a tomato; I have never started my period in public before. I wish I had my sister here to help me. Evie would take the best care of me. I miss her warm rags when I was sick, her healing power that radiated kindness and compassion, and her overall calm demeanor.

After several long minutes, the door opens again. The king holds out a large cloth. "Take this, please," he mumbles, not making eye contact.

"Okay," I say dramatically. He slams the door right in my face. "That was rude," I huff out, feeling more than annoyed with him.

When I take a step, more liquid runs down my legs, apparently, my Fae nature has come into full-bloom. I have never bled this much before turning Fae, I wish I had someone to guide me through this. I finally look down at the red warmth that has saturated my pants. I wrap myself in the large cloth and open the door, seeing a large white tent has been set up.

"How did this happen so fast?" I wonder aloud.

Wolf comes up behind me, and I jump. "Because you are the queen now. The king ordered it, so it shall be done," he slurs.

"Are you drunk?" I smell whiskey on his breath.

"Maybe," he admits with hooded eyes.

"Drunk Wolf isn't a good Wolf," I say in a singsong voice.

He smirks. "You know, there was a time when you wanted me." His breath makes me lean away from him. My eyes widen, and I'm reminded I need to clean myself up.

"There was also a time you would have done anything for your brother," I retort.

He just plows on through as if I have not said a word. "You are a queen now, though."

I feel as if I shouldn't be involved in this conversation. I turn to go into the tent, which I believe is for me, but he grabs my wrist. "Would you have picked me?" His eyes narrow on me, his grip tight. His question catches me so off guard, I don't know what to say at first.

"No," I manage, then turn on my toes to leave. I won't be entertaining any talk about what could have happened. Especially not with the person who failed not only me but his longest friend.

I can't call them brothers anymore; neither one of them would consider the other a brother, either. It makes me sad to think about. Sailor once had everything he could have wished for, only to have it all ripped away from him because of me. I might have lost a lot, but he lost everything.

The tent is large enough for a small bed, a bath, and that is it. The bath is already drawn with steaming hot water. The smallest table in existence sits beside the tub. A note sits atop it.

Food will be brought to you. Clean up and relax for tonight. Nothing is going to get you. I promise. I will be near if you need anything at all.

AAH

Chapter 18

The tiny burning fire in my tent is the only light source, and the moon doesn't seem to reach us here in hell. I swear I hear screams from miles away, then when I look outside the flaps, there is nothing out there other than the men drinking themselves to death. They laugh so loud I cringe every time I hear them. Apparently, they are actually enjoying the time here, according to Barnett. He brought my food an hour ago; nothing much, just enough to keep us alive for the time being. There is a shield around our camp, keeping the noise in and the monsters out. I don't know who is doing the air shield, but they must be strong to maintain it for this long. The priest has yet to leave his carriage; he claims the Gods will punish us for coming into the lands they use for their prisoners. I, for once, agree with him. It seems foolish to go through the lands they have made for beasts they no longer care to keep as weapons.

I haven't had a period in so long, I had forgotten how much Evie helped me through it. She would heal the cramps away, she would warm me up when I felt empty. I don't know if this is a fae thing or not, but my period brings on the most horrible mood swings. And I can just tell this will be the worst one yet. My lower back hurts so badly I could cry out in pain. I won't, but I could. I hadn't ever transformed into a fae before; it's as if all of the fae changes are coming on quickly now. My body feels foreign to even me; I don't feel like myself anymore.

"I want my powers." I moan out in pain, wishing I could heal it all away, even though it feels better when somebody else heals me. After hours of not being able to sleep, I pop my head outside the tent. I see a few guards asleep, but most of them are awake and walking around the perimeter. My pulse spikes rapidly when I notice Barnett is walking around with them. I care almost as much about him as I do Sloan.

I go back into the tent and moan out in pain again. "I want this pain to stop," I cry out softly before putting my fist into my mouth and biting down. I know I can't take another moment of this, so I go lie back down to twist and turn some more. I pull into myself, going into a fetal position on the small bed.

"*Where are you?*" I scream down the bond. A moment later, the king comes in, black mist and all. His tall form almost snuffs out all the light in this tent. I wouldn't mind. I feel tired but unable to fall into the blissful darkness I crave.

"I am here. I told you I would be around. Do you, uh, need something?" He seems unsure of himself in a way that is strange to me.

"Yes, I need you here to distract me." I grip my belly. "I am in pain!" I cry out, feeling so vulnerable in this moment. I hate that he's the one seeing me like this. I hadn't ever realized how much my siblings had helped me be strong. Juniper with pushing me and my powers to my limit, and Evie always being there as a constant healer, but even something like a mother to me. She taught me how to heal with warmth and kindness. My fae darkness might be trying to pop through, but I was raised human.

His eyes flicker with concern before he reaches into his pants pockets and grabs a vial. I scoot away immediately. "Oh no." I shake my head violently, which causes pain to erupt in my temples. "No more potions from anybody." I wave my hands out in front of me.

"Will you just trust me?" He steps towards me slowly; he seems to be struggling to catch his breath. He inhales through his nose and out his mouth several times before taking another step.

"What's wrong with you?" I ask him accusingly, the space between my brows crinkling.

"I can...I can *smell* you," he says, as though that is explanation enough.

"And?" I urge him to continue.

"I can smell your blood. It calls me to, um, *mate* with you." His eyes are planted on the ground, as if he can't look at me.

My mind whirls with his words. "My *period blood* turns you on?" I eye him warily. In and out, I watch his nostrils flare, feeling hot myself. I am actually grateful for the momentary distraction from the blinding pain.

"Not exactly your period blood, darling." He chuckles deeply. "The scent that is coming from you does, though. I can smell it, and since we are bonded, it is stronger than it would normally be." He hands me the vial; I take it from him without asking any more questions. "It's fae nature to try and procreate. Babies are hard to come by, so when females are in heat—" I wince when he uses that animalistic term. He must notice and adjusts himself. "When females are on their *period*, it will prompt naturally stimulating hormones from both males and females to come in full blast. It's nature's way of trying to help fae have babies." I wish I had a huge book about everything Fae.

When I turned twelve, Evie walked me through the birds and the bees for people. Everything I might need to know about my body, or any boy's bodies I may be touching. I thought I had learned all there was to know, even though now it seems like some of that could be wrong. I know next to nothing about fae, and yet I am going to be their queen someday. Hopefully...if their war doesn't kill them before I get there.

"So, I will be turned on *more* than normal because of my period?" I ask in disbelief as I eye the vial. "Because I will tell you, I am in so much pain I will do anything to make it go away." I rock my hips, trying to force the stabbing sensation to leave my body.

He tilts his head to the vial still resting in my hands. "You are turned on often, then?" He bites down on his lip, seemingly unaware that he is flirting with me.

"Often enough to know that this is going to be awful." My eyes dart to the vial in my hand. I ignore his question, opting for a conversation about the potion I'm holding.

He bites down on whatever he was going to say to me and instead settles for, "Drink up. I am going to get you some food." He turns to leave, and panic settles in my belly.

"I don't want you to leave. I have already eaten dinner. I just want you to stay with me," I say in a hurried voice that does not belong to me. It's shy and uncertain, unlike me at all.

"If I stay in here with you tonight, you will end up doing something you do not want." His eyes ripple with a mixture of hurt, confusion, and lust. Pure lust, as if his own calling to demand my body is too much for him.

"Who says I don't want it?" I challenge him.

"You will," he promises. But the thing about promises is that they are never guaranteed.

I roll off the cot and stride to where my enemy stands. My husband and my mate and the very male who will completely ruin me. The only being that I have ever thought might truly bring me to my knees. His eyes finally meet mine, and the raging fire in them tells me all I need to know. He wants me just as much as my body is telling me I want him. I throw back the liquid from the vial, and it burns my throat going down. I grimace slightly at the taste, then drop the vial onto the ground.

I push my chest into his stomach, knowing exactly where this will end, fully embracing what I must do for Mirahalm and for my plans. I need this just as much as he does. Hormones or not, I have known since my wedding where this was going to go. I agreed to it the moment my blood mixed with his. The liquid I just took is already soothing my tender joints.

"My body is aching for yours. *Please* ruin me, consume me, crush me if you must, just *touch me*," I beg, knowing that is what he wants me to do. I lift up onto my tiptoes and press my soft, full lips onto his equally swollen and pink lips.

He doesn't kiss me back for a moment, as if he is waiting for me to change my mind. I don't. My entire body is entranced with him. I feel as if I am ensnared by him, like there is a pull to him that I can no longer deny. He is not my friend; he never was. I had known there was something about him, even when he was Aldrich. I just didn't know what it was.

Finally, I feel the snap. The cord that was keeping me from giving myself completely to the bond is gone. The last and final straw that held me back from giving myself to the mating bond. The warmth of the full bond is almost overwhelming; it feels as if he and I are one and the same. Like my body is no longer just mine, but his as well.

As if he can feel it, too, he moans into my mouth. "Are you mine?" he asks me against my lips, then his tongue sweeps against mine. Our mouths open wider for the kiss. This is our breaking point, the moment we accept the bond completely.

I pull back slightly. "I am," I answer, even though I can tell he already knew it.

"Prove it." He grips the back of my thighs, pulling me up his body, and even though I know there is blood between my legs, it won't slow me down.

I wrap my thighs so hard around his hips, I could hold myself up. His fingers dig into my flesh as if he is scared I will leave and never come back. I grind my core into his midsection, needing the friction.

His mouth peppers kisses along my throat, and the sensitive skin burns hot every place he touches me. His fingers sneak their way to my pants, slithering ever so slowly through every step. I know that in these moments, I am loved and cared for so deeply this male would kill or die for me.

"Come on." I urge him to move faster, needing it in the most primal of ways. I need him inside me like I need my next breath of air.

"We have eternity together, please allow me to love you in this moment." His eyes burn holes into mine, and I see the pleading shining there, urging me to nod my head in agreement. The vulnerability in him is so palpable, I unclasp my ankles from behind his back. My feet hit the ground, immediately missing his warm body against me.

I reach up to unclasp the buttons of his top, and after each and every one, I press kisses to his firm chest. I rake my nails up and down the creases of his abs; the years it must have taken to carve out his body in this way makes me almost feel more grateful that he is willing to share it with me. When I get to the last button, I kneel before him, my eyes latched onto his dark ones.

"Serena." He grinds his teeth, his jaw flexing in a way that shows me my kisses are affecting him more than one might think for a tyrant fae king. I press my lips right above his waistband, the pain of Mother Nature long forgotten. "You don't have to." He tries to pull me up, but I don't allow it.

"You want me to be loved, but when was the last time you felt loved?"

His face is like stone, and any emotions I had seen are gone. "A long time." He blinks several times.

I undo his waistband, my eyes locked on his as I bow to *my king*.

I pull his pants down, and his massive cock springs free. I lick my lips when I see the bead of cum shining in the dim light. I lean forward and press a kiss to the tip, smoothing the liquid over it with my lips. I press quick kisses to his cock before wrapping my lips around him. He groans, telling me he likes it. I slide him farther into my mouth while my fingers play with his balls. His hand fists my hair, forcing my eyes to meet his. "Eyes on me," he demands firmly, so I obey; I keep them there. Eyes never leaving his, I quicken my pace. My teeth lightly graze his shaft, just enough to put pressure. His cock doesn't exactly fit comfortably, and the thickness fills my mouth up so much I almost choke. The way he moans makes me feel as if he won't last very long at this rate.

"I will last all night if that's what it takes to keep you from pain," he grunts into my head. At the same moment, he picks me up, spit leaking from my slightly parted lips. His mouth assaults mine at a brutal pace. Our tongues move as one, no longer in a war but a dance together. Our feet are moving backwards until the backs of my knees hit the bed. I fall onto the scratchy fabric willingly.

Right as I am about to rip my own clothes off, they drift away in a black dust. It reminds me of smoke from a fire my father had me build one time; he would tell me stories of Gods at war. Gods that had no right to give or take from us. *They* had decided our future for us, instead of the Blessed.

Lying naked underneath him, I reach for his thick, long, pulsing shaft. My fingers grasp onto it and run down the length of him.

"Are you ready?" His forehead falls onto mine when he whispers the words.

"Yes."

The pathway between us that once felt ice-cold is warm and open for me. I wonder if he will keep it open to me. Since I don't have my powers, it feels nice to be able to communicate in a way I was so used to doing.

He presses his tip into me, and I squeal out.

"Did I harm you?"

I press my forehead harder against his. *"No. Keep going,"* I plead with him. No more words are spoken, just our bodies moving together and our minds completely in sync.

I adjust my hips to open for him. He pushes more into me, stretching me more than I have ever been. Sailor was huge, but Alwin is *Fae*. As soon as his hips meet mine and he is fully inside of me, I shift uncomfortably.

"Move," I demand.

He chuckles darkly. *"I'm giving you time to adjust, darling."*

I shake my forehead against his. *"I don't need time to adjust, I need you to move right now, or I will explode."*

Right as I say those words into his mind, two things happen.

The first is, of course, that he starts to move his hips. The relief is unimaginable. The bliss of his cock sliding in and out causes my eyes to roll back into my skull.

"Thank you." His hips press in and out, sometimes removing himself completely to rub his head on my slick core. I praise him with kisses and bites along his jaw.

I suck down hard enough on his throat that he moans out. The raw sound alone causes me to tip over the edge. The climax causes full-body shivers; his hair tickles my forehead as the waves of pleasure start to subside.

"Are you ready for more?" he asks me.

When the tingling in my core still lingers, I smirk at him. *"Are* you *ready,* old man?" I taunt him.

He rips me up to stand before turning me around and shoving my head down into the itchy blanket. He growls possessively before saying, *"Mine. You are* mine.*"* I groan out when his knee pushes my thighs apart more. His fingers grip my hip bones brutally. *"Tell me, Serena, who does your heart belong to?"*

Crack. The ice around my heart for him shatters wide. "You," I say aloud, softly and almost a whisper. *"You. I am yours."* I whimper as he pounds into me, his fingers dig so deeply I wonder if not only my skin will have bruises from him, but my heart. I will not recover from this.

The second thing that happens is the bond. It fully snaps into place, I feel as if we are one and the same.

His chest falls onto my back; he pushes my hair to the side when his lips worship my spine. The wet kisses cause goose bumps to spring across my skin. He grabs my hair in a tight knot, forcing me to look over my shoulder. My back arches in a way that hurts, but I relish the pain. I find pleasure in the way his teeth sink into my flesh, and I beg for more.

His pumps start to slow when I feel a rush of warmth inside my mind as well as my body. His seed leaks from me, as he continues showing me what he can offer. He reaches around me, pressing his finger to my center. He plays with my bead of pleasure enough to cause me to push back into him when I scream out in bliss. My eyes shut, and when they do, I see what Alwin sees. *Me.* The curves of my ass still bouncing on him. The moment causes my bliss to spur on for longer than I have ever experienced before.

He waits for several moments before pulling out, though not completely. I start to turn around but feel our combined releases begin to leak out.

"Hold on, My Queen." His voice is stern but soft. He places a cloth under me. "Roll over," he commands. He then pulls out of me completely, and bright red blood mixed with our arousal streams out of my body. My face burns red-hot.

"Don't be ashamed. Your body is perfect." He grabs my chin when I try to look down at the mess.

"That isn't," I huff out, feeling embarrassment creep into me like a thief in the night.

"Everything about you is perfect. What we just did was beautiful, Serena." His eyes are tender, his voice is sweet. "Do not forget that. And do not forget what you are feeling in this moment," he says, almost as if he thinks I might. Warm water runs between my legs as he cleans me up with his power. His large palm grabs onto my upper thigh, and I hiss.

"Are you hurt?" Concern ripples through him so potent that I feel it in my own mind. I shake my head, "No, just sore."

"I can fix that." He smiles, a genuine smile. One that takes my breath away. Alwin is handsome; he is everything I could have ever wanted. If I didn't have a kingdom relying on me, I would think we could live happily ever after.

That will never be my life; happiness is for people who don't have entire kingdoms on their shoulders. Since the moment I was born into this realm I have always caused death and destruction. My life has been about becoming stronger for Mirahalm. Even before I knew what I needed to be stronger for, I was always preparing for *something*.

He wipes away all the blood and pain. He takes away the leftovers of himself while he washes me clean with his power. He doesn't make a mess of it; the water goes where his hands call it to. "Hips up," he demands. I lift them up, and he takes the cloth from under me.

The side of the bed moves when he comes to sit right next to me. "Here are some things you might need." He hands me some small rags that I can line my undergarments with, as well as three vials.

"What are these?" I ask in wonder, while he remains sitting on the edge. One of the liquids is a light sky-blue, one of them is white with bubbles in it, and the last one is lime green and reminds me of another person's eyes that I don't want to think of right now.

"One is for pain, one is for sleep, and the other is if you want, uh...protection. It isn't a hundred percent effective, but about eighty." He runs his hands down his gray, sagging pants. "Also, here are these." He hands me some clean clothes. "I will be right back with some food. You get dressed."

I grab onto his wrist, my eyes searching his. For what? I have no idea.

"Will you sleep with me?" I clench my jaw shut, grinding my teeth with pure anxiety.

His lips tilt up before he nods. "I would like nothing more." He licks his swollen lips before opening the tent flap and leaving.

I stare right into the three vials, not knowing which is which, but knowing I need all three. I may have felt the bond tighten up, I may be developing feelings for this male, but I do not want babies right now. Maybe never. I cannot imagine a time in my life I would want to raise my enemy's child, no matter my feelings for him. I can't think of a day where I would not be mothering a baby with Sailor instead. I rub my wrist out of instinct. Swallowing down any fear I might have, the glass touches my lips three different times.

Chapter 19

I make quick work of washing myself, cleaning off the rest of the blood that trickled down my thighs. The potions are already taking effect. I know because I feel tired, sated, and pain-free. I pull the dark blue pants up to my hips, then drag the white T-shirt over my head, watching it drift down to my knees. I lay down on the too-thin pillow and place my hands behind my head. My eyes shut, but my mind wanders to things it shouldn't.

I wonder what Sailor is doing right now. Has he moved on from me? Does he still worry about me, like I do him? How far along is Evie now? Has Juniper found his way like he always seems to? I need to find Clara when I make it to Darnish; that might be a way to clear my head. Searching for her could be my mission. My distraction.

"Thinking of other men after what we just did is in poor taste, wife." Alwin's gruff voice soothes an ache that was starting to form. I blame it on Evie; she would never allow me to sleep alone, even when I protested that we were too big. That didn't happen often, but I mentioned it a time or two. Soon, I had realized I slept with her as much as she slept with me. We needed each other to feel comfort. She enjoyed taking care of me. My sister will be an amazing mother someday soon. I just hope I get to see it.

"I might have given myself to us completely, but that doesn't mean I can't still wonder about him," I say, not knowing if it is total bullshit.

He brings in a steaming bowl of soup to me, and I sit up in the bed and reach for it. "Allow me?" He raises a brow with his question, and I nod. He sits on the edge, legs hanging off the side. "I like your games," he says, surprising me.

"You do?" I didn't know he enjoyed anything other than killing people, taking over kingdoms, and sex.

"I do enjoy sex with you, too, but I also like how your lips tilt up when you win. Or that when you think you might lose a game, you cheat."

I swat at him, causing some of the warm liquid to spill over the lip of the bowl. Before it can hit my skin, his magic stops it. "I told you...I will not allow harm to come you when I am by your side."

I tilt my head towards the soup, "What a monster that soup is, huh?" I tease, and I regret the words right as I say them. A roar sounds in the distance, loud and long.

"Have we lost anybody?" I ask in a hushed tone, as if I might speak it into existence. I know I can't hear everything outside; he is protecting me somehow.

He gulps. "Let's play your game." He brings the spoon to my mouth and I open for him. In more ways than one tonight, I give him a bit of myself.

"Okay. Which game are you referring to?" I take another bite, then another. Alwin seems to like feeding me, and I don't mind him doing it.

"Questions," he answers.

I like that game; I like getting to know other people. And when I had my power, I liked knowing if they would tell the truth or not. I mostly played with my family, but occasionally Mr. Benson or his son might play with me. I liked testing people, seeing what kind of person they wanted others to think they were. Mr. Benson didn't care for that game much, and I never pushed my way into his head. He enjoyed activities more than games—artwork, gardening, storytelling. Mr. Benson always had the best stories, none of which were ever true.

"You are first," he whispers to me, and I take the concession.

"Have you ever looked into my memories?" I know the answer before he says it. I don't know why I wasted my question on it.

"Yes, I have," he answers right away. I shouldn't be surprised by his truth; he told me it would be honesty from here on out.

"Do you love me?" His question causes unease to form in my stomach; Mother Nature couldn't have come at a worse time. My lips part slightly

I have never felt so emotional in my life. I bite down on the meat in my mouth before I nod slowly. "I think, apart from the bond, I am starting to. If you want the Gods' honest truth, I could have loved Aldrich," I admit, while swallowing more of the salty soup. "I did start to, I think, but you lost a lot of my trust that day." I taper off, not wanting to speak about the wedding day. I sigh loudly, then continue. "I know that my heart has felt conflicted, because Sailor still has an ember inside of it. You have flames, though; I am starting to realize that maybe I might love you both," I admit, even though the words taste like soot in my mouth.

He brings the spoon to my mouth again, and I slurp the hot broth. "What can you tell me about Mirahalm?" I trudge forward, taking my turn to ask him a question.

He places the empty bowl on the ground beside the bed before lying back. He crosses his ankles and puts his arms behind his head, getting comfortable before looking up towards the sky, as if searching for his homeland.

"It is unlike anything you have ever seen before." His voice sounds like he is daydreaming, almost childlike. "If you think the palace is gorgeous, then just wait until you see even just a village there." He shakes his head slightly as if trying to wake himself up from the daydream. "You will someday see the kingdom that the Gods created and cherished. You will fall in love, yet again. Only that time I won't have to worry about it being with a male, just our future." His eyes seem to gloss over as if he isn't even here anymore. I realize he isn't; his eyes are solid black with none of the white swirls I have found myself thinking about.

Right as take notice of that, thoughts are projected into my head. Fields of wildflowers, unlike anything I have ever seen. The most vivid colors—pinks that are brighter than anything I could have ever dreamed, trees that twist and turn in every which direction, vines going all the way up the trees. Some of the plants seem to have their own mind or spirit, maybe. Animals that look like beasts but are friendly—moogroves of sorts. Sparkling oceans and lakes, the deepest parts of them navy blue, with beaches that have crystal-clear waters. It feels as if I am soaring through the skies, and can almost feel the wind blowing my hair back. I can feel the warmth of this land on my face, until suddenly it switches to being ice-cold.

I am looking at a village unlike Darnish; this village is covered in ice. The snow is so thick you would think that the people—no, the *fae*—would die. They look happy, though; there is a castle not far off. The whites and grays look even brighter here than they do in the human lands. The fae all look happy and healthy in a way most people aren't. The brisk cold doesn't stop me from exploring. I don't know how he is doing this, but I am grateful for it. The pull of this land is so strong, I want to throw myself into it with full force. I want to blink myself into the very fabric of the soil. *I want to go home*, I realize.

That is what this place is: home. I might not have been born there, but it's been calling to me for as long as I can remember. The darkness, the urge to just move in any direction. It was always calling me to find home, maybe even to find *him*...

After several more minutes of looking around in a land that *should* be my home, Alwin pulls us back down to the dark reality. The coldness I feel now isn't like the one I was just feeling; it feels lonely in a way that causes my body to curl around his. His arm snakes around my shoulders as he drags me closer. I lean my head onto his chest, my face pressing into him. "Thank you," I whisper to him. He kisses the top of my head briefly.

"What is your favorite childhood memory?" he asks me, even though he could rip into my mind and get it himself. He respects me in a way that I should show him in return. I think about it for a long while before speaking.

"One time, after one of my dad's more severe spells..." I pause, swallowing down the hurt of thinking about my father. "My family wanted to make him happy, so we threw him our own party." I smile into Alwin's chest; he smells so fresh and clean always. "We baked him a cake...well, Evie did, because I don't cook anymore, and Juni wouldn't have baked if his life depended on it."

He looks down at me, his dark eyes shining. Most people would have a double chin just from the angle of his face; he doesn't have one shred of fat on his built body, though.

"I was walking out with the cake in hand, the decorations from Mr. Benson's shop already set up to surprise him." I start to chuckle before I can even get to the good part. I am suddenly unsure if I'll even be able to finish the story.

"What happened then?" Alwin asks through my fit of laughter.

"I got too excited when I saw him coming up the pathway that I forgot I had the cake in my hand. I ran towards him, tripped, and it went flying into the sky."

His eyes widen in shock. "Oh no." He chuckles.

"Yeah, *oh no*. It landed right on his head. We couldn't eat the dang cake," I say in exuberance.

He sits up straighter. "Wait, you weren't upset about your father getting mauled by a cake, you were upset that you couldn't eat it?" He sounds unsure when he speaks, which might be a first.

"Yes. Evie worked hard on that cake. It was our favorite one—strawberry with a light whipped cream on top." I try to level with him, my mouth filling with saliva as I think about how amazing that cake would have been.

His body moves from his own fit of laughter. "You sure are something, Serena." He runs his fingers through my hair. I lean into the loving embrace. I missed this. I realize I missed being loved and cared for. I hadn't ever thought I would need this, but it turns out everybody needs to feel like they matter to somebody. Even a queen needs her king.

"Do you regret following my mother here?" I look up at him. I don't know what he might feel about this, and I don't intend to pry into his mind tonight.

"No," he says immediately.

"Why not?' My eyelids are getting so heavy that they might cause me to miss his answer.

"Because I wouldn't have found you if I hadn't, I would never be fulfilled. I would always have this feeling that I was missing something, and yet, I could never find it. I wouldn't ever be able to have you." He runs his hand over my eyes, urging them to close. "Go to bed now, we can play more tomorrow. I have a surprise for you." My eyes drift shut to the sounds of water running, even though I know we are not near a river.

My sleep is fitful; all throughout the night, I hear screams that I know I should run to. I should be out there helping, but I can't. My body won't move; it is ensnared in the bear holding onto me. He comforts me when I cry out in my dreams, his warmth calms my nerves in a way that feels like drugs. The king *is* a drug to me, I realize. He takes care of me completely and totally. The sounds drift in and out. Sometimes I hear waves or birds, then darkness wafts into the mix. It causes me to startle awake. The king soothes me every time it happens, as if he is watching me sleep.

Roars and growls haunt me in the darkness. I know it doesn't make sense, but I at one point wondered if maybe, perhaps, the girls found their way here and enacted their own type of revenge on me, leaving the beasts here.

They didn't; they *can't*. I know they are dead. They must be; most do not survive Brabble. When the sunlight starts to wander into my tent, I grab for the warm body I know is still beside me. I smile into his chest when my hand reaches his belly. He didn't leave, all night he stayed in my bed with me. It shouldn't cause me this much happiness, but it does. I am happy, and I am selfish for that.

Chapter 20

Why did I do it? I knew it was a mistake the moment I did it. I don't share; she is *mine*. I have worked too hard to find her to just give her away like she isn't the most precious thing in my world. I shouldn't listen to the little voice that tells me I need to do good things for her heart; I don't. She will love me no matter what, I can see it in her eyes. I could kill every worthless soul in this Gods-forsaken kingdom, and she would stand there with me. Wouldn't she? Maybe even holding my hand as we together burned down any who would stand against us. Mother and Father wouldn't like it, but since I was sent here, I haven't cared much for what they have to say.

I hold her sleeping form in my arms, hoping she won't wake for a while longer. I want to savor these moments with her. I want to memorize every pattern she breathes, every face she makes during a nightmare. I enjoy chasing the bad dreams away. It brings me pleasure to give her white noise instead of the screams from outside. I have no idea how many we lost last night, but I know we did lose some.

The monsters here are nothing compared to those in Mirahalm, but that doesn't mean they aren't fucking crazed. The Gods made sure that when they sent the fae to Mirahalm, to send every wicked creature with us. That included sending some of them to the human lands. The Gods like torturing other beings because of what the Fates did to *them*. There is a damned good reason the Gods created dragonkind to balance out the never-ending line of King Ragnar. He was the most vicious God King there has ever been; the only one who has ever surpassed him is his daughter. It's a good thing that humans know little about the Gods and the Blessed Fates.

Fae only know what we do because we were once trapped by them. The Gods thought they were worth more than any other, until dragons came to save us. We were sent away from our captors and into the kingdom we now know as Mirahalm. I learned all about the war that broke the worlds. The war that gave my kind and the humans freedom and power. The fae were granted stronger lands, the very soil laced with power. Fae, unlike humans, get our power from our land, not the Fated Blessed. We have power, even if the Blessed decide we don't need it any longer. Our bodies crave the land; the power felt just standing in my kingdom is indescribable. That's why I haven't been as strong in my most recent years. The longer I am away from Mirahalm, the weaker I become.

I could have helped my men last night; I *should* have. But when I tried to get up from my mate, her tiny fingers gripped onto me. They reached for me. She wanted *me* to comfort her, not *him*.

The more time I spend with her, the more I can feel myself changing. The war caused darkness to seep into me. My parents, and hers, both changed me into a male I don't know. Will I ever be the little fae who once held onto a weaker animal and cried when it passed into the realm of the Gods? Could I even cry now? My family needs me to succeed, because if I don't, worse things will happen than if some human takes my mate from me.

I don't dare waste time sleeping when I know I might not get another chance to hold her in my arms again. I love her, I would do anything for her. Even if that means ripping my own heart out and serving it to her on a gold platter.

She needs my help to get home, to rule over two different kingdoms, but that doesn't mean I have to be right by her every step of the way. I will step back if that is what she wants. I will wait for her. Unlike in my younger years, I have learned the value of keeping somebody like her. She is different than other fae, she doesn't act as if all should bow to her. Even nonroyal fae treat humans as if their lives mean nothing more than a speck of dirt. I thought that for a long while, too.

I had no respect for humans when I first came here to find her devil mother. I didn't have any intention of staying here to entertain anything having to do with humans. They think that because they were pitied and now have weak powers that they are worth something in the grand scheme of beings. I hated them for many years while ruling, in the beginning. That's probably why Serena thought I was a tyrant. I *was* one... I might still be one. But if she wants the humans to thrive, then she will have it. Serena Bloodworthy is the only reason this kingdom even still stands. I am only king to find her and return home. To hell with the humans.

I never cared about what happened to any of them, until one day when I watched a girl step in for another when she didn't have to. She saved him that day; she knew if she were to be caught, it would result in her death...or worse, a lifetime with me. She is the only reason I don't drown this entire kingdom where it lies. She is the reason my heart beats; without her, I am nothing. I mean nothing. Without her, the world should fear me.

Chapter 21

I wake to strong arms holding me against an even stronger, warm body.

"Good morning, darling." Black eyes with white and blue swirls dancing around stare down into my bright blue ones.

"Morning." I wipe my eyes and cover my mouth while I yawn. "Did you sleep?" I don't hear anything outside; that must mean nobody died. One side of his lips tilts up in a half-smirk. It causes my heart rate to skyrocket. I swear I could be flying right now with the way I feel this morning.

"Why would I sleep when I can watch *you* sleep?" he retorts, and I shake my head. "You speak in your sleep. Are you aware of this?" he asks teasingly. I try to slap him softly, but he grabs my wrist, the very one with my sailboat on it. His eyes scan the tattoo; instead of growling, he kisses it.

My jaw might as well be on the ground. I stammer a few words that nobody would be able to understand.

"I am going outside to give you time to clean up. Do you need anything?" he startles me by asking. I have no idea what else I would need. I survived a night in Brabble; most cannot say that. The biggest of the surprises is that I survived a night in my enemy's arms...and even liked it.

"You are not most. Remember that you are going to be welcomed home like a lost princess. Because you are. They will bow at your feet as I have, or die."

I swallow down any response I might have. Instead, I simply nod.

He raises a brow. "So what do you need?" His eyes question me in the same way his words do; they seem to be scanning for answers I do not have.

"I don't need anything," I state plainly. I shouldn't be this nervous around him anymore. "Well, maybe one of those potions for the pain?" I sit up a little, wincing from the aches my cycle has brought me.

Alwin moves at an unnatural speed. "Are you alright?" His eyes are filled with concern.

"Yes, I am just cramping. It's never been like this before," I explain while his white-hot hands touch my naked flesh, healing every bump and bruise he might have left behind. Alwin's healing powers are unlike any I have felt before. I lean into him with a new sense of ownership. He feels like mine; *he is mine*. I am freaking married to him. "Thank you," I say, avoiding eye contact with him. When he stands, he gives me a beautiful view of his ass in his baggy gray pants.

The firm planes are so strong, I feel like he even works his ass out. I giggle a little at the thought of this strong royal fae working out his ass, and as if all he does is listen to my thoughts, he glares at me before pulling his pants up higher on his hips. The material clings to his body, as I did last night. His black hair doesn't look out of place one bit, which makes me growl.

His brows lift. "Something wrong?" His eyes dance with amusement.

"Yes." I nod emphatically.

"What could possibly be wrong?" When he smiles, he gives me a full view of his long, sharp canine teeth.

"You look perfect." I sigh, my hands motioning towards him.

"Is that a problem, My Queen?"

I roll my eyes; he is playing with me. "Uh, yeah. Actually, it is." I stand up, bringing the blanket with me. My stomach isn't cramping as badly anymore after he healed me, but my hips feel out of sorts.

Alwin makes his way back to me, his hand has black smoke dancing around his fingers. When he tilts my chin up, I don't hesitate to look deeply into his eyes.

"Why would me being perfect be a problem for you?" His voice is liquid lust.

I gesture towards his impeccable hair, body, outfit...basically everything about him. "Are you kidding me? You just slept on a tiny bed, and you look like *that.*"

He leans his face down so that his lips are just a whisper from mine. "As if you don't look equally, if not more so, delicious. If we didn't have places to be and people to please, I would be bowing down to you in hopes that you give me another moment of your undivided attention." His words come out low and deep.

How can a king so ruthless say things like that?

"*Because you are the only one worth those kinds of words.*" He presses a quick kiss to my lips before heading out of my tent.

"Stay out of my head!" I yell as he walks away.

"*Never. Your thoughts are my entertainment,*" he teases.

I shake my head rapidly, trying to unscrew my brain from thinking he isn't my enemy. I need him, nothing more. I can use his body to my benefit, but it means nothing. My stupid heart needs to get with the program.

I dress quickly when I hear something going on outside. I rush to put my boots on, but my heart stills when I hear a familiar voice. I feel as though ice has crystallized in my bloodstream. I might have frozen right here in this dirty tent. Brabble may be the place where I have died and gone to the afterlife. That voice should not be *here*. That voice should be safe, hundreds of miles away.

I never would have thought I would hear *him* again. Well, at least not anytime soon. I run from my tent to a full-on fight happening in the middle of Brabble. We are still half a day's ride to the bridge out of here.

"Are you two trying to get us killed?" I say accusingly, my eyes narrowed, and my arms held out to show them exactly where they are. Since, apparently, they have forgotten. Bright blue eyes lock onto mine, and at the same time, he throws a punch to Wolf's face. I wince when blood splatters everywhere. Sailor grabs onto Wolf's shirt, punching him over and over. I look to see Alwin leaning against a tree, ankles crossed, eating something, looking pleased with himself. I scoff. "You are just going to let them kill each other?" I roll my eyes while walking the two feet to the...what should I even call them now? To...the men.

"What are you doing?' I yank on the back of Sailor's soft shirt. "When did you get here?"

He doesn't stop hitting Wolf. "Taking care of business. What does it look like, Honeybee?" That nickname, that voice. The sweetest lisp... I never would have thought I could miss it, but I did. My heart stops, and they keep fighting, although I am suspended in space and time. One little nickname, and I am right back to where I started. I stare at Sailor and Wolf as if it's the first day I'm seeing them. It kind of is. They are no longer the commanding brothers; they are strangers to one another. Enemies.

I am yanked back to the present by none other than Alwin.

"What were you thinking?" I narrow my eyes at him. This is all his fault. It has to be!

He shrugs, a low chuckle escaping his slightly parted lips. "That I shouldn't have sent my mate's plaything away. He has some spice to him that I enjoy." I try and fail to pull from his strong grasp. He leans into me, his breath tickling my ear. "Wait. Allow them to figure this out for another moment. I will step in if it looks like your...*friend* might get harmed." The words seem painful for him to even say, and we go back to watching the two of them fight like animals.

Like the Blessed he will! Alwin would rather watch Sailor die than help him. There is no way in any realm or kingdom that Alwin would ever help Sailor. I have no idea how Sailor even got here, but I can only imagine Alwin's reasons for bringing him back are not decent ones. I blink several times before pinching myself.

Sailor. Sailor is here. "How long has he been here?" I ask, my eyes frantically darting between them.

"I got him when I sensed you were sad without him." Alwin confirms my worst nightmare. I spin on my heels towards this unbelievable male.

"When was that?"

He plays coy while studying his nails. "I don't know," Alwin says as if he is completely bored with this conversation. "Yesterday morning, I went to Clove and retrieved him. If it makes you feel better, he does have his power back. He probably only just woke up, though...hopefully." Right as Alwin says that, Sailor hits Wolf with a mixture of fire and ice. My jaw hangs open as my mind whirls with the possibility that Sailor could have heard something from my tent last night.

"You're really not going to let me explain?" Wolf yells, fighting back in any way he can. Sailor doesn't slow his assault.

"What is there to explain? You betrayed me to Magnolia and let Serena be taken and married off!" Spit sprays from his mouth while he roars in anger. Sailor is bigger than he was when he left; his muscles look far more defined.

"*I am in here, you know,*" Alwin drawls.

I shove him right in the chest. "Get out then," I growl before pulling fully out of his reach.

I am on Sailor in less than a second, my strides strong and sure. His hands have lava oozing from them. The smoke from it burns my nostrils. I catch him off guard by kicking behind his knees. "Leave," I demand of Wolf, right as Sailor's knees hit the ground. I trail my fingers on Sailor's firm shoulders as I circle around him. I walk slowly to face him before I hiss to Wolf when I notice he has not moved, "I will let him kill you if you don't get out of my face right now." Wolf gulps before turning and leaving. A trail of blood gushes from his nose and lip. Sailor kneels before me, not because he can't get up, but because he chooses not to. His head is bowed, but his eyes burn into mine with an intensity that could kill me.

I feel guilty that, just a few hours ago, Alwin had me under him. Sailor seems to calm down enough that his eyes turn back to the shade of blue that I know and love.

"You are here," I whisper, running my fingers down his cheek. My legs give out, and I fall on the ground right in front of the man who first showed me love. "How?"

Slowly, he leans into my space. "Your husband brought me back. He offered me a wonderful position. Too good to refuse." His voice is filled with distrust. I look to where Alwin was standing, but he is no longer there.

"What was it?" I ask, not sure if I really want to know.

"I am to be your personal guard...until my death." His voice has a bite to it.

I chew on my lip, unsure what to say, but I end up going with, "And you wanted that?" I sent him away for a damn good reason; I wanted him to have his own life.

"I wanted whatever it was he would offer me to be with you." Sailor's eyes darken with a promise, I just don't know what kind.

Right as the words leave his mouth, a growl roars throughout the campgrounds. It's then that I realize Alwin had hidden what was going on last night. Bodies are flung in every direction. The tents are torn into tiny pieces and ruined beyond repair. A howl sounds from everywhere at once, and my eyes are wild with panic, just not for myself. No, it's for *them*...for those who will die to keep me alive. I don't want that, nor do I need it.

"It's not safe here. You need to leave," I snap, finally coming out of my trance.

His deep chuckle shakes my body, even though it's just our knees touching. It feels like more, it feels like everything.

"I am your guard, Bee. It's my job to serve you, from now on, with my life." He says this as if it might be a threat.

I clench my teeth before pushing to stand. I extend my hand, offering to help him up. When his hand grabs onto mine, sparks shock my body.

"Ouch." I pull him to his feet. "That's new," I say, unsure why he would shock me.

"It is," he agrees. "I trained every day with your brother—" *Crack*. There goes my heart. It's on the ground, right in the dirt, being stomped on. "We trained knowing I would need to be much stronger than before to keep up with your fae husband." Sailor's throat bobs. There it is again; my entire body reacts to him calling Alwin my husband.

"Stop," I demand, just as a beast comes hurtling through the trees.

I shove Sailor out of the way right as a massive creature hurls itself onto me. Its teeth are jagged and sharp, protruding from the large mouth currently roaring in my face. Spit gets into my eyes, stinging, and I desperately want to wipe it away. Sailor gets up from the rock I pushed him into. Right as he starts to make his way to me, though, the beast literally explodes all over me.

"What the fuck!" Alwin appears in front of me. "I brought you back to keep my mate safe. Can you do that for me when I cannot?" Alwin fists Sailor's black, bloodstained shirt.

Sailor's wild eyes dart between the two of us. "I was about to! Unlike you and your unnatural abilities, I only have elemental powers." Sailor lifts me the rest of the way from the ground. "You okay?" he asks gruffly. I nod, looking around. It appears we have gained far too much attention from the Gods' pets.

"We need to leave...right now." I grab a sword from Sailor's belt before making my way to a huge monster trying to maim our cook. I shove the sword into its eye socket right as it notices me.

"I guess you really did train without your powers as a child." Alwin smirks.

"I wish I had *said powers*, but you won't give them back to me," I hiss.

"For good reason," he replies right as he and Sailor kill another beast. They are coming at us from every angle.

"There are far too many. You need to do something." I swing the sword right into one's neck, not quite cutting its head off.

"What would you have me do?" Alwin blasts a wolf-looking beast with white-hot lava.

"Kill them all," I say as calmly as I can.

Sailor studies us for a moment. "There are over fifty monsters coming at us. If he kills them all right now and we run into more later, he won't be able to help. We are holding our own for now." Sailor swallows, as if the words taste like bile in his mouth. My brows furrow. Is he standing up for Alwin...against me? Right as I am about to ask, Wolf hisses out in pain.

I whirl around to see that Wolf is fighting four massive beasts alone. Sailor and Alwin are caught in a battle with one massive beast. I rush over to help Wolf, not thinking about anything other than helping somebody I once cared for. Somewhere deep inside my body, I know he didn't want to betray anybody. There is more at play here than any of us can see. Maybe even Wolf himself.

The beast pushes Wolf backwards a foot with its large head. Wolf tosses the creature across the tree line with his mind. Another charges at him in that moment, and I swing my sword out, hitting its claws. My back slams against Wolf's.

"Here to help them eat me, Serena?" His large frame towers over me.

"Should I?" I taunt him, knowing I need my powers to actually win this. When I was a child and would train without power, I used power without knowing it. Right now, I am outmatched in every way. My mental shields are the only defense I have, and that is for the enemy to my back. "I would rather you not die here; I don't have fire to burn your body with anymore." I hit the claws of another monster as the fourth gets back up from where Wolf has thrown it. "I don't care for digging either, so it's best you stay alive, huh?" His back shifts slightly, and I realize he is laughing.

"Only you could find humor in this moment, Serena." Maybe Evie was right, and I am actually a glass-half-full kind of gal.

One of the beasts is snakelike. The diamond-shaped head looks lethal in its own way. The body slithers along the ground silently, and scales like a dragon's shimmer on its back. Spikes hang loosely from its spine. This one strikes out at me, and my sword clangs against the sharp edges of the monster's teeth. "Ugh." I wipe green spit from my arm. "Gross." It attacks again and again, and I meet each and every hit, but the power behind the beast shakes my arms.

It keeps hitting my sword, and blood pools in the monster's mouth. That doesn't seem to slow it down, though. Wolf turns towards me, and suddenly the snake explodes. Green blood mixes with the grass. "Thank you," I say, my arms feeling like pudding.

"No problem. You might be the only person here who doesn't hate me." He pushes one of the three monsters left backwards with his mental shields.

"I do hate you." I nod my head to solidify my feelings for him. I turn to stand next to him, our arms brushing, but instead of comfort, like I once felt, there is nothing. He feels blank, dark, unreadable, and dead.

I shiver with the thought, knowing I must focus. "Good. Ram that hate right into the bastards," he commands me. His tone is so harsh, and I listen.

I notice he has a whip in his belt buckle, and I grab it. "I don't think you'll need this anytime soon." I whip it through the air, the sound attracting several other beasts. I swing it over my head before walking forward, out of Wolf's protection. This is my fight, and I do not need a commander telling me what to do. Two beasts make their way to me, three more on him.

Even if he wanted to help me, he wouldn't be able to. I can't help him either. We are all fighting our own battles, in more ways than one. We might all be together, but we aren't fighting the same thing.

I crack the whip again, right by one of the beasts. He snarls at me; I do it right back. I chance a glance at where Sailor is. He is fighting brutally against a lionlike monster. The eyes on that thing promise death, just not Sailor's. He throws water in a bubble around the monster's head, then freezes it. The monster breaks the ice, but not before Sailor throws a long ice shard into its belly. It rolls over dead right then and there. The sight causes me to spring into action; I rush one of the monsters in front of me, and it snaps its jaw at me before I jump as high as my mostly human body will allow. I half toss one end of the whip away from my body and wrap it around the neck of the beast. My thighs squeeze the monster's neck, and it tries to throw me off, but I tighten my knees. I hold firm while I strangle the beast. Its head falls first, then it collapses to the ground. The other two circle me, and I feel as though I am in more trouble than I had thought I was already in.

Black blood pours out. I am covered in different monsters' blood and bits. I almost gag from the smell of it all. "*Where are you?*" I think to Alwin, hoping he will hear me. I don't know if I can handle both beasts, but I know I have no other choice but to be strong. Wolf is in the other clearing now, none the wiser that two monsters are circling me. Everywhere I look, somebody is fighting their own battle, and some have already lost theirs. Barnett has a tree in his hand, ramming it into a group of tiny monsters. Roman is flying above, fighting a birdlike monster that looks more like a hawk than a monster until its jaws open and it sprays him with a thick white substance. I look away right as one of my monsters rushes to me.

"I take it you don't speak?" I ask while circling my whip in warning. It tilts its head to the side. It is studying me, while the other one prowls towards me. They are twins, I notice...brothers. One of them is bigger than the other, but both are standing about ten feet tall. They have white stripes on their fur, and it's slick and covered in some type of oil. I breathe in and out several times before grabbing the sword with my other hand. "Alright, no small talk then."

One of them rushes me, and at the same time, the other circles behind. I hit the slightly bigger one in the jaw, realizing quickly that it has bitten my sword in half. The whip in my hand swings out, trying to hit the creature hard enough to dislodge the sword in its clenched jaw. I pull hard on the sword, hitting its back with my whip over and over again until I finally fall on my ass. The brother pounces, and instead of hitting me, it hits the monster in front of me.

I use this as my opportunity to struggle to my feet, and I rush towards the disoriented brothers, slamming my half sword into one of the beast's heads, right in between his eyes. The brother lets out a piercing sound, almost breaking my eardrums...or maybe it does, I don't know. In the throes of its sadness, it doesn't try to protect itself from me. I think to myself for half a second how these monsters have feelings for each other. Maybe they could love?

"Kill him, let's get it over with." Alwin's leaning against a tree, his ankles crossed again as if he has nowhere else to be. I notice all the other monsters are dead besides this one. I look into its sad eyes and do the only thing I can think of to take its pain away.

"I'm sorry," I whisper while I throw my arms back and cut its head off with my sharp half-sword.

"Thank the Blessed that was all of them," Alwin says, while wiping his hands on his pants. Alwin's strides are sure, but in his eyes? Worry.

"Did you just watch me the entire time?" I toss the broken sword down on the ground. When he shrugs his shoulders, I half wonder if he wants to die right now.

"I had to make sure you were safe," he chirps. I slap him right in the face, and he doesn't stop me.

"Then you should have stepped in!" I yell, gaining the attention of almost everybody.

"I am tired. I didn't sleep well last night," he says in defense. I scoff, turning my back to him so I can survey the damage and bodies.

"That won't be a problem for you anytime soon," I shoot back at him, and he hurries to my side. His hand grips my upper arm in a possessive type of way.

"Darn. I wouldn't have thought that from the way you were screaming my name last night," he says loud enough that I look around. Of course, Sailor walks up right as Alwin finishes his incriminating words.

Sailor eyes us both, but I don't say anything as I make my way to the horses. Luckily, none of them were harmed. Although I cannot say the same about the priest or his carriage. I knew Brabble would be a bloodbath, I just didn't think it would be this bad.

I walk over to a horse that I know is available. His previous rider is lying dead under the trees. My hand stops when I hear a grating voice, my foot already in the stirrup.

"Darling, your carriage awaits you," Alwin says, smirk on his face and all. I pray to the Blessed that I don't make a fool of myself. I hoist myself up and into the saddle with ease. Thank you, Blessed Gods.

"I will not be riding in a carriage with you three," I say over my shoulder before kicking the side of my horse so that he'll run towards Barnett. Sailor and I will have our reunion, and it will not be in front of my enemy and husband.

I chance a look back towards where Sailor stands. His hand is waiting on the carriage handle. His skin is even darker, showcasing the time he has spent in the sun while away from me. His hair is brighter, his eyes seem more alive, and his skin is darker. Sailor seems different, and I hate that I have missed all of it. I hate that he has had to get stronger because of me. I sent him away so that he would live, thrive even. It doesn't even seem like he has rested since leaving on the ship to Clove.

My heart is thoroughly trampled in the ground, no longer soaring in the sky like a lovesick puppy but sinking to the bottom of a deep lagoon with a brick tied to it. Yesterday, I felt as if I were falling in love. Today, I feel as if I have looked at the love of my life and laughed in his face.

Chapter 22

"So," Barnett says softly from atop his horse. I glance at him, feeling my frustration bubble over.

"*Yes*?" I respond, harsher than I had intended.

"How is it going?" he asks, even though he knows full well how this trip is now going.

It has been two entire days in Brabble, and our group of twenty is down to about ten. That is not nearly enough people to keep the tensions between everybody down. In fact, the fewer people we have, the worse it gets.

"How is your boyfriend?" I volley back, knowing it is a low blow.

"He is fine at camp. I also would not call him my boyfriend." His tone is laced with disdain. "I know you don't want to talk about it, but we kind of have to," Barnett says, stating the obvious. Our group is nearing the bridge out of Brabble. If we hadn't been stopped every hour by oncoming attacks, we would have long since been on our way to Saxton. "You only a few more hours until you have to speak to one of them. From Brabble, Saxton isn't too far." He breathes out, clearly reading my sour mood.

"Yeah, I know," I grumble, right as the bridge comes into view. Alwin rides up on his blonde horse, Sailor right on his heels on his own black stallion. Wolf is holding up the end of our group. I am the only female here.

"Ride one behind the other," Alwin orders.

"Why?" I ask, feeling like we should be able to ride side by side.

"The monsters are targeting us; The Gods are playing games. If one gets targeted, I don't want two getting hit." His eyes scan my body in a way that tells me he is hungry for me. The shame I feel when I realize I want to be devoured by him, too, is so potent that when he smiles at me, I am not surprised.

"I mostly care about Serena making it; her boyfriend could fall, and that would help one of my many issues." He smirks at Sailor to his side.

"What other issues do you have, Majesty?" Sailor asks so sarcastically it practically drips from his mouth. "

I would like to go home at some point in this lifetime." Alwin shrugs.

"Right. The kingdom where you want to live with Serena." Sailor rides up next to me, his eyes turning to a light orange color. I have noticed that since he has been back, his eyes are more receptive to changing with his moods.

"What are you doing?" I whisper to Sailor.

"I can hear you," Alwin chimes in. I roll my eyes. Why won't he let me have a conversation without butting in?

"I won't let you cross alone." His bright blond hair seems to shine more than normal.

That's because his hair is dirty, wife. You do not want to get your fingers in that mess.

I almost fall from my horse, I spin so fast. "Stay out of my head," I whisper-yell. He smirks, but pulls his horse's reins back.

Right as my horse steps onto the creaky bridge, I wish I were in a carriage. The bridge swings in a wind that wasn't there a moment ago. My hair billows in the fast, icy breeze.

"Eyes forward, Bee," Sailor's voice orders. "What have you been up to?" he asks to distract me from whatever else is going on. I try to look at him, but he *tsks* at me. "Eyes *forward*. I won't remind you again," he reprimands me. His voice calls to me, and I relax a little in my saddle as I feel others start on the bridge after us.

"You don't have to," I scold him, feeling as though he is sassier than before he left.

"Well?" His voice oozes with banter. I look over my shoulder at him. I can't resist.

He is the epitome of dapper. His outfit is in pristine condition, his hair perfectly styled, and his teeth even look closer together. "Your teeth are straighter," I mention, then realize that could be rude.

"Oh? Noticing my teeth, are we?" He's flirting with me. I know it. He knows it. Alwin knows it, too.

"Well, they are straighter," I say in my own defense.

We are about halfway across when I hear screams. Sailor continues trying to distract me.

"Your husband wouldn't like you noticing my teeth, would he?"

My heart clenches. I rub the wrist that's hidden under my long-sleeved blouse. Of course, Sailor's eyes track my movements. I tune out the screaming, knowing there isn't anything I can do without my power.

"He wouldn't," I agree with him; his mask slips for half a second before he places it right where it is supposed to be.

"I thought so. Again, what have you been up to?" he asks me again, clearly not seeing that I don't want to talk about *what I have been up to*.

"How is Evie?" I ask instead, and my heart breaks a little more knowing I will likely miss her entire pregnancy. If I ever see her again, I will make up for it tenfold.

"She is huge." He winces slightly. "I mean...she is still pregnant. Your brother is more protective of her than a mother bear would be over its cubs," he says while his eyes widen slightly.

I smile a huge shit-eating grin. And it's a real smile. Not some fake queen smirk or grin, no...something genuine. "I'm glad. She deserves the protection." I gulp down the guilt I feel when I realize the protection she needs is because of me.

If my mother had never picked *their* mother to place me inside of, my father would still be alive. Juniper and Evie would have lived their lives in Darnish; their lives would have been normal. The yellow house in the village would have been their home, and whoever I killed the day I was born would have been an amazing person. She would have had incredible siblings. I wish I could have known her. But instead, my life was granted at the cost of two others, just as others pay for it now. I fear somebody will always pay for my life to continue.

We are almost to the end of the bridge when it starts to swing wildly. Sailor curses under his breath before both of us look backwards. Even though we both know what we'll see, there is nothing we can do. The monsters in Brabble have won this fight in more ways than one.

Massive red birds are grabbing at our group. Alwin's horse runs at full speed.

"Run. Once you get across the threshold, they cannot harm you."

I see one of the birds grab onto a man. Wolf tries to chop at the monster with his sword, clearly as drained as everybody else is.

"Go!" Sailor yells at me, commanding me in a way he once had in another lifetime.

"What are you going to do?" I try to turn my horse around like he does, but his eyes plead with me.

"Get across, Serena." Sailor's chest heaves up and down.

My lips flatten into a line. I do not like taking orders, but I will for him. I give him a curt nod before pushing my hips forward, urging my own beast to move.

I make it to the end of the bridge. The land I am on is dead; when I look around, all I see is orange grass. It's as if Brabble takes its life force even from across the threshold. I turn back to watch the only men I have ever cared for fight for their lives. Alwin passes Sailor; his horse is so fast that when a bird tries to get him, it can't keep up. I click my mouth, moving out of his way.

"You aren't going to help them?" I ask frantically, realizing Wolf and Sailor are fighting alongside Roman. Alwin grabs my arm harshly, and I almost fall from my horse.

"I need to get one thing clear to you," he growls, teeth on full display. If I didn't know any better, I would fear him. He is a beautiful monster, with sharp teeth, pointed ears, and power that could rival the Gods. "I only care about *you*. You are all that matters to me, Serena. Us getting home and saving our people is important to me, sure..." His words hit me like a whip. "I made promises that I intend to keep." I open my mouth to ask what these promises are, but he waves his finger towards the bridge, where I know Sailor and Wolf are. "I do not care about them; I will do anything that makes you happy, but it must keep you safe as well. I want our home kingdom and you. That is it. The humans mean nothing to me; they are the Gods' playthings. I won't risk you for them."

I try to urge my horse back on the bridge to help, but fingers made of smoke grab onto my throat; they don't tighten, they just stay there. "Do not." Those are the only words he says to me before commanding both our horses farther from the rest of our group. From Sailor.

I grind my teeth as I watch Sailor rush towards the man whom he once had called brother. A woman I hadn't noticed before pushes her dainty hands out, wind and flames engulfing the group of monster birds as she and Sailor work together.

"GO!" Sailor roars, his voice a sound that I had at one point in my life thought Wolf's sounded like. Like a king's, but unlike the one sitting next to me on his horse. A ruler, and somebody that people would follow. My eyes throw daggers at the king sitting next to me.

"Enjoying the view?" he taunts me, and I cross my arms over my chest.

"No." I huff, just hoping he is reading my thoughts right now.

Sailor turns his horse but waits; he allows the others to pass before him. My breathing hitches. What is he doing? Wolf stops in front of him, and they lean onto each other, whispering some words I can't make out. Damn Alwin, for taking my powers.

I shake my head furiously. Rolling my eyes while I'm at it.

"I have never seen such a sexy female act like a child before. It's entertaining to me." Alwin's grating voice pierces my ears, and I bite down on my tongue, not wanting to fight with him right now.

"I just wish I had my powers to help them, since you refuse to," I retort. The rest of our group—including Sailor—passes the threshold right as one last monster attempts to grab onto him. It hits an invisible wall, and one of the men in front of me falls right off his horse.

"Oh, my Gods," the girl in front of me says when she also drops down to retrieve her friend.

"I'm sorry, Majesties," the man says while he vomits.

Alwin doesn't stop to help anybody, but I do. Some of the men who are left are gravely injured. I don't have any way to heal them, but I do the best I can with what Evie taught me.

Chapter 23

The girl helps me sit the man up, and the rest of the group has moved further away from the bridge. I notice some of the men keep looking back towards Brabble. They either lost somebody in there or are scared the monsters will bust through the barrier. One of the bird beasts sits right on a spike only twenty feet from us. Its eyes track every single person's movements. If I didn't know any better, I would think it was plotting a way to get to us.

"Thank you," the girl says sternly.

I nod. "I'm Serena." We drag the man to sit against a tree trunk. "Is he alright?" I ask, feeling selfish for not keeping a better eye on the guards. Right as I help her sit him against the tree, my cramps come back in full swing. I wince when I stand up, feeling like my entire body is ripping apart.

"Majesty?" The girl almost touches me, then halts herself. "Are you well?" Her eyes fill with worry.

I nod, noticing Sailor nearby and wanting to go speak with him. "What's your name?" I ask her through small breaths while my insides rearrange themselves. I hold a hand against my side, breathing in once and then out through my nose.

"I am Mabel." She runs her hand over her cropped curly hair. As if it was just recently cut.

"Mabel," I say softly, letting the sound of her name play on my tongue. I smile slightly. "I like it." My eyes shine brightly at her. "How are you a guard?" I ask right as Wolf speaks to the group.

"We have ten minutes. Saxton is a far journey from here." His voice echoes throughout the tree line. I gulp down my pain, then train my thoughts on Mabel.

"I pretended to be male. They are so stupid, they didn't ask. Also, the kingdom is short on commanders."

I choke a little bit before asking, "Are you kidding?" My wild eyes scan her, noticing there are small touches here and there of female traits, but not a ton. I only know because I studied people for far too long in my free time.

"No. If men don't think they can fuck it, they won't second-guess it." She shrugs.

"But...they know now, right?" I ask in a whisper, looking around to see if anybody can hear us. She chuckles deeply, obviously having practiced lowering her voice.

"Some do, some don't even know my name after all these years." She shrugs her shoulders, as if she couldn't care any less what they think of her.

I blink several times before blurting out, "But you have breasts."

"Yes, they are small, though." She presses her hands against them, and I quietly gasp, just now realizing I might be coming off as rude to her. "So, enough about me, Majesty. You look not...*well*." Her chocolate-brown eyes scan my body, noticing how I am swaying on my feet.

"Yeah, I am not used to not having my powers to heal me. I'm sad to say I have relied on them more than I should have throughout my life," I admit, even though I do not know this female.

I feel ill to my stomach, but I won't make a big deal about it. I just watched more than half of our men die because of Brabble. A few cramps aren't going to stop me.

She seems to think on it for a moment before tentatively placing a hand on my shoulder. "You, My Queen, are a bad liar. I don't know if you will survive in court. I sure hope you do, though, because I can tell you want to make changes for us." Her voice isn't soft; it isn't kind. I like it, I realize. She isn't flirting with me, she doesn't want something from me, she isn't playing me to win a damn trial.

I half smirk at her. "I am afraid you are correct." I stand up fully now, towering over her. She doesn't act as if this bothers her. "I want to be different than others before me. I want change, I want people to enjoy their lives instead of fighting for them. I see no value in starving my own people." I shrug and she gives me a curt nod before marching away from her friend.

"I never took you for one to take the easy way out, Honeybee," Sailor says from beside me.

I arch my brow, glancing sideways at him. "What does that mean?" I narrow my eyes at him, unsure where he is going with this. If anybody can look cool, calm, and collected after being shipped off to Clove, then brought back just to be dropped off in Brabble with your girlfriend and her husband, it is Sailor James.

Inside the carriage is dark now; the moon has overtaken the sun. The mild temperature day has grown so cold that I can see my breath fogging over. "I just thought you wanted to ride your new friend." His eyes narrow on me, teasing me. His shoulder brushes against mine, and I track every place where his body touches mine. I opted out of riding a horse for the ten or so hours it'll take to get to Saxton's major village. We might make pit stops here and there, but for the most part, we want to hit the major points. I couldn't imagine riding a horse in my condition; my pelvis hurts so badly I almost double over at the slightest pain from my sudden cramps. I have had to change out my rags several times over. Sailor doesn't seem to notice, and if he does, he hasn't said a word.

"He may be pretty, but I don't want to ride anything for that long," I say jokingly. His eyes seem to heat at my comment. The once bright blue, silvery eyes spark to life with a hue of purple and gold. His flames have even changed; the compartment heats instantly.

"I don't remember you having such complaints with me."

I smile, biting into my lower lip. His honey-blond hair is slightly longer, giving his waves room to move about. His hair dusts right above his brows, and the back is cropped closer to his scalp.

"So—" he starts, but I interrupt him, not ready for his questions. I have my own.

"How is my family?" I rush to ask. He doesn't seem to be surprised by my question or me cutting him off.

"I was thinking you were going to try to escape having *this* conversation." He gives me a sad smile, and I gulp down every bit of nerves trying to eat their way through my belly.

A small shake of my head causes my hair to fall into my eyes, and I look to my feet and intertwine my fingers, bracing myself for the conversation I had been hoping to avoid for the rest of my life. "I guess I'm not lucky enough to escape this, am I, huh?" My thumb runs over my wrist instinctively.

"You are not lucky, Serena," Sailor says in the most soothing tone he can. Several moments go by in silence, and I have found that Sailor and I do not mind it. The silence is safe for us. We can still be Serena and Sailor right here and now.

"Your sister isn't like you one bit," he starts. "She is sweet."

I hit his shoulder with mine teasingly. "Hey!" I say more jokingly than anything, and he simpers right back at me.

"She fears everything, really." I blush for no reason at his words. "She doesn't even like snakes."

I laugh breathlessly. "No, she doesn't. I didn't think *I* would like them, you know?"

His eyes look down at his own feet. "That morning on the ship, I knew I would have to leave. I was forced to, actually. I had thought about fighting the compulsion, but alas, I was too weak from my days in the cell." He breathes in softly through his nose, making a sniffling sound. I study his features, as if this might be an important moment for us. "I'm sorry, Serena. I shouldn't have left you." His jaw is tight while he shakes his head in disbelief.

I swallow down my guilt and hurt and stay quiet.

"You didn't ask me," he says softly. "You didn't ask what I wanted. You assumed I couldn't handle sharing you. You didn't give me a chance, Serena. You took away my free will."

I lick my lips, knowing what I did was wrong. Knowing that I have already made so many horrible choices. The weight of them might crush me into dirt. "I know," I say sadly. I look right into the eyes I have fallen in love with, the eyes that take my breath away, the eyes I never want to forget.

Guilt riddles my chest so hard, I lean forward, breaking our eye contact. In through my mouth, out through my nose.

"You slept with him," Sailor says, sounding resigned to the possible answer.

My eyes sting with tears that I try to hold back. I blame Mother Nature. Sailor gives me the sweetest peck on the top of my head. I nod my head when he brings me into his chest. I lean completely into him, needing to feel his warmth against me.

"I'm sorry." My voice cracks, and I wince. Tears start to burn a path down my cheeks, even with me willing them to stop.

"Did you want it?" Sailor asks, the carriage feeling ice-cold. Sailor's arm is wrapped around my shoulders while he holds me firm against his body. I know what he is asking.

"I did." Alwin didn't force himself on me. If I were going to be completely honest with Sailor, there was always a pull, even with Aldrich. I felt something tugging in my chest every time he flirted with me. I just couldn't be sure if it was a friendship or a love connection. Gods, what do I even know about love?

"Do you still want me here?" His voice sounds hollow; I answer him immediately.

"Of course."

My brows furrow together, unsure what to make of this situation. He nods his head slightly, and I grab onto his face. "I love you, I know it isn't fair, but I do, Sailor. I love you. I love you," I say over and over again, knowing what I am doing is selfish.

He shakes his head. "I told you back then that I would stay for anything you threw at me, Serena. I just need to be in your life. If I must wait by as your guard, I will. I cannot live without you." He runs his fingers through his wavy locks. His eyes look at me, tears brimming in them.

I reach out and cup his cheek. "Sailor," I whisper.

He shakes his head. "There are many listening ears, Serena. I just want you to know, I don't blame you. I don't hate you. Gods, you are married to him because of me." He pulls me in as closely as he can without me being in his lap. "I will gladly be your lover, if you will take me?"

And then I do something I know I shouldn't. I do something I will have to explain later. But right now...in this moment...this is what's right.

I press my lips to Sailor's. The kiss is soft and unhurried; it is everything I need in this moment.

"Take from me what you need, Bee. I will watch from the side. If you need me in the game, I will gladly play along. Until then..." he says against my lips, before peppering more kisses along my jaw. I moan, my head lolling backwards. He pulls back slightly, "Your brother sure is a character, though. He is more like you than I would have thought. Considering you two are not blood-related."

Bile rises in my throat. I haven't given much thought to that aspect of my life. I ask what I have been wondering about for a long while. "Yeah, how were the leaders of Clove? Did they tell you anything?" The carriage rocks back and forth on the trail. "They are...secretive creatures. Fae are not like people are. They aren't Gods by any means, but they sure think they are." He seems not to think highly of the fae.

"So, they never spoke to you about my mother?"

He seems to stiffen, but before we can chat more, black smoke drifts into the carriage. I groan, immediately recognizing who it is.

"We will talk later; I just want to make one thing clear, Bee... I am still yours, and yours only. I wasn't with anybody else; I never will be. I know you must test out the waters with your husband, but I don't care. I know you are right for me, but I will give you space to figure things out with him." Before I can respond, Alwin appears in the foggy black mist he has conjured. I scurry from Sailor's lap quickly.

"*Hello.*" He smirks from across us, his voice mocking. Alwin sits with his legs spread wide, his black crown upon his head. It's a statement to Sailor—Alwin is the king. He is my husband and mate. Sailor holds no titles any longer; he isn't a commander, he isn't mine.

Our king looks regal, kingly in a way he doesn't always try to appear to be. I already made several inches of space between Sailor and myself, but that doesn't stop Alwin's eyes from scanning between us. His nostrils flare slightly, a move that I doubt most would have caught.

"Aldrich," Sailor deadpans. Alwin shows no reaction save for his black eyes beginning to swirl with white and silver. It's the only sign of his anger.

"Aldrich is my middle name. You could call me 'King,' though, I suppose. Am I your king or have you already pledged your heart to another?" Alwin makes a show of himself, tapping his chin several times, eyes narrowed on Sailor.

Sailor plays along. "I have no others to pledge my heart to, *Aldrich*." Sailor does not match Alwin's teasing tone. Sailor's tone is icy-cold, matching the temperature in the carriage. I shift uncomfortably, my eyes darting between the two males.

"I—" I start to say, but Alwin cuts in before I can.

"Really? A man like you can't find another king to serve?" Alwin's voice leeches any of the amusement between them. I had thought he was teasing, but now I realize he is baiting Sailor.

"No, I cannot. I am afraid I will stay to serve you eternally," Sailor grinds out through clenched teeth. Alwin rolls his eyes, and the movement in this moment seems childlike.

"If you two—" I start again, just to be interrupted by Alwin.

"We will arrive in Saxton's main village within the hour. The villagers we have passed are not...in a good mood with us. We need to show a unified front, Serena." Alwin is speaking to me, but his eyes don't leave Sailor's. I hadn't noticed anything outside the carriage, and I hadn't heard any shouting. I look to Sailor, realizing he must have shielded me from the noises. "You know...my honeymoon trip that you invaded?" Alwin says, a nasty smile lighting his face up.

"The very trip you kidnapped me to bring me on?" Sailor's voice sounds bored, even though I know he is thrumming with energy.

"Sure. If my mate demands it, I will give it to her," Alwin says so seriously it seems as though he is being genuine in this pissing match.

"Anyway, about th—" I try, just to be interrupted *yet again*.

"I think we should be fine, but I will stay close to my wife, just in case," Alwin says casually, even though the tone he uses is anything but.

Sailor, to my surprise, agrees with him. "Yeah, I think that is a wonderful idea, Majesty. Must have taken a lot of thought and planning to decide to stay with your wife during your honeymoon trip. You won't be able to pick up any mistresses with her at your side, though." Sailor gives Alwin a closed-mouth smile, then adds on, "Maybe you can find another wife if she isn't with you. Everybody seemed to enjoy the trials...that is, until Serena burned half the castle down." Sailor's voice goes from playful to bitter to downright evil.

"I don't need a mistress; unlike my wife, I know what and who I want. She is *mine*, she is my mate. I will be damned if anything were to happen to her. I will never have another, so plan whatever trials you must. I will not be involved. The Gods have finally—"

I decide I don't care to listen any longer. I stand, gulp down my cramps, and flatten my blouse while crouching in the compartment.

I sigh heavily before speaking to the two males who are now staring right at me. "As much as I have liked this, I am leaving now," I state as clearly as possible. Both of them stand up and try to stop me, but I am quicker than they are. Even with Alwin's fae speed, I have one advantage over them both—I hate confrontation, and I have trained myself well to avoid it at all costs. My life has been a series of avoiding situations I do not want to be a part of.

"Ser—" Alwin and Sailor both start to say my name, but it is my turn to interrupt them.

I yank the door wide open; it hits the carriage with a loud thud. Before Alwin can drag me back inside, I leap into the air. I feel free, like I am flying once again. My hair blows in the wind, and I have the biggest smile on my face. Time seems to slow down almost to nothing, as if everything fits right here in this small sliver of happiness.

My feet hit the cobblestone, and I roll with the momentum.

"Serena!" Alwin says from the carriage. He could easily jump, but he doesn't. I see the hesitation from Alwin; his fingers are white as if he is fighting himself back from following me. He can tell I need this small freedom, this small victory. Just because my powers were stolen from me does not make me weak. In fact, I have never felt stronger. What Alwin doesn't know is that he is actually helping me. Sailor looks proud for one small moment before he slips on his mask. He is my guard—he isn't my boyfriend, he isn't even my friend. His job for the rest of our lives is to keep me safe. Now he seems annoyed with me, his eyes flickering to a bright purple before going to a warm blue shade.

I shrug. "I don't like confrontation. I'll see you there," I yell, holding my hands up to my mouth, just to make my voice bigger.

I wave to them both, needing this time to clear my head. I notice one of the guards slows their horse down to a walking speed. I look upwards into chocolate-brown eyes. "You didn't want the company of your lovers together?" She smirks down at me.

"I would rather watch my father be killed again than sit in *that* carriage for another moment." Her deep chuckle causes me to almost trip. Her teeth are pearly white, and her smile is energetic and full of life. "I like you, Majesty. You may be a little messed up, but I like ya."

I smile before kicking a pebble. "Then call me Serena." She nods her head once before we keep on.

The pathway to Saxton isn't easy; there are many twists and turns. The scenery alone is worth it, though. My mind feels utterly blank, which is exactly what I wanted from this. I needed this time to clear my head and just figure some things out. There is a sort of strength in being alone. Well, Mabel's here. I don't mind her company, though. She doesn't say much, and when she does, it's never about the role I play or the powers that I hold. She cares in a big way, one that I might like.

Chapter 24

<u>*Serena*</u>

Saxton is a hostile environment; that is the only way to describe this village. I knew they had started a rebellion campaign a while back, but it was unsuccessful. When the commanders approached me, right as we entered the village, and informed Mabel and me that I was to go nowhere without a guard, it shocked me. I nodded in understanding, even though I know I can fight better than any of my guards.

The looks we earned were enough to make me second-guess walking, even with Mabel. I didn't want to put her in danger, and I hadn't realized just walking down the street would do just that. I would have sat through the carriage ride if I had thought we could be in danger in our own kingdom. She offered her horse several times, but I wanted to walk. I had time to think about my next moves—where I want to go and what I want to do being queen. The walk reminded me of one I had once had with Sloan; my heart aches to see him again.

We walk as fast as we can to get into the inn we are staying at for the night. The commanders trail us at our heels, as if thinking we might truly be in danger here. Mabel hopped off her horse right after she noticed we were being followed. Soon after, we were shut into a room, as if prisoners in my own kingdom.

"Your hus— Uh...the king says we should meet them downstairs in about an hour."

It is well past time to go to sleep. I know we don't have a dinner tonight; somebody already brought us sandwiches and tea when we were shut in here. We are instead meeting for a luncheon tomorrow to celebrate Saxton.

"Did he say why?" I ask curiously from my perch by the windowsill.

I had informed Mabel during our walk that I do not want to speak about Sailor, Alwin, or my relationship with both men. I don't need the distraction from my current mission.

"He just said to meet him whenever you were ready," Mabel answers as she makes herself comfortable on my bed. I don't mind. The hours' worth of walking got us talking, and it turns out we have a lot of the same interests. She likes animals; she prefers them dead instead of friends, but still, she likes them. She agrees that eating ten times a day can be needed in some cases, and most importantly, that fruit does not belong in dessert. I will try anything, but that doesn't mean I *like* everything. Fruit in desserts is one of those things I don't care for.

I pull a clean shirt over my head, completely aware I just flashed Mabel. "What do you think he wants?" she asks me while I jump to pull my pants over my hips.

"I have no idea. I can't ever tell with him; he seems to throw new things my way every time I get my footing."

She chews on some jerky while watching me get ready. "You know, I never thought I would be good enough for the King's Guard," she admits. Her eyes look like they are lost in some history I wasn't a part of.

"How come?" I slip my foot into one of my boots while I wait for her to answer.

"I just never was strong enough; my wind power wasn't ever useful."

She pats between her legs for me to sit down. I do, so she can help me with my hair. Her fingers twist my hair in an elaborate braid of some sort. I can't see it, so I have no idea what she is doing, nor do I care.

"I was always smaller than the other kids in my village—" She pulls my head to the side. My scalp is used to this kind of torture, so I don't say a word about her rough handling; it feels like home. "So, when I snuck out and went to the training camp, my parents weren't happy at all. My father has a decent telepathy ability. I thought he might force me home, but when I promised him I would be okay, he agreed. I had to prove to him I could do it." I look over my shoulder towards the guard who keeps surprising me. The pride that shines in her eyes makes me excited to have her as my guard.

If she didn't already have my respect, she has earned it now. "I wasn't powerful, but I wanted it more than anything. In Langford, there aren't a lot of people...uh, like me."

"Like you?" My voice is deep and sure. I am not faking any friendships, and I am not trying to impress her. I can be myself around this person; she is safe. Mabel pats my back after finishing my hair.

"I like girls."

I turn my head to face her. She chews on her lip for a moment. I nod my head encouragingly.

"Okay," I say in response. I twist my body towards her, holding myself up with one hand planted on the firm bed.

"Well, most people from Langford aren't as open-minded as you. They didn't like that about me, so when I went to the training camp and could be more myself, I felt like I had finally come above water and took a breath of fresh air." Her eyes are glued to the floor.

I smile thinking about her finding her place in this kingdom. Being an outsider isn't easy in a world filled with people who just fit in. "You shouldn't have ever felt like you didn't belong, Mabel. I'm so sorry." My voice is softer than usual. I want to emphasize that I accept her for who she is. Who she loves doesn't define her as a person, as a strong female. "Do your parents accept you?" I venture more than I might have before, but with her admitting that to me, I want her to know I care.

"They know about it; it has been a bigger pill to swallow than me going to training camp. When I was accepted into the commander's program, I think they realized I could fly freely in the palace." She shrugs, carelessly. "Then I did so well that I was promoted quickly to the Guard." Her eyes finally meet mine, and I give her a big, comforting smile. "As I am sure you are aware, being a commander is hard even for strong men. That meant I had to work ten times harder than anybody else to make it physically. They didn't make it easy for anybody, let alone somebody my size. So I did, even though some refuse to see me as a woman." She clears her throat. "I wanted to prove to myself that I wasn't wrong. I could do it, and I did. I don't need anybody else feeling proud of me...because I am enough."

Emotions clog my throat because I can relate. There have been times I wanted to please Juniper or Evie, but I didn't agree with them. All I wanted for so long was to be good enough for them and Father, but now? I just want to do what's right, not even just for my birthright, but what I truly believe in for my kingdom. I am beyond strong enough to make my own dreams come true, with help or no help; I will do it.

I sit next to her on the bed, listening to her stories. Some are sad, tragic even. "There was a time in my commander's journey, I was paired with another commander in Mickle. He was attacked by a group of men too drunk to know any better. I couldn't save him; my power wasn't what it is today. I wasn't strong enough, and I think that day is one of the biggest regrets of my life." Tears build up in her eyes before she quickly swipes them away. I stun even myself by placing a hand on her back and rubbing in small circles. I don't know what causes me to do this, but I want to give her comfort in this moment. I don't have my empath power, but I feel as if I don't need it right now. Like, I am becoming powerful without it. "I think back on that day...I try to replay what happened and what I could have done differently to save him."

I shake my head furiously. "You were outnumbered and your power was limited. It isn't on you, May," I say, trying out the nickname. "Langford didn't deserve you." I hug her right as a knock on my door halts our conversation.

I rush to open it, and when I do, I am faced with two problems. "Hello, mate," Alwin says, looking better than he ever has. That is my first problem. My second is that I have lost my ability to speak. Alwin waves a hand in front of my face. "Hello? You there?" he mocks me, knowing full well I am. I just can't speak! He looks so handsome, I think my jaw is on the floor. "Are you ready? Because your hair could use some work." His eyes narrow on whatever Mabel has done to my hair. He grabs onto my braid, playing with it. I swat his hand away from me.

"Hey, I worked hard on it," Mabel says from beside my bed. Alwin blinks as if just now realizing we have a guest.

I release the breath I had been holding. "What are we doing? It is almost midnight," I say harshly, trying to remind myself that he is still an enemy. His eyes gleam with mischief.

"Do you suddenly have a bedtime?" His head tilts downward to me since I am shorter than him—not by much—enough for his forehead to almost meet mine. If I leaned up just enough, our lips would brush, just barely, and the thought is enough to cause shock waves throughout my body.

"I do not, but I need my beauty rest," I insist.

"You are too stunning for your own good. Maybe you need less so the village girls don't try to kill you out of spite." He holds his hand out in offering. I don't take it, but I do say goodbye to Mabel and walk into the hallway of the inn.

"Yeah, sure," I say sarcastically, taking the stairs two at a time.

"Slow down there, or I might think you are excited about our little date." He smirks from behind me. I know this because I am learning his different voices. Sometimes he decides to be friendly or playful, sometimes he sounds downright evil. But with me...he taunts me, he challenges me, and when he has *that* voice it means he is smirking at me.

"I am excited about seeing more of our kingdom." I look over my shoulder as we step into the outside world. People are still milling around, but my eyes are on my king. "What are we doing?" I ask again. He steps up next to me, grabbing my hand.

"You wanted this tour of our kingdom, remember? You wanted to see what they all needed and what they were about, down to the core. I want to show you just that, but I also want to show you who you married. Tonight I wish to show you something truly special to me." Shock ripples through me as he interlocks his fingers with mine, gently rubbing his thumb against mine.

Alwin pulls me into his arms before just picking me up. "You know I could walk much faster if you would just give me my powers back."

I could get down, but I enjoy not having to walk. I look around, noticing we don't have any guards tonight. I wonder where Sailor is?

"Your boyfriend is in his room, like the good little boy he tries to be." His tone drips with jealousy and possessiveness.

"He isn't my boyfriend," I say harshly. "I am married, you know?" My voice is filled with disdain.

"Yeah, I might have been there." His hands grip my thighs so hard that one might think he is scared of me falling.

"You're kidding." I roll my eyes, feeling annoyed that he pulled me from my bed to walk around the dark woods.

Alwin has a single flame hovering above his head to guide us to wherever he has decided to go. The yellowish-orange flame moves wherever his mind tells it to. His unconscious magic is truly inspiring; even at my best, I still had to think about it. He is power itself; he is strong, more than what I had thought. As the days move on, he seems to gain more power.

Right as I am about to speak, my jaw crushes any words that might have spilled from my mouth. My eyes widen in wonder.

"What is this?" I jump from his strong arms faster than most humans can move. Rushing to the black sandy beach, I kick my boots off, then, when I bend to pull my socks from my feet, they disappear. I don't even take the time to thank him. My bare feet sink into the soft, dark sand as I run towards the water. I press my naked feet in the glowing pond.

"Back home has water like this. There is a place I often went as a child," he says from behind me. My eyes are trained on the warm water washing around my ankles. I can't stop walking towards the deeper water. Sand moves under my bare feet, as I venture out farther from shore.

"What causes this?" I ask in wonder. Every fish in this pond glows a bright light blue. Some have spots on them that are pink or purple, but every single one of them glows so bright my eyes strain to keep watching them.

Breaking my focus from the creatures swimming at my waist now, Alwin holds onto my shoulders. He reaches around me and hugs me from behind. "My parents would let me swim all night if I just asked. It turns out being a prince had its advantages."

I look over my shoulder into eyes that are normally onyx; tonight, they aren't. They are every color of nature. Blues and greens, browns and reds. They keep changing before my eyes, and I reach behind me to cup his face.

"Thank you for bringing me here to show me this." I gulp down feelings I know I need to suppress.

"I wanted to show you that at some point I was a child, too. I didn't begin like this; I wasn't always a king with responsibilities. I was a child who watched the fish, hypnotized, like you are now." I look back down at the dark water, and the glowing trail the fish leave when they swim by.

He isn't wrong. I am mesmerized by this. I have never seen anything like it. "I think the Gods wanted to give the humans just a little taste of our world." He looks out into the water, his eyes glossing over to another time. "They gave them some of our power, but nothing compared to what fae can do. I think this was their way of making it up to the humans for not giving them longer lives. For making them weaker than us. I don't know, but I have my theories about the God Queen Capri Ragnar."

I turn in his arms, and his scent is so strong I almost forget where I am. "What are some of your theories?" I whisper, feeling as if I talk too loudly, something might ruin this moment for us.

"That the Gods are cruel and play games with all of our lives, but *she* might have been different." His eyes flicker with hatred for just a moment before his chest moves up and down, then he keeps on. "That our parents do not force our hand, Serena. We can be anything we want to be. I can be good if I want to be."

I place both hands on his face, forcing him to keep looking into my eyes. He takes another moment before he continues on. "That you were made for me, even though you are everything I am not. You are generous in ways I wouldn't even think to be. You have been in my life mere months, and yet I am not the same male I was before you," he says with a hot passion.

"I think that, even with Sailor in your life, we can make this work. You and me...*and* you and him, if need be."

I start to look away, dropping my hand before he moves and picks me up behind the knees. My face looks down into his as he holds me against his front. I try to wiggle from his grip.

"Listen to me," he commands. I clench my teeth, not liking being told what to do.

"Fine," I agree, for now.

"I believe that no matter what, you are so stubborn that you will make anything work. I can tell that you don't give up. I just hope that includes with me, too, because Serena..." His eyes are pleading with me now. He is silently begging me to listen to not only his words, but also his body. "I want to be worth it for you. Whatever I need to do, I will."

My emotions clog my throat, causing me to be unable to speak. I do the next best thing instead; I bend my head down to his and press my nose against his.

After twenty minutes of watching the glowing fish swim around, I look to Alwin. "Did your parents allow you to actually swim?" I half smirk at him. He sits beside me on the soft onyx shoreline.

"Not usually," he answers, clearly knowing where I am going with this. His eyes glide over to me, looking at me suspiciously.

"Would you like to?" I stand before letting him answer, and rip my shirt off my body. The problems I was thinking about earlier are long since forgotten. My breasts are bare to him as I slowly back up into the warm water. I wade ankle-deep as my fingers barely graze the waistband of my sleep pants. My hands move slowly as I drag down my pants and undergarments with them. Alwin's eyes scan my body lazily, lighting up with hunger. His hands are buried deep within the sand, as if he is trying to hold himself back.

"You can sit there all you'd like, but me...?" I bite down on my lip before turning to run into the unnaturally warm water. "I swim, every chance I get. I swim even if there is no time for it." I dive into the water, realizing I am not a fish. I am no turtle. I am nothing but me, and I like it. I may have to go up for air, but I hold my breath until my lungs burn so hot I feel as if they might explode. My head breaches the surface for a moment before I dive back down as quickly as I can.

I go to the bottom of the pond, grabbing a shell that still glows brightly. The farther into the water I dive, the cooler it gets. To my surprise, Alwin is right in front of me when I surface. He treads water, like he isn't very skilled at swimming.

"Is this what you wanted?" he asks as a small wave goes over his head. "Me, naked, in the middle of the night?" he taunts me. I enjoy the banter between us. I like playing his games because I have finally found somebody who can keep up with them.

"Maybe," I respond with a sultry tone. I place my hand in his, leaving the bright sky-blue shell in his grip.

"What is this?" He brings his hand above the water to investigate the shell.

I laugh at him. "What? You haven't ever seen a shell before?" The color is something I haven't seen, and I have entire collections of shells.

"Of course, I have seen them. I just don't waste my time on collecting them," he chastises me, and I shake my head.

"I am glad I didn't grow up as a princess. I had a fun childhood doing useless things like collecting shells." I splash at him just a little. He uses his water magic to cause a huge wave to crash into me. "Not fair!" I push his head underwater, using all of my strength. When he resurfaces, he spits water into my face.

"I don't have to play fair; I was raised a prince. It's who I am. I get what I want." I roll my eyes, knowing I have known who he is all along. This is still my enemy, the tyrant king. The only difference is that now I know I was wrong about one thing. He does care about one person in his kingdom.

I swim right in front of him, putting my arms around his neck. We sink under the surface of the water. Before the water can flood us, Alwin casts an air shield around us. We continue to sink down, no longer getting wet, though. I wrap my legs around his waist so that he holds me up. We sink and sink all the way to the floor of the lake. I wouldn't have thought it would be this deep, but from down here, it looks like we are a good hundred feet below the surface. It must dip down quickly, because when I went to the floor earlier, it wasn't nearly this deep.

Alwin's excitement pushes at my entrance, and I don't stop him when the tip glides against my core. My body welcomes him when he teases me, biting on my neck while I watch in amazement at the large fish swimming right by us as if we are nothing to them. His cock lines up with my core, and before he pushes completely in, his eyes look into mine for permission. I nod my head before leaning down to press a kiss to the corner of his mouth. I moan into his lips when he not only opens our kiss but at the same time pushes all the way into me. His thick length stretches me more in this position than I was ready for. This isn't like last time; this isn't animalistic. He is making love to me—no blood, no pain, just pure *love*.

His pace is slow and deliberate; his hands cradle my head while his shadow hands help hold my weight up. I no longer look at the fish or the blue rays of light. My eyes don't leave his unless he is kissing me or I am kissing him. I don't know when, but a tether of some sort slips into place. I teeter on the edge of bliss when my core rubs against his navel, and when he whispers the words "I love you," I fall over. He follows right behind me. I can't stop my mouth from moving when I respond, "I love you, too." Tears that I don't dare let fall burn my eyes.

We lie at the bottom of the lake, in a bed of sand. The black soft sand is fine, although lying on Alwin's chest is better. He lies on his elbows, pressing kisses to the top of my head. He murmurs stories about his childhood, reminding me of a time he had once told me a fairy tale about his life. Every time a bit of sand gets into a place I don't want it, Alwin removes it from my body. My legs spread across his, just admiring the nature and the simplicity of this life. The illumination from the creatures in this water lights up his eyes in a way I wish I hadn't noticed. The blue lights at the bottom of this lagoon will follow me forever. When I close my eyes, I don't open them again in fear that this will have all been a dream that I don't want to wake from.

Chapter 25

"Morning, Honeybee," Sailor says from his perch next to the bed in this Gods-forsaken inn.

I groan, wishing I could sleep more. I don't know how I got into bed, but I can only imagine. "Go away." I throw a pillow at him before rolling away to try and get a few more minutes of sleep in.

"I wish I could. Seeing how delicious you look when you drool is cruel. Alas, you have business to attend to. Saxton folk do not like waiting."

I sit right up, noticing the sun is fully up, and Sailor is shirtless. My eyes narrow on his bronze chest. "Where is your shirt?" I quip, glancing at his sweaty abs. They are more defined than even before he left for Clove.

He sees me looking and smiles. "Like what you see?" He tilts his head in a way that is begging me to run my fingers through those blond locks.

"I wish I were looking at a plate of food," I volley back, pulling the blanket over my chest.

"Feeling shy, are we?" He licks over the now smaller gap in his teeth, clearly playing with me.

"We are obviously not feeling shy, since you walked into my room with nothing on." I yank the sheets off the bed and bring them around me as I stand up.

"I have shorts on." He sounds offended.

"Yeah, Sailor, shorts count as an outfit," I respond sarcastically. I walk to where Mabel laid out my outfit for today and smile when I see she left me some pants and a shirt instead of a gown and a crown.

"Have a new friend?" he asks as he walks up behind me.

I look over my shoulder into the brightest sky-blue eyes. "Too early to tell." Sadness sweeps over me in a tidal wave at the thought of Birdie, and her betrayal. "How is Mary Lou?" I ask, trying to change the subject. I make my way into the bathing chamber to change. Well, actually, I slept naked, so I just need to get dressed.

"Is Mary our friend now?" He sits down on my bed, making himself comfortable. I throw the soap bar at him, and of course, he blocks it right away. "Hey! That could have hit my face." Yeah, if only it had. I dress quickly, knowing I am on a time crunch.

"That would have been tragic, wouldn't it?" I respond, while slowly prowling towards him. He yanks me onto the bed, and I let him. He tickles my sides; I almost choke on a fit of laughter. I shove at his hands. "Stop or I'll do it back," I say in between fits of giggles.

"Good, at least then your hands would be on me," he says as he clenches his jaw.

My smile falls instantly. "Sailor," I say quietly.

He shakes his head. "Let's get you to this luncheon." I nod, knowing we need to talk more but not knowing if we will have a chance anytime soon.

The walk into the village center isn't far. The buildings have moss all over them and I find myself studying each and every one. For such a hostile village, it *is* pretty. The rooftops are all covered in thick brown grass. Nature is everywhere here; they use it in every aspect of their lives. I see one woman rubbing some thick green goo on an elderly man.

As soon as I see the tan building I am to meet our king at, my heart rate spikes. I maintain my breathing even though I feel as if I might bolt. I tap each of my fingers against my thumb one time to calm myself down. "One, two, three…" I count each finger, trying to distract myself from the very real possibility that these people could attack us. Wolf follows us, while maintaining his distance.

Even though I am no longer worried for myself, my list of people is growing. Mabel is somebody that I keep trying to get out of my head. She isn't really my friend yet, but it feels like she could be. Birdie burned me, but not everybody has, and I need to remember that. Mary Lou ended up being somebody that I care deeply for, even after my childhood.

My hand waits on the doorknob. Just one more moment of peace. I can already hear the voices from inside Saxton Hall, which mostly sound calm and cheerful.

Sailor and Wolf both walk behind me, shoulder to shoulder, right on my heels. Their boots echo throughout the now still Hall, and some people clear their throats, trying to draw attention to my arrival. The crowd stops speaking when we walk in. Heads turn to watch as I make my way to where my husband sits.

Alwin is at the head of a deep oak table with a man I don't recognize. They are the only ones still speaking, and they seem to be in a tense conversation. My husband's knuckles are white from how hard his fists are clenched together. His irritation is sent directly into my head, and my senses are automatically on guard. Alwin stands when he notices me a few feet away, his body rigid.

Our king's eyes send daggers to every person who isn't standing for me. As if he commands them silently, most do. Chairs scrape against the floors so loudly, I cringe. My eyes glance around the room, realizing that some still remain seated. In reality, I do not mind. I haven't earned their respect yet. That comes with action and change for the better of the kingdom. Which I intend to do. The uncomfortable, tense air feels heavier the closer I get to the man who was speaking with Alwin.

Alwin bows his head, the dark hair tumbling over his forehead. Just like when he stood and others followed, every head in Saxton Hall bows for me.

"To our queen." Alwin raises a glass of bloodred wine, and some others murmur with him, but mostly they all stare under their hooded eyes. Alwin seems to mind far more than I do. His eyes land on one man I know didn't stand or speak any words. I watch as his eyes darken to the deepest onyx I have ever seen, but the man doesn't notice. I gulp down any nerves I might have, and smile at my king before he starts a fight...or worse, *kills* somebody.

"We're here," Wolf announces, clearly reading his king's mood as I have.

"I know." Alwin's response is clipped and harsh. I keep walking until I make it to a seat I think is for me. I have no idea what the custom is here, and I feel out of my depth because of that. I should have been doing research instead of moping about my love life.

I sit in the seat across from the burly man, and right next to Alwin. When I look around the room, people have begun speaking again, but it's hushed. I can tell they don't feel comfortable around me. I watch their body language, the way their eyes sometimes dart to mine, or maybe the way they quicken the pace at which they were eating. All small signs they don't want to be near me. I was a girl from Darnish...who wasn't well-liked at that. Then I won the kingdom in trials and proved how powerful I was. They may have lost somebody in the weeks of our trials. Five women went, and I do not see any familiar faces here.

Mabel sits farther down from me, and I desperately wish she were next to me, considering the girl she is talking to hasn't stopped laughing since they sat next to each other. I move my food around my plate, wishing I had something else to eat. Apparently, this is a customary dish here in Saxton. The slop has meat bits in it that look raw, alongside some mini corn. The grayish sauce in it smells like it came from a monster in Brabble's butt. My fork sifts through the mush until I make it to some lettuce at the bottom.

Alwin eats it but looks half a second away from vomiting. Sailor chews on some lettuce that they put to the side of the dish, presumably for decoration. Wolf just watches everybody, his valley-green eyes scanning everywhere. After the fourth time I watch his slow, meticulous stare hit every single person, I decide he is looking for something. Maybe he is waiting for something to happen.

"You should relax," I whisper to him, having to lean forward and say it across Sailor.

"I wish I could. I just...I don't feel good about this." His proper voice is coming back. The more time he spends away from Magnolia, the more he seems like himself.

He isn't joking, though. Wolf is more tense than I have ever seen him before. He sips his wine once more before saying, "They are being too polite."

I narrow my eyes because I do not feel as if they are being polite. "Isn't that good?" I ask, feeling confused on so many levels.

He shrugs. "Last week they were in full rebellion. Now they are feeding us and conversing as if they love you two. It doesn't add up." He shakes his head; his black hair is tousled in a way that tells me he has been running his fingers through it.

I take another bite of the garbage in front of me before the man speaking to Alwin leans across the table, extending his bulky arm my way. Alwin, Sailor, and Wolf all stiffen before realizing the man is trying to shake my hand.

"I am Haadgar." His voice is so deep, it almost startles me.

"Hi, I am Serena," I answer simply, while shaking his beefy hand. He gives me a curt nod, dropping my hand in favor of his wine.

"Yes, you are the bride from Darnish." He licks his lips while staring at my chest. I clear my throat, then straighten my back.

"I am," I confirm with a regal tone. It sounds unnatural coming from me.

I decide to go the easier route here and just ignore the fact that he didn't address me as his queen, nor has he looked into my eyes. "Serena," I say again, trying to get him to look me in the eyes.

"You are prettier than the last one." His mouth is full of food, some of it falling from between his teeth as he speaks. Alwin grinds his jaw, clearly not wanting to kill this man in front of me. I don't seem to struggle with that issue.

My temper has remained in check until this moment. Alwin has told me bits and pieces of our late queen. She may not have been for him, but I have figured out that he cared for her. She wasn't perfect, no. But she didn't deserve to die. All Alwin will tell me is that she died during childbirth. Something that happens far too often for a kingdom that has healers everywhere. Even with powers, healers cannot fix a mortal giving birth to a fae baby. Especially if that baby drains the mother, like what happened with the woman my mother put me into. For a long while, Alwin had thought he would give up on finding his mate, me. He could live with his human bride and be happy. He tried to ignore the pull to see me, but when she died, he said it became so strong he had to hold the trials. He had to find me. I dragged that information from him during one of our nights in the inn.

"It would seem manners are not a requirement for leadership here in Saxton." I sigh.

The man's coffee-colored eyes flash with irritation. "I am simply stating what every person here was thinking. You are a much better-looking queen."

I put my mug down on the table with a loud thud. "To speak ill of your *late* queen is treason. Are you asking for death today?" My voice is ice-cold, and if every pair of eyes wasn't already on us, they are now.

"Whatever you want to do here, I have your back." Wolf's voice surfaces in my head for the first time in a few days, and I embrace it.

"Of course not, Majesty." The man grinds his teeth before gulping on his wine.

"Good," I answer sweetly. "And Haadgar?"

My eyes narrow on him, and his glaze over as he hums. "Hmm?" Alwin watches so closely, I swear, if he doesn't kill this man, I will be shocked.

"My looks have nothing to do with how deadly I am." My voice is just slightly louder than a whisper. His eyes flash with fear for one moment before going to my neck. He gives me an evil smirk...worse than that, a knowing smirk. His fists are clenched; his knuckles are white. Before he can comment on my necklace that leeches my power, somebody down the table clears their throat.

"Here is to a long, healthy life for our queen." They hold up their goblet and others follow. The man across from me does the same; the only problem is that when his eyes lock onto mine, I see a man who wants death.

When the meal is over, I don't walk around the market. Barnett, Roman, and Mabel all follow behind me while the others pack things up and say goodbye. I pass out coins on my way to the carriage, but I do not stray from the path. Haadgar steps out from an alcove, blocking my way. His large frame takes up my entire viewpoint.

Barnett and Mabel are instantly in front of me, Roman to my back. The large man chuckles deeply, not in a funny kind of way but more of an intimidating one. "I had heard your beloved took your powers away." He shakes his head.

Barnett growls. "That's a lie." He spits at the man in front of us. I know Barnett is strong with his power, but this man has strength, too, and I don't want to see who would be stronger.

"What do you want?" I ask from behind the two members of the King's Guard.

"I want a lot of things. What I *need* is another." His voice chills me to the bone. He looks over Barnett and Mabel, right into my soul. "Pretty necklace. Did the king give that to you?" His tone is laced with venom, as if he already knows what is in the necklace. The necklace that took my power from me, but also gave me the strength I didn't know I needed.

"That doesn't matter. It doesn't concern you where she gets her jewelry from," Barnett says stepping into the man. Haadgar towers over Barnett, and worry hits my belly like a block of cinders.

"I see. I also heard a little rumor that our beloved king likes to share you. Is that true?"

Barnett growls at his insinuation, and my face heats.

"No," I snap, losing my temper completely. He tries to reach out and touch me, but Barnett grabs onto his hand harshly.

"Try to touch her and I will kill you," Barnett growls, showing teeth and all. Mabel has her hand on her sword, ready for anything. Roman is gripping onto my hips, ready to take flight if need be. Ready to leave behind our friends to fend off this burly man.

Haadgar doesn't seem to care that three guards are here, and he chuckles before saying, "I guess we will see when a baby pops from ya if it looks like our *dear king*."

I sidestep all of them, pulling away from Roman. I don't want or need anybody getting harmed for me. "I guess we *will* see, although, you will never be around my babies." I swallow any hateful thing I might have said before becoming queen. Now I have my people watching, seeing how I handle conflict. I can't let them down; I need to help them, and the first way of doing that is proving I am not who and what they think I am.

Chapter 26

The carriage rocks back and forth, lulling me to sleep. I wish it wouldn't. Nightmares plague my dreams, thoughts of darkness swirling around my fae mother and father. Scenes of them killing thousands, me right beside them. The killing never seems to stop, screams from children and mothers. My eyes aren't my own; they are black like Alwin's. The difference is that mine do not change. They stay in the darkness. A male I don't know is in blurry scenes in my head.

My mother looks like me; her body doesn't look a day over thirty, and my father looks forty. There is something wrong about them, but I can't seem to pinpoint what it is. When my mother walks up to me in a bloodred dress, her bright blonde hair swishing against her back, she presses her hand to my chest, causing it to push into my body. *"Hurry, honey. We need you home to help with the war."* Her voice is eternal. I scream in my dream and in the carriage.

Big hands are on me, shaking me awake.

"Serena." The voice sounds scared. "Open your eyes for me." I thrash against the strong yet gentle hands. "I'm here." The kind tone shocks my system. My eyes open to the unlikely green ones in front of me. I pull away as soon as I can.

"What are you doing here?" My chest heaves from breathing so fast, and my eyes narrow as I continue scooting back.

"Alwin and Sailor are riding ahead, scouting to make sure nobody followed us from Saxton," he explains to me, his eyes filled with worry.

"I see." I grab the waterskin and take several sips. "How long until we stop?" I run a hand over my sweat-slicked hair.

"Soon, just a few hours out now." I rub my fingers over the fabric of my pants to distract my mind.

"Have they found anybody?" I ask absentmindedly.

"No," he answers right away.

"Good," I say hollowly.

"What was that nightmare?" Wolf's voice seems caring.

I shake my head. "I don't want to talk about it," I mumble under my breath, feeling as if I am speaking to my brother.

"Okay then." He purses his lips before handing me a muffin, and my brows furrow.

"What is this?" I ask stupidly, knowing it is a muffin, but unsure why he is handing it to me.

"I know you, and your stomach was growling louder than you were screaming."

I grab the muffin and murmur my thanks.

"I know now is not the time, Serena, but I would like to explain what I did." His voice cracks on the last word.

"I would like that." And before he can explain himself, I decide to give him a little more. Wolf may not be able to feel my emotions, but it's clear I am starting to give in to him. "I had a dream about my parents. But they weren't how they normally are. They seemed different somehow." I shake my head, knowing it sounds crazy.

"Like what?" His green eyes scan to the muffin in my hands, and I wonder if he, too, is hungry. I break off a piece and hand it to him. He takes it without hesitation, and I half smile at him. And then I'm brought back to what my parents looked like in my dream.

"They appeared...evil." My voice sounds distant, even to me.

"But they aren't, right?" The carriage hits a bump in the path; I almost drop my muffin before shaking my head back to reality.

"No, they aren't," I confirm.

We arrive in Earsgorg right as the sun is starting to come up. My stomach fills with more dread...our next stop is Darnish. I can't for the life of me figure out how I want to handle that. My panic almost swallows me whole before Wolf places a hand on mine. The carriage stops abruptly, jolting me forward.

"I know I haven't been clear about this, based on my actions, but I would like you to know something." His bright green eyes shine more than they did a moment ago. "I am your friend; at one point…I wanted to be more." He shrugs, at the same time showing me his pearly whites. "I think anybody with half a brain could look at you and want more than friendship." He breathes out for a moment before adding on, "Then, of course, once they get to know you…" His eyes widen slightly, as if thinking about the hidden version of me. "They will fall helplessly in love with you."

My breath hitches. I pray to the Gods he isn't professing his love for me. I would get up and leave. I have no more room for another romance.

He must notice I am feeling uncomfortable, so he saves me from my panic. "There are things I can and cannot say to you, Serena, but here is one of my truths." I wait in anticipation. "Any person with eyes can see how much you care for both Sailor and Alwin, and them for you equally. I have lost the right to call Sailor my brother; I will mourn that loss forever." I watch his throat bob. "I can feel the amount of love they each share for you. When I enter another's mind, I can sometimes feel their thoughts. It's overwhelming the amount of love they each have for you." Confusion pours into my body.

"Why are you telling me this?" I hear voices outside and know we need to join them.

"Because you need to know…I care for you as a friend. I don't ever want you to think we are not on the same side here; we both want this kingdom and its people to thrive. I can see how much you care for it even though you don't have to. You have an entire kingdom where you're from to claim, and yet you are taking the time to help *us*." He runs his thumb over my knuckles. "I just wanted you to know, I see that. Others may not, but I do. You have my loyalty. And if you're questioning their loyalty, you shouldn't; they both know what they have signed up for." His voice is hoarse, unlike his natural, proper, commanding tone. I open my mouth to speak, but the door is rammed open.

Sailor stands at the entrance in a regal navy-blue outfit. His eyes scan over where Wolf's hand is holding mine. I pull away from the friendly gesture to place my hand on my own lap. Sailor pauses for a moment, as if thinking about saying something. Then he shakes his head, his blond locks moving with the motion.

"Alright, I can share you with a fucking *king*, but I am not going backwards here, Serena." He throws his hands up in defeat.

I giggle while jumping from the carriage into his waiting arms. "Don't worry, SJ, I don't want your girl," Wolf says while stepping out into the village center. I look around, seeing Earsgorg is closer to how Darnish looks than any of the other villages have been. The people don't stop to say anything, but I don't mind that.

"What are our plans today, Majesty?" Mabel asks from beside Barnett, and I smile brightly, knowing today needs to be a good day.

"What does our king have planned?" I ask Barnett, because he seems to track the itinerary more than anybody else. He then pulls a piece of paper from his pants pocket.

"We have a dinner and a ball tonight, but other than that, we are free. His majesty has business to attend, he says he will see you as soon as he can." I see Mabel trying to cover her mouth from laughing at our friend.

I watch the villagers, and they seem friendly. There are children running around the village square. All laughing and having a good time. I never got to do that as a child. My father always feared I would expose myself and be taken from him. I guess, in the end, he wasn't wrong.

"I have an idea." I smile, biting down on my lower lip. Sailor groans when I whack his stomach. "Catch me if you can!"

His eyebrows raise to his hairline as I take off into the village, sprinting as fast as my fae legs will take me. I run around children who stop their own playing to watch me carefully.

"What are you doing?" A little girl asks from an open doorframe, her mother right behind her.

"I am playing a game." I stop right in front of their home. My simple light-blue dress swishes against my ankles. I lean forward into her space. "Would you like to play with us?" I whisper, not wanting Sailor to find my spot. She nods frantically, then looks to her mother for permission. The mother grants it, and before I know it, every child in Earsgorg's square is playing a thrilling game of hide-and-seek.

"Serena, you may not have invisibility anymore, but damn it, you are good at this game," Sailor says from somewhere far away. I laugh from inside a partially full garbage can. The tiny child with me laughs loud enough that I know Sailor had to have heard her. I hear boots pound the cobblestone until they are so close I hold my breath. He walks right next to the can, running his fingers up and over it.

"I wonder, where are you, little Bee?" His voice is right next to our location.

I have won every round up until now; I am the only one who hasn't been "it." I love to win, I always have. I never would have thought that the most important game I would ever play…I might not have wanted to win. Alwin might be my mate, but selfishly, I wish I hadn't found him yet. I know I would always find him, but I still wanted more time with my commander. Sailor brings me so much happiness and joy, it's hard to picture a life where we aren't *Sailor and Serena*.

The child's giggles interrupt my thoughts about my future. Sailor kicks the can, causing a loud echo to sound.

"I guess we have lost, yet again," Sailor says slowly, clearly messing with me. I knew I shouldn't have let the child talk me into hiding with her, but I also wanted to include the kids here. They struggle enough as it is. Why not add some happiness to their lives?

I might be their queen, but the most important job as queen is to make certain they thrive in my kingdom. I can't do that if they fear me, I can't do that if they don't know me. I need to earn their trust, I need to show them I am on their side. Not everything needs to be a huge ball with the commanders or the wealthy. Most of my work will be dirty, unnoticed, and most importantly, *fun*.

When Sailor lifts the lid of the garbage can, the little girl who paired with him screams, "I found you!" I laugh, silently fuming that I lost, while standing up and brushing some trash from my skirts.

"You ready to get out of here?" I ask the tiny child as I lift the girl into Sailor's arms. As soon as her feet hit the cobblestone, she is off with her sister.

"Are *you* ready?" He tilts his head towards the can.

"I am *beyond* ready. I believe I have been sitting in rotten fruit for the last twenty minutes." My nose crinkles from the smell. Sailor scans my upper body, then places his hands on my hips as he lifts me from the tall can. He holds me against his chest a moment longer than necessary, before Barnett runs over to us.

"Finally, somebody got you." He wags a finger in my face, and I irrationally want to break the thing off his hand. "You lost!" he yells in my face. If he knew what was good for him, he wouldn't taunt me.

As if Barnett realizes I don't like what he is doing, he wipes the smile from his pale, freckled face. "Uh, I'm sorry. You have rubbed off on me, and I think I got a little too competitive." Sailor laughs while grabbing onto my hand. When his bright ocean-blue eyes hit mine, I swear I may not take a breath.

He leans into my space, his lips brushing against my ear. "I believe you are *it*." He whispers so softly, it tickles everywhere his exhale touches. My lips go between my teeth, biting down on any remark I might have made before becoming queen.

"I am, and I'll find you all in record time," I swear. The kids all run before my friends do. Sailor is the last to leave, his eyes warning me. He wants to ruin me; he wants *me*. I just don't know if I can give myself to him in that way, maybe ever again. It feels wrong now. I feel wrong dragging him alongside me.

"Cover your eyes, Honeybee." I do as he requests, my hands going over my already shut eyes. "No cheating, even if you are losing," his voice taunts me, and I stick my tongue out at him like a child I saw earlier. I may not be able to see him, but I will always feel Sailor James. He walks around me, and I track his footsteps circling my body. He stops at my back before leaning into the groove of my neck, whispering in my ear, "I want that thing in my mouth." His dirty words cause me to clench my thighs together; he chuckles deeply enough to tell me he notices my sudden mood change. As fast as the heat came, it leaves when his boots move further and further away.

I count to the number we agreed upon—fifty—before I rush off in search of everybody playing. I find three kids before I even hit the first shop. They weren't hiding very well, but still, I play along. I act as if they had the very best hiding places, even though they didn't. I find Mabel behind a shop owner, who doesn't seem so happy with our game, but right as I turn to leave, he gives me a card. I shove it into the pockets of my dress, not having time to read it right now.

I find Barnett and Roman hiding together in an alcove, in the dark, suspiciously close together. Barnett throws his hands up while sighing so loud that anybody could hear it. "I swear, you may not have your powers, but you are dang good at games, Serena," Barnett grumbles harshly, seemingly as unhappy with losing as I was.

"It isn't my fault you picked a bad partner to hide with." I glance between the two of them, and Roman elbows Barnett's side. Barnett mumbles something under his breath about not even wanting to hide together, but Roman followed him there. I roll my eyes before leaving them in the darkness. I stop walking in the middle of the village path, the cobblestone gives away more than others might think. I wait and wonder, feeling for anything, listening.

I make my move as I hear footsteps rushing in and out of different shops. The variant sounds tell me exactly what I need to know. I run on my tiptoes, as softly as I can. My feet move so swiftly I doubt any human can hear me unless they have the Gods' hearing ability. I round a corner just to come face-to-face with Wolf. The smirk on his face when he shoves a few kids behind his back is devilish.

"You've got me." He lifts his shoulders slightly, giving me a sheepish grin.

"And them." I claim the children behind him, too.

He shakes his head, whispering under his breath, "You couldn't let them win?" He sighs dramatically.

My mouth droops, and my eyes widen tremendously. I look shocked, I know I do. Because I am surprised... Allowing them to win when they didn't wouldn't help anybody.

"Who would that help?" I say as my eyes narrow on his. I turn in search of the last person, knowing he won't make it easy for me.

I rush around the village, knowing the time for games is ending as quickly as the moon chases the sun away. My feet move faster than they should be able to as the minutes tick by.

"Sailor," I yell when I hit the village limits. I study the tree line, wondering if he quit the game early. Right as I spin on my heels to do something I don't want to do, I am picked up from behind. I laugh loud enough that every person within a mile probably hears me. "Put me down." I hit his large hands which grab possessively at my middle.

"Tell me I won," he practically growls in my ear.

Through fits of giggles, I answer him. "Never. I won it fair and square."

He puts me on the ground, spinning me so quickly I become dizzy. His hands shove firmly against my shoulders until my back hits the hard bark of a large tree. My eyes go wide with what he might try to do when his hands go to either side of my head. He licks his lips before saying, "I mean *you*." His eyes burn white-hot. No longer blue, they are white with possessiveness. "I want *you*, Bee." The desperation in his voice causes me to pause.

"I—" I place my hands on his hips, putting some distance between us. "When I touch you, I feel like I'm cheating on him, on our bond, but—" His eyes don't dart away; they stay locked on mine. The glare in them promises sweetness later. "But also, when I am with him, I feel like I am betraying you. I don't know what to do," I admit, shame coating my tongue in a bitterness that's hard to swallow.

"I don't care what you do with him; I care what you do with me. Are you mine?" He leans forward, his sweat-slicked forehead pressing against mine.

I don't know how to answer his question, because my heart feels torn. "I know I want you," I say as tears sting the back of my eyes. "I know that my heart loves you both. And I know that isn't fair to either of you."

He shakes his head against mine, stopping any words that might have left my mouth. His blond locks fall slightly, and I reach up, slowly adjusting them.

"Serena, you have permission to explore from both of us; neither of us wants to make you feel cornered. Now, if you want to add another in, I may not be able to handle that, but I am man enough to let you figure your shit out." He presses a kiss to the corner of my lips, the same spot tilting upwards.

"What if I can't figure it out?" A single tear escapes its prison. Sailor wipes it away before it hits my rosy cheeks. "What if I love you both forever?" My voice is full of questions. I have never even had a boyfriend, and now I have a boyfriend and a mate/husband.

"My body, soul, and mind are yours only. No matter what I am to you. Your boyfriend, your lover...anything you need, I am there for you. Always and forever, Bee."

This time, when he presses my back against the bark, I don't balk. I don't back out of his touch. I embrace what they are offering me...time to figure it all out. Me being queen, my love life, my fae nature, everything. They are giving it to me, no strings attached, and my selfishness will take it all. For now, I will accept what they are both offering me.

Chapter 27

<u>Serena</u>

The room at the inn is like every other one, housing a small wooden bed with a scratchy blanket. I sit in a rickety, old wooden chair in front of a cracked and distorted mirror. The reflection comes back a rusty brown. I know the world isn't like that, but at one point, I had wished I could see my life in a different color. I stare for far too long at my tinted self.

Mabel wanted to help get me ready, but I told her I was fine on my own. Before all of this, I enjoyed time alone. I would hone my skills—my powers—and even just sit and relax. I don't remember the last time I was truly alone for an extended time. Certainly well before the trials happened. My father would call me a recluse, because other than at nighttime, I would go into the woods for hours on end. I didn't need or want people around me. Now that I don't have to hide who I am, I find that I don't enjoy the silence as much as I once did. I like talking to people, getting to know them. I find that learning their different stories is exciting and welcoming. I have learned that having friends who care for you is powerful in itself.

After spending less than ten minutes in front of the mirror, I feel pleased with my general appearance. My hair swims down to my lower back in large waves, with a single braid by the front of my face. I pull apart the large braid, as Evie had once done for me. My face is bare, aside from some black charcoal on my lashes and a small splash of the maroon paste Millie said would look good on my eyelids. There is a dress lying on the chair next to the bed with a note lying on top of it.

Serena,

You will look stunning in this. If you choose to wear pants to the ball, I won't fuss. Although, this gown will give me easier access to play later... I am so deeply looking forward to seeing you dance tonight. I want to see the real Serena, the version of you I have pictured in my head. The wild, carefree girl I imagine you to have been. I hope we are able to let loose tonight. We deserve it, don't we, darling?

AAH

I smile stupidly at myself before holding the gown up. The gold fabric twinkles in the candlelight, thanks to Sailor for the dim lighting, his fire making a warm glow. The plunge in the front is severe enough that it will show off more cleavage than I would typically prefer. I do like the slit up to the thigh, though, which makes for a different kind of easy access than Alwin is referring to—it will give me access to my long dagger, though I hope not to need it. I decide to go with simple shoes. Since this gown is made for a queen, it doesn't need anything extra. I leave the black crown sitting on the old bed.

My shoes click on the wooden steps as I make my way downstairs. Barnett is right on my trail; he smells like a powdered grandmother, but I don't care to tell him that.

"At least they like us a little more than in Saxton." My shoulders gently rise. I can already hear instruments from the dining hall as we walk through the main sitting area in the inn.

"I wouldn't call any of them our friends, Serena. Remember that, please."

I look over my shoulder before stepping out into the open air. "You haven't always been this depressing. What happened?" My eyes narrow on him in suspicion. I whirl towards him, my dress spinning with me. He backs up slightly before his face contorts with worry.

"I don't know. I just have a feeling a storm is brewing." The sound of laughter causes his eyes to flicker towards where we are meant to be. "I just want to make sure you are safe, that's all. It's nothing that has happened or been said. I just worry for you."

My chest expands, breathing in and out, before I do something I know people will talk about later. I wrap my arms around his lower back in an embrace. "Thank you for caring enough about me that you would worry about possible future situations." I smile up at him with my face pressed against his chest.

"You aren't only the queen who will save our kingdom..., you are my friend, Serena. I still owe you my life for saving me when you had everything to lose." His hands stay respectfully on my shoulders. I feel myself slowly thawing from a lifetime of denying myself true friendship.

"You owe me nothing. I chose to save you that day, and I will continue fighting for you, and our kingdom."

He rubs my back in a familiar way that reminds me of Juniper. "Let's go." He tilts his head towards the noise.

We walk into the hall, and it is filled to the brim with villagers. I am glad I didn't have to invite anybody; they all seem to be here. I smile as I watch the kids we played with earlier dance around, while a huge man with a long beard and a petite woman sing a song that sounds like a fairy tale.

"Look at them." I point out the kids to Barnett. "They are happy. You should be happy, too." I elbow his side to emphasize the happiness here. "There are also lots of handsome men here tonight," I say playfully and smile at him knowingly. He doesn't take the bait. "No?" I try to get through his walls.

"What?" he asks as if he hasn't heard a word I have been saying.

"I was saying there are a lot of men here tonight." I wave out towards the crowd.

"Don't you already have your hands full with two men?" Barnett says before turning and mumbling something under his breath about finding Roman and Wolf.

"Alright, I will stay here. Don't worry." I look around before spotting the wineglasses. "Also, that is not what I meant at all." I sigh, knowing he didn't hear me.

I grab one glass and then another. Alwin said he needed to let loose, so I may as well have fun tonight. I toss back both glasses. The man with the drinks walks by again, and he gives me a look like I should slow down, but I don't take the hint. Grabbing two more, I sip on one before smelling the scent that brings me comfort.

"Having fun already, Bee?" Sailor whispers from behind me. I smile over my shoulder, then watch him stiffen. His body seems as if it is frozen.

"Sailor?" I ask, worried. I face him fully, placing my palms on his firm chest. "Sailor, did something happen?"

Emotion clogs my throat before he chokes out, "Um...yeah. I'm sorry for worrying you." His bright eyes scan my body, pausing on my chest, which I know looks good. "You look beyond amazing, Serena." His throat bobs, and he licks his lips before continuing. "I don't know how I didn't see you were Fae the moment I saw you. Your skin is glowing. You look like a fucking *queen*." Tears well in his eyes. I step completely into his warmth to wipe the unshed tears away.

"I don't deserve you, Sailor." My chest compresses with knowing I will have to let him go at some point. That point is just not right now.

His eyes dart to the second glass in my hand. "Are you drinking for two tonight?"

I chug the last little bit of my drink, handing the second one to him. "Do you want one?" He takes the glass before tapping it against mine.

"I can never refuse you." His eyes dance with mischief. "Here is to our future, whatever comes of it." I dip my chin, agreeing to whatever may happen.

Sailor pulls me through the crowd, making our way to where everybody is dancing. We join the other people already there. Mabel dances with a girl I have never seen. Wolf taps his foot near the dance floor. Alwin is talking with one of the commanders, his eyes darting to me every now and then. The blue and white swirls frantically swim in his eyes.

The man playing the instrument picks up his pace, and as the tempo of the entire room warms up, we all get swept into the dance. There isn't one face in this hall that isn't lit with a smile. The drinks flow as easily as the crowd does, while bodies all move to a rhythm that sounds like the wild outdoors.

Sailor's hands glide up and down my body as I sway my hips to the rhythm of the song. The night runs along without any hassle, and if that isn't a nice change, I don't know what is. I drink more than I should, allowing myself to live, at least for tonight. As my hips sway to the beat of the drums, my hands run through my hair, not wanting to ever leave this village. The happiness here is palpable; even I can feel the warmth and love.

The partygoers start to thin out as I dance with Mabel and a group of others. I don't know the last time I have ever been this truly happy. There isn't anything on my mind other than my friends. I finally know what carefree means. I realize that I love it; I can be myself, and people may or may not like it, but I will not change who I am. I will never go back to hiding what I am.

"May I?" a deep husky voice asks, in between my sips of wine. I look into the eyes that I have begun to find mesmerizing. A smirk lights up my face before I dance backwards, holding up my hand and motioning him to follow.

"You may." I draw my lower lip in between my teeth before setting my glass down. Alwin grips me in a possessive way that holds my attention.

"You drank tonight," he says stating the obvious.

"I did. I wanted to have fun." He nods his head in understanding.

He leans in to whisper in my ear, "It won't always be this hard." His breath tickles my neck enough to cause goose bumps; he seems to enjoy doing that to me.

There are only about twenty or so people still here. Sailor walked a mother and her family home a while ago. Wolf left with Mabel and Barnett. Roman is flirting with a pretty redhead somewhere by the dessert table. It is just Alwin and me in our little area. The way it always seems to end up with us.

Alwin draws me closer to him, my body flush against his. Our bodies move fluidly together, like they may be one in the same. I stumble some, but he holds me up.

"How are you feeling about Darnish?" he whispers in my ear, as if voicing the question louder might cause chaos. I lift my crystal-clear glass and chug the contents quickly before placing it on a passing tray.

"About that good." I give him a sad smile. The gown shows the entirety of my arms, my tattoo on full display. His eyes scan my wrist before I cover the tattoo with my hand. I don't want him to see it in this moment.

"It will be alright, and even if it isn't, you will always have me," Alwin says while still looking to where my hand hides what he has already seen. His eyes slide back to mine, where they seem to be more often of late. I lean my head into his chest, wanting to just lie on him.

"Can you hold me tonight?" My voice is weak; I *feel* a little weak for asking him to hold me. I shut my eyes, unable to look at him during this moment of pathetic vulnerability. His soft touch causes my eyes to flutter open; his eyes are on my lips.

"I thought you would never ask." He sweeps one arm behind my knees, scooping me into his strong body. My arms wrap instinctively around his neck before a cloud of black mist delivers us to my puny bed in the inn. The bed creaks as he adjusts his large frame in the tiny, flimsy bed. I eye him warily, unsure what his next move is going to be. That is my major setback with him—I never know where he stands.

Alwin sits up to take off my shoes. "I told you this dress would be a heart-stopper," he drawls as he places the shoes to the side.

"I didn't need to stop hearts, Alwin. I want to make the villages happy and healthy again," I deadpan.

"Well, you did both. I was told you even played with the children."

My dress disappears, instantly replaced by a long T-shirt that smells like green tea and sage. Alwin rolls from the bed.

"Where are you going?" I ask him as I watch him walk away. The warmth from his body stays with me, as his dark shadows curl against my exposed flesh.

"I told you long ago, Serena...I am not a God. I still need to use the restroom." He peeks his head from the bathing chamber, a shit-eating grin on his face. "Have you grown so fond of me, you wish to follow me everywhere now?"

He is only teasing, but my face heats from his question. I realize it's because he isn't wrong. I sigh. Even though he is onto something, I won't admit that.

"I was just curious if you were getting a snack," I lie through my teeth, knowing he won't call me out on it.

"Are you hungry, wife?" His gaze heats as he leans into the frame of the bathing chamber. Alwin stands shirtless, no shoes, and his pants still unbuttoned.

"Possibly," I say on a breath. His head tilts in a predatory way; he's studying me, I realize.

"For what?"

My forefinger finds its way in between my teeth. "You," I whisper.

Alwin stalks towards me, his body moving silently. I have seen monsters move the way he does, right before they go in for a kill. Alwin is an apex predator. I just can't tell if I am his prey. He looks at me as if he would devour me whole, and I don't think it would be unenjoyable. He snaps his fingers right in front of me, dragging me from my lust-filled thoughts.

"The children, Serena...did you have fun with them today?"

"I did. It was a good day. Where were you?"

He sits on the bed beside me, the mattress creaking even more. "I had business to discuss with the commanders. I wanted to let you have your fun."

He puts an arm behind my head, and I lean fully on him. My hand spreads out on his chest, my leg going right over his. "You sure are more like a bear than human or fae, aren't you?" He pushes my hair out of my face before pressing a kiss to my head.

"I like snuggles, what can I say?" The candlelight is the only light in my room, causing this moment to be more romantic than it should be. Alwin is only in his unbuttoned pants from earlier. My hand trails to the smooth skin right above his open waistband. He grabs my wrist before I can get any further.

"I wouldn't touch you in the state you're in right now." I roll my eyes before thinking how sometimes his honor is annoying. "Consent is not annoying, Serena. You deserve more than drunken sex." I know I would agree with him tomorrow, and yet, right in this moment, disappointment fills my body.

"Stay out of my head," I hiss before settling into him.

"Never," he promises.

I close my eyes, still wanting to talk with him. "Are my parents alive?" I ask, even though I know the answer. His body tenses under me, causing me to pop one eye open.

"Why are you asking that?" His tone sounds wary.

I close my eyes again. "I had a dream about them. It was different from before; they were alive and well. But they weren't what I thought they were—they were killing innocents." My words slur together. I know I shouldn't have drunk this much, but I also know tonight would have dragged on if I hadn't.

"There will be a time to speak about Mirahalm, and it isn't when you are drunk. Go to bed now, and we will talk about it tomorrow."

I open my eyes once more. "Do you promise?" His jaw clenches before his fingers dust over my eyes.

"Shut these pretty eyes, and I will give you anything you desire." The last thing I see is Alwin's eyes shimmering a dark, deep blue.

Chapter 28

<u>Serena</u>

Today is the day. Today I am going home. Instead of being in a carriage, I am vomiting on the side of the pathway. I have been throwing up for a solid ten minutes, anxiety eating away at my insides.

"You good?" Barnett rubs small circles on my back as he crouches next to me.

"Uh-huh," I say, in between fits of vomiting acidic bile.

Alwin clears his throat. "Serena, darling, I need you to sip this." He hands me a liquid that looks like my vomit and makes my stomach even angrier. The contents of the vial are green and earthy, and the thickness makes me gag.

"I don't think I can." I shake my head. I knew before I took my third drink last night that I would regret it in the morning. My body hates me for last night's choices. If I had my magic, I would be healing myself, but even with power, a hangover is a hangover.

Wolf kneels next to me. "You are scaring the horses." His comment causes me to laugh enough that Sailor shoves the vial down my throat. Wolf grabs my jaw and forces me to keep my mouth shut until I am able to swallow down the entire drink. My belly is instantly soothed. I breathe in through my nose several times before standing on my feet. Sailor steadies me long enough to get my bearings, but even still, my head feels fuzzy.

"Can you go on?" Wolf eyes me with a concern that I don't like.

"Yes, just give me a few more minutes." I press my palm into a thick tree trunk, stabilizing myself. They all give me space to regain my composure.

After ten minutes, I am on a horse and riding into Darnish. The woods feel like home, just not one I ever wanted to come back to. My heart rate spikes when we make it to the village center. Mr. Benson is standing in the middle of the pathway, waving his arms around like a lunatic. I slide from my horse before the beast even stops.

"Serena!" Barnett yells at me, and Sailor drops from his horse as if he thinks I fell or something. I don't stop running until I grip onto the man who might as well be my last family here in Darnish. The old man grabs onto me as well, tears welling in his eyes. My fingers grasp onto the back of his shirt with all my might. They couldn't pry my dead body from this man. I hadn't realized how much I would miss him until seeing him just now.

"How are you?" I pull back, then register that every person with me is armed to fight. I clear my throat, feeling embarrassed. Every person in Darnish is outside, pointing and whispering about us. "There is no threat. Put your fire away," I tell Sailor, at the same time, telling the rest of the king's guards.

After assuring everybody that I am, in fact, okay, I walk arm in arm with Mr. Benson—my longest-standing friend, the man who watched over me as an adventure-seeking toddler, and into my teenage years of figuring myself out. "How are you?" I ask him again. We make our way to his storefront at the end of the street, where so many of my earliest memories were made.

He sighs deeply before speaking. "Serena, I have missed you." His voice cracks, which causes tears to sting my eyes.

"Are you alright?" Alwin checks in with me.

"I am. Just an emotional reunion." With my assurance, Alwin makes himself scarce.

I didn't expect to be so emotional seeing Mr. Benson; it just hit me. He is the last little bit of my family here. "I missed you, too," I say softly, sniffling.

Sadness drains any happiness from his face. "I am truly sorry I couldn't help your sister and father."

I wipe a stray tear from my face. "It wasn't your fault," I tell him, grabbing onto his arm and squeezing tightly.

"No, it wasn't. I had been checking in on them, though." He gives me a closed-lip smile. "I was worried about your sister going into preterm labor out there."

He says it so sadly that guilt grips my throat. I have tried not to think about her pregnancy much. There isn't anything I can do for her from here, and she is safer away from me.

"She is okay. Do not worry about her. How have you been?" I clear any and all sadness from my body and try to fill my head with positive thoughts instead of sorrow.

"My son is getting help from the clinic. Evie set it all up before...uh, before it happened. They say with treatment, he could get better." Mr. Benson sounds hopeful, which makes me feel lighter. I pick a long piece of grass from the garden, just trying to distract myself from any and all thoughts about my family.

"That is amazing news." I rub on my wrist as I drop the grass and watch it spin down to the ground. "How are the new commanders?" I ask, keeping my eyes locked on the green garden Mrs. Benson loved so dearly.

"They are fair. Stern but fair. I suppose I have you to thank for losing Mary's father?"

I smirk down at my feet before meeting his chocolate eyes. "You do," I confirm.

He nods his head, understanding filling him. "You know, I had always thought you were special, Serena."

I clench my jaw, hoping it doesn't snap from the force. "Funny, I have always thought the same about you," I joke with him. He has a serious look in his eyes, though.

"I'm serious. Please believe me when I say I always knew you were somebody I would follow one day." I know he means what he's saying. There aren't many times this man is serious, but I can tell right now, in this moment, he is. "There was this one night that I thought I saw you, but then you disappeared. I wondered for a long while about that...until this one time, when you were real little, your father brought you in, and I thought it was strange how you could hear even an insect outside. I chalked it all up to my imagination; there was no way a child could be that skilled in their power already. I didn't want to cause any harm; I never did. I never mentioned it to your father because I didn't want him to think I would cause you or your family any danger. I love you guys like my own family."

I reach into my pocket and hand him a heavy bag. "What is this?" he asks as he opens it, and then gasps. "I will not take any coin from you, Serena. I do not need it." He tries to put it right back into my hands, but I brush him off.

"No, you aren't taking it from me. That is your payment," I say so softly, I am not sure he can hear me.

"For what?" His brows crinkle as he questions me. The bag is filled to the brim. It will last him his lifetime as well as his son's.

"For being the best person I know. For always looking out for me and my family, for everything you did for them while I was gone. For everything." I gulp down anything else, because I can't say any more words about them without crying.

"I would have watched over you all, no matter what," he swears, and I believe him.

He finally relents and keeps the bag of coins. "Plus, I would have left it on your countertop had you not kept it," I joke with him.

"You have a nasty habit of that," he accuses me right back. I nod in agreement.

"I do, but it is never to offend you. I just don't want you to struggle anymore. You don't have to. Let me help you, when I couldn't help my father." At the mention of my dad, my heart cracks wide open. The patches I had put on my heart break at the thought of him. Lifeless at the home where we had once thought we could live forever, safe. Me with my dog, he with his hobbies. I never would have thought this would be my life.

"Have you seen Clara?" I ask after sitting for a while in silence. The day has dragged on like I thought it would.

"Do you want to stay the night here?" Alwin's voice pierces through my mind.

I didn't even want to come here; I was so scared to. Now? I don't want to leave without getting what I need done first. *"I would like to."* My response is immediate, but his is even faster than mine was.

"As you wish, My Queen. I will make arrangements. Would you like my help?" The sun is setting, the day is almost over, and I have spent it exactly how I wanted to. With my best friend remembering the good times and the hard times.

Mr. Benson clears his throat before speaking. "I have not, but I think I might know where she could be." He chews on the side of his mouth.

"Want to fill me in?" I ask him, since he isn't giving me the information.

"I think you already know where she is." In the back of my mind, I think I had always known what happened to her that night. I nod, then stand with him.

"Please, don't leave without saying goodbye to me, Serena. You are family to me, and have been longer than you ever considered." His lip quivers.

I wipe a stray tear from my cheek. "You are my family, too." I hug him before asking Alwin to pick me up. Alwin's dark, warm shadows take us to the inn I never would have thought I would be staying in. Darnish is my home, but no longer does it feel like a prison I am trapped in.

Alwin gently kisses my forehead before I fall asleep in strong arms that have begun warming more than just my body. I have no nightmares, as if the Gods are taking pity on me. They know my next journey will be a hard one. I need more rest than just tonight for what is to come.

Chapter 29

<u>Serena</u>

I was up and ready to go before the sun was even out. I didn't tell a soul where I was going or when I would be back. My nerves were so high this morning when I sprang out of bed, I threw up everywhere. Alwin slept right through it; he must have been tired from the night before. Even in his sleep, he is a regal fae prince. He doesn't snore, he doesn't drool, he looks like a king in the fairy tales I read as a child.

My body moves through the trees as it has for my entire life. My mind doesn't have to tell my feet anything; they move without direction. My mind, soul, and body all know where we are going. The insects chirp, the birds sing, and the dew-slicked grass wets my boots. I whistle while listening to the songs I didn't even know I could miss. The twenty-minute walk to the clearing in which my cabin had lived a full life is a full twenty-minute walk this time. Maybe even more since I am stopping every few minutes to just stare. I hadn't known how much I would actually miss this—the simple life I had gotten to live during my childhood years.

I pick flowers on the way; my hands are both filled with different types. Purple, blue, pink, and white. Bugs crawl from their homes and fall to the ground at my feet, no longer wanting to stay in the plant I have taken from the ground. Squirrels follow me, probably remembering a time I would have shifted and played. Bunnies chase at my feet, and I giggle to myself, trying not to step on them. "Watch it. I can still skin you." I don't know if they can still understand me, since I don't have the ability to speak directly to them anymore. I walk right by the pond on the outside of the clearing. I set the flowers down for a moment and just watch the calm water.

The dark skies open to the most beautiful sunrise I have ever seen. Pinks and oranges chase away the darkness. Light always wins in the end. Light has always been prettier to me, even when the darkness promised the most beautiful release. The colors that dance together in the rising of the sun force a smile onto my lips, even though I feel anything but happiness in my hollow heart.

I sit for a while longer, not ready to face the memories from that night. I skip rocks across the pond, remembering a time when my family had all tried to make one skip fully across the water and onto the bank across. I could have done it with my strength, but I didn't. I let Juniper win that round, knowing he would throw a fit if he didn't win. That day, Father had been happy. He had gotten up from bed in a good mood and his mind clear of any sadness. It had been a good day.

My thoughts go on for a while, and I sit just past the lapping water at my feet. My toes dig into the rocky shoreline. I watch fish swim up to me, begging me to play. Begging me to just be happy, but I can't for the life of me smile anymore. My stomach knots with unease and nausea threatens to take me again. The sickness I feel is caused by my spiked nerves. I toss one more rock, throwing it as hard as I can, then a sad smile slips on my face when it makes it all the way across, even without power. I did it. I am strong without the gifts the Gods gave me.

At one point in my life, I would have thought the tears that prickle my eyes were a sign of weakness. I wipe them away, knowing that the reason they are falling is in fact a strength some people will never know. I know it is because I am crying over a lost loved one. A lost life I could have had, a father, a friend, myself. I died that day with him. The difference in my death and my father's is that he stopped breathing. I continued even though my soul didn't.

Like a phoenix in the ashes, though, I stood up. I will fight as I have been to get my people the life I had once wanted. Happiness, health, food, protection. I may have taken a minute to dust my ashes off, but my rise will be something they will study one day. I will save my kingdom, even if it kills me. I will embrace whatever end the Gods have deemed for me.

I dust off my butt, pick up my flowers, and walk. My feet feel heavy, but not too heavy to lift any longer. I make the short distance to where I need to say goodbye. A goodbye to more than just my father, my powers, and my family; a goodbye to the life I had envisioned. Because the new Serena will not stand for any injustice. I will fight for every person who can't. I will save the kingdom that was given to me during my birth, and the one I earned by living with the humans.

Ashes, dirt, and cobblestone. That is all that is left of my family home. The scorch marks from my fire are still there, where my father's bones were burned so hot they are no longer. I place the dozen or so flowers where he passed away. I stay kneeling there, my fingers buried in the dirt. Just trying to feel closer to him in this moment. "I'm sorry, Father," I whisper, my voice barely audible. "I know you didn't want this life. I know I am the reason you lost your wife, your child." I chew on my lip, unsure if he can hear me from wherever he is. I swallow whatever I have left, whatever shame or guilt I have, and say what I have been wanting to say to him since I watched his flesh burn to nothing.

"I know you were not my blood, but you were more a father to me than that male would have been. I am proud to say I wouldn't have wanted anything different. You were the best dad I could have asked for." I pause, tears sliding down my face. "You taught me kindness and compassion. You taught me that just because you fall doesn't mean you can't stand up again." I take deep, calming breaths. In and out. In and out. Swallow the hurt, swallow the bile threatening to spill out. I must be strong now, my time for wallowing is coming close to an end. "You got up and raised three children after losing a part of yourself. I don't know how you did it, Dad." My voice cracks. "But I will follow your lead." Plump tears hit the top of my hand. "I wasn't sure I could survive without you. Without Juniper and Evie by my side. But it turns out I can. Thanks to you for teaching me that even with the hurt, I can be strong still."

I wipe the snot from my nose and stand tall. I had once wondered if I would be able to stand up again after being chopped down; it turns out I grew taller. I close my eyes, knowing I will likely never come back here again. "I love you. Thank you for raising me as you did. Thank you for everything. I will see you again soon." There is a promise in my voice. When I turn away from the life I had once thought I needed, I know I was wrong. My heart knows that the pull I had felt as a child wasn't ever going to allow me to stay in one place. It was calling me home. To Mirahalm, to my people. Even if my mother and father are dead and gone, that is still my homeland, and I have every right to stake my claim against Alwin's parents. I will rule my two kingdoms as my true father would have wanted. I will protect my people from harm; I will give them the life they deserve to live.

Chapter 30

<u>Serena</u>

I walk towards a den I have been to thousands of times, just never in my own flesh and blood. I was only ever accepted in wolf form, but alas, I do not have my wolf form today. I hear a low growl a moment before a large white wolf jumps out from behind a tree. I had heard him prowling in the distance a mile back. I didn't want to draw attention to him, since it seemed like he was hiding.

Large, sharp teeth snap in my face, but I tentatively reach towards his snout. "Hello, Haggot. Do you remember me?" When he doesn't growl, I decide it's safe enough to run my fingers through his thick fur. A chunk of grayish white fur comes away between my fingers. I shake my hand out, trying to rid my body of the itchy wolf coat. "I see your winter coat is shedding." Some of the long fur blows into my mouth, and I try to spit it out. It still sticks to my tongue, but I don't dare try to grab for it. I don't know if Sloan's second has truly recognized me. I also wouldn't put it past him to just eat me for coming here. "Is...Sloan around?" His ears perk up at the mention of his alpha. I look towards where I know the den is. Haggot growls low at me before outright trying to take a bite out of my leg. I don't move and I do not dare to speak, knowing that if he wants to kill me, he will. I slowly back up, tiny steps.

The large white wolf stalks towards me, his claws out and on full display for me. His large, heavy paws crush anything he steps on, while his claws cut into the earth. When I take another step backwards, I hit a large rock and fall to the ground, right on my tailbone.

I have grown up with this pack, but that does not mean anything in this moment. I know Haggot on a surface level, but that doesn't mean he knows who I am as Serena, the fae. Right as he pulls his front paw back, getting ready to claw my arm off, I hear the voice I knew I would find.

"Oh my golly!" Clara rushes over to me, completely ignoring the beast in front of us.

Clara's once blonde hair looks light brown because it has so much dirt in it. Her kind face is covered in mud...I hope. My nose crinkles when I inhale and smell something foul wafting from her.

"Haggie, you cannot attack Serena!" Clara chastises the predator as if he were a small puppy. She rushes to the five-hundred-pound beast.

"Uh, Clara, I wouldn't," I warn her before his hazel eyes narrow at me. To my surprise, he allows her to touch him. I hadn't known this particular wolf to be kind to anybody. So, when he nuzzles against her hip, backing off my body, my jaw drops wide open. She brushes her face against his, and my face contorts in discomfort.

"It's okay, buddy. She is a friend," she coos to the wolf I have known my entire life.

I roll my eyes and stand up, just to be tackled back to the ground by the biggest wolf I have ever seen. Instead of growling and teeth, a sharp tongue licks up and down my face. I giggle and laugh in the dirt, not caring that his tongue is cutting into my cheek. My fingers intertwine with his fur. I scratch his head, just deciding to go for it.

My arms wrap around his thick neck without faltering. I squeeze tightly around my friend. "Sloan." I don't expect to hear from him, so when he responds to me, shock ricochets throughout my body.

"*My friend,*" Sloan's deep voice echoes in my head. Yyette comes out from the rock den, a load of cubs following behind her. Clara walks over to a red wolf cub and picks it up. My eyes train on Sloan.

"You can speak to me..." I say in wonder, since I have absolutely no power in my body.

"*I have always been able to.*"

I arch my brow. "So those times I asked you questions, and you didn't answer me, you were ignoring me," I accuse, and he blows a deep breath out. A few of the cubs interrupt us for a moment, playing with their alpha. I watch in amazement that Clara is just blending in here; they have completely welcomed her.

After several minutes of playing with his cubs, Sloan prowls over to my legs, brushing against them as his cubs follow suit and all jump on me. I crouch in the dirt, giggling, before looking over at Clara. "You saved her," I say softly.

"I did," he agrees.

"Why?" One of the cubs bites down on my finger, and I yelp. As I stand up, Yyette and Haggot both howl. The cubs' ears perk up, then the two adult wolves turn to leave. The cubs follow right behind them, yipping and chewing on the ankles of their mother. The cub Clara is holding squirms in her arms before she gives him a kiss and places his already moving legs on the ground.

"Do not kill bunnies unless you are going to eat them, Bear!" she yells at the small cinnamon-colored cub. I narrow my eyes at her. "What?" She tilts her head.

I raise my shoulders. "I don't know...you *named* him," I state the obvious.

She looks at Sloan before saying. "Yeah. They claimed me, so I claimed them. I love them."

It's my turn to look at Sloan. *"She is your family. I promised I would protect your family as you had mine for many years."* I walk over to a rock that stabs me in the butt when I sit on it, but I don't complain.

"Okay, explain." I nod slightly.

Sloan stalks towards me and sits right in front of me, his head falling into my lap, a silent request to pet him. Clara wanders over to me, sitting crisscross next to the massive wolf. She leans into him before he starts to speak to both of us, a skill I had no idea he possessed until now. I can tell he speaks to us both though when her eyes zero in on him.

"When you left, I had done what I promised you I would. I watched over your family, and for the most part, they did well. Your father had his days, as he always had when he wouldn't get out of his bed. I watched this one—" His head tilts towards Clara before continuing. *"—attempt to make him happy. Your sister and her mate played games with your father, and he seemed to get better. One night, I saw Clara go to the cabin, so I followed her. When I saw guards at the tree line ahead, I didn't feel right. I knew they weren't supposed to be there, so I pulled her to my den. I tried to go back for your father and sister, but by the time I got back to them, you were already there, and the males were there."* His head tilts down, as if he is thinking back on those horrible memories. *"I knew you would be protected, so I went back to calm her down. I've kept her ever since. The villagers talked about harming her*

because they thought she knew about you all along. I couldn't allow it. She is part of my pack now. As are you, my friend."

I start to chew on my finger, pure anxiety pumping through my body. "Don't bite your nails, it's not healthy," Clara chastises me.

I eye her before asking her my own questions. "What are you eating out here?" I ask curiously, while looking around the deserted woods.

"Berries mostly, some fish. I have learned to scavenge most things. Some tree roots have protein in them." She shrugs as if that isn't impressive.

"Have you gone into Darnish since...that night?" I dare to ask.

"I have...once. I didn't go back." Her voice is hollow, unlike the cheerful girl she is.

"Do you want to stay with the pack, or do you want to go to Juniper?" I clench my jaw because I am unsure if she'll want to leave the wolves. Sloan stiffens slightly, but allows her to speak. As an alpha, he could demand she stay here. Even though she isn't a wolf, she is a part of his pack. He has accepted her; she could stay and live out her life here with them. But he pushes his head into her chest and lets her think about it a moment before answering.

"I miss Juniper. Where is he?" She doesn't answer my question, but I will give her what she needs to make the choice.

I tell her all about Clove, and Juniper getting there. I tell her everything I know...or think I know. She sits and listens while petting Sloan, maybe out of habit. They seem so close.

Haggot and Yyette come back with the cubs an hour later. Sloan excuses himself to eat whatever animal they have dragged in. The cubs follow behind, fighting over a dead deer. They tear at it from all angles until it finally rips apart. I shake my head, trying to regain my focus. Clara and I are alone as the wolf pack eats their meal in the den.

"So." I venture to start our conversation again. "What do you want to do here, Clara?"

Her face falls from a soft smile to sadness. "I don't know. I love Juniper, and I want a life with him. But I also love them... They saved me, Serena." I reach out to grab her arm, something I wouldn't have done a while ago. The surprise shows on her face, too. "Serena, you have changed." Her lips purse as if thinking about saying something else, but she stops herself.

"I wouldn't blame you either way. Juniper loves you, he wants you with him, but he would understand either way, Clara." My voice stays level, even though I want to urge her to go to my brother. He needs her. Right as she opens her mouth to tell me her choice, Sloan—along with the entire pack of wolves—walks up to us. We both freeze and wait to see what they will say.

"Clara is in our pack, as I have already said." Sloan's eyes dart between us. I know he is also telling her what he says to me. She wipes snot from her nose, sniffling. *"That means she is ours. My pack stays together no matter what."* Clara chokes on a sob. If it's happy, I have no idea. *"My family has claimed yours, Serena. Your family is gone from these lands, though, so my pack will follow. My pack is loyal to our queen. Wherever she goes, we go."*

My eyes widen in shock for a moment before I school my face. "Are you saying you want to leave Darnish?" Yyette comes up next to Sloan, but slightly behind him, as does Haggot. The other wolves follow suit until they are all standing in front of us. Then, one by one, their front paws bow to the ground. As if a beacon is signaling them all to come, more animals follow suit until there is nowhere I can't see an animal bowing down. I realize they aren't bowing to Sloan—their alpha—but to me.

"I go where I am needed. My family will follow," Sloan swears before slowly pressing his paws into the ground to bow to me. The alpha of the strongest wolf pack...bowing to me. *"Because your blood is worthy of much more than you have been given. In my lifetime, we will watch what the God Queen has planned for the one they promised would save us."*

Chapter 31

Serena

After a long conversation with the wolf pack, and more tears from Clara than I ever thought were possible, I now must do something I hate doing. I have to ask Alwin for a favor. My nails dig into my palm so hard, I know there will be crescent-shaped red marks on my hand.

"*I need you,*" I say softly, down our bond. Alarmingly faster than I would have thought possible, he appears. I slap his arm when his black mist dissipates.

"Hey, what was that for?" He pretends to be harmed by my hit, rubbing his arm, and not even where I softly hit him.

"You were listening in on me!"

His dark, deep, blueish-black eyes flash with something I don't recognize. "I was," he confirms, then holds his hands up while shrugging his shoulders. "But look, you said you needed me, and I am here," he says in defense, as if it excuses the behavior.

"I do not want you to listen in on me. Stop doing it," I scold him.

A voice clears from behind me, and Clara steps out. Alwin looks as if he knew she was there the entire time. "Hi." She reaches out to shake his hand, but he doesn't take it. Instead, he looks at her as if she disgusts him. I can't really blame him, though; her scent is something else.

"What do you need me for, My Queen?" He half smirks at me in the same way Aldrich once did. His eyes lock onto me and scan my body slowly as if searching for any injuries. Clara lowers her hand, playing it off as best she can.

He doesn't even register that he just fully ignored Clara. Alwin smiles big at me now. Flirting with me, tempting me.

"I need a favor from you; one you cannot hold against me," I say evenly.

"Do I need to kill the fae prince?"

I look back towards Sloan, crossing my arms over my chest. "No, not yet," I yell over my shoulder. Alwin looks between me and Clara before his eyes scan the trees behind us, finding the wolf pack in its entirety.

"Tell the alpha he could try." Alwin looks smug as he says the words. A low growl leaves Yyette, and I realize I need to speed this process up.

"I need you to take them to Juniper."

I watch his jaw tick before he gives me a slight nod. "Anything you want." Alwin's voice sounds strained.

I sit watching Alwin take as many wolves to Clove as he can. "Are you doing okay, Serena?" Clara asks softly after Alwin leaves for the fourth time. The tiny red cub Clara had called Bear nibbles on Alwin's earlobe in the midst of the black mist. I stifle a giggle as I look around, seeing that there aren't many wolves left. She is about to leave me. Sloan sits next to me, watching his pack depart.

I run my hands absentmindedly through his fur. He nudges me every time I stiffen. "As well as I can. I thought coming here would destroy any progress I had made." I look up to the sky for a moment. "It did the opposite. I feel stronger than before, even without my powers." My mouth slams shut before she puts her hand on me.

"Hands off," Alwin growls as he picks up another few cubs. Clara just glares at him, not taking her hand from my body. I half smirk at him, knowing that her ignoring him bothers him. He disappears into his mist again before our conversation continues.

"I knew about the powers. I didn't know they were taken, though. What happened? Did the Gods realize they made a mistake?"

I shake my head. "No, uh...I just don't have them right now," I respond, not wanting to voice what happened to them. Even though he shouldn't have taken them from me, I don't want to say the words. Which is crazy, because Clara clearly doesn't like Alwin already. Why do I care if she hates him? I hate him more often than not.

"But why?" she presses me, not knowing she is pressing my sorest spot right now.

I clear my throat, running a hand over my face. "I lost them; I am working on getting them back." Alwin appears suddenly, and I realize there aren't any wolves left other than Sloan.

I kneel down right next to him, hugging his neck. He nuzzles into me. "I love you, you know?" I whisper into his thick, soft fur.

"I know. You are loved as well, fae princess."

I nod frantically. I feel like this may be a final goodbye for us. A small part of me had always liked the thought of the pack being here, just in case. I stand and turn away from yet another friend of mine. Alwin takes Sloan when I make my way to Clara.

I wrap my arms around her tightly. "Tell my brother I love him, will you?" Her hair smells like shit, and I hope she bathes before seeing my brother again.

"I will," she promises, and I grab onto her wrist while Alwin waits patiently.

"Evie is going to need a sister. Please help her with the baby. Be her sister for me. *Please.*" My voice breaks, alongside my heart. Clara's bottom lip quivers violently, though she doesn't cry. Her empathy abilities are impeccable.

"Nothing will ever replace you in their lives, but I will help her until you are able to, Serena." Alwin waits until I nod for him to take her.

I wait in silence for just a moment; the woods seem to mourn with me. He gets back to me faster than he had every other time. When Alwin's mist thins out, we stand a few feet apart. He watches me, as I do him. Just us standing in the eerily silent woods. I fall to my knees from the weight of the day.

King Alwin Henry

I rush towards Serena, catching her before her body hits the ground. I yank her upwards and into my chest. Tears stream from her eyes, and I kiss them all away before they can leave their mark. "It was a hard day," she whispers into my chest. I nod in understanding, not wanting to tell her that our days will be hard for a while. So, I lie to my mate even though it kills me. It won't be the first or last lie I tell her.

"I know. It will get easier, I promise." I kiss the top of her hair. "Your brother's...*friend* was reunited with him," I inform her. I had thought about leaving her far from the village in Clove, where they all live, because she smelled so poorly. I didn't want her to kill them all. Then I thought about it and realized I don't really care if they all die.

"How do you know?"

Unease trickles through my body. I don't want to tell her that the Gods have shown me what we will face. The Gods are cruel, but have promised that if everything goes accordingly, we will fulfill our destiny and rule over our two kingdoms. There will be death and loss, but the Blessed Gods have promised they are looking out for us.

"I just do." I smooth her hair out; it's getting in my mouth. I love her wild, untamed, wavy hair, but I don't wish to eat it right now. Maybe other parts of her...

Emotions make me uncomfortable. Normal fae do not show love of any sort. We do not show weakness; Fates, half of my kind were raised by dragons. We are strong creatures until the very end. That is why we are in this situation. Two sides of fae are at war right now in Mirahalm. Our families will kill the others; each side thinks they have a right to the throne. If I thought Serena was ready for that conversation, I would tell her. I just can't crush her more than I have already.

As if an elemental were standing in front of us, she changes from burning-hot to ice-cold. Right in front of my eyes, she starts hitting me. I let her because I am sure I deserve it tenfold. I don't even hold my hands up to block her anger, and she is strong.

She lands a punch to my jaw, and damn the Gods for making her so naturally strong. "I hate you!" she screams as I scurry to my feet. "Why did you have to pick me?" Her voice cracks with the words. She doesn't slow her assault; if anything, her steam gets hotter as she too stands tall. "I never asked for this. I didn't ask for a kingdom. I just wanted to *live*. I didn't even need to be accepted."

I would kill the Gods for the pain they have given her if I could. I would take it all from her if I thought she would fight for our people without it. I know she needed to lose those closest to her in order to get to this. This anger is what's going to get her going. She needed this, even though it killed me to let it happen. After I intervened in the games, the Gods gave up on me doing the right thing for her. They stopped giving me visions of our future. I worry about what else they may throw our way, in their own sick way of preparing us to take what is ours.

"Are you listening to me?" she roars at me after hitting my face. I wasn't listening to her. I was worrying about what's going to happen to her.

Lately, that is all I think about. This trip has strengthened our bond more than I ever thought it could. I don't know when it started, but at some point since my fucked-up wedding, my views changed. Mirahalm is no longer the goal, going home is no longer a priority, because home isn't a place. It is *her*...Serena Bloodworthy. I will do anything to make her happy. I care about her well-being more than I care about anything else. For her, I will give our people the life she wants for them.

I would let them all die if it kept her safe, but she wouldn't look at me like she has been if I did that. I need her to look at me like I am the hero in her story, because I no longer want to be her villain. How she looks at the commander, I need her to do to me. So, I will fight for the people she wants to be strong for. I will stay in this kingdom my entire life if that is what she wishes. Even though home is calling, my parents are insisting, and others are breathing down my Gods' damned throat.

Her tiny hands grip my shirt so hard, I swear it might rip. "You aren't hearing me." A single tear streaks down her face. I let it fall, allowing the emotions to sink in. I need to see it, to make certain my brain knows these tears are for this kingdom.

"I am." I calmly assure her that I have, in fact, heard her.

"What did I say?" She sucks in a breath like she might not get another. Over my dead body will she be harmed again. I can't watch her lose anybody else. I cannot let her fail at being queen and claiming her birthright. It would kill her. So even if she doesn't feel like she can, I will drag her to the finish line.

"That you hate me."

She nods, and her plump pink lips purse while she thinks about what her next move will be. I don't know what I expected, but it wasn't this. She pulls my face down and presses her soft lips to mine. The passion and hunger I feel is undeniable, I just don't know who feels it stronger.

Hot tears brush against my face; the discomfort causes me to wipe them away. I grew up in a royal fae court, opposite of the life she grew up in; although, I would have fit into her family more than my own. She opens our kiss, greedily taking what I am offering her. My tongue sweeps out and brushes against her. She moans in my mouth at the contact.

"I need you to take it away. All of it," she says against my lips. I shake my head because I can't do that. I have the empath ability, yes. I hate every time she feels sorrow, but I also know she needs to feel this. These hard emotions are what's going to keep her alive. And I need her alive, because if she isn't here with me, the kingdoms wouldn't be safe from my wrath. The Gods wouldn't even be safe from me in their realms. I would kill every being responsible for taking her from me.

Her fingers scratch at my shirt, urging me to take it off my body. She doesn't have to ask me twice. My shirt vanishes alongside any clothing she was in. Within the same second, she is on me. Pushing me against the tree. I will accept the pain that laces my back if she keeps touching me like this. She kisses up my sternum, hot and passionate.

"Please," she begs, as I once had told her she would do. I smirk, then wipe it from my face before she can see it. Now is not the time for being right; now is the time for making her feel better. That I can do; I can make her feel better, physically.

"Hands and knees." I conjure a quilt on the ground. "Now, darling," my voice taunting her. Her silvery blue eyes shine with amusement, and we stare into one another's souls for another moment before she listens to me. She slowly lowers herself onto the blanket, facing away from me, and she places her hands out in front of her. I take a few moments for myself to just look at her. Her tanned skin, her long blonde hair. She is all *mine*.

"Good, darling." I walk around to her face. My fingers grip her chin before tilting it up to meet me. "I can't take your pain away from today, Serena." I feel the faintest sting in my eyes, but I blink it away before I can even register what that might mean. "I wish I could. For you, I would do almost anything else. I will give you anything else. But that pain you feel?" I point to her chest, where her huge heart is. I don't even glance at her breasts before I meet her eyes again. "It is going to make you a better queen, the one you desire to be. I promise it will; the pain will fuel you. Your war against those who will challenge us begins and ends with what you're willing to do." I lean into her space, our lips so close to touching, but not yet. "Tell me what else I can do for you, right now, other than take your pain." Her eyes burn with an emotion I know all too well. Lust. My head tilts, patiently waiting for her to voice what she needs in this moment.

"You," she whispers. My fucking heart beats faster than a hummingbird's wings flap. I don't know who moves first, but I'm in her faster than seems possible.

She looks back at me, and I lean forward to brush my tongue against hers. My chest is against her back as I slam into her. Over and over again. I pull my mouth away, and her head falls back to cry out in bliss. I grip her hair in my fist, wrapping it around my fingers. I pull her to look at me as waves hit her blissfully. "You are mine; I will protect you, Serena." She shakes her head, as if thinking of saying something that might ruin this, but she doesn't say anything other than whispering my name.

I have listened to fae songs before. They are magical. Females have sung for me. Their voices were carefully crafted by the Gods. None of them compares to right now, hearing my name on her lips as pleasure overtakes her again. My hand softly rubs against her core, trying to make her release last as long as it can. My fangs pop out watching her ass bounce against me. I can't help it; my body needs to mark her as mine in every way possible. My animalistic urge to claim my mate is far too strong. The closer we get, the worse it will get. By nature, I am possessive with her. After this, I will be *ruthless*.

Unbridled fae nature shoves its way into my chest, so hard that I do something I am not sure she will like. My teeth sink into her, and she cries out when my black magic coats her flesh. My mark will forever be where my teeth had just been. I spill myself in her at the sight of me permanently having my own mark on her. Not some small sailboat that will wash away in a storm. My mark is forever on her body, and in her soul. I reach down and pull her body flush with mine. My hands grip onto her breasts, my thumbs play with both her sensitive buds. My bliss hits me so hard, I don't think I will ever get over the waves of pleasure she has given me.

I hold onto her so tight, one might think I am completely losing myself to her. That would be crazy, though. I am still Fae. Fae mates can be complicated; just because you are mates doesn't mean you love one another. Love in Mirahalm is a laughable word. I know humans enjoy it. They say it to animals, even. But for fae? That word is sacred. But I know I feel it for her. The pull to be with her always is so strong that I find myself searching for her in every moment. I find myself thinking of her after just being around her.

"I don't need you to protect me, Alwin," Serena says from in front of me, lying on the quilt I may keep forever.

"Oh?" I laugh while we search the skies for more glow bugs.

"I'm serious." Her tone is so stern. I shouldn't laugh at her, I know I shouldn't. She is funny, though.

"Okay, you don't need protection. I believe you." I do believe she thinks that, but without her powers, she needs *some* help.

"Alwin." She growls my name and Gods Blessed if my cock doesn't spring to attention for her. I hold my hands up in mock surrender. My eyes stray to her large breasts. She snaps at me, and I try to focus on her cute little fingers.

"Huh?" My brows raise almost to my hairline.

"Pay attention or else I will get dressed and leave." My brows furrow now, then I smirk. Right as I burn her clothes to ashes. "Okay, well, now I can walk through Darnish naked." She shrugs. I hadn't thought about that. And Blessed, she will do it.

"Fine, I will stay out of your head," I promise, even though I know it might be impossible. Our mating bond is so strong that I can't help it sometimes.

She smirks as if she has won, lying back down. Granted, she has. At one point, I wouldn't have ever spoken the words "I love you." Now I am whispering them into her ears as if I am a fool for her. Goose bumps linger on her skin before I watch her eyes flutter shut. Every night, I watch her fall asleep, and sometimes I watch her dreams. I regret that often. When her eyes finally stay closed, I blink us into the inn room. I gently lay her body down onto the bed; she barely makes an indentation.

I sit with her a moment longer before I do what I have done every night since coming to this Gods-forsaken kingdom. I speak to the only being that knows how to get home.

Chapter 32

<u>Serena</u>

Standing in front of Mr. Benson's shop hasn't ever been sad. I have been worried, yes. But standing in front of his shop, saying goodbye when it could actually *be* goodbye this time, feels painful. The old man has never seemed old to me, he was always just my friend. Now, he looks his age. My heart feels like it's a bunny running from a wolf. I don't want to go inside and see him again. These long weeks apart aged him more than I was ready for.

"Serena?" Sailor asks from behind me. Wolf is off talking to Alwin about something neither one of them wanted to disclose with us.

"Yeah?" I ask, trying to hide the sadness in my voice.

"Are you going to stand here or go in?" His hand rubs against my back in small soothing circles, as if Sailor always knows when I need true comfort.

"I'm going to go in. I just need a moment." I look over my shoulder at him; he is closer than I had realized. "I just...I'm not ready." Swallowing down the bile rising in my throat, I step onto the creaky, worn-down steps. "I promised him I would have these fixed," I whisper to myself, but of course, Sailor hears the words fall from my lips.

"You know, you don't have to have the entire kingdom on your shoulders. Give somebody else some of that weight."

I bite my lip hard, trying to break skin. "It will crush them," I say sternly.

"Better them than you." His response is swift. I take the rickety steps into the shop I have gone to my entire childhood.

"Serena." Mr. Benson smiles at me, an old, withered smile. But still, a good one.

"Hi," I say on a small sigh. Sailor waited outside to let us say our goodbyes. I clear my throat, picking at my nails. I don't like this; the sadness feels unnatural in my body.

"I suppose it is time to say our *see you laters*?" Half his mouth tilts up. My eyes scan the store, looking at anything besides him.

"Are you going to keep the store open?" I ask instead of answering him. He moves some things around awkwardly. I don't look at what he is doing.

"I don't think I will. I might travel some, though. I think it will be good for me, something different than the last few years. My son can handle the store; he belongs here."

"Will he?" I grab an apple and bite into it, knowing I have paid tenfold for this delicious fruit.

"He will. He is doing well in the clinic. They are all so kind and hands-on with him. He needed that, and he will need this. And I need to leave. I miss Mrs. Benson. I would like to do what we had once dreamed of, and leave." I hadn't known they had wanted to travel. They always seemed so happy here. "But—" His voice cuts through my thoughts like a knife. "I think what *you* need is to put away the thoughts that you must take care of everybody around you, child. For once, take care of yourself. You cannot be the queen we need if you are constantly giving more of yourself than you have to give."

Mr. Benson grabs a burlap sack and places different items in it. I watch while he works, finally looking at him. "Are you packing already?" I say, shocked. He doesn't stop to answer me, he just keeps adding things into the bag.

"No, this is for you," he finally says. My eyes bulge before I'm shoving off the counter I was leaning against.

"Oh, no. I don't need anything," I try to assure him, but it doesn't seem to work.

"You will take the bag because you care for me. I have been waiting for you to come home to give you the things I didn't give you before you left for the trials." He shakes his head once before continuing to pile things in the bag.

I glare at him for another moment before I concede. "Okay. What do you have for me?" I ask curiously before trying to sneak a look into the bag. He yanks it out of my line of sight.

"It's a surprise." I hate surprises more than most people. Typically, surprises are not good. They are finding your father decapitated, finding your new friend in a weird sex dungeon, and being tortured. Surprises are never good in my life. Finding out my husband was the one fucking me instead of my boyfriend is the top of my list for bad surprises.

"I hate surprises," I mumble under my breath, right as he clicks his tongue at me.

"Serena, you never were a pouter. Why are you doing it now?" His chocolate eyes search mine as he grips the sack in his hands.

"I don't know. I guess I'm just tired," I answer honestly.

"Are you not sleeping?" His voice sounds concerned.

"Not that kind of tired. I just feel…I don't know. Worn down?"

My eyes burn from crying; yesterday took it out of me. "You went there?" His voice sounds unsure if he really wants to have this conversation. I nod my head slightly.

"I did. I found Clara, too," I admit to him. Unsure if I should tell him about Clove.

"I see. Was she alive?" His words are small, whispering almost.

"She is." I nod slightly.

"Good," he says cheerfully. "I had gone out there several times, too," he says after a few minutes of silence.

"You did?" I don't know why this surprises me. After Father lost his wife, the Bensons were the only family in Darnish who cared enough to keep following up with him.

"I did." His eyes gloss over almost. "You know, I had known your father his entire life." My teeth sink into the juicy apple. I chomp down on it, relishing the fresh fruit.

"I had a feeling," I answer, even though I hadn't. He smirks as if knowing I am lying.

"He was always a good little chap. He helped around the shop like you did, and he would fix things around here. He would even work for free. Kind of like a little girl I knew." I avert my eyes. "One day, he met a girl, and they fell in love. They started to grow a family. A boy and then a girl." His voice is filled with wonder, as if living a life, a long time ago, right in this moment. "They didn't think they would have another baby. Imagine my surprise when she became pregnant with another. Only to have twins." Pain fills me so full, it might tip right over.

"Mrs. Benson had gifts, you know. She had elemental magic. Earth abilities…it would speak to her, tell her things. Such as ways to tell the gender of babies, how many a woman was having…" His voice trails off.

My eyes narrow on him, zeroing in on his tone. "You knew?" I ask suspiciously.

He shakes his head. "I have no idea what you are speaking of. All I am saying is that your father was a generous man, and I knew he would be an amazing father for you. He loved all. You couldn't have asked for a better one, really. He was always so sharp, too." The words hang between us, what he is implying.

"Hmm." I hum in wonder, hoping he doesn't see my reaction as an admission.

"Now, I don't know anything for sure, but I do know he loved the little girl the Gods gave him. He treated her as a princess. He would have loved her forever, no matter what," Mr. Benson says slowly. My father may not have known who and what I would become, but he raised me to know exactly how to handle ruling a kingdom.

I rush over to Mr. Benson and hug him. It isn't a soft hug; I wrap my arms around his midsection and squeeze. "Thank you." I gulp down everything I want to say but won't. I won't put him in more danger than he already is.

"I didn't do anything. I just told you about a little boy I once loved who raised a child that I love even more so." He places the sack in my arms before pushing me away. "Make sure you eat and sleep, Serena. People like you do not do well with little of either."

Chapter 33

<u>Serena</u>

I never would have thought that I would be sad to leave Darnish. But as I sit in my carriage with Wolf, Sailor, and Alwin, I'm miserable. I don't want to leave Mr. Benson. I wish I had dug more into his past. I feel as if I might not have known the man very well. I also feel like I might not have known my father. I rest my head on my hand while I watch the trees thin out.

"Whatcha got there?" Wolf points to my bag, while Alwin and Sailor ignore him.

"A bag," I deadpan. He rolls his eyes, then shuts them as if trying to figure out how to have a decent conversation with me.

"Yes, I see that, Serena," he says sarcastically. "I mean, what's in it?" He runs a hand over his face, his stubble grown longer than normal.

"Why do you want to know what's in her bag?" Sailor says. His tone is even, and that almost makes it more cruel.

"I was just trying to spark a conversation...a clearly *unwanted* conversation."

Truthfully, I haven't even looked in the bag yet. I want to be alone when I do. Which sounds crazy, considering it is probably fruit and sketch pads. Maybe a book. I don't really know what all he would put in here. All I know is that I don't want to open this can of worms until I can process everything.

"Are my parents alive?" I try my best to shoot down the bond with Alwin, and not Wolf. Alwin glances at me, then looks down at the ring on his left hand. The black ring

that, to humans, symbolizes our marriage. He found it for himself. He doesn't have to wear it, but he does. He spins the ring a few times before looking out the window.

"What do you think?"

I think if I *knew*, I wouldn't be asking him. He rolls his eyes at me, even though he shouldn't be listening in on me.

"How have the commanders in Grove been handling everything?" Sailor asks Wolf, completely unaware of the conversation being held right in front of him.

"Well, I do not believe there has been another outbreak since before the tour." I have no idea if Sailor and Wolf have spoken about what happened, but I think Sailor would tell me if they had. I would hope he would.

"I think I want you to give me an answer." My tone leaves no room for argument. I wipe at my eyes, fatigue from the journey hitting my body in ways I wish it wasn't.

"I haven't been home in decades. I have no current knowledge of who is alive."

I roll my eyes. *"No, seriously. You came when she came here. Did you kill her?"* Guilt slams into me, then peels back as if he didn't mean to throw those emotions at me.

"Do you believe we will be welcomed?" Sailor asks Wolf. I am curious, too, so I listen in on them.

"I would believe so. They have wanted more food, grains for their gardens, and less taxes."

"I see," Sailor says, and I notice he still has a ghost of a lisp. I doubt anybody else would still be able to hear it, but I notice everything about Sailor James. "We agreed on lowering their taxes, so I would assume only good things can happen while there." I look at Sailor and see him worrying his lip. I place my hand on his arm.

"Is something bothering you?" I ask softly, before noticing the compartment is boiling hot. I realize it is because Alwin's eyes are locked on where I am touching Sailor. I quickly place it back in my lap.

Sailor's eyes darken slightly before he says, "Not anything in particular." He then mumbles softly, "I just feel uneasy. Like this has been too easy. The villages aren't usually this forgiving of being abused and forgotten." Sailor's bright eyes narrow on Alwin.

He isn't wrong, the villages haven't liked the king's rule. "Maybe they are giving me a chance to prove I can make a change," I say positively, and all three sets of eyes look to me.

"Possibly. Although even a pretty face won't get them to forgive the years of neglect," Wolf replies. Alwin and Sailor both glare daggers at him.

"She isn't just a pretty face, and you'll do well to remember who keeps you alive." Alwin's voice is ice-cold, while Sailor's gaze is white-hot. The two of them are complete opposites, and I do not know how they will live together.

The rest of the journey goes by so fast, I don't even think before I jump from the carriage in Grove. "Where are you going so fast?" Sailor asks from still inside the too-small carriage.

"Barnett and I have a date."

Alwin's eyes almost fall from his face. "A date?" He hops out of the carriage so quickly that I giggle.

"A-a what?" Barnett stutters out.

"Yep." I grab onto his arm and pull him into the masses of people that part for us.

I don't even wear a crown, and they know me. Unlike the other villages, though, they bow their heads in respect. "*Queen*" they whisper as I pass. Some even touch me.

"What are we going to do?" Barnett asks right as we reach Mabel on her horse.

"I was thinking we could have some fun." I smirk at both of their unsure faces.

"What kind of fun, Majesty?" they ask simultaneously. My answer is immediate.

"Grove is known for its beautiful mountains. I haven't ever gotten to hike them, since I could always fly. I saw we have a few days here, so why not?" I shrug. Alwin has already decided he has business to attend to here. We will be in Grove for three days, which is more than enough time. "Come on, guys. Let's have some fun!" I urge them to say yes.

"I don't like sleeping in nature, Serena," Mabel says before she adds, "But for my queen, I will do it."

"Sailor should come." Barnett glances over my shoulder to where I know Sailor is standing.

"Sure," I agree. I could use more time with him.

An hour and lots of convincing later, Alwin agreed that we could go hiking and camping for the night. Grove is holding a dinner for us in two days' time, so we will have plenty of spare time for fun activities. The green grass under my feet is so soft, it almost makes it hard to walk. Nobody talks while we walk towards the mountain. The birds are singing their songs. The world is whole again. I am in nature, right where I belong. It calls to me in ways I didn't understand at one point. Now? I know it's because I am a fae.

Fae—in some of the books I have read—are creatures that form major bonds to the land the Gods gave us. Fae are more powerful than humans because the Gods gave them more. Although, no other fae in their history have as many powers as I know Alwin and I both have.

"How much longer?" Barnett moans for the tenth time.

"The top is just up that way." Wolf replies in annoyance.

"Why did you come again?" Mabel asks Wolf, and I cover my mouth to hide my laugh. He clearly hears it because his valley-green eyes meet mine. My eyes widen slightly, in a show of my sarcasm, at the same time I lift my brows.

"I came because I didn't want to listen to our dearly beloved king sing his own praises for the millionth time."

Sailor's eyes scan Wolf's body over. "Isn't he your favorite person?" The tone he uses isn't kind, but it also shows no signs of jealousy. Wolf's eyes glass over, as if he isn't even here anymore.

"He isn't, and you know that." His tone is harsh.

Sailor kicks a rock, then plays with his water power, presumably to make the time pass faster. He forces it into different symbols and shapes. "I know nothing, because you won't tell me the truth." He throws his hand out, tossing the water away before it turns to steam.

Sailor walks to me, gripping my hand in his tightly. "We're almost there, Maymay," Sailor teases our friend.

"Thank the Blessed," she says, clearly out of breath.

"I thought you guys had to be in shape to be a commander." I chuckle at her, even though I am breathing as hard as she is.

"Have you seen some of these commanders?" Her hands extend in a show of how big some of their bellies are. I chuckle, but the boys don't.

"Not everybody needs to be in shape if they can kill you without moving," Wolf says sternly.

Unease creeps through me. Mary Lou's father never used his magic on us unless he was helping us. He was always stern with us, though. Sometimes, he made laws that the king didn't know about. Typically, it was to give his family more coin than they needed. But I am now realizing, I may have had it good. My thoughts go back to the commander in Saxton; chills run through my body thinking of his words.

"Are you cold?" Sailor asks, placing his extremely warm hands on my body to warm me up. I shake my head in answer.

"I was just thinking how grateful I am that I never have to see Haadgar again."

His jaw clenches. "He isn't somebody you should worry about."

I swing our arms, noticing Wolf watching us. "If I had my powers, I wouldn't be scared at all." I sigh, still feeling bitter about it. My fingers brush against the cold metal of my necklace, once, then twice. "See, this is still on my neck. Therefore, I would have to fight somebody hand to hand if they came at me." Sailor tilts his head, studying the strange metal. I know my blood is in the crystal, but other than that, I haven't found anything out about how to remove the dang thing.

"We're here," Barnett says from the top of a large boulder. I drop Sailor's hand, rushing over to where a pond sits right past a mountain of boulders. I jump right into the sparkling water, clothes on and everything. Wolf moved our small bags here while we were walking.

"I guess you were useful for something." Sailor slugs Wolf in the arm. I can't tell if it's playful or not.

"I'm coming in!" Barnett cannonballs right next to me, the biggest smile I have ever seen on his face. When his head resurfaces, his cheeks are so big that I should have guessed he had water in his mouth.

He sprays me with said water right as I splash at him. "Stop it! Gross! You don't know what lives in here!" I yell playfully. His face scrunches like he wasn't thinking about what sorts of things poop in this water before now. Sailor runs and jumps from the biggest boulder there is, and his splash causes waves to follow his body. Mabel sits by Wolf on the beach.

It isn't *really* a beach, some rocks here and there, a grass spot maybe, but this place may as well be paradise to me. I smile, looking around at the people I would have never thought could be my friends. The people make all the difference to me; they are why I care about Nymphamera so deeply. I look around, even to Wolf, a wild card right now, and realization strikes me right in the head. I would do anything for any one of these people; they are family to me.

"Are you coming in?" I ask Mabel. Wolf shakes his head in answer, though. I tread in the water.

"I didn't bring other clothes," he answers.

"I can't swim," she admits at the same time. I laugh.

"Are you kidding me?" Sailor swims up from behind me, grabbing onto my waist. If it weren't for his power, we would be sinking to the bottom of this small pond. I look over my shoulder, and his blond hair is falling into his eyes. He shakes his head to get the hair off his face. The blond locks send water droplets everywhere, including into my eyes.

"You're getting water in my face," I hiss out and pout. He leans in and bites my lip, drawing it into his own mouth. "Ouch." I laugh into his mouth, then shove some water into his face to get him to let go. His eyes widen slightly before a playful glint lights them into a fiery purple.

"You'd better swim, Honeybee," he says threateningly, and my eyes widen in fear at what I have started.

I go under the water; I'm a quick swimmer. Even without being a fish, even without power, I am faster than Sailor. Unlike me, though, he *has* his power. He catches up to me within a minute. Fish swim by us, but it doesn't matter. My eyes are only on him. This blond man, who has vowed his life to me, in every way other than marriage. As if I would ever deserve him and his loyalty. I wrap my arms around his neck, pulling our bodies flush together. My lungs are burning with the need for air, but all that matters in this moment is my sailboat in the storm. As if reading my mind, Sailor casts an air bubble around us.

"Thank you." My arms tighten around his neck, fingers dancing in his hair.

"I wouldn't want my favorite person to drown, especially here of all places." He looks around in the murky depths. The air gives a little bit, and I fall. I yip when Sailor's arms snake around my waist, pulling me up and against his chest.

"No, I guess that wouldn't bode well for you, considering your only job is to keep me alive." My feet dangle in the uneven air at our feet. Sailor stands solidly as ever. I rub my wrist behind his neck, my favorite pastime.

"Oh? Is that my only job, then, Serena?" He purses his lips together, as if thinking about it.

"Well, no." I roll my eyes sarcastically.

"No, it isn't," he confirms. "Because—"

I push away from him, going to the edge of his air bubble. My weight dips from the amount of effort he is using to keep us afloat. "Sailor, I don't want you to feel trapped here."

He leans against the invisible wall of air. His ankles cross instinctually. "Well, we are underwater in an air bubble. So, we kind of are."

I make my way to him, grabbing onto his shirt. "You know what I mean. You deserve a different life than this, Sailor."

He chews on his lip. "You have already had this conversation with me; you sent me away without speaking to me first." His eyes burn into mine. "I won't allow that to happen again, Serena. I also won't tell you this again." My chest heaves, my breathing is ragged. "While I was away, my body ached to be home. Then, the more I thought about it, I realized my home is you." I avert my eyes before he drags my attention back to him. "You are it for me, Serena. I don't care if we never fuck again, I just need you. I am drawn to you in a way I have never felt before. I will not live a life without you in it. I don't care if I am just a guard and am forced to watch you have children with another male. All I am asking is that I am just a part of it." He pauses, but I don't dare speak. "I can't live without you again. Please don't ask it of me, I would hate to disappoint you." I press my nose against his and shake my head gently.

"I hear you. I can't give you any type of answer right now on what our lives will look like, but I don't want you living apart from me either." He looks up, then kisses the very edge of my lips.

"Are you ready to join the others? They may get the wrong idea about this moment."

I can't even think about what they might be wondering. "I am," I confirm before breaking through the barrier of the air shield.

I breach the water's surface and notice Mabel standing on the bank. I swim over to her before Sailor can drag me back under. "Come here." I wave to her as I walk in waist-deep water. She shakes her head so vehemently that I chuckle at her. Her cropped hair has grown slightly, and the tight curls dangle by her ears now.

"No way in Blessed realm I am trying that."

I walk right up to her and place my hands on her shoulders. "If you think I'll let my favorite of the King's Guard drown, you are crazier than I thought."

Her eyes widen in shock. I'm not sure what shocks her more, my words or Wolf sitting up from his green grass patch and saying, "I thought I was your favorite." He is clearly trying to play around, and I will take it for now.

"Close second," I holler back.

I know there is dirty-smelling air between us, but for the next twenty-four hours, he is a friend to me. *"I appreciate that."* His green eyes dance with amusement, seeing me get annoyed at him in my head.

"I never knew how many times I would have to beg somebody to get out of my Blessed head!" I yell at him. He seems to find me funny enough to lie back down, placing his muscular arms behind his head.

"Damn...if I didn't like women, he would definitely be my type," Mabel says from right behind me, and I glare at her because his smirk tells me he heard her. As if his ego isn't already way too high.

"I hear he has a small dick," Sailor says from the water.

Wolf sits up faster than he should be able to. "Would you like to compare?"

He starts to stand before Barnett cuts in. "I can prove you all wrong. Everybody knows gingers have the biggest—"

I hold my hands up. "Wait a second. You were seriously about to whip your dick out to measure it against his?" I ask in disbelief, pointing right at him. They all stare at me like I am the one who sounds crazy.

"A queen shouldn't say *dick*." Barnett sneers at me. My jaw drops.

"Unbelievable."

They all start laughing at my expense. "Who says I won't still whip it out? Sailor, you want to see?" Wolf asks teasingly, and Sailor glares at him. I turn to leave, Mabel right on my heels.

"I am changing into dry clothes. You all better have your cocks in when I get back." I say over my shoulder, then look at Mabel. "Can a queen say *cock*?" I ask seriously, but the way her lips tilt tells me everything I should have already known. I am a joke.

"I think a queen can say anything she wants to," she says sternly, even though her face is lit with a large smile.

Chapter 34

When I come back in dry, clean clothes, I notice Wolf and Sailor standing next to one another. They haven't spoken outside of the group since being here at the campsite. "I wonder if there are competitions for who is the funniest in the King's Guard." Mabel continues on her rant about how much better she is at jokes than everybody else. She is on this kick of wanting to win an award.

"I'm sure somewhere in the palace they do, maybe Hollow. They have too much time on their hands as it is," I say, shrugging my shoulders while I sit down next to where Mabel kneels.

"You could always make one," Barnett says excitedly, his strawberry hair shining.

"Way too much time on their hands," Wolf agrees brazenly, nodding his head sharply.

"You would know," Sailor says in a tone that suggests he wants to fight. Wolf's clean-shaven jaw clenches so hard and fast, I almost think his teeth might shatter.

They stare at each other for so long, I wonder what is being said without my knowing. Clearly, they have not aired anything out. Mabel pulls a quilt out from the bag strapped to her side and lays it right next to the fire. "I know we are far away from Brabble, but I am not taking any chances. I need my knives right by me," she says sternly when she catches me staring at her. I wipe my hands off on my pants and stand to get my things. This stills any silent conversation Sailor and Wolf are having. Sailor is up and next to me in half a second. When our eyes meet, I feel the sparks I hadn't known I would feel again since my mating bond set in fully. My breath hitches; I feel like I can't inhale. Sailor's ocean eyes ensnare me in a way that feels like the tides might drag me under. Sailor might drown me. I may let him.

I have to tell myself that my duty is to the kingdoms I have sworn to protect, first and foremost. "Are you following me?" I smirk at him, watching him trail directly behind me.

"Eyes forward, Honeybee. You might trip and hurt yourself."

I shake my head before walking over to where I put my bag. "I may not have been looking forward, but I was looking at something so much prettier than this destination." My arms go out in a show of the woods we are currently standing in. I missed my Sailor. I hadn't let myself truly think about how much I did, but right now, looking at him with nobody else distracting me, I know it. Our journey first started in the woods. Without the palace clouding my vision, I see him for what he is to me. Deep in my heart, no matter what happens with Alwin, I will love Sailor, no matter what. My heart beats for two very different males. I feel as if I am a tree in a jungle, my roots growing in two separate directions.

"Does your wrist itch?" His tone is laced with humor, as if he already knows what lies on my skin at the very spot he is looking at. I glance downward to see if my tattoo is showing, but it isn't. My thumb strokes the spot underneath my shirt, the very same.

"No," I answer right away. His face contorts in a way that shows me how playful he wants to be. I take off into the woods, running away from this. I am not ready to show him how messed up I am from losing him the first time. He runs right at my heels, nipping at me. I giggle and chance a glance behind me. Which is my fatal mistake, and he grabs onto me as I trip over a massive log.

"I've got you. I will always catch you when you fall, Honeybee." The air that leaves his mouth when he speaks tickles my neck, the goose bumps that raise on my arms don't show, but he knows. Sailor doesn't have to see anything on my body to know when something is different or off. "Show me." His tone is gruff.

"Never," I declare, attempting to squirm out of his tight grip. His arms snake around my body, a hold that promises to never leave.

"We'll see about that, Bee." His lips graze against the soft skin at the base of my ear. I shiver in his arms. "Now, I know you are not cold, baby." His hands are so warm I couldn't be cold even if it was chilly.

"I'm not." I shake my head, showing him how serious I am.

"Then why do you act as if my touch does something to you?" he whispers in my ear. I turn around in his arms, my chest heaving against his. I press onto my tiptoes, invading his space. My lips are only a few centimeters from his.

"Because it does."

Our lips brush against one another for a small moment, and everything lights back up in our world. *Sailor and Serena.* For this small amount of time, it can just be us against everything else.

Chapter 35

<u>*Serena*</u>

My quilt lies between Mabel and Sailor. Wolf was fast asleep when Sailor and I got back to the camp. I know we have much to talk about, but I want this small detour to be about fun. We have the rest of our lives to hash out everything that has happened. He is, after all, my personal *Queen's* Guard.

The stars glow so bright tonight, I would like to think the Gods are giving us something pretty to look at. Maybe they are feeling bad for us and the trials they have put us through. Mabel lies next to me with her hands behind her head. "Thank you for coming on this little camping trip," I whisper to her.

Barnett pops up from his spot across the fire. "What about me?" he says defensively. I roll my eyes.

"Of course I'm glad you came. You didn't really have a choice, though." I know I sound exhausted. Mabel tosses a stick at him, which hits him square in the forehead.

"Hey!" he cries out, and I can't help but laugh. "Why are you laughing? She just assaulted me for no reason. That stick could have caught fire and burned me." Barnett says, panicked. Sailor covers his mouth to stop Barnett from hearing his laughter.

"Oh, come on. She barely hit ya. And we all know you wouldn't burn to death," Sailor coos, trying to calm our friend. Barnett's brows comically rise to his hairline, which is far way.

"Could have blinded me, easily," Barnett mumbles.

"I highly doubt you would have gone blind, but sure, buddy." Sailor's voice is pleading.

"Thank you," Barnett mumbles. The fire stays lit all night long. Sailor's doing, I'm guessing. For the first time in a long time, I sleep throughout the night without any nightmares, no dreams, and not being held by Alwin. I never would have thought that the king I am supposed to kill would bring me so much relief. Unfortunately for me, though, he brings more than just relief.

When I wake, Wolf is already up and cooking something. I walk over to him, seeing that he is alone. Everybody else is still asleep. Sailor's body ended up curling against mine on the outside of my quilt.

"Gone hunting already?" I question him. Wolf startles slightly, as if he didn't hear me coming.

"I didn't have to. I moved it from Grove this morning before I got up." I guess I should have guessed that. I can't see Wolf going out and hunting on his own. For some reason, he just seems too proper.

"Too low of a job for you?" I taunt him, clearly playing with him. He doesn't bite, so I decide to just go ahead and ask the question I have been waiting to ask. "Wolf, what happened?" His bright green eyes meet mine for half a second before he cracks a huge egg on the sizzling pan over the fire. "I wish I could tell you. I wish I could tell *him*." His head tilts to where Sailor lies asleep. "I can't, though." He shrugs. I purse my lips, trying to think about what he is saying.

"Okay." I nod before sitting next to him. "Then say what you can."

"Somebody is in control. They run everything from behind. The family that I still have is somewhere in the palace." His scattered words make me more confused than before, but one thing is for certain.

"Your sisters." I sigh. "Wolf, if you are being held hostage for them, don't do anything you'll regret. You don't know if they are even ali—"

He cuts me off, clearly upset by my words. "*I* know. I have seen them." He tries to take a deep breath but fails. "I know they are. They are my little—" His face contorts in pain, as if he is physically hurting from trying to speak the words. "I just *know*, okay, Serena?" he hisses at me.

I hold my hands up in surrender. "Alright, I believe you. So, is that why you betrayed him?" I tilt my head towards where a sleeping Sailor lies.

"One of them." His voice is as sharp as rocks and as cold as ice.

"Okay then. Nice chat." I stand, but before I can leave, he grabs onto my wrist.

"Just sit down." He blinks several times, slowly, before I finally cave in and sit back down.

Wolf hands me a plate of steaming food. "Thanks for the food," I say in between bites.

"I sort of have to feed you; I am your guard after all." I smile overly large, food falling from in between my teeth. "Very *queenly*," he teases me, and I take another bite, not caring what I look like. "You know, you need to learn to actually fight without your powers. Gods only know when he will give you back your magic." He isn't wrong, but that's why I have fought and trained without power my entire life.

"I have practiced without power before," I say defensively. "I'm not some spoiled princess, Wolf. I know how to fight. I think you forget where I came from." My tone is even and controlled, unlike how I feel inside.

"I know you aren't spoiled, and I will never forget where you came from. I watched it burn right alongside you." His callous words hit me hard enough that I want to hurt him back. This weird feeling of pain lacing throughout my body causes hate to spill over into my next words.

"Yeah, the night you allowed Sailor to be beaten and left him in a cell. You watched as I had to beg my pregnant sister to leave our childhood home and father." He doesn't even flinch, as if he knew my next words would be pure venom.

"The very same." He chews on nothing while he sits there, clear-eyed and unaffected. I am about to respond right as he beats me to it. "I have nightmares about your scream," he admits, not meeting my gaze.

I don't say a word, so he continues. "Sometimes I can still picture you grabbing his head. I had seen that sort of thing before...Blessed, just a month earlier on our trip. My friend. Seeing somebody I cared about as deeply as I do you, though..." He shakes his head as if trying not to picture that night. His thick dark hair blows in the morning breeze. He blows it from his forehead.

"I still care about you," he continues. "Even though I know you and Sailor may never know what I have done to keep you both safe...I have tried. And I won't stop keeping you safe from behind the scenes." I don't know why I move my hand to his, but I have every instinct telling me he needs this touch. He needs a friend. I rub my thumb on his fingers.

"I don't know what you're going through, and I won't until you can tell me. But I would love it if you would teach me some moves if you're willing." I know I can kick his butt in half a minute, but I will play into this if it makes him happy and wanted. Judging by the smirk he gives me, I think I have done exactly what I have set out to do.

"I would love nothing more than to train my queen."

Half an hour later, Wolf and I stand in a circle made of rocks. We have each moved about ten so far. Of course, we woke up everybody in the camp. None of them offered to help, though. Sailor wasn't too happy about my wanting to train with Wolf. Even now, Sailor sits on one of the boulders right outside of our circle, eyeing Wolf like he may just try to kill me.

My arms dangle at my sides while I secretly watch his feet move. "Are you ready?" he taunts me. I can tell he truly believes he will win, as if he doesn't remember our training sessions just mere months ago. He moves before I can answer him, kicking his strong leg out towards me. I grab onto it before trying to twist it, but I can't. I am not strong enough, I realize. He yanks it from my touch. "Not as easy as you thought it would be, huh?" His proper voice doesn't belong in a fighting ring. We circle each other several times over. My fists are clenched right in front of me.

"It's nice to say that, as you have your powers," I hiss. The metal of my necklace is almost choking me. I want my powers. I *need* them.

"You do not need them, Serena. You are strong enough; you just have to believe in yourself," Wolf says, invading my thoughts.

"Don't do that." My tone is a warning. My mental shields are up; he shouldn't be able to get through them.

"What will you do to me?" He smiles at me, and Sailor growls from the sideline. I eye him sideways, in clear warning. This is *my* fight.

I kick out at Wolf; he rolls forward and is back on his feet before I can even turn around. I dance on my feet, never staying still. I move all around him, and he does the same to me. "Am I getting into your head?" he teases, while anger builds up in my system.

Wolf plays unfairly; he fills my head with so much anger I might explode from it. I punch out several times, and he blocks each and every one. I move in tune with his feet, his speed. It's all evenly matched...that is, until he pours more thoughts into me. I kick out at his abdomen, hoping to land a blow, and I do. He grunts out right as he grabs my head and throws me to the ground as if I am nothing but a schoolgirl's doll to play with. I roll away before he can get on top of me. I'm on all fours when he pierces into my brain, and a mind-shattering noise breaks into my head. My ears start to bleed; I can feel the warm liquid seeping out of them.

"*Hey*! NO power if she can't." Sailor stands, but I wave him off.

"He never said he couldn't use them. He just said *I* didn't have any. I'm training for if I have to fight somebody without my power," I manage to say while I grind my teeth together. I don't know if I want everything to end or if his power is just so strong that it is burning down any defense I had in my mind. I pull on my knee and then try to stand. I almost can't. I watch him move through blurred vision. I think I have tears streaming down my face, but I can't be certain. The fire in my mind is burning so hot that I wouldn't be surprised if my brain completely melted from my head.

Wolf doesn't halt his assault on my mind; I almost think he may be trying to kill me.

"Enough." Sailor is right outside our circle now, about to walk in, when Wolf looks at him. That is when I attack. I grab a sharp rock from the ground and move faster than any human can. I know my fae nature is helping me move faster. I know my fae bloodline is the only reason I am not passed out on the ground. I grab the back of his neck before he can even realize I have a hold of him. I hold the rock against his head.

"Now, unlike you, I do not want to truly harm you. I could hit you over the head with this rock, but I will not. So, do you give?" My ears hurt so badly from whatever he has done to my head, I almost think he may have caused permanent damage.

"I give." He sighs. I can tell he isn't happy about the distraction, but before I can do anything else, Sailor is in the circle and holding Wolf by the throat.

Chapter 36

"If you want to fight somebody of your own caliber, fight *me*." Sailor doesn't lessen his grip when Wolf looks stricken that Sailor would even lay hands on him.

"Seriously? You'll fight me because of her?" Wolf sounds more offended than I figure he should. He is the one who betrayed Sailor.

"*She* didn't leave me in a cell to rot. *She* didn't disown me or cause others that we love harm. You know what has happened to them?" Sailor hisses the last words as if they physically pain him more than any fight could. "They are *dead*. Anybody we were friends with is dead. If you are doing this for your sisters, *she* will kill them before you ever get to see them. You must know that." Sailor's eyes burn purple and red. I know the words hit Wolf like a pound of rocks because I cringe hearing them myself. I watch Wolf's face cave.

"They are alive, we both know it," Wolf replies immediately.

"Yeah, yeah. I have heard that time and time again. And what shape would you consider alive, Sylas?" The use of his proper name is a dig in and of itself.

"I don't care!" he roars, spit flying out of his mouth. "I don't care if they are *vegetables*, I will get them out of there, Sailor!" I believe he thinks he can. *I* believe he can do it, but not if he is being controlled. Not if he isn't strong enough to fight against the mental hold on him.

Barnett finally steps in. "Okay. Everybody, calm down. We can hash everything out, but it doesn't have to be violent." He tries to remove Sailor's hand from Wolf, but Sailor's fingers are too tightly wrapped. "Guys, come on. If anybody needs to be training Serena, it's me," Barnett says, trying to help the situation. They both look at him like he may have just suggested they kiss it out. "I'm just saying...I have strength and can work her muscles out." Sailor looks five seconds away from killing the poor ginger. "I just mean, I can help her get *stronger*," Barnett says defensively.

Mabel steps into the circle. "I would like to train, too. Why don't we spend today training? Maybe one day *I* will be the one to save Serena." Everybody takes a moment before we all agree. Mabel fights against Wolf. Barnett, and I take turns with Sailor. I figure Barnett would rather be taking turns *with* Sailor, but here we are...fighting in a makeshift circle of rocks, which feels like it may be the most healing thing during this trip.

"BB, you can do it! I believe in you," I encourage Barnett, and Sailor's eyes glue to mine, betrayal written in them. I ignore him and focus on helping Barnett. "Go for the knees!" I yell right as Sailor drops Barnett to the ground with a loud thud. The day has gone by faster than I would have liked. We leave first thing in the morning, right back to the real world, I am glad we extended our trip another night. I think all of us could use it. The problems here? I can fix them. I can hunt, fish, fight, and swim. Anything I would need to do here, I can do. Being a queen in the middle of a love triangle that I can't see an end to? I don't know how to do that.

Sailor makes his way to me, fury apparent in his eyes. The way his body moves and commands the forest to bow to him does something to me I would rather not admit out loud. "You ready for round two, Honeybee?" His sweaty fingers grip my chin. I try to yank away, but he grips me harder. I pout. "Upset?" he taunts me. So I do what I do best—I punch out, right into his stomach. I land the surprise blow, but as I'm pulling my arm away, he grabs onto it, twirling me around so that my back is against his chest.

"This must be your favorite position or something," I tease.

"You would know. I'd gladly show it to you again, if you'd allow me to?" I gulp down any shame I feel when his excitement touches my back. I try to move my hips forward. "Running from me?" I hear him lick his lips, and in turn, my ear.

"I don't run away from my battles." My response is short-lived when he spins me away from him.

"Pick it up." He tosses a stick at me, it's long and thick. I arch a brow at him.

"You want me to beat you with a stick?" The curiosity must show on my face because he then grows a branch and snaps it off with his foot. He rips his shirt over his head and off with one hand; the entire thing is hotter than it should be. Sweat glistens from his perfect body. The form in which he moves is more attractive than anything else I have ever seen.

"Stop drooling and defend yourself," he chastises me, and I wipe at my mouth, knowing it had been hanging open. I kick the stick up and grab it in one swift movement.

"If you want to fight, I'll fight, but don't forget this is what my entire childhood looked like." The stick fits in my hands perfectly, as if Sailor had thought it through for longer than I had seen.

"I know all about your childhood. I got front row seats to all the embarrassing stories of Serena Bloodworthy's memorable adventures." Ouch. He hit his mark, and he knows it. He swings out, but I am ready for it. I hold my stick up, my hands precisely positioned away from each other to make the hit not as hard. I grunt from the force of shoving him off me.

"Nice try, but I have thought about nothing besides you, my father, and my siblings for months. I have cried all the tears in my body out," I say as I swing my leg. He dodges, but I hit out again and land a blow to his stomach. He grows a vine and wraps it around my ankle. I kick out hard to break the vine from the ground. He tries to tighten it while swinging assault after assault at me, and I meet each and every one of them. I bend to try and get away from his earthly abilities. The vine is cutting my circulation off, as my nails dig into the unnatural earth at my ankle. Sailor doesn't slow his attacks at all. If anything, he tries harder. I can feel eyes on us instead of the sounds of the others fighting.

"I didn't want your tears, Serena. I wanted *you*. I *want* you." I don't focus on his words; I know a distraction when I hear one. "I love you, and that won't change. Even when you try to send me away to whatever hell that place is," he spits.

My stick swings in a circular motion in my hands before I hit it out towards him. He blocks it. I hit again and again, pushing him closer to where I want him. He strikes out, I go left. I meet every step he takes, trying to get two ahead of him. "Do you even have a plan here?" Sailor's tone has a bite to it that makes me think he is no longer trying to say things to distract me.

"I can't plan for something I know nothing about." *Hit*. I hear my stick crack just a little, and I know the next blow will break it in half. Kind of like how my heart feels. Like each blow he makes will somehow cause further damage. "All I can do here, Sailor, is be a queen that the people need. They need food, they need more coin, and they need safety. I can only help what I know. I can't plan for something I have no knowledge of. I'm doing the best I can." When he hits my stick, it cracks wide open just as my heart does. Not for the man standing in front of me. Not for the male back in the village. For my people whom I am not doing enough for. I take the two parts and use them both against him. He doesn't see it coming. The emotion I use behind the attack fuels me even more. Finally, he walks backwards, right to where I needed him to be.

He falls over a log, and I push him even more, so he hits the ground harder. I straddle him while pushing my two sticks into him. One at his throat, pushing down, the other I hold at his side, pushing slightly in case he gets any ideas.

"I didn't want to leave you, and I should have been given a choice." His jaw is clenched so hard, I worry he might cause another gap in his teeth.

"I didn't give you a choice because you would have picked the wrong one, Sailor," I hiss out in his face. He turns red with anger.

"Staying to help you isn't the wrong choice. Like you said, you have no idea what you are doing. Fates' sake, Serena, you didn't grow up knowing anything about either kingdom you are to rule." His words hit me like a beast in Brabble would. The pressure on my chest is so tight I feel like it might kill me. I may be having a heart attack.

"I told you, I didn't think it was fair to you. I still don't, Sailor. I wanted to give you—" My words cut off when he bucks his hips up and pushes me off him.

"You don't get to tell me what I need to do. If I want to stay here and watch you fall in love with your husband, I can and I will. I will stay, Serena. Because no matter what, I am *yours*. My heart will be yours, even if you pick him. You may never be mine again, but I will always be yours. I will watch you grow old with him, I will not move on from you." He seethes, his chest heaving up and down as we sit facing each other.

"What kind of life is that, Sailor?" I ask in shock as he stands to pace in front of me.

I am fully aware of the show we have created, I just do not care. After years of hiding everything from everybody, I no longer want to do that now. I am who I am, and sometimes vulnerability is strength.

Sailor walks to me, his strides sure and true; he doesn't falter. "A life worth living, Honeybee." Bending down onto one knee, he reaches for the dagger he keeps in his belt. When he retrieves it, he cuts deep into his wrist.

"Sailor!" I hiss out. Wolf comes to us now, but not before Sailor's eyes look into my soul. Blood trickles from his arm in deep, red pools.

"You are my queen, you are my soulmate, even if I am not yours. Hear my words, Serena. I am yours entirely." Bright, red blood seeps from his wrist, but he never takes his eyes from me. "I will be *just* your guard, if that is what you decide. You are not stringing me along. I am fully aware of what I am saying...I just have to be a part of your life." He holds his arm out to me. I am unsure what to do with it. "I pledge myself to you, Serena Bloodworthy. I will until my very last breath protect and serve you. If you will have me, I will give my life to you. And we will never have this conversation again." His eyes finally drop to where the blood runs down his arm. For some reason, I feel as though I know what he is asking me to do. Blessed Gods forbid, I bend down, my fingers gripping his arm. I lick where his blood is running to.

"Sailor." Wolf's eyes are wild with disbelief. "Do you know what you just did?"

Right as his thick, hot blood hits my throat, I feel a bond form. I don't know how, because I have no magic. Wolf looks to me. "Even though King Alwin took your power, it doesn't take away your natural fae powers. This is a *blood bond*. Sailor will have to serve you as whatever you deem for him for his entire life." Wolf shakes his head as if he is disgusted by this, but when I look at Barnett, he shrugs.

"I may not do that..." Barnett says immediately. I chuckle to lighten the mood. "But I do pledge myself to you, Serena." Barnett comes to me and kneels on one knee. Sailor moves out of the way; Wolf brings a clean cloth to him and starts to bandage him. All the while, hissing words to him I can't hear.

My entire focus is on my body; I barely even see Barnett on his knee in front of me. "I will protect and serve you, Queen Serena. Until my dying breath, if you will have me." His eyes plead with me to agree; the uncomfortable feeling I feel in this moment is pushed to the back of my mind.

"I will," I agree, seeing the want in his eyes. Even though I don't want any of them risking their lives for me.

"I would like to serve you, too, My Queen," Mabel speaks up.

"You are all already serving me enough; it's my turn to serve you," I say, my thumb rubbing my wrist. The prickling sensation in my body thrums more than it ever has. Is that because Sailor's blood is coursing through my body along with Alwin's? I just hope their blood gets along better than they do.

Mabel shakes her head, and the slightly longer curls bob. "I want to pledge my life for yours." She bows completely on the ground. Her chest is touching the dirt, her face to my feet.

"I should have done that," Barnett mumbles, and I roll my eyes. Mabel shoots him a look that promises that if he ruins this for her, she'll skin him. I believe she would, too.

"I will give my life to you, Majesty. I will protect you over my own life." The words taste bitter to me when I hear them. I bend down to look her in the eyes.

"I hope you know I would protect you as well. With *my* life," I declare, needing her to know this isn't a one-sided agreement. "For any of you, I will fight. You are worth just as much as I am." Sailor shakes his head in disagreement, but I continue. "I'm serious. I love you all. I will do anything for this kingdom, but more so for you." My words are a promise to them and my people. I am gearing up for a war.

"Group hug?" Barnett smiles, teeth on full display. Everybody besides Wolf joins in on the group hug. That's about how the rest of the trip goes, us as a group, while Wolf is apart from us.

Chapter 37

"You smell like shit." Alwin takes another deep whiff of me. "What did you do?" His black eyes search me, and I shift uncomfortably.

"I went camping with my friends." His eyes narrow before he takes a bite of his toast.

"I am well aware of what you did, I just wasn't aware you would be playing with blood." If I didn't already look guilty, I know I do now. "Relax and eat, Serena, you look stick-thin. Did you eat there?" I had, I just didn't eat a lot. The meat tasted wrong for some reason. Alwin starts to pile breads and pastries on a plate for me. The pile is so ridiculous, I snort a laugh, and his amused eyes meet mine. "Not to your liking, wife?" Wife. I am *his* in the eyes of the Gods. Even in my eyes; increasingly, every day, I feel closer to Alwin. But I want them both...and they both seem okay with that...

"I just find it funny you think I just want junk." I gesture towards the plate he's holding.

"Well, I need you to not starve to death. We have business to attend to today." He sounds happy, which is surprising, because when I got back to him, he grilled me five ways to charcoal about everything that happened during my little trip. I was grateful he didn't put up more fuss. I had expected a fight with him; I was ready for it.

I grab a muffin and start eating it, already feeling better with the food in my belly. "What do we have to do today?" I take another large bite, not caring that I am shoveling food into my mouth at this point.

"You are going to help me gain the favor of the people." He sits back in his chair and just watches me eat. His feet go on the table, ankles crossed, dirty boots and all. I push at them.

"You know, for a fae prince and a king, you are not mannered."

Alwin continues on as if I didn't just offend him. "I was raised by a nanny. She taught me everything I needed to know to survive a war. I'll live if somebody has a problem with my feet on a table that is the perfect height for me to relax." I use this chance to dig into his childhood. I have tried in the past, and that has gotten me nowhere.

"Oh, so your parents didn't raise you. Is that because they were busy starting a war?" His eyes narrow on me, brows furrowed, and then, as if snapping out of a daydream, he shakes his head and moves on.

"I was raised to rule a kingdom that is rightfully mine...now look where I am. Prime position to rule *two* kingdoms." He smirks at me, and his tone is humored.

"Mommy and Daddy must be proud of you," I taunt him, knowing exactly what I am doing.

"They are," he agrees with me, too quickly.

"Do your parents know we are married?" I question.

I watch Alwin carefully, trying to figure out if I can read him. "They are aware, but not because of me, though." So somebody may be higher up than even he is; Wolf isn't wrong then. Interesting. I had thought Wolf had been making things up.

"Who told them then?"

His chair scrapes against the floor before he answers. "Somebody that I don't like very much. They are none of your concern, though. We need to get going. Did you eat enough?" His eyes scan the almost empty plate, as if the entire thing isn't laughable. "You know, I went through a phase where I didn't eat meat either," he claims. I stand and walk right next to him, looking up at him in wonder. Alwin is more complex than I had thought, he shares such vulnerable things about his childhood that I can't help but wonder if I might be slightly wrong.

He wears his ears and fangs on display to the villagers. They all watch as we walk hand in hand. He wears his crown; I do not.

"Why?" I finally ask. A child runs up and hugs my legs, and her mother yanks her from my pants.

"No, honey," she says to the child, and I note the scared tone she uses. I bend down to speak to the kid, but the mother rushes away.

"They fear me still," I whisper, emotions clogging my throat. Alwin studies my face for a moment before he decides to speak. I never truly know what is going to come out of his mouth.

"They don't know you. They know what happened at our wedding; other than that, they are judging you. They always will. Every move you make will be studied and lectured on. It's not an easy life to live here. In no realm is being royal easy, but with the humans...?" I stop in my tracks when I notice a certain somebody in the village center.

"Sounds nice," I say, so sarcastically and high-pitched that several people stop to look at me. I try to look closer and see if it's really who I thought I saw. Alwin gains my attention by pulling my face to look into his dark, navy-blue eyes.

"I don't enjoy meat because in Mirahalm animals are sometimes fae. I don't like cannibalism, honestly. Some don't have a problem with it, though. I do. I enjoy friends."

I blink several times, not expecting that answer to my initial question. "And what were you saying about the humans?" I clench my mouth shut so I can listen to him.

"Humans will never trust us. They hate what the Gods gave us. They think we are power hungry and will never put them ahead of our own good. Humans do not forgive the mistakes of the fae." I hear his words, and I can even understand them. I didn't forgive him for being the king he was; how can I ask them to give *me* a chance?

I watch as kids rush from the cobblestone pathway through the village. "How can I change how they see me?" I can't help them if they are terrified of me more than they trust me to take care of them.

"You cannot change their perspective, Serena. You can just give them another version of yourself. People like to hate you; it gives them a reason to talk. They will never truly be happy with you, and you just have to accept that. You must rule them no matter their feelings for you. You might have to make choices that impact them negatively, but you will still be their queen." He walks up to a storefront, walking up the three steps into the shop, and he looks over his shoulder expectantly. "Are you coming in?" I follow him into the unknown; it seems I have been doing that more often than I would like.

When I walk into the shop, it turns out it isn't *just* a shop. Alwin walks to the back of the small blue room. There are white and pink clouds painted on the walls of the clothing shop. I don't see anybody in the room with us. Alwin continues to walk; he doesn't even stop to see if I am following him. My feet follow dutifully behind him without even thinking about it. I do stop when he opens a cupboard that opens into a sprawling room. There are cots everywhere, strung out all over the space. I duck into the small cupboard and stand fully when it opens into such a big space that I can't see the back.

"Where are we?" My arm brushes against Alwin's.

"We are in Caramoor." That doesn't really answer my question.

"But...how is this building so big?" I ask in wonder.

"Magic." His answer is short, and that irritates me.

"Whose?" He doesn't answer. Instead, he walks over to a table with plates and hands me one.

"We just ate." I may not be hungry, but I am intrigued for sure.

"It's not for you, princess. Look around, what do you see?" I do as he asks, and I see families. People who appear injured, I see some who may be sick.

"What are we doing here?" I ask while looking out at the people.

He shoves the plate into my chest. "Exactly what you signed up for. We are making a difference here. You wanted to do more, and I agree. I should have been helping more than I did. Before meeting you, all I wanted—" He pinches the crease of his nose. "I craved finding you. It was all I wanted, other than going home. My body wouldn't slow down until I could find you. I regret marrying Lillaphe. I wish I hadn't listened to...my advisor. You were always my goal, as soon as I could feel you. Now, I want to do right by you and our people that I have hurt." My jaw is slack on the ground.

"So, you created this? For them?" My voice shows how unsure I really am.

"I used my downtime to create a safe space for them, yes. But not just for them, for you, My Queen."

I look around, suddenly seeing stuff I know he would have brought here, and laugh. Rugs from the palace that are just pretty, but have no use here, though. Blankets that aren't thick enough for Grove's harsh winters. But he tried. Alwin wants to be better for our kingdom, and maybe he will be.

"When did you do this?" I ask while looking around.

"While you were taking your time in the woods." My mouth opens slightly.

"When I was camping?" Guilt eats away at me.

"Yeah. I had to keep my mind busy, so why not start making a difference while I worry about what you're up to?" His sarcastic tone tells me he really didn't want to do this. "You are quickly rubbing off on me, wife." I take the plate this time and follow his lead.

"Yeah, well, same for you," I whisper before going to the table that has food piled high. Some of it is decent-looking. The folks already eating seem to enjoy it. "How will you keep this up after we leave?" I ask without looking at him. I'm too scared of what I'll start feeling if I watch him give small children food.

"I have hired people. The commanders will pay them accordingly. This village will no longer struggle; none of them will. I promise you we are going to help this kingdom." His chest presses into me; I startle slightly, then lean into him despite knowing I shouldn't, at least not in here.

"Majesty," Mabel says from a cot across from me.

"Hi. Where is Barnett?" I don't want to ask about Sailor or Wolf. Tensions between the two of them were at an all-time high when they got into a fistfight on the walk down into the village.

"Oh, um." She looks around before pointing to Barnett, and my insides turn to molten lava.

"Who is Barnett talking to?" I know my voice has a bite to it because her eyes widen so much it would be funny if I weren't upset.

"I believe her name was Tiana, but I don't know for sure. She's pretty but not my type," Mabel says nonchalantly.

She *is* pretty. Her skin is perfectly smooth; she has a button nose and rich, choco-late-brown eyes. Her long brown braids complement her rich brown skin tone. The tips of her braids are a lighter brown, probably from sunlight.

"How did she get here?" The words rush out before I can even think about how I might sound.

"Oh." Mabel chuckles. "Are you...*jealous*?" I bite my lip, which draws blood when I notice Alwin walking over to her, too.

"Excuse me, Majesty?" A little girl comes up to me, reaching for the plate in my hands. I hand it to her and pat her head. I am not thinking, I am running through all the motions.

"Holy Gods' balls, you *are* jealous of that girl. Why?" Mabel teases me.

"She is the king's ex-lover."

Mabel looks to where Alwin is talking to Tiana, then back at me. "I could see it," she admits, which doesn't help in any way.

"Thanks." I make another plate of food before handing it to the next person.

"Thank you," a small voice says, and I stop right in my tracks. This little boy is all alone. No family with him, just by himself. His small face is speckled with dirt, and his clothes have rips in them.

"Hi." I squat down to be eye level with him. "Now, who are you?" All thoughts of jealousy are gone from my heart.

"My name is Ram," he says more strongly than I would have thought a tiny child could.

"Nice to meet you, Ram. What a name." I smirk at him.

"It's because I can turn into a ram." So, a nickname then.

"Where are your parents?" I ask, looking around for anybody who might be close by.

"They are dead," he answers plainly before turning to leave. I reach out tentatively to place a gentle hand on his shoulder, and he stiffens.

"Who are you living with?" I ask shyly.

"Myself." His tiny voice is harsher than it should be. "Thank you for the food." He tries to leave, but I stop him again.

"Where at?" I question him again. He seems annoyed with my pestering, but I keep on. "Also, how old are you?"

"I am nine, way old enough to be on my own. I don't need your food; I just like it better than mine. I am good and well-off on my own." I have no doubts about that, but this headstrong kid reminds me of somebody else.

"Okay, where do you live?" I ask again, hoping he will tell me.

"In the woods, as a ram," he deadpans, while blinking slowly.

"Could I come visit before I leave?" I don't think he expected me to ask that, but he nods and tells me right where he lives in his animal form. I let him leave for now, feeling creepy trying to get him to stay with me. I make a mental note to tell Sailor about the child to see if there is anything that might help him. We keep on working for a long while after Ram leaves, serving people and giving vials out with different herbs to help them.

"So, are you gonna do it?" Mabel asks, looking like she is ready for a show. We have fed everybody and helped all the injured or sick. I can't see why Evie picked this as her job. Yeah, she is a healer, but still, it is horrible. People coughed in my face, one person threw up on my boots, I have blood all over me, and it isn't even mine.

"I guess I have to, seeing as though they are working together like a well-oiled water mill." She smirks at me before lifting her legs onto a cot with a sleeping man on it. I gape at her. "Mabel, you can't put your feet there," I hiss at her.

She places them back on the ground before mumbling something under her breath that sounds a lot like, "Well, he won't be waking up anytime soon after the dose I just gave him, so it makes no difference to him." I huff out a breath while rolling my eyes.

Chapter 38

Serena

The grating sound of feminine laughter pierces my ears so hard, I look around to see if Wolf is trying to test me. Tiana's giggles sound like what I would imagine birds' songs sound like. She is everything I am not. Tiana is girlie, she is soft and sweet. She is charming in a way that even I seem drawn to because I can't take my eyes off her. I'm annoyed, to say the least.

"That did not happen." She playfully hits Alwin's arm. I see red. I am on her like a moth to a flame in less than half a second. "Oh my." She startles and pulls away from Alwin.

"Serena, what are you doing?" Alwin sounds amused. He finds enjoyment in my despair. "Tiana was just helping here since we needed more hands."

"It looked as though she was trying to harm you." I know I sound jealous, I know I sound stupid. For some odd reason, I feel possessive of him. I don't even want others to look at him, let alone touch him. He is _mine_. I have no idea how he seems so relaxed about Sailor. I'm grateful, but I have no idea because seeing this girl standing next to him causes anger to almost boil out of me.

"I was doing no such thing," she hisses before pulling out of my grip. I almost want to tighten my fingers around her dainty little arm, just to harm her. I don't, but I would like it. I don't have to look to know Mabel is laughing at my expense.

"I would like to speak with you, please," I demand, turning to Alwin and seeing exactly what I didn't want to see on his face. Enjoyment. He likes watching me squirm. I believe that is one of the reasons he made me go through the trials to begin with. I didn't have to finish them. Really, we didn't even need to have them at all. From my understanding, he knew who and what I was from the moment he saw me.

"The moment I could smell you, if you wish to be accurate, darling."

"I told you to stay out of my head," I reprimand, then notice that Tiana is still standing next to us. I glare at her, wishing I could blink us away from her very presence. "What are you still doing here?" I ask in a tone that is biting and cruel.

"I was having a conversation with him, but it is unfinished." She wishes to die. I think that's what she is saying to me. Fury must show in my eyes because she backs up, and I step forward.

"*I* am having a conversation with him now. You may be excused."

She looks to Alwin, whose eyes are on me. I snap at her, trying to get her to listen to me.

"I just need to tel—"

"No, what you need to do is listen to your *queen*." I sound as if I am scolding a baby. My tone is condescending, and everything I wanted to portray to this woman. She looks between the two of us before finally leaving without another word.

His mouth opens to say something, but I cut him off. "I would suggest you tell your girlfriend not to stay around you when I am in the same room." His eyes widen, his smirk grows, and Gods bless, my freaking heart hammers. He steps into me, and I step back. Again, and again, until we are in a dimly lit room at the back of this large room.

"Are you jealous?" he asks firmly, not one hint of teasing in his tone. Denial rears its head, but I decide to go with the truth.

"Yes," I say softly, still meeting his gaze.

"Good." He tilts his head before crushing my mouth with his.

His kiss is searing my lips; his swollen lips claim every ounce of my willpower. I hitch my leg up on his hip. He grips my thigh hard, claiming my mouth with his. His tongue sweeps against mine with a fever that might kill me, but I will die happily if it means I get to feel his hard body pressed against mine. I push my hips into his, and he grinds against me. His hard length is pulsing even through his pants.

"We can't here," I whisper, and he chuckles against my lips.

"If you believe I would allow them to even see you hitched onto me like this, you do not know me well enough yet."

When I look out at the room full of villagers, there is a small shimmer in the light. Only around us. "They can't see us," I say softly. I pause for a moment, realizing that no matter what, I could never beat him with power. I would have to train every day for the rest of my life. If I am to win against him, it will have to be by outsmarting him.

As I look out at the people roaming around, he claims my neck, kissing and sucking on the sensitive skin that instantly makes me wet. He teases me enough that I am pulling and ripping at his clothes in a desperate need for more contact. The animal inside of me is telling me this primal need is normal.

"Because it *is* normal for a fae, baby," Alwin whispers in my ear right as he pushes his hand into the front of my pants. "Back home, there are even celebrations for mating bonds where large groups gather together." His fingers brush against my slick core, and I gasp right as he hits the bead of pleasure. His finger plays with it as he explains. "Sex isn't like what it is here. Back home, sex isn't something that is always private, unless mated pairs want it to be. Some females have two males to themselves. It just depends on their exact bond." Jealously rears its head again.

"And what about ours? Do you want to bring Tiana into our relationship?"

He stops licking my neck, pulling away, and I almost regret asking the question. Until I see the passion written in his eyes. "I want what you want, Serena. If you want to add another, they will not be our mate. They will be yours to play with, but we are mated by the Gods. We are paired together; none other can be mated to either of us. I want you happy and sated, if that includes another male or female, it is for you to decide." He pulls my shirt down, exposing my bare breasts. "I have had my fun; you didn't get to do that. That is the only reason I am allowing you to explore now." He pulls my already hard nipple into his mouth, his sharp fangs brush against the skin, and I gasp again. "I am possessive of you, yes. I want you all to myself, but if I cannot have that, I only ask that you let me watch." My head lolls back, hitting the wall behind me.

His dirty words continue as he takes me with his hand. His fingers move with such ease that I am finding myself grateful for the practice he has had.

"I don't want you to have another female," I say in between gasps of pleasure.

"As you wish," he agrees without hesitation.

"That easy, huh?" I ask, unsure, fully aware that I am being loud. None of the people in this room seem to hear me, though.

Alwin teases me with his teeth, tongue, and fingers. I fall apart on his hand, and then he picks me up in his arms, caging me in his large frame as if wanting another stolen moment of being alone. I reach down to please him, just trying to return the favor, but when I get to his pants, I find they are already soaked with his seed. His grin is boyish and innocent, which is the exact opposite of what we just did.

"I told you, all I need is to see you fall apart, and I am a goner. You have completely ruined me, Serena." My legs grip tighter around him, and instead of a passion-filled kiss, I give him several long, hard pecks. Somehow these kisses feel more intimate than even him finger-fucking me. They feel like more, like maybe this moment causes our bond to tighten even just a little bit further.

"What were those for?" he asks me, seeming unsure, which is crazy considering he is a king to one kingdom and a prince in another. When he looks at me, though? I see a male who never got to live a life of his own. I almost feel bad for him living the life he had, and me getting to live the life I did.

"I wanted to show you what I feel when I look at you." I must imagine it, but for a second, his eyes stay navy blue with only swirls of white and silver.

Chapter 39

Serena

I am not excited to be leaving Grove. I like it here. I feel like we have finally made a difference. Instead of a ball or formal dinner like we had planned, we sat with our people. Learning about them and their stories, who they are, and what struggles they have. I feel fulfilled in a way I hadn't pictured I would. The people run after my horse, kissing my feet, even though I have told them not to do that. We spent the rest of yesterday giving them things they might need. I taught several of the little girls how to use their powers. That is one thing I have noticed among the villages...they are grossly undertrained. I had always known the schools don't teach powers like they should anymore, but I didn't realize how negligent they have gotten with teaching basic skills.

Alwin moved some new commanders in here, and they are under strict instructions not to harm anybody unless they have truly broken a law. Even then, Alwin told them he would like to hear about anything that would result in death. Unless it is a rapist or murderer, everything else will be a proper punishment for them. For stealing, they will have to work in the village center for a month. Alwin is going to look at making this an entire kingdom rule when we get back. It will increase the number of coins, but he promised he would figure it out so that taxes aren't being pushed any higher than they already are.

"Sailor, what did you do with the tiny child?" Mabel asks him from atop a blonde horse. She likes to switch it up daily. She shows no loyalty to any particular horse. She enjoys them all, like she likes her women. She informed me that she isn't picky, but she does have a type. They *cannot* like men. That is the only answer she gave me last night during our drinking game. I had played truth or dare with her, only the two of us, and she informed me that the only type she had was a woman who knows exactly what she wants. If they pretended to like men but secretly like girls, she isn't interested. I have to respect her for her boundaries; she doesn't want somebody to hide their feelings for her. She makes her choices and doesn't care who hates it; she is going to be herself no matter what. I feel deeply similar in that aspect.

"He is going to meet us whenever we get to Groke. Wolf is bringing him up after the new commanders are feeling good about everything. Shouldn't be more than a day or two behind us." Sailor wasn't too happy about leaving the boy, but it was for the best. Langford isn't somewhere he should stop at; the riots there are getting worse every day.

"Do we have a plan for whenever we cross the border?" Sailor asks Alwin, looking up at him. The height difference between the two, even on horseback, is staggering.

"Well, I would assume none of us wants to die," Alwin says coolly.

"I would assume *not*." Barnett sounds offended. Alwin glares at him. None of us wanted to ride in the carriages today. As the honeymoon trip continues, we all get closer to one another. It's like a family; I just wish Juniper were here, though. He would like it. He would fit right in. I can't imagine what he and Evie are doing to keep busy in Clove.

One thing I made Alwin do was to send Nolan to Clove to be with Evie so that he didn't miss the birth of my niece. I know I will miss their lives, but Nolan didn't need to. Alwin did it without hesitation, which I was grateful for.

"I think we can only do what we can. It will depend on how the people react to us being there." He shrugs; Sailor doesn't seem to like that answer.

"But they are all aware that we will be there." Sailor slows his horse down to be right next to Alwin, and I am following behind the two loves of my life. One from my human time, and one for my fae life. I can't seem to separate the two.

"Of course, the commanders in the villages know. What they chose to tell their people isn't up to me." Alwin's voice isn't kind, but neither is Sailor's.

"You are *king*; you should be in control of everything, as you have been for decades." Sailor's response isn't about just tomorrow, and the people not knowing about us coming.

"What are you trying to say?" Alwin speeds his horse up just a little to be in front of Sailor slightly. Sailor does the same until both of their horses are now trotting.

"That you should have always been looking out for your people. Not just now that you have Serena. She can't be the only reason you step up," Sailor hisses through his teeth, which makes Barnett chuckle at Sailor's lisp. I snare Barnett with a look that tells him I will push him from his horse if he doesn't stop laughing at Sailor's lisp.

"Hey, guys. You are causing the horses to get scared and rush. I don't want our carriages to crash," I say in a calm voice, trying to get them not to fight.

"Serena is not the only reason I am working on fixing my mistakes. She is a big part of it though. Before her, I didn't value anything, and now I see the Kingdom's worth." Alwin says with hate behind his words. "We are a partnership, she and I. She has opened my eyes wider than they ever have been." Alwin adds on for good measure.

"Listen, you seem to have a problem with being honest with people. Just don't forget that I have been to Clove and I do not struggle with keeping stuff from her."

My ears perk up at that. "What are you talking about?" I kick my horse's side, urging him to catch up with them. Now we are all full-blown running through small trails. What could possibly go wrong?

"Nothing!" both of them yell back to me.

"I am just saying you need to rethink what you think she should be responsible for and what you think she can handle." My attention is fully on Sailor's words. "She can handle more than you are giving her; she isn't some fragile little girl. Tell her, or I will," Sailor swears.

I almost feel betrayed. What were they talking about? When I tried to bring it up with Sailor later, he mumbled something about needing to pee and rode off. I asked Alwin what he was hiding from me, but he did not seem inclined to share anything. He acted cagey when I brought it up to him, so I stopped. We arrive in Langford in less than half a day's ride because each of their horses were forced to race.

Our welcome is less than joyful. They glare at us enough that I almost wish we were back in Saxton with their evil commander. Even the new commanders hate us. They are young, but they have seen enough still. When we crossed into the hostile village, there were six men strung up in the trees. They were dead, had been dead for a while, even. Their bodies were filled with maggots; flies were swarming them. I threw up, and my stomach has still not recovered. It reminded me of the time with Millie. I will never look at maggots the same again.

None of us speaks to the other; the fighting, the laughter, everything comes to a halt.

"Majesties. Sorry for your welcome here, we didn't know when you would get here, and we had some men that...did some things," the thicker commander says, almost as if he does feel bad.

The other one laughs. "Yeah, one of them was fucking livestock."

My brows furrow. Firstly...*gross*. Secondly, they hung him instead of placing him in a clinic?

"And the other five?" Alwin asks without emotion. I almost gag while the men list off the atrocities those men committed. Although, the other five seem a little worse than the one with the animals. People here are violent; most of the people who live here have offensive powers. They have a lot of mental powers, breaking abilities, and some can even cause sickness in others. I cringe thinking about the stories I have just heard.

Most people's power is given to them based on their personality. The Gods know who you will be before you're even born, so they know which power is good to have. Healers are typically kind people. They care more about others than themselves. That's why they have a high rate of suicide; they care to the point that when they can't help, *they* would rather die. Some powers are for selfish people, like Nova and her mental power. It could only be used to hurt others. I don't like to think about her, though.

"I will show you all where you'll be staying," the thin commander says. His arms stretch out in a way that tells me his power is elasticity. He grabs my trunk with his long arms and stretches it back to his body. "Follow me." Alwin and I both follow him side by side. Sailor trails behind us while Mabel and Barnett stay to talk with the other commander. Roman circles up ahead, watching carefully, just in case.

"So, how come things have gotten so out of hand here?" I ask, then regret it when Alwin looks at me as if I have just punched a puppy.

"We just got here four months ago, Majesty. I believe it has always been this brutal here, though," the commander says. Right. Just before the Queen Trials, Alwin sent in new commanders. I guess I had always thought the new commanders were the ones who traveled with the girls to the palace.

"Oh." I nod in understanding, even though it didn't answer my question at all.

"I must warn you, though…they aren't happy about their daughters being sent to the palace. Some of them even heard that there was no reason for it."

I bite my lip, trying to find something else to focus on other than the fact that this commander is insulting Alwin. Sailor steps forward.

"Serena wasn't picked beforehand. They should be honored their daughters were sent." I'm shocked he is defending Alwin.

"No, but they have heard enough about the wedding to know that she is Fae and their wedding was also a bonding ceremony. The talk is that our king knew who he would pick," the commander says brazenly as if he were wishing for death.

"Is that so?" Alwin questions, and the commander doesn't seem to notice the difference in tone he is using. I do. I grab onto his arm, fingers digging in.

"Do not kill him. It will not look good on us," I think down our bond, hoping it doesn't hit a wall. It doesn't, but it does go unanswered. "It would seem as though these people want more trials," Alwin says harshly.

Finally, the commander must hear the danger he is in. "Oh, no, sir, they don't. I was just rambling on. Ignore me," the commander says, trying to backpedal.

"It sure sounded like you were warning me that I have done something wrong."

Even Sailor has the good conscience to step back. The commander tracks Sailor's movement and gulps.

"I wasn't saying that." His eyes widen drastically. "I was just telling you what these people believe. I don't think that, sir. I was top in my commanding training, I swear it."

Alwin grinds his teeth for a moment before relenting. "Sure. As my kind and beautiful mate pointed out to me, I wouldn't want to kill you." The commander goes gray. "It might look bad if I murder you on my honeymoon. If you would be so kind as to show us where we will be staying, then you can be on your way." The guy nods frantically before walking faster.

We make it to the place we are staying in. It has open doors and open windows, and I almost wonder if they just enjoy being outside so much that they wanted to leave everything open. I had noticed the shops were the same. Nothing is completely closed off here.

"Here we are," the commander tells us before rushing away, probably scared that Alwin might kill him.

"Well, isn't he a bright chap?" I say before walking right through the frame of a door that is not there. "So, they just leave these open then?" I ask while walking into the room that houses ten beds. Each looks way worse for wear; the blankets look worn, and some are in ribbons. I watch Alwin as he surveys the scene in front of us. If he was expecting anything nice, he doesn't show it. Instead, he walks to where the commander dropped my belongings and places a book on the bag that Mr. Benson gave me.

"Sailor and I have some business to attend to. You will be safe here until we get back. Barnett will be here shortly," he informs me hastily.

I pick up the book, investigating it. "What is this?" I hold the large leather-bound book in my hands. The thing is thick; its deep-brown leather is smooth with oil on it. It's tied shut with a small piece of yarn. There are swirls all over it, but what catches my attention is that it feels warm in my hands. It thrums with energy; I blink several times before I ask, "Is this from Mirahalm?" My words almost seem silly. But right as I am about to take back my question, he nods.

"It is. I thought you might want to read about where you are from." Alwin chews on his lower lip, the only sign he might be nervous.

I hug the book to my chest. "Of course I do. Thank you." He kisses the top of my head. Sailor doesn't seem pleased by this but doesn't say anything. Instead, as Alwin walks away, Sailor comes and gives me a huge, tight hug before plopping a wet kiss on my lips.

"We will be back soon, Honeybee. Don't get into trouble," he warns before walking off.

I swear I hear Alwin taunt him, saying something that sounds a lot like, "*Oh, Honeybee. Be a good girl and do nothing while you wait for us.*" But surely not, considering that would be below a king.

Chapter 40

The Book of Fae: How to Live Your Life Properly

I open the leather-bound book and chuckle. Who names a book that? Fae must have some sense of humor. I plop down on a bed, and it squeaks underneath me. I almost feel as though the bed might have bugs in it. I scratch my thigh, knowing there isn't anything on my body, but still feeling like I need to. As I hold the thick book, it feels like magic is coming off of it. I might find answers about who I am in here, what exactly I am, who my family is, or...was. I lose all track of time when the pages start turning, completely getting lost in a book. Like old times.

Dunamis is a plant that the Gods gift fae. It can only be grown in Mirahalm. This plant, paired with royal fae blood, will mute any being's ability to use raw magic. This plant can be contained in a crystal of fae making, a potion, or sometimes in food. If made improperly, it will kill the user.

Well, isn't that wonderful? He could have killed me. I skip through some chapters about geography. I may need them at some point, but not today. I clutch the book in my hands as tightly as I can. It seems like this might be my only real thing from home. I stop when it gets to the royal families, slowly reading each word.

The two purest bloodlines are the Bliza line and the Verdaisil lines. The Bliza line is strong; they have females and males throughout every generation. The ruling family is of the Bliza line, consisting of Thalia Bliza and her consort, Eldrin. They are parents to an unborn twin, whose name is unknown, and a male offspring. He is named Cormac Bliza, his powers are vast, although not as strong as the prophecy suggests his twin sister was to have been. She died during childbirth, unnamed.

Oh my Blessed, is this my family? A twin? I try to come up with anything to make sense of my mother keeping one child and leaving me. I try to piece this together, but it just doesn't fit. My mother wouldn't leave me here, alone, just to take one baby home.

The Verdaisil line is secured as well, and they pose a threat to the current ruling line. The Verdaisil line is strong thanks to the young male that Princess Amaris gave birth to, she being the consort of Prince Nyvariant. The birth of the strongest male we have seen in recent three hundred years is reason why there is uproar in the kingdoms of Mirahalm.

I realize this book is old, but Alwin would have already been here when it was written. The book is dated only a few weeks after my birth, although it acts as if Alwin was still there when I know he followed my mother here. I have more questions than answers from just a few chapters of this book. I skim through the family trees, not caring about dead grandparents I will never meet. However, they died at an old age. One of them died at eight hundred years old, which seems to be a common age of death. This book suggests that at one point, our worlds were interconnected. That might be why Alwin could travel so easily between the realms. At some point, it was locked by somebody, and I get the feeling it wasn't Alwin.

Mated pairs

A mate formed by the Gods is irrevocable. A mated pair is destined for one another from the moment of their birth. Each will seek the other out until they find one another, even if it takes decades to do so. They will not feel at ease until they are together and bonded. This bond can never be broken; once mated, the two become one in the same. They will share feelings, powers, thoughts, and even truly powerful ones will share death.

There must be a blood sacrifice large enough to show the Gods of the faes' faithfulness and loyalty to them. The pair must each show their gratitude in blood; this does not have to be at the same time, but within weeks of each other. The Gods will grant the bond if they see the sacrifice is fit for the pair. The stronger the bond, the more blood must be shed.

I feel sick to my stomach, that's why he did the trials. He had to kill enough people so that the Gods deemed it fit for our bond. He killed them for me. How would we even know how many to kill? We didn't know how strong our bond would even be. I could scream at how unfair that is. How unjust the Gods are. I continue reading, even though I feel as if I have read enough.

I never thought I would think this, but I hate the Gods more than I ever hated Alwin. It seems like fae might live a more carefree life than humans do, but they are held to a much higher standard of rules than humans are. Humans cannot mate apparently; they are not worth enough for the Gods to even pair together. Mating bonds are sacred, according to the Gods. I do feel the pull deep inside the marrow of my bones to Alwin. All throughout my life, I had felt like there was more. I had felt a pull to travel and find my missing piece of home. I had just thought it was my need to have fun and explore. I never thought it would be to my mate who the Gods made for me.

Mates are almost always equal in their power and strength. They will complement each other in every way possible. Mates will be possessive and protective. Unnatural emotions will come with a bonding that is strong and growing. Urges to kill other fae who even glance at the other's mate wrong can overwhelm even strong fae. Stronger bonds will cause mates more trouble in the beginning—they will not be able to hold in their urges. Lust, jealousy, and protectiveness will come as second nature to pairs that the Gods have given the strongest of bonds to. These bonds can be beneficial.

There is no way to unbond a pair once bonded; their connection will only grow from the moment they have their bonding ceremony. The blood share will join them as one being, no longer two halves. They will be one whole.

In extremely rare cases of mating bonds, when one of the pair is harmed, they both will become harmed in the same way. This is unlikely to happen, due to the fact that the Gods would grant this bonding of the highest esteem. This is the rarest bonding experience, and there are no records to show this happening in fae history. This has only happened in dragon history once.

I keep on reading, but I don't read about mates any longer. I don't need to. I think deep down I always knew he was mine and I was his. I didn't need to read all of that to know. The power sharing is interesting, though... I do wonder which powers I don't have, and he does. I also wonder which of us is the stronger one in the eyes of the Gods. I can only assume it is him. I haven't had a chance to test that, though. I learn more about my homeland, realizing the dreams I have had are dreams of home. The way this author describes the lands is pure magic. I can almost smell the salt from the ocean there, the dirt even. I feel as if I have been there, although I haven't. I haven't had any more walking dreams or nightmares with my mother since my bonding.

I fall asleep reading about the beings that live in Mirahalm. It isn't just fae; there are tons of different beings I didn't know even existed. I hold the book tightly against my chest when my eyes finally close.

Chapter 41

I know two things when my eyes shoot open to find the hand of a burly man covering my mouth. I know for a fact Alwin and Sailor are not here yet. I also know that Barnett *is* here. I don't know what kind of state he is in, but I know he is here. I can hear him grunting, probably from being kicked in the stomach, if I were to guess correctly. I struggle against the hold, groaning from the sheer force this man is holding me down with. I hear many voices, all male.

"Shut it, girl," the man hisses at me. "You are no queen to me. You are a dirty-blooded fae and you deserve to die. Just like he said." He says all of this while his hand covers my mouth. I can't respond if he is waiting for me to. "You'll die for what you are," he says, and then my eyes scan to where Barnett lies in a pile on the ground.

Please don't kill him, I think, hoping this man has the ability to hear my thoughts. For the first time ever, I hope somebody is in my head. I start to struggle and another man comes and holds me down alongside the burly one. I begin to panic because I have no power, but the next thing I know, Alwin's black mist swirls into focus through my watery eyes. I see many shadowy figures, but don't recognize any of them.

"You are both fucking dead," he growls through clenched teeth. "Take your Gods-damned, unblessed hands off my *mate*. Right fucking *now*!" Alwin roars. The sound pierces through to my ears. The men take their hands off my body immediately before Alwin throws shards of ice at them. One of the shards hits the one man in the throat, and bright red blood sprays everywhere. His body thuds on the ground in a horrific, echoing sound. The gurgling noises reverberate in my ears. The other shard hits right in between the eyes of the man who was holding me down.

One of the men tries to run, and Alwin blows fire at him. He catches ablaze before he even gets through the door. "Wait," another man says, his hands held up in surrender. "I wasn't a part of the group; I just wanted to avenge my daughter. She was in the trials," he says, out of breath. I can't help but feel bad for the man; he lost his daughter. It gives him no right to harm me for it, but still, I feel sympathy for the guy. Alwin doesn't give him a chance to beg for forgiveness before the man is relieved of all the oxygen in his body.

Alwin, within the blink of an eye, has killed more than ten men. Right as the last man falls, Sailor, Roman, Mabel, and the two Langford commanders come rushing in. I am already making my way to Barnett. The scrapes and bruises on my body forgotten, I just need to know BB is safe. I bend down to check his pulse. He looks pale, even more than he naturally is. As soon as I am about to ask for a healer, his eyes open slightly. I sigh in relief that he is indeed alive; he may be bruised, but alive is more than enough for me.

"Are you alright?" Sailor rushes to me, and I nod frantically while trying to help Barnett sit up.

"Nice of you to finally show up," Alwin hisses at Sailor. Barnett rubs his face; his eyes are black, his ribs look broken, but he is alive.

"Damn." He breathes out, wincing when he tries to stand. I hold his elbow so hard, I may be bruising him. I just need to hold my friend because I could have lost him today.

"Are you alright?" I ask in the softest voice I have.

"I am just going to relax a minute. I'll be fine, Serena."

Alwin is on him faster than I can even process, shoving him out of my grip and into a wall. Pieces from the crumbling wall fall into their hair. "Like the Blessed you are. What the fuck happened?" Alwin sneers right in Barnett's face. I rush to yank Alwin off Barnett, but Sailor is already doing it.

"This is not his fault; those men planned this out," Sailor says. The commanders nod their heads in agreement but don't voice their own opinions.

They are cowards, so I speak up. "Barnett has done nothing wrong, Alwin. He is my friend, and I do not want him blamed for the mistakes of uninformed men." I glare at the men they call commanders. Now I know if women could be commanders, I would be one. My balls are much bigger than any of the commanders I have ever met. He stops his assault immediately, his grip on Barnett lessening just a little. Alwin softens in a way I didn't think he could; his body appears to slow down, as if realizing we are not at war right now. His emotions are feeding into mine; I don't know if I can actually tell the difference between the two anymore.

I grab onto his face, fully aware that his skin is steaming from how upset he is. One thing I did learn from my reading is that mated pairs are unable to harm each other.

"Hey," I say in a soothing voice. His eyes are still frantic, searching for another to kill. The white swirls in his eyes simmer when his dark pupils finally meet mine. "I am okay," I say, nodding my head. "I wasn't even harmed. You got here in time." My voice seems to calm him in a way that warms my heart more than my hands are warmed from his skin.

"You're okay," he whispers in disbelief, his eyes slowly blinking. I nod softly so he can follow my movements.

As if snapping out of a trance, he finally zeros in on me like the predator he is. "This should have never happened." His tone is detached and cold. I would be scared if I were on the other end of those words. He starts to scan the damage in the room. My sheets are all out of sorts; Barnett's bed is shoved into a corner. The struggle from their entry is apparent.

"The men were upset about their daughters, Alwin...they had a reason to be. I read the book." His eyes snap to mine.

"You did?" His head tilts in a slow, curious type of way. There is an unasked question in there that I can't figure out for the life of me.

"I did." Relief pours into me as if he can't help but shove it down my throat. He wraps an arm around my shoulders.

"I'm so glad." He kisses the top of my head before looking to the group. "We will be leaving from here. There is no need to stay," Alwin commands, and everybody dispatches.

I pack my things up quickly. "I still think we should stay the night," I say for the thousandth time.

"You don't want me to kill anybody else, you said so yourself. So we will leave," Alwin answers, happily, as if we weren't talking about murdering others.

"Just because I don't want you killing somebody doesn't mean we shouldn't stay and figure it out. I just think we are moving on too fast; we should figure out who the 'him' is that the man was talking about, don't you think?" I give him doe eyes. Sailor grabs my trunk from my arms, and I rush to grab my blanket from the top.

"Listen, Honeybee. I hate to agree with Alwin, but I think we should move on, too. The danger in staying is far too great. This was more than likely a rebel attack. They have been planning attacks for a long while; the trials are only one reason they have for coming after you."

They have voted against me...again. I can't believe it. Sailor and Alwin are a team against me, it would seem.

It takes two and a half days to get to Mickle. Once we were out of Langford, I felt so sick I could hardly ride. I rode in the carriage some and the other time I spent trying to nurse my wounds. Not physical, but I think I have exhausted myself from the travel. I don't have my powers to recharge, and I am not eating much due to the meat tasting like ash in my belly. Sailor has spent the better part of the trip playing games with me to distract my mind from the unease I feel.

"Thank the Blessed we are finally here." I step out of the carriage feeling lighter than I have for the entire two days leading up to this.

"That was rough," Mabel says, looking as green as I feel. This wasn't as easy as some of the other pathways we have taken. The mountains were uneven in places; there are intricate cave systems that sprawl throughout the mountain ranges here. The forest is vast and mostly untraveled due to the steep terrain you must take to travel throughout it. "I never want to come back to Langford again," Mabel swears, and I agree.

"I can't say that since I am their queen, but I secretly agree with you. I see why you left here May," I whisper in her ear. She chuckles.

"This might have once been home to me, but what I saw tonight isn't what I remember it being. I am sorry, Serena."

"I am sorry you didn't get to see your family or friends," I say, sorrow hitting me in the gut.

She slaps my shoulder playfully. "I am glad you are safe, my queen." Her eyes sparkle with amusement; she is quickly becoming somebody I trust. "Also, I didn't see any females worthy of flirting with." She says, happily changing the subject.

"That must have been the real reason you wanted to leave then, not what happened to me." I tease.

She sighs dramatically before saying, "Serena, if you were to ever want to add a fourth, I am game. Please do not think I don't take what happened to you seriously tonight." I laugh because she is funny. I also know she knows that will never happen.

I start to trot behind Alwin and Sailor, Barnett taking up the end. Roman flies overhead, searching high and wide for any traveling groups. He doesn't talk much anymore. I wonder why that is.

"I would rather die a horrible death than add another to this strange arrangement," Sailor says over his shoulder.

Mabel looks to me before whispering, "Sounds like he might think about sharing you. You in?" Her brows move in a wave motion. I stifle my giggles because I can tell she is taunting him. She's funny, in a way that feels inclusive. Mabel is my friend, and it feels like coming up for air when you hold your breath for too long.

"Only if you are." I'm teasing her, and we both know it. I don't want to add anybody else to my love life; I don't even want it to be the three of us.

"I would be stupid to turn you down, Majesty," she says in a high-pitched voice.

"You are a gem, Mabel. Whoever you end up with is going to be one lucky person." I smile softly at her while she and I continue to make jokes at the men's expense. Alwin turns to roll his eyes at me every time I snort a laugh. We are just trying to lighten the mood after what happened in Langford. I keep telling the jokes Juniper once told me nobody would laugh at. Mabel laughs at every single one.

The villages are filled with tension; they aren't happy about the trials still. I wouldn't figure they would be, but our welcome to Mickle is a much better one than Langford.

Everybody we come across grabs my hand and kisses it. They thank me for being their queen and stepping up when they needed it. Alwin sets up another station for them, this one more temporary than the last one, but once the new one is built, it will be amazing. There will be a chemist, healers, and even a station to train others who are empaths looking to learn basic healing skills. Kind of like what Evie did in her free time at Darnish's clinic. Potions and other amazing skills will be offered as free classes. They will easily be able to sustain them after we leave, which was the goal for every village. Mickle is nice in a way that other villages haven't been. The homes don't have vines on them, but they are well-kept, and for the most part, the shops appear to be newly built. We aren't near the coast yet, but I can almost smell it. The closer we get to Groke, the more I can feel Sailor becoming tense.

"Are you alright?" I ask from atop of the horse I am riding. We only stayed in Mickle's village square for two days. We set everything up and informed the commanders of what needed to be done. I think they will be able to follow through with it. Wolf is bringing up the rear with Ram; they will check in on Mickle when they pass through.

"I am," he says simply enough. I know him, I know he isn't, but I won't pry.

Groke's main village is right on the sea. The closer we get, the lighter I feel. I enjoy the sea, I enjoy the beach, and the sand. I never would have thought that, growing up in the woods, but my heart calls for the water. Even before I had shifted into anything that has gills. I have always loved to be under the surface; it's a freeing feeling.

"Sailor, you know you can talk to me. Right?"

I try to make sure I even out my time between the two...Alwin and Sailor. I don't know if I am doing this right; it doesn't feel right to me. All I know is that Sailor holds too big a piece of my heart to let him go. I think I would die if I did.

"I know, I just don't want others to listen in," he says evenly. I look to where Alwin is watching us closely.

"I told him not to intrude on my thoughts; he hasn't since then," I inform Sailor.

"So he says," he fires back, and my defenses flare even though I don't want them to.

"I guess, but I trust him."

He purses his lips, clearly weighing his next words out carefully. "I see. What is your reason to trust him?" Sailor narrows his eyes at me. I sniff, feeling like I have something in my nose.

"I can tell when he lies to me. I believe him when he says he will stay out of my mind." I tread carefully, knowing I don't want to fight with Sailor.

"I guess you have no reason not to trust him then." He utters the words more to himself than me.

"Is there something I should know, Sailor?" I finally ask him, my voice laced with unease.

"No. I just don't trust him, Serena. He killed those women for no reason. He lied to you and made you kill those people, and for what?" He laughs darkly. "A bond that you didn't want or need. I just don't trust a male who sits back for decades and allows his kingdom to suffer while he stuffs his mouth and cock with anything he pleases. How do you know he isn't still fucking that Tiana girl?" My jaw drops, and I don't know what to say. I blink several times, then wipe the tear that had fallen from my eye. As if realizing he has overstepped, he stops and tries to backtrack. "I'm sorry. I didn't mean that. I'm just jealous and pissed off. I haven't gone home since I left. I don't know what to expect." Poor excuse to treat me like that, but I understand, I guess.

"*I don't,*" Alwin says sharply. My head snaps towards him, and he isn't even looking at me.

He is speaking to Mabel, and they are laughing. I can't imagine what she has said to him to cause him to laugh, but I find myself wishing I knew so that I could watch him smile like that again.

"*I wasn't in your head; you two talk loud enough that I can hear you even without using my fae ears,*" Alwin informs me. Sailor raises a brow and then says sorry again.

"I accept it." My voice is soft and unsure.

"*Of course you do. You are perfect in every way possible. That also means you are far too forgiving for your own good. I will teach you what you need to know about forgiveness.*" His words hit me hard. I never had to work on forgiveness because I didn't have friends growing up.

"Just a few more hours and we'll be there," Sailor says, changing the conversation. Thank the Blessed.

"I'm excited to see where you and Wolf are from," I say, more cheerfully than I feel.

Sailor eyes me warily. "So I am not forgiven then," he deadpans. I eye him right back.

"What makes you say that?" I sound suspicious.

"Hmm...let me think about that, Serena." I hate it when he says my name. I don't know why. *Honeybee* just sounds better on his lips. "Probably because I am getting *fake Serena.* You are never cheerful if you are tired or hungry—and I know you are both—yet you just sugarcoated your voice, raising it two octaves, and smiled at me when I know damn well you are not in a smiling mood."

I enjoy having friends. I never would have thought I would say that, but I do. In this moment, though? I wish my friends didn't notice me so much. I spent my life in the shadows; I was content with living the rest of it like that. And now? Now the problem is that my friend knows when I am being fake based on the sound of my voice. I gulp even though I can feel him studying me.

"I just think we are all tired and ready to be home. *I'm* ready to be home, at least." I shrug, then internally hit myself. That is the last thing to say to Sailor.

"The palace is your home, then?" He sounds offended. Ugh, I cannot win right now.

"He is being petty. Shove him from his horse and move on from the human pet," Alwin says cheerfully.

I can't help but smile, then I wipe it from my face. I look at Sailor, and when my eyes land on him, he looks sad. "Are you nervous to be back?" I persist with this conversation even though I cannot seem to say the right damn thing.

"I don't like being on the outs with Wolf," he admits to me. "I know something is going on that we can't see. He wouldn't just betray me like this. He even seems more like himself, but then there are things he is compelled not to talk about. I don't know who is strong enough to do this, but I have my thoughts." Sailor sounds broken.

"We'll figure it out, Sailor...together. But for now, let's visit your home." His shoulders finally relent, the tension leaving his body.

"You are right, we will always figure it out together, won't we?" He gives me a sad, half-smile before leaning over into my space and kissing my hand.

"We will," I swear to him.

Chapter 42

Groke is magical. That is the only way to describe this village. Most of the village itself is buried in the woods, and a small stone pathway leads to the larger, central part. I notice a red brick path right by the raging sea. There are beaches where children play, and shops with all sorts of things. This is my favorite village, even more so than Darnish.

"I can't believe you're from here." Amazement is apparent in my voice.

"Yeah, sure is mystical, huh?" Sailor's eyes scan the crowd, maybe looking for somebody he might remember. "Wolf has been back several times. I just couldn't bring myself to do it," Sailor says, shaking his head enough that his blond locks fall into his eyes. I reach up and move the hair that's blocking his view. His eyes still scan the crowds, and now I do wonder if he is looking for somebody in particular. I understand him in these moments; going to see my burnt-down cabin in the woods was almost as bad as watching it burn in real time. Going back to see that nothing had changed since the last time I was there, even though everything had changed for me, almost killed me. When I stepped into that clearing, and nothing and nobody waited for me, for the very first time in my entire life... I could have stayed there and cried for a lifetime, but I didn't do that. I have people to protect, I have beings to save from themselves.

"I can see why it would be hard to come back; I struggled with that, too, in Darnish," I admit. Sailor turns to me, as if just now realizing I might have been struggling more than

I let on. He hugs my shoulders as we stand in the middle of the stone walkway, people walking around us.

"I'm sorry," he whispers while holding me tight against his firm body. A breeze brushes my hair from my face. I look into his eyes; the candlelight makes them glow. Sailor changed in Clove. He is a stronger version of himself, one that I admire deeply, and I hope I get to hear more about his time there. My heart finally feels ready to hear about my family. Throughout the village, there are strings of lights dangling around, blazing power all around. "Come on, I'll show you where I grew up," Sailor says while rubbing my upper arm.

I grab onto his hand, and not for the first time, I follow him into the unknown. I get the feeling this won't be the last time I follow him somewhere. Sailor James is a sturdy sailboat in unknown waters, and I know he will always be mine.

"Do you believe Wolf's sisters are still alive?" I ask while walking hand in hand with Sailor. We have been walking along the coastline for about thirty minutes. Every time I look out at the harsh seas, I wonder how Juniper is doing. Is Clara happy with the pack there? Am I finally an aunt? Sailor clears his throat, stirring me from my daze. We make our way to his old home. "I can't imagine they are alive after all this time. I have tried to talk to King Alwin about it, but he just waves me off and tells me prisoners are Magnolia's job. If that is the case, then they are long dead," Sailor says almost coldly. My blood boils at the mention of her name. I hate her with a passion that burns so hot it would melt bone. "She plays with her victims in cruel ways. I searched The Harbors Club for them several years in a row. I never found them," Sailor continues, now with more sadness to his words. "I think he needs to believe in them being alive for his own sake. Sometimes, Serena, people just need something to believe in." Sailor sounds sorrowful.

I hope that if they *are* dead, that they were never a part of that torture. His voice is hollow, beaten down, when he continues. "I prayed to the Blessed for a long time for them to come back."

"Maybe we will find them still," I say, trying to remain positive. The sea turns to thick trees before we make it to a swampy area. Exactly how Sailor had described it to me, some time ago. There are trees bigger than even the ones in Darnish here. Vines wrap around the trunks of them, and my eyes spot one of those traitorous spiders that had once caused me some major issues. The very ones that killed his sister.

"This was home." His voice pierces through my thoughts as I watch the massive spider scurry up the tree. They are typically scared of humans. After I was attacked, I did research. They only attack if they feel threatened, or so the book claimed. I watch this one very carefully, making certain it retreats to a safe distance from me. The body of this particular one is as big as my head, which I have found is not even the biggest of them.

The home I walk up to isn't what I had pictured it would be. In my mind, I thought a home where two members of a family died would be haunted by their spirits or falling apart at the seams. This house doesn't look like that, though. It's as if frozen in time. This home has some chipped paint, but the house Sailor would have grown up in is cute.

It once was a light yellow, I can tell. There is even an upstairs window looking out over the swamp. Some of the trees fall over themselves, sloping to the ground like rain made of leaves. They drape over the swamp, which has green lilies floating at the surface. I wouldn't swim in that water, but it's pretty to look at. A light fog skates across the top of it, as if this entire place is in some magical trance.

I step on a creaky stair right behind Sailor.

"You don't have to come, Honeybee." He steps into the home he had once loved.

"I wouldn't let you do this alone. I know how emotional it can be," I say while searching the tiny home. I was raw for days after visiting my childhood home. I don't want him to do this by himself. "You know I would do anything for you, Sailor James." He stops and turns to me, leaning in to press thick kisses to my cheek. His own cheeks glimmer from tears that have already fallen. I wipe them away. "I'm here," I assure him again. I kiss his cheeks before he lifts his hand to my face.

"You are the only family I have left. I lost my brother...I need to keep you, so please stop pushing me away. Let me in, in any way you will allow. Please just let me stay," he pleads with me, his eyes searching for an answer in mine.

"I want you to stay. I need you, too, Sailor." My voice cracks. "I am allowed to try to figure out my feelings, though. It's not every day that somebody not only gains a mate, or husband...whatever he wants to call himself that day." I pause and take a deep breath. "As well as a boyfriend. This is uncharted territory for me. I just want to figure it out without dragging your heart along for the ride. I love you...too much to hurt you more than I already have. I don't want to hurt you." Tears stream down my face, not for me but for the position I have put Sailor in. "I just want you to be happy," I whisper, unsure how much more I can take.

"I am happy with you. That's all we need to figure out for now, Bee. Me, you, and your husband. That's all there needs to be. I don't want to complicate anything else."

I wipe at the hot tears on my face. "Oh, is that all? Just the three of us then?" I joke with him, but not really.

"There are weirder things out there. Your brother saw some crazy shit in Clove. You fae are adventurous with your sexual habits, so maybe you are just acting on your natural calling." My eyes narrow on him. He half smirks at me. "Don't worry, we didn't participate."

I slap his arm playfully. "Good, I would've killed you." It's stupid to think I can have complete ownership of the two of them and expect them to be faithful to me. But a girl can dream for now.

"Here is my humble abode." He wipes any remaining tears away from my eyes, and we walk through the building he once called home.

"I love it." The walls have dirt on them; the floors are filthy, but that's expected after over a decade of nobody being in here. There is some mold in the room with the hearth, but overall, the structure is in good shape.

"Here was my room." He motions towards the small area, clearly meant for a toddler. I walk into the space; there is still a bottle in the crib from the day his mother killed herself.

"Oh, Sailor," I whisper, because I can't speak any louder. I hug him from behind, nuzzling into his shirt. He grabs onto my wrists, pulling them tightly around himself. I nudge my head into his back, knowing that all I can give him in this moment is comfort.

We spend the entire afternoon walking around the house, looking at old toys and clothing from his past. The tiny outfits are strange to me; they are handsewn and even have flowers on some of them. His mother loved him enough to sew him personalized clothes, and yet her mental health deteriorated so much after losing her daughter that she couldn't care for him any longer. Grief hits some in more intense ways than others, and I almost wonder if Sailor will ever struggle like his mother had.

"Did you ever hear anything from your father?" I ask while picking up a piece of paper that has coloring on it. When I open the torn paper, I see there is a drawing of a man, a woman holding a baby, and a toddler standing next to them all.

"I don't care where he ended up. He means nothing to me now," Sailor says while guiding me somewhere else. I don't blame him for his harsh words; his father left his mom at a time they needed him. "One more stop." Sailor steps outside of his childhood home, and right as I follow, his fingers spark to life.

"What are you doing?" I eye his fingers that are dancing with purple flames. I have wanted to ask him how much he truly trained with Juniper to get that purple flame. He has used it before, but I am still starstruck by it now. It isn't easy to get that strong. Sailor may be the strongest elemental in this kingdom; I am including myself in that.

"I think I want to take a page out of the Serena Bloodworthy handbook and burn my problems to the ground." His hands become engulfed in flames. I can't help but stare at them. The sparks are hypnotizing, dancing with purple and blue hues, some green even.

"I didn't burn my home down; the king's guards did that," I remind him, but it's too late, though. One spark to the dry wood, and the house is overwhelmed with flames.

"Wanna watch it for a while, or do you have queenly duties to attend to?" he asks, even though he's already dropping down. I plop down by him, but make certain we are nowhere near that tree with the spider, or the swamp. I find a lush patch of long green grass, and sit crisscross.

"I have nowhere I would rather be than here with you," I say, knowing we both feel the same. We sit and watch the flames break the old wood down. Cracking sounds echo throughout the trees. I watch as fish jump from the water, and birds flutter away. Sailor remains consistent; he stays right next to me the entire time.

"Are you going to ever show me?" his voice finally echoes throughout the silent moments. The house is gone now; only embers remain.

"Show you what?" I play dumb...I know exactly what he wants to see. I just don't know if I am ready to share my last comfort.

"Your wrist. I know something is there. Is it a mating bond?"

I don't look at him when I respond. "In a way." My answer is an evasion; we both know it.

"I see." He stands and holds a hand out for me to grab onto. He pulls me to my feet, and I wipe my butt off. "I still will memorize your body in every way possible one day, Serena. One day, you won't feel guilty for accepting what we are offering you; you will just know you are loved by two instead of one." His words shock me, because he admitted to feeling jealous earlier today. I don't think I can even respond to his words because these complicated emotions clog everything up. Even without my empath power, my emotions are getting stronger; I'm feeling more every day. That's a scary thought. The more I go into the world, the more I seek to understand those complex things. Relationships, the Gods, and why they torment us so badly.

We walk side by side together. "One more stop," he promises again. The sun is setting. The sea is coming into view, and I find I could never tire of it.

"After this next stop, I would like to come back here, please." My request is answered with him stopping in front of me and squatting down.

"Hop on." I jump on his back right away, feeling relieved I don't have to walk any longer.

"Gladly, sir." I smack a huge, wet kiss on his cheek as he carries me away.

Chapter 43

King Alwin Henry

I can smell war. It is brewing somewhere nearby; I need to focus my mind on the ultimate goal here. I have been distracted lately, and that will not stand. I cannot be king with her breathing down my throat. She is jealous and wants to harm me; every misstep is another way for her to walk all over me. She wants to take my kingdoms from me, and if that happens...Gods bless us all. Millions will die under her wrath.

Mirahalm is the goal here, and Serena will find out the truth when she gets there. I need to secure my line and get home. Mother and Father want answers from me, and I cannot give them. I have nothing to report back that is good. This kingdom is falling apart at the seams. No matter how badly Serena wants to help the humans, we cannot. The Gods have forgotten about the humans in total. The powers here are slimming down to almost nonexistent; soon, the humans will have none. I am trying to help them for Serena's sake, but what more can I do? I have given them food, I have given them medicine. There is only so much she is allowing me to do; her tight grip around my throat constricts me more than I ever knew. I never wanted to make a difference here...I didn't care to. Serena has changed that for me; she loves this kingdom with white-hot passion. She is inspiring me to want more, although, I cannot afford to. One of my kingdoms will fall if I can't get a handle on things, and I would rather the humans burn.

I pace back and forth in this inn, which is decent enough. Serena's eyes almost fell out of her skull when she saw it. It could be worse... She doesn't understand how close we are teetering on the edge of a full-out war with the fae. If only I could take her home now, but she won't leave unless forced to. I want to win the war in Mirahalm, yes. My parents need me and Serena to step into our roles there. We must ascend the throne, and soon. But I keep finding myself caring more about what happens to these humans here. Lately, I am doing things that I feel might please her even when she is not with me. I don't know who I am now, but I am not the male who came to this land with the mission of killing her mother.

I haven't had the balls to tell Serena that her mother is, in fact, alive. I don't know why her mother hasn't told her that, or never came to retrieve her. Probably the same reason I have kept my mouth shut. I am here and not there. If I saw the woman who left my mate alone, I don't know if my temper could handle not killing her on the spot. She knows it, as do I. She also knows that with my being here, her evil son has every opportunity to sit on my throne. Serena has begged me for her powers back, and I cannot tell her why I can't do that. She can't have them back because, more than making her happy, I need her *safe*. I need Serena to be okay, and she will not be okay if I allow her to be found. She won't believe it if I tell her, though; she must see for herself. Once she does, I will be there to pick up every broken shard. I will glue her back together, because, in my eyes, no matter how broken she may become, she will always be perfect to me.

Once we are home, I will figure everything else out. I just need the human lands to be able to sustain themselves like they did for years. I need somebody I can trust to rule them in our stead. We must save Mirahalm, though we cannot do that until Serena is ready. Hiding her is the best thing for now.

I had thought about appointing *her* to do it, but she would kill everybody. She is evil; there is no better way to describe her. I know I must do something with her; she is a danger...but she is family. She also holds Mirahalm over my head. I will never go home without her help. Blood is blood, and mine helps each other, even if she has lost sight of that in her blood thirst.

My sister is the reason why I do not care about Serena's pet for now. I may grow tired of him at some point, but for now, he is a welcome distraction for her. If he makes her happy, he may stay. The moment she tires of him, though, he will be disposed of.

I have learned that I must play my cards behind my back. My sister will try anything to kill my wife; if she can't, then she will destroy us. She believes it will make Mother and Father realize she is the more fit ruler...instead of me. I am eager to get back to the palace and see what damage she has done in my absence. I have done my best to keep Serena away from her, and I have tried to keep my sister on a tight leash. This is the longest I have left her alone in years. I check on her, but a few minutes isn't enough to know what she is doing.

All throughout this honeymoon trip, I've made stops along the way. I have sent men to check on her, and they say she might marry soon. I have no clue how she would trick any man into marrying her. It may not be a bad thing, though. She could use somebody taming her down. When she killed my first wife, I thought I had taught her a lesson. But it would seem as though I have not. One might think all this death might force her to see me as I truly am—a monster created by the Gods—but maybe she is a worse kind of monster.

Chapter 44

Queen Serena Bloodworthy

I hadn't expected Sailor's orphanage to remember him, but after an hour of people coming up to hug him, I have realized he is easily lovable. It almost makes me more protective of him. Sailor James is everything I have ever wanted. He is loving to his core, he cares for everybody to a fault. He is funny, kind, and compassionate. He cares about more than himself, and that is why I am not surprised the headmistress of the orphanage has been talking his ear off about where the other kids have landed and who out of his friends had been adopted or aged out.

Sailor and I sit at a dinner table in the main café, and the headmistress is talking his ear off about stories from other kids. I watch the children run around and laugh and play. You would never know they didn't have family. Because they *do* have family. They are not alone, they have each other. They're having fun and smiling, even after whatever happened to them landed them here. My heart warms as I walk away from Sailor and towards a group of small children.

"Guys." One of the little girls with pigtails pulls on another's shirt. The other little girl hisses at the pigtailed girl, and I crack a smile.

"Hello." I sit down with them. "What are you playing?" I ask the group of them. They all look startled before the pigtailed girl speaks up.

"Patty-cake," her tiny voice squeaks.

"Could I play?" My gaze scans the herd of them. They whisper to one another before agreeing to allow me to play with them. We play patty-cake and then decide to play hide-and-seek.

"But you're a queen. You shouldn't play games," one of them says in between rounds, seemingly more sure of herself than before.

"I *am* a queen, but that doesn't mean I can't have fun, does it?" Pigtail girl pulls on my shirt before placing her hands around her mouth. It seems as though she wants me to lean down.

I do as she wishes, and when I do, she whispers in my ear. "If you are a queen, why aren't you wearing a dress or a crown?"

I also cup my mouth with my hands and whisper right back into her ear. "Because not all queens wear dresses, and not all queens have crowns. Some queens need to wear pants, others skirts. There isn't one specific thing to wear for a girl to be powerful, you know," I inform her.

Her brows furrow in confusion before she says to the group, "But Bunky Mason says girls aren't pretty unless they dress up. So, we aren't pretty because we don't have dresses." She pouts, and the entire thing almost makes me chuckle, but I don't because I realize that would be very inconsiderate.

"Bunky Mason sounds like he needs to learn a lesson from his queen, then. Because as I look around at all of you, you are all gorgeous and powerful without a crown or a gown."

A tiny girl with bright red hair and freckles all over her nose squeaks. Another girl whispers in her friend's ear, "The queen just called us pretty."

Then I tell them what I wish I had said to my younger self: "It doesn't matter what you wear...the only thing that truly makes you pretty is your heart. You could look any way, but have a heart of gold and you'll be the most gorgeous girl out there." They all look around in awe. "All you need to know is that you stick together, you love one another, and you always look out for each other. Clothes have nothing to do with what makes you pretty or not. You don't have to look a certain way to please others. Your person will love you for you." The tiny girl sitting right next to me hugs my legs tightly. They all look to me, and I have an urge to tell them one more thing I wish I had known. "But no matter what your looks are, you will all be powerful. Don't ever allow a boy to tell you your looks define you. As I stand here watching you all, I can already tell you are going to be the most powerful girls in the kingdom." They all giggle and whisper to one another.

A hand lands on my shoulder, and I look into the brightest blue eyes I could have ever seen. "Are you ready, My Queen?" The girls all whisper and squeal about how handsome Sailor is, and he definitely is. I grab onto his hand on my shoulder.

"Of course. Did you talk to everybody you wanted to talk to?" I ask before saying goodbye to the girls. "I will come back, I promise. And even though you don't need them, I will bring dresses when I come." They all run to their headmistress and scream, telling her all about their time with me.

When Sailor and I leave the orphanage, I feel a pang of sadness at leaving them. "I enjoyed it there." His thick blond brows arch. "I just mean, the kids are great," I amend.

"Yeah, they are. They deserve loving homes," he agrees. I grab onto his hand, inter-twining our fingers.

"They will get one someday. They will all have loving families," I say cheerfully.

He shakes his head. "How do you do that?" he asks in disbelief.

"Do what exactly?" I narrow my eyes at him.

"Be positive all the damn time. I mean, I love it about you, but I just wish I could do the same." The candlelight from the sky is bright enough it lights up the stone pathway.

"If I let everything that has happened in my life bring me down, I would never get back up, Sailor. I have to think positively in a world where Gods think we are nothing. Our lives are expendable to them. If I stayed down every time I got hurt, then I think I would die."

He kisses my nose before pressing a softer kiss to the corner of my mouth. "That is one of the many reasons why I love you, Serena." His words are whispered against my lips.

"I love *you*, Sailor James."

He smiles at my admission, and my blood warms from whatever bond we have forged.

We spend the rest of the evening strolling through the village. It's such a nice place, I could see myself living here forever. Everybody here is so kind and considerate. I am shocked that what happened to Wolf's parents even happened at all. I can't even picture anything bad ever happening here.

Sailor walks me to my room. "I think Alwin is still in a meeting with the commanders here. Would you like to come in?" I offer, knowing where this is going to lead.

"I would love nothing more than that, Honeybee. I have missed you."

I bite my lip. "We have been together nonstop for weeks," I tease, and he gives me a knowing smirk.

"Not *that* kind of missed." He pushes me against the door, his knee going between my thighs. "I am ready to give you all of me...my blood, my soul, my heart. Take it all, Serena, because I may not be your mate, but you are as good as mine.

I kiss him with a passion I have long felt but have held myself back from. "Gladly," I answer before leading him into my room.

Chapter 45

"Girl. I don't know about this," Mabel says when we sneak out from the inn.

"Why not? Don't you want to explore more of Groke?" I question. Alwin didn't come home last night, but he sent Roman with a note. Sailor was still in my bed when I read it for the first time.

Wife,

I am deeply sorry for this, but matters that need attending to have come up. I will come back as soon as I possibly can. Stay with your pet and do not get into trouble. Or do… You know I like punishing you when you disobey me…

AAH

I read the note several more times before finally standing up and facing my friend. The morning sun shines brightly. "What did your honey say?" she taunts me.

I smile slightly before correcting her. "He is not *my honey*." I climb out the window and down the hay rooftop that I am unsure will hold Mabel, too, jumping before I can test that theory. The morning sun burns hot and bright, and I want to explore. I saw a flower shop that had books in it down the street. The perfect combination for me. I don't like flowers, but Sailor does, so I can grab myself some books and him some flowers. He prefers wildflowers to carefully curated and mass-produced bouquets that you can find anywhere. He says that he likes them all to be different, unique.

Mabel thumps right next to me. I think I hear her knees crack against the stone. "You good, Granny?" I tease her.

"I am younger than you are, thank you very much." She looks around as if searching for somebody to find us. I roll my eyes while motioning for her to follow me.

"Come on. They aren't going to figure it out."

She seems to be skeptical, but then she agrees. We walk to the seaside cobblestone pathway, where I know I saw the shop.

Not seeing the florist yet, I decide to stop in a sweet bakery. Some bells ring when we enter, and the smell of sweet morning treats wafts right into my nose. I order a bunch of different foods before sitting beside Mabel at a petite circular table outside.

"So where are your boyfriends?" Mabel chews on a blueberry tart. The blueberry jam inside it is so bright blue that it looks dyed.

I almost choke on my double-chip chocolate muffin. "Boyfriends?" I sip on some hot chocolate, then wipe at my mouth.

She doesn't stop eating and repeats the question, just in a different way. "Yes, Majesty. I thought *I* was a player. You have milked the cow, cooked the cake, and are enjoying *all* the benefits of that milk."

"Excuse me?" My face crunches in confusion.

"You got yourself a whole husband, or mate…whatever you wanna call him. You got a boyfriend, and then another sidepiece." She slams her hand on the small table. I hold my hand up, stopping her there.

"I don't have a *sidepiece*," I correct her immediately. I don't want any rumors to get started.

"What do you call Wolf then?" She tries to grab my next muffin—cinnamon banana—but I swat her hand away.

"No way. Don't touch my food," I say gruffly. She gives me a look that says, *Do you really need another?* She doesn't voice any of those words, though. "You are more protective of your food than your men," she says with a stern face. I swallow another bite of my muffin before grabbing my burrito.

"I haven't felt good traveling; I need the food!" I defend myself. I have lost weight since leaving the palace. I didn't eat much on the journey between villages. The rocking carriages and no powers to heal myself weren't good for me. It turns out I have motion sickness, because my body thoroughly disagreed with eating on the road.

"Right." She doesn't seem to believe me, but that's alright.

"Wolf isn't my sidepiece," I tell Mabel as we clean up the table outside the bakery.

"If that's what you say." Her voice is high-pitched, and I don't believe her words one bit.

"I do say. I think I would know if he was coming into my bed." We both tell the bakery owner our thanks, then head off.

"Again, where are all your men?" she asks again.

I look out at the sea; the waves are so large today that the white caps are mesmerizing.

"Earth to Queen Serena Henry." Mabel waves a hand in front of my face, and I again swat her hand away from me. I almost punch her.

"What?" My face whips towards her, and my tone is harsh.

"What?" she repeats to me as if she is confused.

"My last name is not Henry," I deadpan.

She looks at me, super confused. "But you are married to King Alwin *Henry*," she says softly, as if knowing now is not the time to question me. We are very much miscommunicating here, so I need to set her straight once and for all.

"Yes, I am. I am married to Alwin. Sailor is complicated and not a topic I would like to talk about. But Wolf, on the other hand, is nothing more than...I don't know. He is complicated, too, okay?" My thoughts are all blurred. Mabel has thrown me for a loop. "Wolf I would like to still call my friend, but he betrayed me and Sailor. I just don't know how to feel about him," I say, out of breath.

"Do you know where they all are? Are we going to get caught and punished?"

"No. Alwin had some business to attend to, Sailor is with Barnett and Roman working outside of the village for the entire day, and Wolf is bringing Ram to us. I don't know when he'll get here." Just judging by the short communication I have received from Sailor about Ram and Wolf, they are getting on well together. Ram is very outgoing, and Wolf says he is growing on him. Wolf isn't easy to please, so the fact that he likes the little boy says a lot.

"I think that kid will be good for all the commanders," Mabel says, which is what I was just thinking.

"I think so, too, maybe even for our king," I say with a cheesy grin as Mabel shows me a blanket made in patches of different fabric at a nearby stall.

"I think I might buy this for a girl I met in the palace." She holds it up as if sizing it for her body.

"It's pretty. I didn't think you were dating anybody, though," I say with confusion laced in my tone.

If Mabel's face weren't already red from the midmorning sun, it would be red from talking about this new mystery woman. "I am not *dating* her; she is just somebody I would *like* to be dating," she says shyly. I nod while she gushes over some new girl.

"And you say *I* move fast. Do they even know you are a...woman?" Mabel has pretended to be a man to get into the commander's camp, then continued for a year after.

"I think people who want to know, know, but I haven't ever come out. If they haven't noticed, that's on them." She shrugs, and I gape at her, then decided that I agree with her.

"I guess that's one way to look at it." I hand the kind woman coins for Maymay's blanket, a pen, and a ring I liked.

I never gave Alwin a wedding ring, so when I see one in the case that reminds me of him, I grab it. He gave himself a ring to wear after our wedding, but I don't think it fits him as much as this one does. I also feel as though that ceremony shouldn't count for our mating celebration. The onyx ring glimmers in the light. I quickly tuck it into my pocket before skipping to Mabel's side.

"People accept what they want to, Serena. You won't make everybody happy, and that is okay. You aren't supposed to. You do what you can, and that's enough for your kingdom, because I can promise you something..." She stops on the stone path, clutching the blanket to her chest. "You are way too good to let the opinions of people who will never be happy affect you. I have never met somebody as kind and compassionate as you are. You truly care about each and every person in our kingdom, and we are lucky to have you."

I hug her tightly. For the first time in a long time I feel as though my life is complete. I have found my people. My relationships aren't perfect, but they are *us*. It is whatever I, Alwin, and Sailor want it to be. For now, that is good with me.

"And yes, she knows I am a girl." Mabel smirks at me.

"Oh?" I question.

"I wasn't ready to settle down, but now I am. I want to be free, I want to be myself…like you. I want to forget what people might think about me and just be happy."

A woman walks up to me. "Hi. I would like to offer my new queen some herbal tea." She has two cups in her hands; the mugs have a pretty glaze with flowers and vines on them.

"Oh, thank you. What do I owe you?"

The woman gives us the steaming green tea. I can see the shop with the books and flowers, so I want to hurry before they close for the day. I reach into my pocket, but right as I do, Mabel shakes her head. "I've got it." She hands the woman the coins, and we take the steaming mugs of tea to go. I watch the woman walk ahead, then sit down on the pathway several yards in front of us. There is a lemon tang to the tea when it hits my tongue. "Weird flavor," Mabel says as we pass the last alleyway before the stand with the flowers for Sailor.

I take several more sips of the tea until the mug is empty. I bend down and place it on the ground next to the lady who gave it to us. She gives me a weird look, and I almost wonder if I was supposed to keep the mug, but when Mabel places hers down next to the woman, I figure she just isn't the social type.

"Are you alright?" Alwin's voice startles me, even though one might think I should be used to the intrusion by now, I wasn't expecting it.

"Yes, I am fine. Mind your business and stay out of my head, creeper," I say playfully, hoping he can tell I am teasing him. Alwin's darkness shimmers against my mental shield, which I have started leaving down more often.

"I will see you tonight, wife. I am eager to hear about your day."

Mabel looks right over my shoulder as I listen to Alwin's last words. The fear in her eyes shines so brightly that when I look behind me, I am not surprised to see coffee-colored eyes staring at me. The burly man, whom I had wished I would never see again, blows powder in my face, while another equally large man blows some in Mabel's. The last thing I hear is the woman who gave us the lemon tea telling them, "I just gave it to them. You might wait a few hours to take them to the cabin." Her monotone voice irritates me, because I now know I have trusted far too easily.

Cabin...

My mind swirls with confusion as the man lifts me over his large shoulder. The blade is digging into my stomach so hard I feel as though I might vomit. I am grateful to be wearing pants so that my butt isn't being shown to everybody.

"Where are we going?" I ask groggily, knowing my voice is slurred. "Mabel?" I call out. Though, when I see her, she is out cold; her body is slumped over the other man's shoulder.

"She is fae trash, her blood is stronger. Give her more." The man holding Mabel growls. He sounds more uneducated than I am; the way he speaks reminds me of a toddler. I giggle manically for a moment before Haadgar rams some dust into my nostrils. The last thing I do is grab onto the ring in my pocket and squeeze it.

Chapter 46

King Alwin Henry

When the connection goes dark, I almost kill my sister. "Shut up," I hiss at her. My connection with Serena is gone...*completely gone.*

"W-what?" My sister says in disbelief, her face contorting in disgust at being told what to do.

"I said *SHUT UP!*" I roar in her face, spit blowing from my mouth. She has the good sense to hear the threat in my voice.

"*Serena?*" I chant her name over and over again. No response.

"What are you going on about? Mother and Father don't want you coming home unless you are going to do what needs to be—"

I shut her up by removing all the oxygen from her lungs first, then my hand closes around her tiny throat. "I left you here to manage things while I grow closer to my mate," I snarl in her face. "I couldn't give a fuck if we never go back home or not. If you believe I could give a damn about that Blessed war, you have another thing coming. I am *king* here." My laugh is dark and detached. "I don't need to leave to have power. I have everything I could ever want right here." My sister stares blankly at me.

"You don't want to go home?" she asks in confusion.

I shake my head in disbelief. "I must go; I will be back in no more than a week's time. Halt whatever madness you are trying to do and just fucking do what I tell you to do.

Understood?" My sister's purple eyes flash with hurt for a moment before she schools herself.

"I understand what you are saying." There is a threat lacing her tone. I just don't have the time to figure it out. I couldn't give a flying fuck about her feelings; I just want her to control her sick impulses. I find myself having to clean up her messes all too often recently. It gives our family a bad name when, in reality, our family wants peace.

"Great." I blink away to the very last location I felt Serena.

"What the *fuck*?!" My voice cracks from the brute strength of my scream. All heads in the small room turn to me, and some men drop their glasses. "Where am I?" I ask the room. Only one answers me.

"You are at Toad's Tavern," he slurs out.

"Which is where?" I growl through my teeth.

"Oh, uh...on the border of Snolly and Mickle." The tavern is a shithole at best.

"Has anybody seen your queen?" Every set of eyes is staring me down. I smell shit somebody leaks out of their ass. "Anybody?" Black mist swirls around me. I cannot control it when my anger gets to the height it is at. I pull some dark coercion out—even though my mother says it is wrong—and turn it on the entire tavern. They all shake their heads in unison. Fury builds up in me to such a level I can't stand to look at the useless fucks a moment longer. I make my way out of this shit box and into the frigid air.

I then go to my last resort, my anger trailing behind me in a way that burns throughout the forest. "Where is my mate?" I scan the trees as my body zips throughout the sky in a dark mist.

Sailor James

When Alwin shows up before dusk, without Serena, I know something is terribly wrong. Barnett, Roman, and I have been working on making the shelter for Groke. It will be a place where the folks can all come for free food and potions that they would normally have to pay coin for at the chemist. We spent the entire day setting all of this up, and I had left Serena with Mabel to hang out at the inn. I left her with strict instructions that the front desk would notify me if they were to leave. I hadn't really done that, but it was a nice threat. Or so I thought.

"Where is she?" His black mist is still fogging his body when he rushes towards me, grabbing onto my shirt.

"Who?" I question, even though I know exactly who we are speaking of. His black eyes show none of the creepy white or silver swirls they sometimes sport.

"You know who!" he roars in my face. Anybody else might have shit themselves, but I am not scared of him. I know exactly who he is. His eyes are red-rimmed, and I half wonder if he is on potions.

"Serena?" I ask lazily before Barnett tries to intervene.

"Majesty. We have been here all day. Working on the project we discussed." Barnett has grown some balls in the last few months. Roman says nothing and twiddles his fucking thumbs like he is some teenage girl.

"Who else would I be asking you about?" Alwin draws my attention back to him.

"Listen, I know we are somewhat sharing her right now, but I don't want to talk to you about her whereabouts. Also, I don't know. As Barnett just said, we have been here all day." I get the feeling he is fucking with me.

"She will never be yours." Then I see it, the utter rage in his black soulless eyes.

"Why do you look like you want to kill everybody?" My mouth parts slightly. Worry starts to swell in my chest when I watch him struggle to say the next words.

"Our connection...I can't speak to her." His eyes finally go down to the ground. "I figured you gave her a potion to keep me from her mental shields." Shame licks his words, and so many questions flare in my mind.

"Can that even happen?" I narrow my eyes, studying him for a long moment. He is the strongest male I know, and his face looks like it is two seconds away from falling apart.

"There is a drug that can separate our minds. Although the bond is still forever in place, I may not be able to get through to her." His grip on me lessens slightly. "If anything happens to her, it could still affect me—our bond is already strong enough—but I cannot feel her anymore." His eyes don't meet mine, and it's uncomfortable the way we both don't acknowledge we are *with* her. "So, if you didn't do it, then that means somebody else did," he says, fury coating his words.

The sudden realization that Serena is in danger causes me to start sprinting. "Where are you going?" Barnett's voice squeals like a fucking baby.

"To her inn to look for something," I scream back to him.

Alwin is one step ahead of me. He leaves in his creepy-as-fuck black mist, zooming on through me like I am in his way. The mist causes my body to prickle with unease; the darkness within him is so cold I have to heat my body back up after he departs. Barnett and Roman are both on my heels. We don't even tell the Groke commanders we're leaving. I am not wasting a single second if she is in danger.

Chapter 47

When my eyes open, the first thing I see is Mabel tied up next to me, a sock in her mouth, a black eye, and still passed out. My eyes scan the dirty room we sit in, and the darkness is the first thing I notice. It is completely and utterly black outside the window, which means several hours have passed. Sailor or Alwin will come looking for me.

My hands are tied behind my back. I try to pull them free, but without my powers, I can't. I am not strong enough to break the rope. I try to see out the window, even though I know, with night in full bloom, I won't be able to see anything. But I still have to *try*. I need to figure out where we are, and I must do it before they come back. I listen for footsteps, and when I don't hear anything, I try to scoot away from Mabel and look. I only make it a few inches before her body thuds to the ground. I wince, hoping the men are not here, and if they are, that they didn't hear that.

I scoot across the wooden floor that catches on my pants. It pulls at the thin fabric on my legs, and small pieces of wood embed into my skin. It doesn't even faze me, and I just keep going. Right as I make it near a chair, I hear hoofbeats outside. As fast as I can, I scurry across the room, away from the window, wishing I would've had more time. My ankles are tied tightly enough that they are being ripped apart by the magical rope.

I have come to the conclusion that somebody knows more magic than a normal human should. This is fae magic. I had been reading all about how the fae have their own ways of making objects magical. Even without a potion, they all have basic magic, apart from their powers the Blessed gave them at birth.

I hear three people out there, but only two step through the door. I have just made it back to Mabel, still passed out on the floor, when the coffee-colored eyes look at me. They are completely natural; nothing about them is abnormal, so I can't believe *he* is Fae. Really, neither of them look fae. Maybe the third male outside is.

"I see you've woken up. Your dirty blood burns through that shit like it's water," Haadgar says cruelly. I don't know what he is talking about, but I do know that whenever I try to find Alwin in my mind, it's completely silent and dark. I can't even *feel* the bond in my mind, and the coldness chills me to the bone. Panic starts to build up, and I almost hyperventilate. I breathe in through my nose and out through my mouth. I calm myself down while I watch the two men walk around the dirty, beaten-up lounge. Haadgar plops himself down as if he has nowhere better to be. He glares into my eyes for a long moment before the other man draws his attention in the other room.

"Want one?" The man's accent sounds unlike any other voice I have heard.

"Yes." This beast of a man never allows his eyes to stray from mine. "You know what I find strange, Wren?" Haadgar calls to the other man. I stare right back at him.

"What Gar?" His nickname for him makes sense; this man is a slippery beast of a person. He is nothing but a monster that should be locked in Brabble.

"This girl claims none of the boys in her village ever touched under her skirts. Do you believe that?" He smirks at me as he says the words. My blood turns to ice. I have no idea what their plan is, but I do not feel good about this. Haadgar stands and slowly walks up to me. When his thick, chubby fingers graze my jawline, I shake my head furiously. This only makes him chuckle at my expense. "No matter what your blood is, your body sure is nice to look at. If only you didn't wear these Gods-awful combat pants, so I could play with our little king's pet."

"Here, sir." The other man looks at me in disgust; thankfully, the feeling is mutual. For now, Haadgar stands and takes his hands off my body. "I don't think I would ever believe that whore was a virgin. I hear the king shares her with his favorite commanders. Would you call yourself a favorite, sir?" the man called Wren says. Haadgar sips on the amber liquid until his eyes roam over my body in a way that I know far too well. He is sizing me up. His gaze leaves a burning trail on my skin, and not in a good way.

"I think I am his *very* favorite. And I am due some Gods *damn* respect, Wren."

I growl at him, which just causes him to laugh. I want to scream, I want to demand reason as to why he hates me so much, I want to *fight*. I can't. I don't have my power; I don't have my voice. I am completely stripped clean of any and all defenses I might have had. I am completely powerless over these men in front of me. I will not give them the show they are asking for, though. I will not allow them to best me.

"I think we should test it out. Don't you?"

My heart slows almost completely to nothing. I watch with concern, not knowing if he would truly rape me. When the man named Wren looks at Haadgar, I know my fate before Haadgar grabs onto my ankles and drags me into the room with the dirtiest bed I have ever seen. I try to grip onto the doorframe, then remember my hands are useless behind my back, tied with a rope that had to have been made by the Gods. It is impenetrable. My body is tossed onto a mattress that is no better than solid ground, but my soul and mind are elsewhere.

Chapter 48

When we made it to the inn, the keeper said she didn't have any memory of the girls leaving. That got her killed. Alwin has never been this angry before. I know that because there is a trail of bodies in his wake. I have sent Barnett and Roman to look through the woods.

"Where is she?" Alwin throws a chair, and it shatters against the wall of the shop outside. His temper continues to spike; this is the last thing we need to happen. I don't do well with temper tantrums. I grab onto his shoulders, hoping he respects Serena enough not to kill me outright for touching him.

"Listen. We will not find her if you kill everybody in Groke." The fury in his eyes subsides for a moment before I notice his nostrils flare.

"I smell her," he claims, as his nose flares several more times.

He blinks out of my grip before appearing in front of a homeless lady not too far away from me. She looks to be about thirty-three, but before I can ask her anything, Alwin is gripping her throat tight enough to pop her damn head off. I rush over to him.

"If you kill her, she won't tell us where Serena is," I grind out, trying to get his strong fingers off this woman.

"Tell me what you did." He presses his nose into her hands and inhales.

Alwin has a temper... Aldrich was funny and calm and collected. "Bring in Aldrich. Come on. If you care for her at all, you need to calm down and think about this logically."

I am trying to reason with a demon. His eyes flash with hurt. I know the look because I have felt that same hurt before—when I watched the love of my life marry my enemy. My heart shattered into so many pieces that day, and I wasn't sure if I could ever glue them back together again. But that was what her brother taught me: I didn't need to glue the pieces together, I needed to grow a new one. And that is what I spent two months doing. I learned things from the fae. I learned to have an open heart for the one I love. I have learned many things in my time of growing. The number one thing I learned, though: a male with a broken heart is a distraction. One we cannot afford right now.

Suddenly, the king we all know and hate shifts into Aldrich. The funny, curious, and sometimes creepy cousin to the king. The black hair is replaced with brownish-auburn. The king's chiseled, tanned face is now a freckled pale face.

"There you go," I coo, like a parent might. I look at the frightened lady now clutching onto her throat. There are bright red fingerprints on it; they will bruise, but she'll live for now.

"Have you seen the queen?" I take a small step towards her, holding my hands out to show her I mean no harm. I step in front of a steaming Aldrich, putting myself between them.

"I-I was compelled to give the queen and her commander a tea." She shakes her head while pulling on her hair. "They took them. I don't know where they went, but I know it was more than just those two men involved. I saw them talking to somebody else. They told me I could remember because whenever you came to ask, I was to tell you something." I can feel Aldrich losing it. I know he won't stay Aldrich for very long. I don't blame him, really. I want to burn the world down to get to her, but not if it she goes down with it.

"Calm." I try to soothe him before I ask the woman what she was supposed to tell us.

When the words fall from her mouth, I want to kill her myself. She smiles cruelly, her nasty teeth showing hues of yellow and brown. "It's your fault, both of you. You took her powers from her and made it easy for us to steal her and keep her. She cannot fight back, and we will get what we need from her. Thank you for that." The way she speaks is methodical. I know it's part of the compulsion, but still, it doesn't help her case. "And you." Her head tilts to me, and I listen to the words I know will sting. "You made her weak. You showed her love instead of pushing her to be the hardest form of herself she could be. So, we will do that for you." Her deep, unnatural voice sends chills down my spine. I want to leave to search for Serena, but I know we must listen to her last words.

"We won't give her to you until she is totally and completely drained. You will not receive the same female you once knew. We will return her, though…just fractured."

Right as her words end, Alwin's black smoke kills the helpless woman. I should have seen it coming. My patience is wearing thin with him. I need to get a handle on myself if I am going to be able to find Serena. Right as I question if I should just kill him myself, Wolf rides up on a horse with the kid riding next to him, a huge shit-eating grin on his face.

The poor kid doesn't see it in my face, but when the man I have called brother for my entire life hops off his horse, he sees it. Wolf's strides are confident, and I am not surprised when my knees give out in his arms.

"What is going on?" His words are so simple, and yet it breaks the floodgates in my mind. My entire composure shatters, my world is flooding, and I just need my Serena to be here. So, I will take the next best thing. My ex-brother.

"She's gone. She's been taken." My broken words are hushed.

Wolf's body is as hard as a rock. The stiffness in him tells me he knows who I am talking about. "How?" Panic fills his tone.

"They fucking *took* her," Alwin roars, then starts blinking in and out between the king and his cousin, or whatever that thing is.

"He is falling apart. There is a body trail. We need to do something with him," I holler down the connection I know to be his. Wolf starts to do what he does best—he stands up and begins to lead. Leaving my body on the ground to fall apart as he is taking control.

"Alright. Let's not be rash." He points to Alwin/Aldrich. "The last place she was is here. Can you scent her?" Wolf takes on the assertive role all too easily.

"No. They have given her something. I cannot even speak to her. She is gone!" Alwin screams.

The kid, Ram, is smart enough to watch from his horse. I crawl my way to stand next to Wolf. "What is the plan?" I ask him, not for the first time in our lives.

"We find her. Alive." His voice gives me the confidence I need to nod my head and trust him for the first time in a long time.

Chapter 49

I watch Haadgar and Wren eat their second lunch. It has been two and a half days of beatings and things I would rather not think about. Mabel's face is a pattern of bruises and cuts. Her only reprieve is that they still believe her to be a boy. My stomach grumbles so loudly that it gains me the attention of the men. Luckily for me, I spent my younger years hurting myself so I could patch myself up. I may not be patching myself up now, but I am no stranger to pain. I haven't shed one tear for them. Mabel can't say the same. She hasn't been through years of torturing herself to prepare for this type of moment. I can't blame her; most seven-year-olds don't need to know how to fix a broken arm without healing it.

"Hey, *trash*." That is their kind nickname for me. Haadgar takes the sock from my mouth for the first time since...*the room*. My eyes dart to where Mabel sits slumped against the fireplace. It's the only thing that is pretty in this shithole. The red brick has been my only focus since we have been here. I stare at it for hours on end, making plans and schemes to get Mabel out of here.

I lick my lips, hoping to wet them enough that they don't continue to crack. "Ready to kill me?" My voice comes out broken and thin; I hate it. I don't want him to think he has anything on me.

"Ready to use you for my pleasure, maybe." His voice is grainy and hoarse. I almost throw up. When I start to gag, he grabs my face and forces me to look in his ugly eyes.

"You're lucky *I* use you. Wren isn't as kind." His coffee eyes dart to where my friend lies limp. Mabel groans, and I wince. I try to divert attention from the female sound that just came from her mouth, but it's far too late for that. "Ah. I had thought this one was too small to be a *real* man." Haadgar motions for Wren to come over, and he stands to his full height, a large butcher knife in his hand.

"No. No, no, no, no. Take me," I beg Wren, but he drags Mabel away. She fights and screams against her bindings. Her tiny body thrashes as he tries to steal the last pieces of her.

I scream, pulling against the rope that has long since cut deep into my flesh.

"Shut up." Haadgar slaps me so hard that blood starts to pour out of my nose. My lip splits open again. "Shut the fuck up!" he roars in my face. I listen to her scream; I can hear them through the walls and the sock that is in her mouth.

Haadgar watches me with amusement glinting in his eyes. "Oh, I see now." He crouches in front of me. The smell of alcohol wafts off him; it could make me vomit. "You hurt more from your friend being harmed than you do yourself. That's why you haven't cried. You don't care about yourself." His eyes are wide as he says the words. My brows raise in challenge.

"You want my tears? My sorrow?" I ask sternly. He chews on something in his mouth; I didn't see him put anything in there. I know it is such a weird thing to focus on, but it's the only thing. The bricks are starting to blur together as I focus on him, but when Haadgar calls to Wren to bring Mabel back in, I find that the bricks are the best thing to watch.

"Stop!" I cry out. I watch the man drag her small, naked body back in. "Stop it!" I scream. "You do not deserve to just take what you want, you worthless fucking pig!" I scream so loudly my voice cracks.

"There is some of that emotion I wanted!" Haadgar claps his hands manically. "You are a vile, selfish fae, and from where I am standing, you are the only worthless one I see." He sneers at me. I don't respond because I know anything I say will be taken out on Mabel. When Wren starts his own sick games with her, I don't shed a tear. I will not give him what he wants; I will remain strong.

"What about now, Serena Bloodworthy?" Wren grabs her hand and, without warning, chops her finger right off. Blood sprays, she screams, and I scream through my teeth.

"What do you want?" I hiss, and his face crunches in disgust.

"For the fae to never walk into our kingdom again." Hatred laces his words, and for the life of me, I cannot figure out why he can't stand me. They take turns with her, my friend, torturing her in ways I have never seen before.

I made it through trials that were designed to kill me. Even if I live through this, I will not be myself. After a while, I zone out of the pain and suffering, and I can't hear her screams any longer. I can't hear my screams either, because I no longer have a voice. Finally, blissful darkness overtakes me when I get hit hard enough to black out.

I am grateful for the moments of rest. I have no idea what happens to my body while I am sleeping, but without being knocked out, I wouldn't have slept. I stay asleep for another day before my swollen eyes open to wailing sobs.

I notice Mabel no longer has her gag in. "Mabel." My voice cracks. My throat is dry and sore from screaming. Her face is streaked with tears and blood. The cracked blood is all over her; when her eyes meet mine, they look like they have accepted death. I shake my head, "No," I say sternly as I watch another tear fall from her eyes. "No. Listen to me. You will make it out of here. Do you hear me?" I sound harsh, I don't mean to, but I also need to make sure she knows she has a reason to live.

"I don't know if I want to, Serena." Her usually happy self is gone, replaced with a version of her I don't know.

"What about the girl you want to go home to?" I remind her, hoping to give her something to fight for.

"They ruined that for me. I am ruined." She sounds hollow inside.

"You are not ruined, Mabel. *They* are," I hiss, trying to point to the door, but my hands are still tied. I fight and fight against the rope.

"Stop, you're going to attract them back in here," she says between sobs. I groan before hitting my head against the brick. The pain doesn't even faze me. I know how bad I look, but Mabel looks worse. She is missing whole fingers, like Sailor had at one point. "I will get back everything they took from you. *I promise*," I swear, trying to fill her with hope. She doesn't look like she believes me. "Hey. Let's play a game." I try to entice her; but she doesn't take the bait. "Close your eyes. I'll watch." She scoffs; I don't blame her. I can't protect her here.

"Serena, no matter what you do, they will still hurt us. They will still beat us. They are going to kill us; you don't have power, and I have *failed* you. I am so sorry, Serena." Tears stream down her face. "I wasn't strong enough to save you." She gulps, and her throat bobs.

"That isn't true, Mabel. We will make it out. We must be strong. Can you be strong for me?" My words crack, my voice barely audible. Instead of answering me, she shuts her eyes.

Her declaration echoes throughout my mind. She finally passes out, which I am glad for. I sit there until the sun comes up, thinking of ways to escape. The men don't come out of the room, but another man walks in. I pretend to be asleep while he wanders around. His boots squeak when he walks. The man makes eggs, and my stomach churns with a need so powerful I feel like my insides are burning. I am starving to death; if they don't beat me to death first, I will die from not eating. The man has a knife on his waistband that seems to glow a white color. It hisses and has swirls on it.

Suddenly, I think back to the book Alwin gave me, and realize I have seen that knife before. If I am right, and I can find a way to catch this man off guard, I could steal it with enough time to cut our ropes off and get away. I just need to get up. I decide I'm going to spend the day scheming. I let Mabel sleep until the door closes, and the man leaving finally jolts her awake.

"What?" she startles, and I shush her.

"It's okay. He is leaving, not coming in. It's okay." I try to give her comfort, and when she sees I am telling the truth, she relaxes some.

"Okay," she whispers to me, nodding her head. Her voice is barely audible due to the screams we have both yelled.

"I think I have a plan." I inform her of what I think the knife is and what it can do. "I don't know how they got these ropes, but if I am correct, the only thing that will cut through these Blessed things is that knife he is carrying. That's probably why he stays outside." She finally perks up some before hell starts over again.

Chapter 50

Queen Serena Bloodworthy-Henry

"Now that we have established you two are worthless in our eyes, I would like to try something." Haadgar sneers at us.

"We have not established anything of the sort, actually. I think it is the opposite." I scowl at him, knowing it won't get me any points, but I can't help it. His dark laugh prickles my skin. I go still when he brings from behind his back a long metal poker. Mabel starts scooting back, as if she can get away from this next torture. I position myself in front of her.

"You know, I have heard you fae are protective. I just didn't think you were stupid." He spits at me, and I grimace. "Oh, you think I am gross?" He grabs the back of my hair and yanks me from my seat. Mabel jams her eyes shut right as Wren comes up behind her, and I wish I hadn't seen her flinch when his hand grabs onto her face and forces her eyes on me.

"Eyes open. Or else I will cut them out of your skull," he threatens her. Her eyes stay open as Haadgar rips my pants from my body. We're no longer taking my pants and the ropes off, putting them back on, apparently. When Haadgar puts the poker in the fireplace and I watch it turn from black to white, I know what he plans to do.

Mabel starts to curse, and Wren yanks the small amount of hair she has, screaming something at her. I can't hear because right as I am about to try and focus on his words,

Haadgar presses the poker to my upper thigh. I don't scream; I bite down so hard on my lip I taste the metallic tang on my tongue. I know I have bitten through my lip.

"Scream, girl." The way he calls me girl causes me to snap.

"I am your fucking *QUEEN*, and I am no *girl*!" I roar while spitting blood in his face. He backhands me before putting the poker back into the fire. I squirm, trying to get away from him. Wren comes over to hold me down. "I am no girl either," I snap. "I am a Queen."

"I know. That is what I am testing right now." Haadgar presses the poker on the opposite thigh; my body convulses with pain. Sweat beads on my brow, and I can't take much more before I am good and truly broken. I need to be strong for Mabel. I need to get her out of here. That is the only thing causing me to continue to stay, because I think I could easily entice this man to kill me. No healing power? The pain could end. My body wouldn't fight back any longer. At one point in my life, that was all I had wanted. The end. Swift and smooth. Not like this, though, not leaving her behind.

"I have only met five fae in my life," Haadgar says with a menacing scowl.

I should look away when he places the hot poker on my flesh, but I can't. I watch as it boils my skin, the flesh burning and assaulting my nostrils. I close my eyes and picture something else. One thing I have learned in my years of pain is that pain isn't always the worst thing in the world; sometimes it's the *lack* of pain. It is the numbness that overwhelms your body and forces you to stay in bed for days on end. It is the complete and utter helplessness in a world where I am supposed to be an apex predator.

"Would you like to know what I have learned?" he taunts, but before I can answer, Mabel whines and draws Wren's attention.

"Shut your trap, girl, or else you'll lose whatever small value you have." The way Wren speaks to her causes my body to jolt. I try to kick with my legs tied together, attempting to harm him in any way for the things he has done to my friend.

I barely miss his face by the tips of my toes. My feet are wounded but in decent condition. "Ah, ah, ah," Haadgar tsks at me. He slams my legs down, and before I can fight, Wren is speaking.

"Show her a lesson she won't forget." Wren shoves an apple in my mouth so that I can't scream past it, but when the poker goes between my thighs and inside of me, I scream. Spit spills from my mouth on either side of the apple. My hands and arms strain from being held behind my back. Fury builds up inside of me. He is burning me in ways I cannot repair.

After an hour of being burned and tortured, Haadgar has Wren take Mabel to the other room. For what, I try not to think about.

"So, anyway," Haadgar starts. I lay on my side, shaking violently, my arms hurting from the weight of my body being on them for so long. "The reason you are so special is because normal fae wouldn't heal themselves after all of this. They wouldn't survive this. Trust me, I would know. It is my understanding, little girl, that you've got yourself in a jam by being something special." He slowly runs his fingers up my thigh, the very flesh I haven't been able to look at yet. I stay deathly still, hoping this man will just stop. He doesn't. My prayers are unanswered, yet again.

"And yet, even without your healer powers, you *are* healing. Yes...slowly. Maybe not even perfectly, but your cuts are closing faster than a human's should, and faster than most fae would be able to accomplish with no power. Most powerful humans, and even strong fae would die from what I have done to you. That is why I had to test you. See how truly powerful you are." He shrugs as if that is it. Then he leans down, cuts into my arm, and licks my blood clean off my skin. When he looks at me, he smiles; his teeth are red from my blood, his pupils completely dilated. "You aren't just a *normal* fae. Yeah, you're royal, but you're *more*...and you are mine," he sneers.

I don't think too hard about what he's saying, only that his eyes gloss over as if he is high. Then he passes out on the couch. The thumping in the other room continues for a long while, until that, too, stops.

Chapter 51

<u>King Alwin Henry</u>

My mate's boyfriend threatened to kill me five times yesterday. One of the times, I wish he had. My body is sweating; my stomach is burning with a hunger I know I don't have. How could I be hungry while she is out there being tortured?

"What are we supposed to do with him?" the one with the black hair hisses at the blond one Serena likes so much. I can't even think of their names right now. My body aches so badly I want to die. The pain I know she is going through is blinding, even for me. I know what she's feeling because I'm experiencing it, too. When I get my hands on those motherfuckers, they are *dead*. I will kill them, bring them back, and then kill them *again* and again until my bloodlust is sated.

My body pulses as new welts form on my arms and legs. The searing pain engulfs me like the waves I watch. I know I am lying on the ground because the hard surface is the only thing I know for sure that my *own* body is feeling. Aching, throbbing pain pierces my skull, as if I am being bashed across the head over and over again. The wounds come and go as quickly as my body heals them.

"What does this mean?" Sailor asks the other one.

"It means that whatever is happening to her is bad, and we need to find her. Without her powers, she is defenseless."

Sailor comes to my body, and I have to hold myself back from killing him. Everything in me is telling me to do it. I want to, even without the blinding pain...I want him dead.

"Knock him out, we need to find her and can't while he is like this. You have to," Sailor tells his once brother.

"I don't know if I can," the brother says sharply. I feel blood dripping from my nose. I know I seem manic when they both look at me with startled expressions.

"If you think you could keep me down while my mate is out there, you have another thing coming," I hiss between my clenched teeth.

Sailor whispers something into the other's ear. I growl, the low rumbling sound echoing throughout the woods. Right as I am about to get off the cold ground, I feel the sensation I know all too well before Sailor's face comes into my view. "You need to listen to me carefully." My eyes are trained on the man I hate, but I am starting to grow towards. "We have to find her. If you're in this bad of shape, she's gotta be worse off. We have to get to her, and you can't make it." I gulp down the next round of pain lacing up my body, it hits me right in the base of my spine. My head is thrown back in sheer agony. I know he is right. I hate the thought of him being right and doing the right thing, but for her, I will swallow my pride.

If he doesn't find her, I know we will both die. I can feel her resistance waning. I know I feel her giving up, even without her in my mind. I know it in the marrow of my bones. She is losing her will to live. I nod once; it's slight, but he understands.

"We can't just leave the fucking *king* here, Sailor," his ex-brother says before the ginger steps forward.

"I'll stay. But you'd better find her. I'm serious, SJ. *Find her.*" Sailor grabs the ginger's shoulder before pulling him into a tight hug. I hate it.

"Barnett is going to watch over you," Sailor promises, like I am some child he has to check in with. I might fucking wet my pants from the damn pain in my back, though. "Do not kill him, do you understand?" he asks me with venom in his words. I grip his wrist so hard I am shocked when he doesn't wince or flinch away.

"Find her, *please*. Take this." My shaky hands reach into my pants pocket—past where the shell she gave me that night in the lake resides—and I drag out the vial to give back to her what she needs to survive. This vial will bring the war, but it will save her, and that is all that matters to me. *She* is all that matters to me. "Give her this, and the necklace will fall. Be ready to run. We must make it to the palace walls, or we'll all die. Make it back to me." I search his eyes, hoping he sees that we both want what's best for her.

Sailor takes the black vial; my blood swishes in it along with my own flower. The complete opposite of hers.

"Don't kill him, promise me you won't. She will kill you if you do," Sailor says, trying to reprimand me; the ginger pales even more than he was before.

"Bring her back to me." My voice is hoarse; my throat is sore. Even though I know it isn't my own ailment. It's hers, from screaming.

Sailor takes another moment before he tells me, "I will bring her back for *us*. She is *ours*." The passion in his eyes is all I need to see to know he will save her. I nod slightly before attempting to sit up. If I must share her, he isn't a bad man to share with.

Chapter 52

<u>Queen Serena Bloodworthy-Henry</u>

Seven days. I have watched the moon rise and fall seven times.

It is afternoon, I believe, and the leaves outside are orange and yellow.

They are dying just like I am. The man outside hasn't come inside in two days. I keep waiting for him, but he doesn't come.

"How much blood do you need before she can die?" Wren asks from the table where they are eating lunch.

"I don't know if I'll ever have enough. Her royal fae blood isn't like the other fae I have killed. It is far more powerful. She has lasted much longer than they did, too." I look to Mabel, who is barely hanging on.

"You have only kept three others; there isn't much to compare her to," Wren responds.

I know I need to get Mabel out of here, so when the door opens, I take my chance.

"Serena?" Mabel whispers so softly that I almost don't hear her.

"It's okay, May. I am getting us out. You just have to stay here, okay? We're going to be fine," I whisper, though speaking at all is almost impossible. I push up and onto my cut-up feet. The day before yesterday, they cut into my feet so deeply that I thought they would cut them clean off.

"Her blood gives me the power that I need. You see this?" He shows the other man his arm. "There was a scar there; it's healed. I could sell her blood and live the rest of my life in luxury."

Mabel watches me with hope in her eyes.

My hands are still tied behind my back; my legs are tied together with a rope that is impossible to break. I push on, for my kingdom, but mostly for my friend at my side. I make it to my knees, hoping the men are so distracted they will not even notice me.

"See this? She is fucking powerful, and that damn king made it easy to take what we need. I say we keep her," Haadgar says with his smug look on his face.

"Well then, we gotta start to feed her more than we have been or else she will die," Wren replies as if he has made the biggest discovery there is.

Really? I want to say, but I don't dare because I push with everything in me to jump onto my feet. The floor creaks under me, but neither of them seems to notice. Mabel's eyes widen before she nods frantically. Urging me on. The man with the knife that glows from the Blessed went into the torture room. I softly hop my way into the room, but neither of the men turns around to see me. Each light hop, I stop to make certain the men don't notice me. The sound of urine hitting a pot rings in my ears as I swiftly make my way to where the other man stands with his pants down.

"What the—" He doesn't have a chance to finish his sentence because I catapult myself with everything I have left in my body to kick him. Both my legs meet his throat, and he sputters. My body thuds onto the hard, creaky floor, but I roll quickly, flipping onto my back and using all my strength to get back to my feet. "You bitch," he spits before I hear chairs scraping against the floor. I rush as fast as I can, with my ankles still tied tightly together, before hopping on his balls to stop him from moving. He slithers on the ground, moaning. I fall onto my butt before the darkness inside me tells me what I need to do. There is a loud ruckus outside the door, but I can't stop now. I kick and kick his head with both feet until he stops fighting me. I turn around, not meeting his mangled, bloody face. My hands scramble to get to the knife. When my fingers touch the warm handle of the knife, it hums; the sound of the afterlife rings in my ears.

"How did you get in here?" Haadgar snarls at me right as the knife slips through the rope like butter. My hands are finally free, and they know exactly what to do. I slice through the rope around my ankles and watch. I watch the blood drain from his pale face. I watch the liquid leak down his legs, as I have watched Mabel do the same. I watch the apology fall from his mouth, and I watch from the outside of my own body as I strike.

My body moves without instructions. I slice at the man who has kept me and my friend for days on end. He wanted to leave his mark on me, but it looks as if I might leave one on him. I strike at his body, his face, his hands, everywhere my knife will slice into. "Stop!" he screams, speckled with blood, and his spit sprays as I continue to avenge my friend and myself. My chest is heaving as I bend down to where he now lies, his arm covering his face.

"I may not have my powers, but that does not mean I am powerless. You underestimated me, and you will die for it." My hands move before I can tell him all the ways he hurt me. He doesn't need to know the permanent damage I have sustained from him.

"No. Please...wait." My fingers grip his wrist, currently trying to cover his throat. My knee digs into his side, shoving so hard I hope his last moments are as painful as the last few days have been for Mabel.

"It is fitting your last words are to beg me for life, when you don't value living for anybody but yourself." His eyes drain as understanding hits him. The sharp, hot blade slices into his throat as warm, bright red blood seeps from him. His sliced-up hands try to cover the cut, but it is far too deep. When his head hits the floor, eyes still open and wide, I make my way to where my friend is.

"Stay back," Wren yells at me. His hands that once seemed so massive look so small as he smashes Mabel's face to the wooden floor.

"Serena," she tries to croak out, but he shoves her face to the floor again.

"I know." My eyes watch her frantic ones.

"Stay the fuck back or she is dead," Wren screams. My eyes dart around the room, scanning for any way to fix this. To make sure she makes it out. I don't care about myself; I need her to have a good life. I hear the other man start to move around in the room with the piss pot. I can't imagine he's moving very fast. Wren looks at his friend and must see the damage my feet caused because Wren presses his knee directly into Mabel's lower back. "I'm telling you, I will do worse than kill her. Get out of this house, let us leave, and she will stay unharmed." Wren looks like a cornered animal in this moment, which is never a good thing. I try to weigh my options, but when the other man walks through the doorframe, hate in his eyes at what I did to his face, I know there isn't another way out. They won't let us leave alive, and we can't let *them* leave.

Wren must see my train of thought, because he presses so hard onto her spine, her screams pierce through any resistance I had. I move before he can even blink, throwing the dagger right in the middle of his eyes. The magical steel doesn't even hesitate before smoking right through him. The other man rushes to the door, and it slams against the wall as he sprints away. My only concern right now is Mabel. She lies on the floor completely lifeless. Wren still lies half on her, his dead weight crushing her.

"May?" I drop the dagger and fall to my knees. They sink into the floor that will forever haunt me. "Mabel?" My voice finally cracks completely; tears stream down my face for the first time since being taken.

"My Queen." Her voice is so small, such a devastating difference in the woman I know and love. Her eyes remain shut.

"I'm here. They are gone. We're okay," I promise her, as my hand takes her good one and squeezes tightly. Tears stream down her face, her chocolate skin coated in cuts and bruises. I gently place my other hand on her cheek while she shakes her head slightly.

"I can't make it," she croaks out. I fiercely shake my head in denial.

"No, I can carry you," I demand, sternly.

"No, you can't. You aren't much better off than I, Majesty." She convulses in pain, her body shaking so hard from the adrenaline leaving her system. I choke on my sobs.

"Do not call me that," I say between my pitiful sobs, my bottom lip pouting as snot and spit flow from me during the worst cry I have ever had. "I am not your queen; I am your friend. You are my *family*. Now and forever," I declare, and she gives me one small nod.

"Promise me something?" She asks so quickly I almost can't hear the words. I grab onto her hand with both of mine, before her eyes open slightly.

"Anything." I can feel snot dripping from my nose in pools.

"Take Taryan the quilt, please. Tell her how I felt, and that if I had..." I watch her throat bob as she struggles to get the words out. "If I had been a better woman, I would have told her myself a long while ago." That must be the woman Mabel is interested in back in the palace. She has mentioned her several times, but wasn't ready to commit to anything. Our late-night conversations are all rushing into my mind.

Tears so thick I swear I might have called the ocean to me drop onto her hand before her body stops moving. "*No*. No!" I shake her body...nothing. "Please don't leave me," I whisper. Her chest doesn't move again, her swollen eyes stay just as they were. My lip quivers as I say my last goodbye.

I sit with Mabel's body until the moon chases away the sun. "I will tell her," I tell my friend, my last promise to her. Darkness engulfs everything; the only bit of light is the stars.

I hold the onyx ring I found for Alwin against my chest, which means more to me than it ever has. The tattoo on my wrist burns to be touched, but it is a mangled bit of flesh now. It no longer looks like my sailboat; it looks like destruction. I grab the quilt May bought for her love with my spare hand and clutch it to my chest, blood drenching it completely. When I stand, I wrap my naked body in the quilt.

"I will come back with reinforcements. I will not leave you here with them." I bite my lip, knowing that once I leave here, this is the end. She will be dead because of me. I wait for another moment at the doorframe. "Thank you, Mabel, for being a loyal friend to me. I have never had a girlfriend to share secrets with until you, and for you I am eternally grateful." My stomach cramps so hard, I think I might finally fall over due to starvation, and the Gods will finally take my body.

My bare feet crunch leaves under their path. I walk throughout the night, not caring about the roars in the distance, not caring about the monsters lurking in the shadows, because I am the biggest monster out here. I hold the knife of the Gods so close to my chest, I fear that if I trip, it might cut straight through to my heart. Even though I know I have left my heart on the ground of that cabin.

Chapter 53

<u>Sailor James</u>

"I hear her," Wolf says, his voice happier and more sure than he has been in days. We have been searching these woods for more than three days straight. I don't know how long it has truly been since we left Alwin, but I know when he says he can hear her, he can.

"How far?" I look around the tree line.

"That way." Wolf's strides are so fast I almost can't keep up.

We run for about twenty minutes at full speed before he stops. "She's that way." He starts sprinting. Even though we have been going at this for days, he acts as if he can't be stopped. I respect him for it, and I will owe him. I know he is pushing through for me, mostly. "Right around—" We both stop when our eyes land on her.

I don't move, and neither does he. "Serena?" My voice comes out hoarse. She is walking, yes, but barely. "Serena." I rush to her before she even realizes we are there. Both of us run to her, but she flinches backwards as if scared of us. She doesn't say anything, only points.

"She wants to take us somewhere." Wolf interprets for her.

"Baby." My voice cracks at the state she is in. Her eyes are almost completely swollen shut, and her lips are cracked so badly that blood trickles down them. She is naked underneath a tattered quilt that's red from all the dried blood in it.

"She wants to take us to where Mabel is." Wolf steps up to her, placing his hand on her shoulder tentatively, before she gives him a slight nod. He draws her into a small hug, and then I wrap my arms around her, too.

I clutch onto her and Wolf for the longest hug I have ever been a part of. I can't think of ever letting her go now that I have her back. Serena pulls away before she turns and leads us to a small cabin. The door is wide open, and the stench from inside almost makes me cover my mouth. Wolf coughs to cover up his disgust.

"Apparently, Haadgar brought her here with a few followers. They wanted her blood, claimed hers could give them powers," Wolf informs me. *"She won't speak about anything that happened to her, but she believes they think the blood of the fae will give humans the power that the Gods are taking from them,"* he says down our connection. *"Just go slowly...give her time. Nothing else matters right now."* Wolf's eyes scan to mine; this moment feels like so many we have had before.

I could see why somebody who has nothing would risk everything for more power. Worry eats my insides, knowing there might be more to come for her. She walks right up to the small cabin, as if she knows nobody inside will ever hurt her again. I follow Serena inside and watch her walk over to a dead, stiff man.

Wolf goes to check on the man while I clear the rest of the house. My blood almost boils over when I go into a small room and see the bloodstained mattress. My Honeybee didn't deserve this; no person does. My vision turns red to the point where I must turn away from what I can't even begin to imagine, or else I won't be able to be there for her. I finish clearing the tiny cabin, clearing my mind as well. I need her to heal, and she won't if I can't help her.

Serena stands close behind Wolf as if she is scared to get too far from him. She hasn't said one word to either of us. Wolf looks at her and then at Mabel.

"Serena?" I ask lightly, and both she and Wolf look to me as if startled by my being here. It is so silent in here that my voice seems to boom. I walk over the dead body of a man that I then decide to stomp on, shattering his skull. That seems to make her somewhat happy because she smiles slightly. I shake off the blood from my boots before walking up to them. "What happened?" I don't take my eyes from hers. Her eyes glaze over as if reliving these past few days is too much for her.

"Let's bury her body, get back to the king, and then we can figure it all out," Wolf says in his commander tone.

I nod my agreement and allow Wolf to take Serena outside while he carries Mabel's body. I watch her closely. She holds the quilt to her chest, as if unable to let go. I can't look away from her. I can't seem to let her get farther than a few feet from me. I stand in the doorway of this small, shitty cabin and look one more time at the damage here. Burning this place down would be much more kind to these men than their bodies deserve. The blood speckled everywhere will haunt me even more than my own time being tortured. I slam the door and follow my brother and my soulmate to bury her friend.

"Are you going to give her the vial?" Wolf asks me, dragging me from my morbid thoughts. I look to where the dirt pile lies, where Serena seems to be mumbling things to her lost friend.

"I am," I confirm. I pull out the black potion and uncork the lid.

"How fast can we get to him from here? Her powers probably won't come in right away. It'll take a while for her to be healthy again," Wolf says, more timidly than before.

I watch her, seemingly still so strong after what I can't even imagine has been done to her. "I don't know. I'm thinking by the looks of her, she hasn't been fed since being taken. She probably hasn't slept much either. Her powers are very much reliant on her health. It could take days, but she won't make it that long, even with her body healing itself. We gotta get her home to rest," I say, knowing how strong she is to even be alive right now. The cuts along her body are deep. I am shocked she can stand on her feet, the bottoms of which are ruined.

My brother and I give her time and space to say goodbye to her friend before we walk over to her. I hug her from behind, not hard, but enough to make sure she knows I am here with her. "I will never allow you to be harmed like this again. Do you hear me, baby?" I whisper against her neck. Wolf kneels in front of her.

"Are you ready?" he asks her out loud, even though I know she responds inside his head. He nods once before I slowly pour the vial into her mouth. Her eyes widen so drastically that her pupils completely dilate before she grabs onto my wrist and digs her fingers into my flesh.

"I know, baby. I'm here." Goose bumps prickle my entire body when she finally slumps over and cries, and I know her sobs will echo through my mind forever.

Chapter 54

<u>Queen Serena Bloodworthy-Henry</u>

The first power that comes to my body is my flames. I almost scorch the quilt Mabel has trusted me with. The next is healing, and my body immediately begins expelling all of the horrible things that had been done to it. They just keep coming in waves after that, overwhelming power flowing into my body at a rapid pace. If I hadn't had a similar experience as a toddler, I would've been scared these powers would kill me. Everything from chirping insects suddenly blaring in my ears to the emotions I had gotten so good at ignoring comes blasting into my head.

I try to distract myself by walking. The soles of my feet are finally healing to the point where I don't wince when I step on a stick. Sailor has offered to give me his shoes. I didn't know how to tell him that while being held against my will, I had been kicked so badly with black boots like his that I couldn't look at the damn things. Wolf had offered to carry me, and so far, he is the only one I have been able to talk with. Not because I don't want to talk with Sailor, but because my voice is gone. Words are failing me because every time I try to mumble them, it brings back the memories of the late, hushed conversations with Mabel. She told me I was the only thing close to a true friend she has ever had, and she was mine.

We have been walking for a little over four hours now. Wolf gave me some food, but we didn't want to overdo it and cause me to get sick. I haven't eaten more than a cracker or rotten bread in over a week. So, I shouldn't be surprised when my stomach starts to clench. Pain isn't always something that has to hurt, I learned that this week. I could think of something else while the worst things were happening to me, and I could live through it. A future with Alwin and Sailor, children running around. Wolf being forgiven for his betrayal, and my family living side by side with me. Those visions are what got me through this last week.

Another hour goes by. *Where are we?* I ask down the open connection. Wolf is walking right in front of me, while Sailor won't let me out of his sight. Sailor keeps his distance but stays close enough for me to feel him right there.

"You were in the valley. So, just before the mountains. That's why it took so long for us to find you," Wolf explains. Snolly. They brought us to the mountains; they had intended to keep us there. Fear starts to clog my throat when I think about staying there forever. Cramping begins in my lower back and belly. "We searched everywhere. Alwin...he, uh...he was losing his mind; everything that happened to you happened to him." My eyes blink, and for a moment, I am looking through Sailor's eyes by accident. After months of having no power, controlling them all again overwhelms my system. My power is warming my body, but not enough when my knees hit the cold, hard ground.

"Serena?" Sailor gathers me in his arms. I still have the quilt wrapped around me. When I feel the thick, hot liquid seep onto my thighs, I know. I just know. *NO.* I want to scream out, I want fury, I want to say something. But when the cramping doesn't subside and the liquid continues to trickle out, I meet Wolf's eyes.

"What's going on? How can we help you?" Wolf asks, and Sailor nods into my hair. He is pressing kisses to the top of my head.

"Serena, are you okay?" Sailor sounds defeated as I groan out in pain and sorrow. I still have blood all over me, but the cuts and bruises are gone. Sailor had asked to clean me up, but I wasn't ready for it. Now I wish I had been.

When I say the next words to Wolf, he stills so solidly that I think I might have accidentally frozen him. So, I say it again out loud this time.

"I am having a miscarriage."

Sailor goes still, everything is silent, and I almost think maybe, just maybe, I am dead finally. I look to both of them before squeaking out again, "Did you hear me?" My voice is raw and broken. Wolf nods, but Sailor speaks.

"What can I do?" he asks into my hair. I lean back into him and cry. I cry for the baby I am losing. For the friend I have lost. For the girl I once was.

"Hold me," I say on a moan.

Suddenly, as if hearing my cries or feeling my pain. Alwin appears in his thick, black foggy mist. It encases us completely. His blackish eyes glow with blue rims, and I realize right away that Wolf isn't in our circle, but Sailor is; he is still holding me from behind. Alwin drops to his knees in front of us. "May I?" His voice is filled with despair. His cheeks are hollowed out, as if he has not eaten either. Alwin appears frantic, as if had I told him no, he would respect me, but it might kill him. I give him a slight nod before I feel not only Sailor holding me from behind, but now Alwin is standing and holding me in front. The black mist keeps all the light out. It's swirling around us like a tornado, but all I feel is safety.

"You're here," he says from one side of my face, while Sailor whispers on the other side, "And safe. She's safe." The three of us sit there for a long while. Alwin comforts me while Sailor cleans me with his water, all while I sit here and mourn the losses I have experienced this last week.

"I—" I start, but can't get the words to form in my mind.

"I know, darling. You don't have to tell me. I know." His own voice cracks as if he is also mourning a child we will never meet. "We don't have to talk about any of it if you don't want to. But if you do, I am here, Serena. I want you to be able to tell me anything at all." The love in Alwin's words and eyes fills me up completely. All of the emotions I have not been allowed to feel for months are almost deafening. The sorrow I feel coming from Sailor and the absolute fear wafting from Alwin almost chokes me. When I am certain I have passed everything, I tell them, and Sailor picks me up and carries me out of the circle.

When we make it out of the black mist, the light is almost blinding. I cover my eyes to keep them from burning.

"What's going on?" Wolf stalks towards us, slowly, but the same commander I have always known.

"Our honeymoon tour is over, isn't it?" I ask, knowing something else is going on.

"It is," Alwin confirms, while stepping out of the mist. Not that I would have finished this trip anyway. When Alwin's mist clears from around him, I swear I see a tear drop from his eyes before the king stands in front of me. Clear eyes and a clear mind, he walks to where Sailor holds me tightly in his arms. "Listen to me very closely, Serena." He tilts his head, and the black waves of hair cascade across his forehead.

"Okay." Fear... This is how he tells me somebody else is dead. The absolute desolate look he gives me does nothing to help me.

"You will have time to heal, I promise you, Serena, but we must get back to the palace. We have a visitor." His face is grave as he speaks.

Confusion must be apparent on my face because he cups my cheek, his fingers softly stroking my face. "Please. I need you to be okay, but I just need you to be strong today. Tomorrow we can fall apart...together. We will, okay? Today, we must be the strongest versions of ourselves. I will take the brunt of all of this, alright?" He continues to speak but doesn't answer anything for me.

"Who is here?" I ask, narrowing my eyes at him.

My heart plummets when he tells me, "Your brother. I can and will explain, but we do not have time right now. We will at the palace, I will explain everything. Fae do not naturally have kindness towards humans, alright? He is here to see you; if he doesn't or he sees you as weak, he will kill everybody and everything."

My mind stops working completely. "What do you mean?" I croak. He shakes his head, then looks to Sailor as if they have already spoken about this.

"Honeybee, your brother came in through the sea dividing Clove and us. That's where the portal to Mirahalm has been; Magnolia hid it from Alwin. She brought your brother back. She is Alwin's sister and has been working with *your* family against her own family."

I have another brother, and he is alive and here. Reading about him and hearing that I will meet him are two very different things.

"Your brother is your twin."

I had already read that, but hearing it again strikes me.

"Your mother didn't die when she fought Alwin, but she wasn't able to transport you both into the woman's body. So, she kept him and raised him as a prince in Mirahalm." Sailor speaks as if he has already known all of this.

She left me and took him with her? I had hoped the book was wrong, that somehow my mother wasn't the evil queen I was reading about. Wolf looks like he is two seconds away from taking me from this mess.

"You can't be serious," Wolf says in disbelief.

"I am," Alwin responds before looking at me. "I know this is a lot, and I'm sorry," Alwin says again. I can see it. He truly means that. "Your brother and my sister are threatening to bring the fae war here if you do not go meet him," he explains, but I am stuck on something. Magnolia is his sister.

"What?" I say, feeling dazed. I feel the irritation coming off him, but he smooths it over quickly.

"Your mother was always able to track you through your powers, Serena. That's why I took them from you. I wanted you to be safe while we figured things out," Alwin says in a lower voice.

"Safe from who? You?" My brows raise; I squirm to get out of Sailor's arms. "I don't understand." I shake my head again, trying to clear all of this up. "How did he get here?" I ask anybody. Wolf shifts uncomfortably on his feet. Sailor stands right at my back.

"Magnolia is my sister; she has been working with your family for a few years. She wants the fae to be the only beings with freedom in Mirahalm." He waves his hands as if it is all too confusing for me. But I latch onto one thing.

"My family works with her?" His eyes soften slightly. I can feel the truth coming from him. "Are you saying, in the war with our two families, my family is on the wrong side of things?" This cannot be.

"I am. I am also telling you that your powers were a beacon for them to track you. They have been your entire life. I didn't have a blood connection with you until our mating ceremony, so I could not find you...to keep you from them, so they couldn't use you as a weapon."

"Okay. But I am still stuck on Magnolia being your *sister*, Alwin." I can move past my mother being evil. I felt that in the carriage ride when she spoke with me before the trials. There was a darkness to her that felt so cold, I didn't know if it was me or her. I guess this is my answer.

"She is, and we can discuss this later. Right now, your brother is on his way to our throne room to meet with my sister. We need to be there, and we have to be strong." That isn't the first time he has said that, and his eyes are pleading with me.

"Why wouldn't I be strong?" My voice cuts through the thick tension. Sailor's hand rubs small circles on my back.

"Serena." Alwin levels his eyes with me before I sniff away any of the remaining snot from my nose.

"I'm fine." I wipe the back of my hand to my face and steel my mind and emotions. I have my powers, I feel alive, and I'm not cut off from nature any longer.

"Now, I am not saying you have to be fine, just pretend, for today. He needs to see us as a threat," Alwin says calmly.

"Is my mother coming? Because she's obviously alive. She has spoken to me before." My eyes feel heavy, and I need food.

"She is not coming. Mirahalm is in war, Serena. Your family wants freedom to be taken from the lesser fae and other beings that live there. They want more humans, everything you had accused me of, they are doing there. The difference, though?" He waits a minute before continuing. "They are killing any and all who disagree with them. The fae had had enough, and my family stepped up. My mother and father are fighting their hardest to help the cause." I still have so many questions, but I know there are pressing concerns right now that need to be dealt with.

"Well then, let's go meet my brother," I respond, even though I feel as if I need to be asking harder questions. Alwin engulfs all of us in his black, fury mist and leaves the very woods I have found I hate.

Chapter 55

"You're back!" Millie beams. Her bright face and short brown hair haven't changed. She looks the same.

"I am, and I need a bath," I tell her, walking right up to her and giving her a long hug. "After my bath, let's catch up. Alright?" Her brows raise comically high before she places the back of her hand on my forehead.

"Are you ill?" She doesn't mean to hurt me, but it does nonetheless.

"I am not. I am just peachy. Let me take a bath and get all the dirt and grime from my body before going to meet my brother. Shall we?"

"Oh, your...uh, Juniper, you mean?"

I don't have the energy to explain to her what Alwin tried explaining to me. I walk past her, and she follows me. "I'll get a water bender to fill it up for you." She stops in her tracks before she can even finish her sentence. "You— Your powers are back!" She claps her hands.

"They are," I say softly. When she sees I am not over-the-moon excited, she knows something is wrong.

"Are you sure you're okay?"

My gaze goes downwards. "I am fine." I give her a soft smile.

I shut the door in her face, and she mumbles something about how she thought we would have a better reunion, but I don't have the energy for a do-over. I place the clothes that were given to me in Groke on the ground. I dip my toe in the steaming water before lowering my entire body into it.

It fills with dirt right away. Sailor had already cleaned me with his power, and still, my water is tainted with the blood of others. I scrub my skin until it's red, then scrub again. It doesn't feel clean. I don't know if it ever will. After soaking in the tub for a little over ten minutes, Sailor knocks on the door. I can hear the difference in his footsteps and Millie's. Millie is still pacing outside my bathing chamber doors. "Come in," I call through the thick wood. She huffs and hisses something at him about me not letting *her* in.

"How are you?" Sailor sits by the tub, his fingers barely dipping in the water.

"I am fine." I lick my newly healed lips.

"Be honest." His bright blue eyes swim with all the promises I will never get.

"I am broken," I admit softly. Hurt floods into my heart from him.

"You are no such thing, I promise you. I have seen broken Serena. You are strong and you will survive this."

I brush my fingers against his in the water. "I want to be strong, I just don't know if I am anymore." Shame coats my words. His fingers tighten around mine; the motion is small, but it means everything to me. He isn't pushing me for more, neither of them are.

"You are Serena Bloodworthy. You are a queen, and a Gods' Blessed princess. I bow to you, because you are the strongest female I have ever known."

My eyes hurt from being so tired, but I still meet his hopeful gaze. "Am I ruined?" I know I sound small, but he doesn't miss a heartbeat before responding.

"You could never be ruined, Honeybee. You never were and never will be. There is a reason I fell in love with you, and it is not the power you hold in your blood but the person you are." The raw emotions coming from him make me uncomfortable. I try to soothe the ache by rubbing the place on my wrist where I know—no, I *knew*—I could find comfort.

"It's gone," I tell him, not even looking at the smooth skin now.

"I know." His words shock me.

"You knew?" My brows furrow.

"Of course, I knew. If you didn't think I have your entire body memorized from each and every strand of hair to every scar you have given yourself and forced yourself to keep, you are crazy." His bright eyes show so much passion that his words are almost overshadowed by them.

"You saw it?" I bite my lip.

"Yes, and as much as I love tattoos and the meaning behind yours, you don't need that tattoo to have me anymore, Bee. I will never leave again. I'm yours...forever." I lean my head on his shoulder as tears stream down my face. He nuzzles against my face, rubbing the tip of his nose against mine.

An hour later, I am dressed in a gown fit for a queen. Because that is what I am today. I am not the helpless girl I have been in the past. I am a queen fit to rule her people. Sailor and I snuck in some time to talk. Apparently, he and Alwin have become somewhat allies when they both realized they are on the same team. Sailor also found out that Magnolia has been holding Wolf's sisters over his head since the first time in the woods that she came to get me. She had told him to visit her that night and has been using him and controlling him since. I shouldn't be surprised, although I really wonder where she keeps them so well hidden that neither Sailor nor Wolf could find them for years.

When I look in the mirror, I don't see myself. I don't see the scars that should litter my body; I don't see any of the stains on my skin. I see a woman who has been through enough, a queen who is ready to fight back for herself, for her kingdoms, and for those who cannot fight.

My heels click against the onyx tiles; my black gown drags behind me. Wolf and Sailor are on either side of me. With my power back, I don't really need them, but I want them. I want to keep them safe from whatever happens. I want to keep them all close so that I can protect them like I couldn't Mabel.

Glen waits for me to give him permission to open the doors. I wait there, knowing that after this day, everything in my life will change. I will no longer be able to deny that I am Fae; I cannot deny the connection between Sailor and me. I also can't say I don't love my mate. That's why, when the doors open and I walk into a room where my exact face is printed onto the body of a male who looks like me but isn't, I have to pretend. Something I know I will get very good at soon.

The male standing in the death room glances at me, then back at Alwin, who is already sitting regally on his throne. When I walk through the doors, though, Alwin stands and bows his head. A show of respect for me, and our bond.

Alwin's black ensemble is the ultimate king's outfit. He looks polished and clean; his shadow of a beard is now completely shaven. He looks so young and fresh, unlike how he appeared earlier. This is the male my life is tied to. I smile slightly. My dark red lips contrast so harshly with my white teeth I fear I might scare my new brother.

He doesn't bow; he doesn't even look at me longer than a few seconds before continuing his conversation with Alwin. "As I was saying, my parents would like their daughter back now. What will it take—other than the throne in Mirahalm—for you to give her up?" The male's posh voice rings in my ears. He doesn't sound like I do. I walk right next to my blood relative and feel nothing for him. I had once compared Juniper's looks with mine; I had thought we looked like twins. Now, looking into the eyes of my exact clone, I see I was wrong. The only true stark difference between us is that he is male, and I am not. He *is* slightly stronger-looking than I, but I bet if you put us in a ring, I could hold my own.

"Hello to you, as well." I stop walking. Sailor and Wolf stand at the base of the dais. I kiss Alwin's cheek, but don't sit yet. "I noticed you didn't bow to me. Is that a custom in Mirahalm?" I ask in a sarcastic tone. His bright, silvery-blue eyes meet mine. I can see another difference—he is smug, and I don't like it.

"What?" His voice is proper to an annoying level.

"I *said*...do you not bow to your king and queen in your homelands?" My harsh tone causes Alwin to send ripples of happiness down our bond. Since being connected again, he hasn't left the bond alone. He toys with it, sometimes with me. When I feel the invisible wall tingle with shadow fingers, I know I have his support if I want this to go down in flames.

"In *our* homelands, you mean?" he tries to correct me. I look into his mind with ease. He doesn't even have shields up and I see visions of his life and his childhood within seconds. I see the life I lost and realize the one I had here was much better. I cough, trying to hide my giggles.

"I mean...*your* homelands. I will claim them as my own one day, maybe if I desire them. These lands that you are standing on?" I motion out the door and to the large glass windows. "They are mine, and I will not be leaving them," I declare. I see several of the guards shift uncomfortably.

"I see." The male standing in front of me then looks to Alwin.

"As I was saying. We will end the war, no more fighting, and give your family leave to come to these..." His face contorts in disgust. "These human lands. If you agree to send her home."

I scoff before answering for Alwin. I place my hand on Alwin's chest as a show of dominance. "I am not some child to be dealt with. I don't know who you think you are, but you are no brother to me. I have a brother, and I can promise you he is a much better one than you could ever be—"

He interrupts me, taking a step towards me. "I do not wish to share secrets and braid your hair like some children. Mother and Father need you home now; we have business to attend to." The male speaks loudly, as if he has grown up believing one day he'll be king. Sailor takes a step towards him and I shake my head.

"*Do not engage.*" My powers may be rusty, but getting into Sailor's mind will always be easy. I do not need my honor to be fought for over this male.

"Again, I am not some mule you can bargain with. I am a queen, and bonded at that. I will not leave here, and I will not be leaving my mate."

Challenge glints in this male's eyes. His fangs are on full display; his ears are so pointy I swear they could cut you. "Does she speak for both of you then?" His question echoes throughout the chamber. I glance over to the place where, at one point, there were dozens of people standing for my mating ceremony with Alwin, then there weren't. They were red mist, exactly what I am about to do to this male.

"What is your name?" I ask randomly, because I want to know who exactly I will be killing. He ignores me...again.

"Alwin. Does she speak for you both?" He seems bored and annoyed at the same time.

"She does. She is my mate, Cormac." *Thank you, Alwin.* I smirk at him; he smirks right back. "We make choices together. We do not want war, but if you threaten war here again, that is what you will get." Alwin's voice is ice-cold. I nod my agreement before stepping forward.

"I will also warn you against attempting to steal me. I will not go home and be your puppet for whatever games you are playing there. I will stay and fight for my people, I will one day soon save the people of Mirahalm from our family's wrongdoings," I declare sternly.

Cormac's face turns red with fury. I tilt my head slightly. "I wonder, do you have as many powers as I do?" His face turns from red to white instantly at my words. "Huh, I guess the Blessed Gods wanted to give me something then. What is your power?" I ask in a threatening tone. He grinds his teeth down, loud enough to hear the crushing of his canines.

"My power is strong enough to go against you," he declares, so I challenge him.

"Would you like to test that theory?" I take a step down the dais. Alwin stays; he allows me to fight my own battles.

"I would not. I am here to speak with a king and queen, and clearly, they are not here. So, this is my last warning... I'm serious, Alwin. Take the deal if you do not want war killing your people." He has a bite to his words, an icy undertone.

Alwin steps down a step, then two, then he is right in front of Cormac. "Do not threaten me and my people. I have fought stronger males before; I will survive you, too." Alwin's voice doesn't betray any fear, but I can see in his posture that he is nervous. My confidence slackens slightly before Magnolia steps forward. In fae form, Magnolia is almost unrecognizable. She goes from being a middle-aged woman to being as young as I am. Red fog swims around her until a tight dress clings to every curve of her body. I feel Wolf stiffen and instantly become protective of him.

I blink right to him and Sailor and stand protectively in front of them. She chuckles a sultry laugh before moving her curvy hips towards us. "Serena darling, if you do not go to Mirahalm and do what must be done, then I will kill every villager you have ever met. Starting with Mr. Beanstalk and ending with *I don't give a fuck*." Her lips are painted black, and even with that blackness, she looks gorgeous.

"You wouldn't," I hiss. She presses her lips against Cormac, leaving a black kiss on him.

"I would. I don't care about any of these humans. Haven't you figured that out by now?" The way she treats them as disposable toys is abhorrent. "You killed the only one I cared for." Her voice leeches of hatred. *Nova*.

"This is clearly not going very well. Would we like to reconvene for dinner?" Alwin says while sitting back on his throne, seemingly bored and pleased at the same time.

Cormac scowls for a moment before turning to leave. "I will bring him," Magnolia chirps, then follows him into the hallway. I turn to face Alwin, just to realize he is right behind me.

"Oh." I stumble backwards. He smirks at me before moving a stray hair out of my face.

"So, I think that went fairly well, don't you?" he asks while running his fingers through my hair. My mouth falls open.

"No, I do not. Also, I remember Magnolia talking about wanting to *get* with you. What's that about Alwin?" Disgust riddles my body.

Sailor coughs, but it sounds more like he is trying to cover up a laugh. Alwin's gaze darkens at Sailor before turning towards me once more.

"Yes, she was very good at theatrics throughout the years. I have tried to keep her at bay, but not too long ago, I found out she was meeting with your brother. She wouldn't tell me why, but I knew. She has become bored here—after you burned her club down—and I guess she escalated things."

I blink slowly several times. "Bored?"

"Yes, I knew some of her silly games, but not all of them."

Wolf steps forward now, his green eyes are bright and clear of any and all fog. "Did you know she took my sisters?" Wolf asks fiercely. I can feel the sting behind my eyelids when I shut them. This is all too much.

As if reading my mind, Alwin places his hands on my shoulders. "You don't have to come to the dinner. We can make an excuse." His tone is soft, unlike how he was just speaking to Cormac. I shake all of it off and then tighten my shoulders and harden my heart just a little more.

"No more excuses, we need to end this. Wolf needs his sisters, Alwin. That's a priority to me." Alwin looks at Wolf, then back at me.

"If you say it is, then it is, and we will find them. I will tell you, though, my sister is cruel. She is just like any other fae. They taunt and play games; my parents don't live that way. That's what caused the war in the first place. Your family thinks that lesser fae and other beings live to serve us. When I was sent after you, to hopefully bring up a new queen who would fight for the lower's rights, Mirahalm was in bad shape. From what I have heard, it's not in any better condition now than it was then."

I think about that for a while before finally responding. "So, your hope was to kidnap me and raise me to be a queen that *you* could manipulate?" I arch my brow.

"Well, no. Not exactly. We just hoped you would marry me and help bring peace to the kingdoms." I don't think he even hears what he is saying.

"That is kidnapping, Alwin."

His face furrows in confusion for a moment before he schools it. "No, I knew you were my mate when you were born. I couldn't find you because of your mother. That evil litt—"

I slam my hand over his mouth. "You are not helping yourself," I say harshly. Sailor chuckles.

Alwin scoffs. "No matter, we will still have to defeat them in order to gain peace in Mirahalm."

Way too fast, my mind goes back to the cabin. No longer are cabins a safe memory for me. My recent experiences have shown me I might not ever step foot in another one. I zone out as conversations continue around me. Sailor comes up behind me and places a hand on my lower back.

"What if you went and took a nap?" Sailor asks. I look to Alwin, then nod my head. I haven't truly slept in Gods knows how long.

"What time is this dinner going to be?" It's still early, so I could try to sleep for a few hours.

"We have time," Sailor says before anybody else can respond. Alwin walks up and grabs both our shoulders.

Right as we blink away, I vaguely hear Wolf mutter to himself, "Yeah, alright, I will just stay here."

When we land in my room, Alwin discards my gown, and a shirt is thrown over my head. Sailor kicks his boots from his feet and lies down on the luscious bed. He pats right next to him, and I crawl into bed, not thinking about anything other than getting some sleep. Alwin crawls to the other side of me. They both hold my body so tightly that when I close my eyes, I know I am safe. But I also know *they* are safe. I wouldn't ever put them in danger.

"Sleep, Serena. We have time to discuss the things that take up space in your mind. For now, we all need rest," Alwin soothes.

I fall asleep in the middle of two males who love me so much they are willing to put aside their differences for me. They are both willing to love me, as I am them.

Chapter 56

<u>Queen Serena Bloodworthy-Henry</u>

"So, what will it take?" Cormac asks Alwin right as he sits down. I sit at the head, which causes several people to glance sideways at me. Sailor and Alwin sit across from each other. Magnolia tried to sit next to Wolf, but he got up and moved. Barnett and Roman just got in and joined us, as well as Millie and Arlo. We are all almost here. My heart drops when I see the spot I know would have sat Mabel. I didn't let anybody sit there because I wanted to save her a seat. Ram is in a cottage, far from Cormac and Magnolia.

"Let's enjoy our meal for a moment, shall we?" Alwin tells Cormac. Even though I don't doubt my blood brother is fuming about not getting this over with, he doesn't argue.

"The human food is disgusting. I don't know how you have lived here this long without coming home," Cormac says brazenly.

Alwin's knuckles turn pure white with anger. "Because my sister has held me hostage here." His tone could cut through glass. "She has taken memories from me as to how to get home. She wouldn't help me find you either, actually, every chance I tried to find you she would get in my way."

"I see. I am sure she had her reasons."

Magnolia gives Cormac a large and pretty smile. If I didn't know her, I would say she is drop-dead gorgeous. She looks like Alwin, but female. Her curves hit in just the right places, her teeth are perfect, and her hair is lush. If only she weren't a soul-eating bitch.

"You allow your wife to sit in your seat, King?" Cormac says with a biting tone.

"I don't *allow* her to sit anywhere." Alwin sips from his mug. "She is my queen and will sit where she pleases." Alwin smirks as he responds.

I decide to show my teeth in this fight. "Really, I can do anything I want here. I sit where I want, I eat amazing foods, I sleep with whomever I want."

I shrug before Cormac mutters, "Yeah, I can tell." The disgust in his voice is apparent. So, I keep on.

"If you have issues with this kingdom, I am queen, so speak to me." Cormac looks to Alwin again. I decide I have had enough of the disrespect from him. "Eyes here, *brother*." My voice is full of command. I force his gaze to meet mine with coercion. His jaw ticks, once, then twice, before Magnolia tightens her shoulders. "I don't really see the value in going to our homelands until I can rule both of them." I study my nails, pretending to be bored.

"If you think you are coming home to usurp our own family, you are wrong." He is getting flustered; little does he know, I have been through worse than an uncomfortable dinner.

"Let's just calm down a little bit," Sailor speaks up. Magnolia sneers at him, which causes my rage to spike to an all-new level.

In half a second, my hands are in her thick, pretty hair; I am shoving her head into the plate right in front of her. "I am done with your disrespect, *Maggie*." The casual use of her name causes her to hiss at me, showing me all those bright and shiny teeth. "Be careful, I am not some small village girl anymore, Magnolia. I am your queen in any realm you try to escape to. If you think you can ever disrespect my friends again, I will do much worse to you than end your sorry excuse for a life." I push harder, hoping it might kill her.

Cormac looks as if he is liking this, then he claps. Alwin, Sailor, and Wolf are all already standing, wide-eyed, but not stopping me or questioning me in front of our guests.

"Apologize," I demand, knowing full well her face is covered in food.

"To whom?" She acts as if she doesn't know who I am talking about. I push a little harder, and she starts to squirm then.

"You know who."

My teeth are bared. I can somewhat hear Cormac saying, "Maybe she is Fae after all. We had all worried about how she might be raised here." I will deal with him in a moment.

"Oh, your whore?" Her eyes glance to Sailor, then Wolf. "Which one?" she says in a joking tone. Alwin then moves and yanks Magnolia up, holding her by her throat.

"Leave." His voice is harsh and cold. Nothing like he would speak if she were truly family in any real way to him.

I stop her when she tries to obey Alwin. "You still need to say sorry to him."

Her eyes are filled with hate before they soften somewhat. "I am deeply sorry for offending you, Sailor James." She winks at him before leaving the throne room.

Millie and Arlo both sit slack-jawed and in complete shock. Roman is smirking, and Barnett looks disgusted.

"Are you alright?" I go to sit back down while waiting for Barnett to answer me. Alwin guides me with his hand on my lower back. I leave the bond open between Barnett and me to communicate.

"As I was saying, Serena, dear sister." Cormac's smug voice pierces through my thoughts.

"I am not your sister," I hiss before taking a sip out of my mug.

"I just found out what happened to you, Sailor told me. And Wolf's sisters are being held by Magnolia. I am just processing." He sounds hollow. I try not to hone in on Barnett, but it isn't easy to focus when one of my last living friends looks on the verge of finding his own fight. *"I'm sorry, Serena. Are you alright?"* he says softly, his eyes red-rimmed.

I gulp down any and all emotions coming up my throat. *"Thank you."* His eyes glisten with unshed tears.

"I am just trying to be reasonable here, Alwin. We both know you both belong home. We can put our family differences aside, can't we?" I can tell Cormac has years of experience being a diplomat. "Also, Serena, I hate to break it to you, but we are not just siblings but twins. I did have a good laugh when you declared the humans your family. I didn't know you would be this funny. They are not family to you." I swear, I might kill both mine and Alwin's siblings today. My eyes narrow before Alwin speaks.

"We are not here to discuss families. We are here to discuss what it will take for you to leave without Serena and me, with no bloodshed."

"I am okay." Barnett doesn't look convinced, but he gives me a nod.

"You always are. But know, whenever you are not, I am here." Warmth spreads through my chest.

"Nothing, I already told you. We do not require *you*. I was attempting to be kind by inviting you." Cormac moves his food around before finally placing his fork down on his plate.

"I will not allow my mate to go to Mirahalm without me," Alwin says sternly.

Cormac looks between the two of us for a moment. He chews on his lip before saying, "You allow your mate to sleep with others? That is very human of you, Alwin." The jab doesn't go unnoticed by me or Sailor.

"What if he is mine?" Alwin lifts a brow, his tone challenging. I almost laugh, then realize he is trying to protect me from shame. I don't need it. I hold my hand up.

"I don't need your input on my life after, well, forever of not being in it. I just would like to know why you think you need me." I don't want any small talk. I just want to get this over with and send this male on his way.

"Well, as Magnolia tried to tell you earlier, we have people all over the kingdom who are willing to kill those you love. But I would assume the only ones you truly would go to war for are those you called siblings. Correct?" My heart stops beating for a moment. I don't give him anything, though; I keep calm, cool, and collected. "That's what I thought. I would really love to meet your brother and sister. I guess I will get to, considering the fact that the leaders of Clove are on our side of the war."

All the oxygen is snuffed out of the room. I clench my jaw shut tightly. *"Is this true?"* I ask quickly into Alwin's mind. Alwin looks as stiff as I am.

"I have no reason to believe he is lying. The fae in Clove had come here after I was announced king; they said that they were seeking refuge and wouldn't cause harm. Apparently, I am too naïve."

"So?" Cormac presses on as if he didn't just shatter the very ground I am standing on.

"I thought that the leaders had followed Maggie here for safety from the war. I have never met them. When I went to get Sailor for you, your brother and sister were both fine."

Amusement spills right out of Cormac, and I realize the king I had once thought Alwin to be describes Cormac instead. "I sent them our safe word, and now they are all safely in my palace back home. I am being told your sister looks about ready to pop, though." His face looks disgusted. "They will stay that way if you agree to come back and help fight our war. We are close to finishing this."

I look to Alwin before realizing he is letting me decide. "What do you need from me?" I ask, because I still don't understand.

Anxiety is rolling off Wolf and Sailor. "Simple. You come to Mirahalm, end this war, then come back here. Easy peasy."

I roll my eyes. "I don't trust you."

"I don't either," Sailor chimes in, and Cormac looks at him as if just now noticing him.

"Mistresses don't speak at royal events," Cormac says condescendingly.

"It's a good thing this isn't a royal event. This is a dinner between friends. Right?" Alwin is good at trying to keep the peace, I realize.

"Anywho, I just need you to end this once and for all. As well as sign a small decree" Cormac purses his lips.

Alwin stands up. His fists hit the table, causing Arlos's drink to spill. "Drop the bullshit, Cormac. She is not signing over her claim to Mirahalm. She is not ending the war that is tilting in favor of my family. She won't do a damn thing without me, and she for Blessed sure isn't killing our people for your family's greed."

Cormac then disappears. I look around and see he is indeed gone. Alwin plops down in his seat. "My Blessed Gods. I hate my brother-in-law." He sighs before chugging the rest of his mug.

"Where did he go?" Barnett asks, looking under the table.

"He teleports. Far, further than any human could. He can travel between realms. It's his main power," Alwin says before pouring another mug.

"Nervous, sir?" Roman asks, and I blink several times, attempting to figure out if he is crazy and has lost his mind.

"Very. I don't know what they will do if we do not agree to go," Alwin says, before looking at me nervously.

The table goes still for a moment, right before Millie has a bottle brought to the table. "Um...Arlo and I have something we would like to announce," she says hesitantly. My eyes go to her stomach. "We are getting married and would like to have the wedding here," she says quickly. My chest finally releases the oxygen it was holding.

"Oh my gosh, Millie, that is amazing." I stand to hug her.

"So sorry about the timing, but could would that be okay?" Barnett and Wolf are both giving him their own side hug.

"Of course," Alwin says before striding out of the room.

Chapter 57

<u>Queen Serena Bloodworthy-Henry</u>

I knock on the door that leads to Alwin's private quarters, suddenly feeling unsure why I am knocking. "Come in, Serena." His voice is soft through the thick, white wood. His door has accents of gold and navy blue. I step into the dim room, not seeing him in the bedchamber. "In here," his voice calls to me from another room. I walk right into a dark room, and I almost have to squint to see.

My fae vision is good, but this onyx room is *dark*. The walls are dark, the tub is dark. The only light in here are the many candles littering all over.

"What's going through your head?" I ask as I make my way to the tub where Alwin sits. His tanned skin glows in the candlelight, his abs going all the way down to his navel. The weight he has lost is in favor of his lean body.

"My mind is currently on the way you are looking at me," he says as his fingers grip the lip of the tub. I lick my lips before telling him something I never thought I would admit to him.

"I don't think I'm ready." My eyes go down to the ground, and shame coats the inside of my throat.

"Look at me," he demands as his fingers grip my chin. I meet the gaze I had once hated, and now I seek out. "You don't ever have to again, if that's what you want. I could go the rest of my life without having sex with you, so long as you are happy and feel safe." His eyes plead with me to see the truth in his words. I nod, knowing he would do exactly that.

"I don't need forever, just a little bit," I claim, even though I have no idea how long I will need. I grab a cloth from beside the tub and dip it into the water before rubbing it on his back.

"Take the time you need to heal, take whatever you need from me...it's all yours anyway," he says as his head lolls backwards and hangs.

I grab onto the soap before spraying some water from my hand into his hair, and his head stays backwards. I scrub his scalp with my fingertips, and he leans into my touch.

"I had always wondered why you smelled so good. Your soap isn't from here, is it?" I ask. He opens his eyes, and man, his eyes are made directly from the Gods themselves.

"No," he responds, and I kneel down on the floor. My knees are on a thick cloth to protect them from the hard ground.

"What's on your mind?" I ask again after allowing him to soak for several minutes.

"I just don't understand what they think they can get from you going home. It doesn't make sense; no matter what, I will have my claim. They need you for something else, and I don't think they intend to allow you to come back here." He stands, giving me a glorious show of his package. He wraps himself in a towel before offering me his hand to help me off the ground.

"I don't know what they're planning, but if they have Evie and Juniper, I need to know." I stand chest to chest with him.

"I know, but if they have them, Serena..." He shakes his head.

"Don't say that. My parents may be some evil fae, but I have spoken to my mother before in a dream. She can't be that bad, can she?" Even as the words come out of my mouth, I know she could.

"What if we come up with our own deal?" I ask, interrupting his raging thoughts.

"What are you thinking?" He wraps his large arms around me, the scent of his soap engulfing me.

"Let's agree to *all* go there. I will help end the war, and I will bring my siblings home, and we will let them live there, as your parents rule." He eyes me narrowly. "He never said I had to end the war in favor of *them*. I read somewhere that a bargain is a bargain. If your parents are ruling Mirahalm and we rule here, I would feel fine with leaving the fae lands. Wouldn't you?" I know he has more to lose than I do. I never lived in Mirahalm; those were never my lands.

"I think that's a great idea. Trick the trickster."

We make it to bed, both passing out in old T-shirts. When my eyes open, I am in the middle of Sailor and Alwin. Barnett and Wolf are on the floor, and Roman stands at the door. "I didn't want to wake you all, but your brother— Oh, um..." Roman shifts uncomfortably. "I mean, *Cormac* wishes to speak with you."

When I get up, I have to tiptoe around all the bodies. Of course, right as I get out of bed, Alwin is already right on me, Sailor right behind him, stepping on Barnett. "Ouch," he hisses at Sailor. Sailor doesn't even give him an apology. Barnett then mumbles, "That was my arm."

Alwin doesn't look his way but says loudly enough to wake Wolf up, "Then don't sleep on the floor in my Gods' Blessed room." Barnett seems dumbfounded.

"What's happening?" Wolf asks.

"Cormac wants to speak with me." All of them stand up and head to the door.

"Just her," Roman informs them as a group.

"We heard you; I am his king while he is here. I am also the crown prince of Mirahalm. I will not be told where I can and cannot be," Alwin hisses. Roman takes a few steps away from Alwin. Smart man.

"I am going as her guard," Sailor says. Wolf and Barnett immediately agree. Roman rolls his eyes before mumbling something about how weird we all are.

I couldn't care less about how anybody views my relationship with Sailor and Alwin, my friendship with Barnett, and even my newly reforming relationship with Wolf. I know Wolf will show us we can trust him again. Since he is out of Magnolia's mind control games now, it should be easier for him to withstand her torments. She had been playing with his head in ways I didn't know were possible. The stories Sailor told me Wolf disclosed to him made my stomach churn with unease. I had no idea he was going through all of that during the trials.

"What's your plan?" I walk out of the room in my T-shirt before materializing a gown right on my body. My steps don't slow or falter; I walk right to where I know Cormac is. I can hear his proper voice from miles away; I want to scream at him. Tell him life isn't always fun and games. People and fae have feelings and matter more than he has ever viewed them. I hate that my family is on the wrong side of things. I hate that they started this war for power, coins, and greed. They want others to suffer so that they can have more. Well, not if I have anything to do with it. I may be their blood, but I am no longer anybody's but my own. I do not belong to a single soul.

"Well, other than me," Alwin chimes as he walks in step beside me. Sailor and Wolf take up the back, and Barnett on their heels.

"Not even you. I belong to myself; I loan my body and heart to you sometimes. If you're a good boy, that is," I taunt him. Alwin may be one of my more fun games.

"Don't forget your soul, that is on loan to me as well. I'll have it checked out forever," he adds on. Sometimes I forget that Alwin and Aldrich are not really the same; they are, but they are not. Alwin has responsibilities while Aldrich doesn't. He enjoys life in a way that Alwin can't. I see why he made Aldrich. I see why he tricked me. I love both versions of him.

"Do you have a plan?" Sailor asks from behind me.

"I'm more of a let's-roll-with-it kind of gal. So, let's roll until we can't roll any longer," I answer. Alwin sighs loudly, telling me exactly how he feels about my plan, but I feel pride coming from Wolf. Since finding out Magnolia had snared him in the woods that first day, I have been trying to forgive him. It's easier for me than it is for Sailor. I can say that I know my feelings for Wolf were always going to end as a friendship, maybe even a best friend.

"Then, let's do this." Barnett huffs. I know I have five strong males with me, but they also have a powerful female looking out for them. The most powerful thing in the kingdom isn't the one that's the biggest; it's the one with the most passion—the most desire to win—and I am hungry for this war to be done, for my loved ones to be safe. I will do anything to protect the ones I need to, to protect the ones who have no voice. I won't have another Mabel... I can't lose anybody else, and that desperation to keep them safe is what makes me truly dangerous. I don't care about my mother or father; they are not mine. Cormac or Magnolia do not matter to me. I can pretend to care until it is time to do what's right, though.

When we walk into the throne room—Cormac's choice since he won't eat the food here—Magnolia stands beside him in her fae form. I do wonder why her human form aged so poorly compared to Alwin's.

"It's because she uses more dark magic than I. I only use it for necessity, while she uses it for her fun and play. Her body can't keep up with it here."

Cormac stands poised and proper. His back is so rigid I almost feel like he has put a stick in his shirt and plastered it to himself to force his body to be this firm. I had once thought Wolf acted as if he wanted to be king with how he acted and spoke, the way his body moved like a royal, but of course, he doesn't hold a candle to Cormac.

"You wanted to see me?" I bring out my *play nice* voice. It's sweet, almost bitter, and high-pitched. Magnolia cringes in the most dramatic way possible.

"I did." His tone is clipped, as if he cannot stand to even speak to me. "I have given our last few conversations much thought, and I have come to a conclusion."

Alwin motions his hands for Cormac to continue. "We don't need theatrics. Let's get this over with, Cor," Alwins says, and that gets a chuckle from Barnett, then Wolf is elbowing him in the ribs.

"What? I'm not used to him being funny," Barnett says defensively while rubbing his side.

"He is *Aldrich*...you know that, right?" Sailor says, arching a brow. His eyebrows are darkening slightly from bright sunlight-blond to dusty-blond. You can see them more now; I like the darker.

"I know that, but they are still separate," Barnett says in a whisper. I look back, glaring at them.

"Hush," I scold them.

"Anywho, I believe I have a proper deal for you." Cormac steps up the stairs of the dais while Alwin and I take our seats. Sailor and Wolf stand at the back of our large throne. Barnett and Roman stand at the base. Magnolia follows Cormac.

"Okay," I urge him on, feeling as though he is trying to make this into a show.

"I have spoken with Mother and Father."

I nod before interpreting. "You went back to Mirahalm because you were hungry and needed Mommy to give you advice," I supply. His blue eyes darken slightly, the only sign of his anger.

"I went home, yes. Mother has given me two options for you, because she still finds some joy in having a daughter." I don't like the way this is going already. I can tell Alwin doesn't either because his knuckles are white, clenching onto the armrests of his throne. "I will set war here, in the human lands. I have somebody already waiting for the word to set everything here in flames. You may try to save it—you do have lots of elementals here—but the being I have holds far bigger power. The Gods gifted the fae stronger powers than humans for a reason. We are the better species." I clench my teeth, unwilling to respond.

"The other choice?" Alwin asks.

"The other one would be that you and whoever you want to bring back to Mirahalm come for one year. You would have one year to end the war once and for all with your dear sweet mate's line. Obliterate his mummy and daddy and any and all of their supporters. If you succeed, then your siblings, you, and anybody else you bring can come back to live out the rest of your years in the human lands."

Is he joking? I can't tell.

"Agree, Serena. When we get to Mirahalm, we can actually see the damage and come up with a plan. If anybody can play the games of the royal court, it is you," Alwin's voice booms throughout my silent thoughts. I don't know what to say.

"Some deal you have there. You intend to back me into a corner then?" I tilt my head, my crown almost falling off.

"I don't make deals with human sympathizers," he responds. I swallow any retort I would like to make.

"No, I see that you don't." Nothing I say will ever make them see that they are not better than anybody else. Humans have a wider range of emotions. "I think that your offer is kind, but I would like to suggest an alternative. I will go to Mirahalm with you. I will bring whomever I please, and we will all be safe and well cared for during our stay. I will do what I can to end the war, but you must give coins and food for my kingdom." I take a breath before continuing. "I have a week in my kingdom before we will be called to Mirahalm, and in that time, reinforcements will be sent here for us to divide out as we see fit." Cormac smiles as if he has won, then Magnolia steps forward.

"You will fight for your family in the war," she declares.

"Yes, I will fight for my family," I agree right away.

"Deal. We will keep your human pets until you arrive to tend to them."

I want to ask about Nolan and Clara, but I don't want to give them away if they are safe somewhere.

"I am glad you have agreed. I had already picked out which village I was going to have burned. It would have been pretty, but we will save that fun for when you get home."

Home. My home is wherever my family is.

"I have one more request." My voice bellows throughout the room. "I need Wolf's sisters from your pet." I tilt my head towards Magnolia. "If you do not agree, I will go to war against you right here and now. And we will see who the better fighter is in our line." My voice is commanding, regal.

"No way." Magnolia shuts it down right away, but Cormac grips her throat hard. Her face turns red immediately.

"Give them up. Now. If you want a marriage with me, you will do as I say," he threatens.

Whoa, a marriage? That's why she betrayed her family then. She thinks she can gain more power that way. Fae are like that, it seems...greedy and power hungry.

"I want them back, alive and well. Today." Wolf's heartbeat is so fast it sounds like a hummingbird. Sailor's pride hits me so strongly I almost smile, but I keep my stoic mask on.

"Fine," Magnolia concedes before leaving. She rubs her throat as she makes her way out of the throne room. Wolf leaves on her heels. Sailor follows as well, then Barnett and Roman.

"You don't trust her, do you?" Cormac asks with a slight chuckle.

"I do not," I concede.

"For good reason, she is a good and loyal fae. You wouldn't know anything about that, seeing as though you are bonded to a fae who left his parents to die in a war he helped create." Alwin growls, showing his teeth, his canines lengthening slightly.

"Watch your mouth, Cor. You were just a babe during that time; let's not speak about your mother forsaking her own flesh and blood for power," Alwin says, disgust licking his words.

I feel as though I should be more hurt from that, but I feel numb to it. When Cormac steps towards me aggressively, I flinch. I have flashbacks from the cabin. Alwin notices the difference in my posture, but so does Cormac. My body trembles slightly from fear, and I hate that Cormac sees it. Alwin steps protectively in front of me.

"Oh, I had always thought because of your powers, you would be the stronger twin. It seems as though your time in the human lands has caused you so much trouble, you may not be a threat to me after all. Maybe once this war is over, I will take both lands as you had intended to," Cormac taunts. Alwin blasts white-hot lava at the male. He blinks away, the place he was standing in melting away before my eyes.

"Are you alright?' Alwin cups my face. I nod frantically.

"It just—" I gulp, swallowing the bile rising in my throat. "The way he came at me. I-I don't know why it affected me," I stammer, unsure why it did that to me. I can fight for myself, so why was I so scared?

"Serena, we can do this, okay?" His eyes are the softest they have ever been, and for one moment, they are blue. It's a very deep and dark blue, but blue nonetheless.

"I trust you," I mutter the words that, at one point in my life, I wouldn't have ever said to him. But he is my family, and I will fight alongside him.

Chapter 58

Four Days Later

Millie is wearing a gown the seamstress created just for her. The gown hugs her curves in all the right places. The bodice is a second skin for her; the pure white looks amazing against her bronze skin. Her short brown hair is down in small waves, pearls braided into it. I stand with pink flowers, bundled with some pastel colors, all in a large bouquet. It's evening and the breeze is just right...thanks to the elementals she threatened if the weather wasn't perfect.

Everybody is in attendance, save for Wolf. His sisters are in the infirmary, and he hasn't left their side since finding them. We have no idea where Magnolia had them, but they weren't in great shape. The younger one, Isabella, was in slightly better condition. The older one, Katherine, hasn't spoken a word since being found. Alwin sits front row, right next to Sailor. Barnett stands on Arlos's side in a tan suit that looks awful on his body, but Millie forced him, saying, "The bubblegum pink Serena has to wear will look Gods-awful against any other color." So, Barnett had to pick between tan and cotton-candy blue.

I look out into the crowd, not sure where all of our futures are going to take us, but knowing they are all worth saving. They are all worth going to war for. Nobody ever deserves to be held captive like I had been, and I will fight to the death to ensure they never will be.

Millie and Arlo have the most profound wedding vows. Tears stream happily down my face as I listen to them promise forever to one another. Alwin and Sailor both stare at me in awe, me in return at them. I can easily say that I love them both for different reasons. I know this will have to end sometime, but for now, I will cherish them.

Millie grabs Arlo's face in a far-too-long kiss, but people cheer for them; people I have never met before. Millie, it turns out, is very personable. She could make friends with a rock. Getting her out of her village and into a more open and welcoming space is exactly what she needed. When we walk to the reception area, Alwin hangs back to speak with a royal advisor I have never seen. He is a younger man, from what Alwin just told me, and he is strong, too.

"It was a pretty wedding, huh?" Sailor eyes me, his gaze gliding down my body like butter on warm toast.

"The prettiest. Much better than mine," I joke. He cringes slightly, and I push his shoulder a little playfully. "I'm serious, I am glad she picked a little bit more extravagant day. She deserves the happiness, so does he." I say, because it was far better than mine. He runs his hand through his blond hair.

"I have something I would like to do, will you go with me?" Sailor asks softly. Millie steps onto a small stage that she must have had built just for this event. Her wedding is over-the-top, but everything she deserves. She has a long, slim glass in her hands, and she holds it up as servers bring everybody a matching one.

"Thank you," I murmur. Sailor takes one, too.

"Hello, everybody." Her voice is loud already, but when she speaks, it seems to draw everybody's attention to her. "I wanted to thank you all for coming to our wedding." She motions between her and Arlo. The guests in attendance all hold their glasses high. "Today wouldn't have been possible without our beloved queen, Serena Bloodworthy- Henry. Thank you for saving my life during the trials. Thank you for every moment after that, too." Eyes turn to me, and my face heats with the attention. Also, with the announcement of my new name. I added Henry because Alwin is my mate. I can't pretend otherwise anymore. We are going to Mirahalm together; we'll be pretending together. But I need to accept reality. "Our queen has sacrificed much for us, and she will keep doing so to keep us safe. We do not deserve her, but we will always be loyal to her. So, I want to raise a glass, not only for my new marriage but also for our queen, my best friend, and our savior," she declares.

My heart thumps so hard I swear people can see it pumping in my chest. I gulp down the bubbly before Sailor leans down while grabbing my hand in his. "Ready?" His breath smells minty and fresh. I look into his bright ice-blue eyes and nod. Not knowing what I am agreeing to, but also knowing if it involves Sailor, I will always say yes.

"Lead the way." I wave my hand in front of me.

"Actually, will you blink us into the village?"

My brows raise comically before I grab onto his hand and do exactly what he says to do.

We end up in the middle of the palace village. "Now where?" I ask, feeling confused. He smirks at me, a smirk that tells me he is up to no good. We walk right into the tavern I had been in, not that many months ago. I follow behind Sailor, my hand in his. I notice the man in the black hood, and I know just what Sailor is doing.

"Hello." The man eyes both of us and nods towards me.

"Hi." I smile, not sure what Sailor wants. I can't get a tattoo...my power will heal it.

"Thanks for meeting us on such short notice." Sailor slaps down his coins, then waves the barkeep over. "Two whiskeys," he calls out.

"*Nervous, darling?*" I taunt him. He hands me a glass, then clinks them together.

"Never when we are together, no matter what is thrown at us, Serena. We will come out on top together or not at all. These are my vows to you. I know you didn't get to have a wedding like you would have liked, but this is all I can give you." I watch him in awe. "I know you wouldn't have wanted what she got today, but you also didn't want what you and Alwin had either. I just want my own permanent reminder that I am yours always. You may not fully be mine, but I am yours. There are no others and never will be. This is it for me. *You* are it for me." He shrugs his shoulders, then kisses me. The kiss is passionate; he opens up the kiss with his tongue until the man clears his throat.

"Can we get started?" His gruff voice sounds uncomfortable.

I chuckle slightly, then murmur, "Sorry." Sailor sits down, and I watch. He must have already told the man what he wanted because when the male gets started, they don't speak. Instead, Sailor and I talk.

"Do you think Juniper and Evie are okay?" I no longer watch the man tattooing Sailor. I want a surprise. Sailor thinks about my question for a moment before answering me.

"I think your brother is a force to be reckoned with, and he will protect your sister with everything he has."

I nod, without truly knowing what I am nodding to. "But do you think the leaders of Clove were always evil? I mean, I just don't know how I didn't see the darkness in them when I saw them." I sit dumbfounded. Feeling betrayed but also not surprised. I have been reading the book Alwin gave me. Fae are not by nature truthful; they are greedy and want anything that will make them more powerful. I wonder if spending so much time in human lands has helped Alwin. I hope it has, and he doesn't have something sinister up his sleeve.

I sigh before continuing. "I think Juni will play it safely. I think he is too smart to get hurt; I also think that my mother is smart enough to know I will not help her if she harms them," I say, needing it to be true.

"I agree. I think your brother has a brain on him that is built from years of fighting with *somebody*..." Sailor drawls the last word. "He is going to be fine, and he would kill anybody who looked sideways at Evie. I have no idea about Clove or the leaders. When I was there, they were kind. I think that we have a lot of issues at hand, and you can't figure them all out yourself. You need to delegate some of that, Honeybee." He sips on another whiskey.

After two hours, Sailor finally stands and looks at his left arm. "You just had to outdo me, huh?" I taunt him while looking at his new tattoos. He has a thin line on his ring finger, a honeybee on his bicep, and a tilted black crown to the side of the bee.

"I don't know...I think I like the ink. I may do more later. You think the fae have tattoos that will give me more magic?" he asks sarcastically, and I smile. A true smile, not a half-hearted one, not a pity one, but a real one.

"I don't know, I guess we will see in a few days, won't we?" I ask cheerfully.

Sailor grabs my hand outside of the tavern, and we blink back to the full-blown party that's happening. He leans down and presses a hot kiss to my cheek; I lean into it. "I guess we will see," he agrees.

When we walk back into the party, everybody is clearly drunk. They are all dancing; even Wolf has made an appearance on the dance floor. Alwin sits at a table alone. I make my way to him, Sailor making his way to Wolf. They may not call each other brothers anymore, but at least there is some friendship now. Understanding, maybe. It will take a long while for complete trust and forgiveness, but I know they will both work on it.

"Enjoying yourself?" I eye the mug in Alwin's hands. His black regal outfit looks dashing on him, beyond dapper. I lick my lips and swallow just from looking at my mate.

"I was not...now I am, though." His black eyes shine with something I don't want to put a name on yet.

"Why is that?" I take the mug from him and sip on the amber liquid in it. I choke a little before he takes the mug from me and draws me into his lap. I wrap an arm around his neck.

"I don't know if you know this about me or not, but I do not enjoy people in general. I am their king, yes. I will fight for them now because you wish it, but just because my family, other than my sister that is, are on the right side of this war doesn't mean I like to spend time with them." He tilts his head towards the dancing crowd. He sips on his drink, not even seemingly fazed by the taste. I am still trying to swallow, attempting to get the bitter taste from my mouth. "I do this for you; I would rather have a backstage presence. I wasn't raised like most fae are. You will see that when we make it to Mirahalm. That's the reason for the war. My parents do not believe the fae ways are warranted in this day and time. Your parents disagreed." His eyes darken, clearly remembering something. "We will talk about it later; I just need you to know that I will not allow harm to come to you. So, if we have to end the war, we will do so no matter what, to keep you safe. I care about our people as long as you are safe, but your life means more to me than anything else."

Alwin stands, his hands gripping my waist while pulling me to a standing position as well. His gaze softens when it lands on me. "Let's dance, shall we?" His eyes shine with mischief. I take his hand, and we join the dance floor. Sweaty bodies dance all around us, and Alwin growls at anybody that so much as glances at me, but when Sailor makes his way towards us, Alwin allows him to. I sway between the large males, feeling totally and completely in love and safe. We spend the night dancing and drinking, and end up all three together in Alwin's large four-poster bed.

Chapter 59

<u>*Queen Serena Bloodworthy-Henry*</u>

"You know what you need to do, right?" I ask Millie for the hundredth time in the last few days.

"Yes, Serena. We know what we need to do." She rolls her hands before putting them on her hips.

"No attitude. I need to hear you say it," I chastise her.

Arlo steps up next to her. "We are to spend our honeymoon in Clove, searching for everybody you saved from Magnolia, and your siblings' spouses," he says begrudgingly. I nod, encouraging him to keep going.

"Yes, and?" I urge him on.

"Everybody we find, we bring back to the palace because Clove is now enemy territory...unless we think we can kill them all." Arlo, it turns out, goes to killing way too fast.

"No—" I start, but Sailor's chuckling comes from behind me.

"Serena, he is kidding." Sailor narrows his eyes on the guard.

"I'm not, but okay." He shrugs before going on. "Okay, fine, we just save them and bring them here. Easy enough." Arlo holds his hands up in surrender.

Alwin stands next to his sister; they stand right on the cliff where she just appeared an hour ago. Her hair billows in the wind, her bloodred dress blows. Her ears are on full display, and she looks every bit the threat I have always known she is. The fact that she has enough power to control Alwin to a degree is scary. She continues to smile at me in a way that promises a fight will break out.

I look to where Wolf stands. "Now you." His eyes stray to Magnolia, and I know the look in his eyes far too well. It's the reason I wake up in cold sweats. It's the reason why I have two men in my bed, and I still am scared to be taken against my will again. It is the reason I vomit uncontrollably when I even think about ever having sex again. I don't know if I will heal myself with time or if I may never be touched like that again. But I know the look in his eyes far too well. I grab onto his hand and tighten my hold on it. "It's okay," I whisper, and send warm and happy emotions into his body. My father may have always told me to never interfere with others' minds because it's too invasive, but I have learned a valuable lesson. People are too fragile not to help, that's why, when I can, I send happiness to anybody I feel needs some.

"I am to rule in your stead. I am to keep the palace and kingdom safe while you are gone."

"And?" I urge him on, too.

"And the little girls in Groke are getting all new clothes, gowns, and crowns."

Tears sting my eyes for no reason. Sailor draws me into his side, then Wolf hugs me tightly. Barnett follows suit, and shockingly enough, Roman, the man of few words, hugs us as well.

"I will do my best, Serena. Thank you for trusting me with this. I know you didn't have to. I have my mental shields intact, and everything is going to be okay until you get home. I will continue the programs you guys set in place and will send men out to follow through with our plans." Wolf repeats what I have been instilling into him for days.

Every village will be getting a resource room, which will be fully stocked with things each village needs. Some only a few things, while others aren't doing as well. As their queen, I will not allow them to suffer without things that they need to live.

Wolf looks me in the eyes. "We will be okay," he assures me in his proper commander voice, and I remember the man I once met in Darnish and believe him.

"I know we will be." Knowing this isn't about the villages, this is about me and him.

"Ready?" Magnolia asks. I am not. But I will have to be.

"We are," Alwin confirms for the group of us going to Mirahalm. Barnett steps forward, then Roman, Sailor, and me. Wolf yanks Sailor into a tight hug.

"Come back to me, brother. I can't live without you."

Sailor pats Wolf's back. "I will miss you, too, brother." I can feel the hurt in Sailor when he says the last word, but I know he wants to mean it.

"Come *home*," Wolf repeats.

"Take care of home," Sailor replies.

Magnolia clears her throat. "Let's go." Her harsh tone hisses through everybody's mood. Alwin stands sharply, arms crossed over his chest.

"You ready to go home?" he asks me as I come to stand at the cliffside. My toes dangle over the jagged rocks.

"How do we know she isn't just going to send us somewhere where we will die?" I ask the question that everybody is thinking.

"We don't, but we know your family will make her wish for death if she harms you," Alwin assures me.

Magnolia watches our interaction with curiosity in her eyes. "Alrighty then." I can tell she is used to years of being in charge; Alwin gave her too long a leash. It's going to be a shock to her system going to Mirahalm, where she is a betrayer, even to her own family. "All you have to do is link arms, and Cormac already opened the vortex for us. Just jump." She motions to the sea below the hundred-foot drop. The rocks are sharp at the bottom. If you miss the water, you are dead on impact.

"Are you kidding?" Barnett's fear clogs my throat. I look at him and send some warm love into his body. His tight body relaxes some, but not enough.

"I am serious, sadly. Why are you coming again?" She narrows her eyes at him and Roman.

"They are with me, and I was told I could bring anybody," I say sharply.

"I don't think Cor knew you would bring so many playthings," she says in disgust. I send jolts of pain to her. She drops her brother's hand right away, clutching her head tightly. "Ah. You bitch. Stop." She hisses as bright red blood seeps from her nose. I increase pressure. Alwin sends pride into my system. Finally, I pull back slightly.

"I don't find you funny, Magnolia. If you touch them or harm them in any way, I will kill you," I warn her before taking the pain away completely.

"Alrighty then." Sailor tries to take some of the tension away.

"Let's just get this over with," Magnolia says harshly. We all grab hands, and for the last time, I look behind me at the kingdom I have lived in. The place I have called home for my entire life. I watch Millie hug Arlo, and Wolf stands stoically. I wink at him, just as he did to me once.

"We will be back, and we will heal what has been broken. See you later, Wolf." I smirk at him.

Then I am being dragged over the cliffside. Barnett screams, my hair is flying everywhere, including in my face. We all drop, our hands still locked together. We pass the water level, and right as I brace for impact, nothing happens, as if we are floating through space. It's completely dark once we go below sea level. Tiny light specks float around us, and my body feels as if it weighs nothing at all. I look to Alwin, and he looks like a God.

His black, wavy hair is floating as if in water, though we are not. He winks at me and tightens his grip on my hand. I squeeze right back before our bodies finally thud onto hard, solid ground.

Chapter 60

When we hit the ground, I can already feel the difference. Mirahalm. Home. Or at least, this would have been home to me, had my mother not traded my life. She gave me away to give herself a better chance at a living relative if my brother were to be killed. I try not to think about the sting of that betrayal. Knowing I am completely disposable to her.

I look around at the field we landed in, not knowing remotely where we are. Alwin seems to know exactly where we are, though. His body is tense and tight. I sit up on my ankles before Sailor reaches a hand out to help me up. "Where are we?" I ask out loud, noticing Barnett vomiting. Roman's rubbing small circles on his back, and I almost wonder if something might be happening between them.

"We are home, darling." Alwin walks right up to Sailor and me, looking directly into our eyes. "Mirahalm is not like Nymphamera. Stay by me." He includes Sailor in the statement.

"Alright," I agree, but Sailor doesn't. I elbow him in the ribs hard enough for him to mumble his agreement.

"Okay, yeah, sure."

Magnolia doesn't stop walking when she calls over her shoulder, "Come on, or else you'll be eaten. Mirahalm doesn't have a magic village for its monsters; they just walk around." Her voice is sugary-sweet. We all follow behind her. I run my hands through the tall, greenish grass. It's so soft and wavy, it looks like we are walking through water because the grass blows in waves. It stands about knee-length for me. In the distance, I see some cottages. They look similar to those back home, but also not. None of them have doors of any sort. Some of them look burnt down and torn to nothing. As we make our way through the tall grass, I notice I don't see any fae walking around.

We make it onto the dirt pathway. "We will meet Cormac here any minute. They must have felt us enter," Magnolia says, but I am too focused on my body. Just being here has me feeling more powerful than I have ever felt. My powers feel right at my fingertips. As if living in the human lands muted them slightly, being here, I can feel them at the ready. It seems as if I could be a God. The power like an endless stream.

"That is where you and I differ from the others, darling; no other fae are like us. I don't know why the Gods blessed us more than others, but they did. Our families may be fae, but they are weaker than we are. Remember that even though we are outnumbered, they need you," Alwin says firmly.

"Why does it feel like this?" I watch Sailor help Barnett and Roman through the grass. I stand side by side with Alwin.

"Because The Gods created different worlds. I have heard rumors of dragons, vampires, or even werewolves." My mind whirls with all the possibilities. "There is a God King who created all these different worlds for the species to each have their place in his universe. The Gods felt bad for humans, so they gave them each a power, just to help out a little. The fae got angry when they encountered some humans that got through the vortex and made it into Mirahalm somehow." I listen carefully.

"So, they teleported throughout the realms?" I ask, trying to follow.

"Yes, they somehow did. You know how sometimes, when you blink somewhere, you don't always land where you are supposed to?" Alwin kicks a rock as if bored with this conversation.

"I do. It's happened many times to me."

His eyes light up. "Me too," he agrees, and I try to picture the king, Alwin, the strongest male I know, making a mistake. "So, anyway, the fae realized that the Gods granted powers to humans and got angry. They figured out how to portal into the human lands and started to take them for themselves."

My mouth opens wide, and Alwin chuckles before shutting my mouth with his hand. "Keep that closed, the bugs here will lay eggs in your throat." My face distorts in revulsion.

"Sick," I say, louder than I intended.

He nods his head. "Yes, *sick*. It will make you puke for days," he informs me. My entire body shakes before I try to erase that image from my head. "Anyway, the fae started bringing people here...they made them into workers of sorts." I stop walking.

"Like slaves," I say in disgust.

"Yes. Then they realized that some lesser fae are just as powerful as some people, so their value in our kingdom was next to nothing. And that is what started the war, our kind were basically long living humans. Your parents wanted slaves, mine knew it was wrong and wanted to step up and help."

Magnolia is in front of us, but far enough that she can't hear us if she isn't paying attention.

"Most fae are greedy and tricksters by nature, but half our kingdom thinks that freedom should be something everybody has. Not based on the power you have running through your body." he says. "My mother has a claim on the throne—she is a second cousin of the last king. Your family has a bigger claim than mine, but when my parents saw what was happening, they couldn't sit back any longer."

I take in the village that we are standing in, the rubble, really. I listen intently to my mate.

"I was still young, well...*fae* young. Magnolia was a babe. I decided that since I am stronger than my parents, I would stake my claim instead. My mother didn't want to risk me like that, not so publicly at least. So when she found out your mother was pregnant and had left for the human lands to leave her baby, I was sent to retrieve you." Magnolia turns her head towards us, as if listening in now. Alwin doesn't seem to mind, though. "I confronted your mother. Even though she claimed she was still pregnant, I knew something wasn't right, so when we left, I came back."

Magnolia walks up to us. "Are you telling her the story, brother?" she sneers.

"I am," he assures her before continuing. "I came back and couldn't find you. I couldn't sense anything, so I came home and for years stayed and fought in the war."

Cormac blinks in. Sailor is right on us now. Barnett is being pulled behind him and Roman. "We will finish this later," Alwin tells me, then says into my head. *"Long story short, my parents sent me back when we felt the power surge strike hard when your powers came in. We all felt it, but your mother had put a charm on you, so I couldn't directly find you. I appointed myself king and made them all believe I had been their king for years. My parents sent Maggie whenever the war here got too bad. She saw more than I did. That's why she is the way she is."*

Cormac walks up to the group. He looks around, and his nose wrinkles in disgust at Barnett, Sailor, and Roman. "Ready?" He claps his hands together.

"We are. Are my siblings safe?" I look around at the village we are standing in to show him I know how they treat people here.

"Your friends are being treated better than they were with our allies in Clove," Cormac says sternly.

"Then let's go see them." I slam my hand into his hand hard, hoping it might hurt him enough to cause fear. He doesn't seem bothered by it. We all link hands together, and I look to Cormac. "Are you powerful enough to teleport all of us?" I use the most menacing voice I can muster.

"Do dragons fly?" he volleys back.

"I don't know, I haven't ever met one," I respond. I can feel irritation flaring from his body.

"They do, and I am." Then we are gone.

Chapter 61

<u>Queen Serena Bloodworthy-Henry</u>

When we land, we are standing in one of the most gorgeous gardens I have ever seen in my life. I had thought Alwin's garden at the palace was perfect, but it was nothing compared to this. Sprawling flowers and willow trees line the walls of a white palace. There is a moat surrounding the outside with two different bridges leading into the palace. Each bridge has unnatural vines all over the stone. The grass smells fresh and overwhelm-ingly nice.

"It's magic," Alwin says, confirming my suspicions. "Your mother has lots of workers. She wants it to always look and smell decent, as if she believes it will make her people happier. People die if it isn't to her liking," Alwin says nonchalantly.

"Oh, let's not be dramatic. They would die no matter what," Cormac chirps while crossing one of the bridges. The water in the moat isn't still, but runs in one direction. She must have water fae tend to it every moment to make it run like that.

"They don't *have* to die," Alwin says sharply. Cormac continues until we reach a large, rich brown door. It's arched in a way that reminds me of a fairy tale. There are balconies coming from each room...this place is like my storybooks.

"*You* came here to kill. Do not forget that, young prince," Cormac says, and hatred blasts from Alwin.

"Do not forget I am older than you, and already a king," Alwin growls, teeth on full display. Cormac stiffens slightly before Magnolia comes to walk beside him, brushing her arm against his. I roll my eyes and gag myself. Barnett chuckles at me, and Roman gives him a look. When we pass through the doors, I realize quickly that this is a castle. I live in a palace, which is not this. My palace is small compared to this. My palace could hold entire villages, but this castle? It can hold entire *realms*.

There are gold accents all over the white marble walls, as well as many portraits of various fae. I stop dead in my tracks when my eyes land on a portrait of my family. My mother, father, and Cormac. They look happy, and the title card below reads *The Royal Family*. I don't know why my heart hurts seeing that. When Sailor grabs my arm, I flinch. He quickly takes his hand off my arm and takes a step back.

"I am sorry." Sailor's eyes soften.

Alwin rushes over, pushing Sailor out of the way. "I am fine. I'm sorry. I was just looking at family portraits."

Cormac smirks at my discomfort. "Yes, that is one of my favorites. One of my favorite quotes, though, is the one where history says you died," Corman says smugly.

Sailor clocks him so fast and hard that Cormac's head hits the wall. Magnolia screeches before she tries to attack Sailor, and Alwin freezes her on the spot.

"You listen and listen damn good," he says with a growl in Magnolia's face. "I have allowed you to live, even with all of your sick games, because you are my sister. But I promise you, I will kill you faster than you can blink if you ever charge at her again," he says, and then unfreezes her.

"I wasn't going after her," she hisses.

"*He* is hers and therefore is an extension of her. Do not harm her or whomever she claims." The fury coming off of Alwin causes even the fae guards to pause.

"Everything okay, prince?" one of them asks Cormac, I realize. He rubs the back of his head like a little baby before responding.

"Yes, tell Mother and Father I have brought her." The guard nods before having a not-so-private conversation, but only because I eavesdrop on it. He warns about watching over us. They think we are uncivilized, but they haven't seen anything yet. Alwin comes to me, Sailor standing next to me.

"You okay?" Worry coats his features.

"I am. I am sorry, I just saw the painting."

Sailor stops me there. "No, do not say sorry, Serena. I shouldn't have grabbed onto you without you seeing it was me; that's my fault." Sailor takes all the blame. I shake my head, then Sailor looks at Alwin. He smirks at him. "It would seem as though you, King, have grown fond of me," Sailor teases Alwin.

Alwin regards Sailor with as much kindness as one might a puppy, then slips a mask on. "I like you enough to keep you alive," Alwin responds. Which is saying a lot considering the fact that Sailor is my lover. The words are bitter in my mind. Sailor is more than that, but also, he isn't. I am more to him, sure, but he cannot be more to me.

We follow Cormac, Magnolia trailing right on his heels like an eager puppy. The massive hallways open up to multiple stories. The open space makes it seem endless. There are walkways that some fae wander around on. Just a floor above us, some of them point and whisper. They don't know who I am, but they do whisper about who we might be. I do notice there are humans here, but they are prisoners. I soon realize that they were stolen from their homes. Those Brabble monsters were fae...stealing humans to bring them here. There are even some children among them.

We make our way through the hallways, and I wonder how many people they have stolen and brought here.

"They don't mind it." Cormac notices my gaze.

"How could you know that? Did you ask them that before you stole them?" My voice is as sharp as the sword strapped to Roman's back.

"They live much longer here; their power is stronger, the food is better. The overall life quality is better," Cormac responds as if I should have just known that.

"But what about the ones who don't want to be here? Do you send them back?" I ask pointedly. We make it to a very large set of doors that gleam gold.

"No." He confirms only what I already knew.

"Exactly, you steal them away from their lives for your own benefit," I say with disdain. His face turns pink from anger, and the guards at the door interrupt us.

"Are you ready, Prince?" They don't even look at me. I also do not wear a crown like he does, though. Neither does Alwin.

Cormac's crown is brown, with thin, stick-like pieces on it. Green metal leaves are woven throughout it, and some of the branches on his crown have long white flower petals. I want to laugh; he is no prince. He has no idea how to treat people with respect. He has no idea how to treat his people at all. I would argue that I had a better childhood to learn exactly how to rule people.

"Give me a moment," Cormac says harshly. The guards nod curtly. "Leave," he demands of Barnett and Roman. Maybe even Sailor, but Sailor won't leave.

"And where do you want them to go?" I ask sharply.

"The dungeon, perhaps." Cormac shrugs. Magnolia laughs bitterly.

"Absolutely not." My response is immediate.

"I was just kidding with you; they will be taken up to your wing. It was made when Mother was pregnant with us. She kept it in case you ever decided to come home to us. It was pathetic, really, but Father allowed it." Two human girls walk up and grab them, but Sailor doesn't leave. "Your pet needs to leave," Cormac says right as he sees Sailor plant his feet firmly on the floor. Sailor shows his teeth.

"Do not insult him," I say between my own teeth. Cormac's eyes narrow on me in challenge. Alwin steps in, as does Sailor, even though I can fight my own battles. They know it, as do I.

"Listen here, little sister." His nickname grinds my wheels. "I have no idea why the Gods made this grave error, but I assure you, I have the resources to take you down if you step out of line. So, you should listen to me carefully. We will play nicely together, you will do what is asked of you, and then you will leave intact. You will treat me with respect when here, because I am to be king. You won't ever take that from me. Do you understand me?" he asks coldly.

Then I feel it. The strong urge to go inside to the very sound and scent I know all too well. When I try to sidestep him, he stops me. I freeze when his hand hits my arm.

"Understood?" His voice sounds in my ears, but I can't hear his words. I hear Haadgar's, I hear Mabel's screams. I clench my eyes shut and focus on something else. "Hello?" Cormac tries again. Alwin shoves him off me and against the door. "What the hell happened to you there?" Cormac hisses. Magnolia studies her nails, as if she is bored.

"Nothing happened to her, you hear me?" Alwin's voice pierces through my thoughts. I open my eyes and see only his eyes.

"You are with me, and we are safe," he reassures me. I take a deep and long breath.

"You are here, and I am not there." I repeat it over and over again.

I look to Cormac. "You do not command me. Let me make that clear. Nothing is wrong with me other than the fact I haven't killed you yet." Cormac's face pales, and Magnolia stops investigating her nails as if something magical might come from them. "You are alive because I am unwilling to kill you...yet. But you better believe this—you are not my family. *They* are." I point towards the doors that separate me from Juniper and Evie. I then point towards Sailor and Alwin. "They are what matter to me, not you. So, remember that the next time you want to insult me or them. Remember that I may not be a normal fae, but I am just as protective of them. And I have baggage to carry around that I can easily chuck at you if need be," I threaten.

Cormac seems to understand that I will kill him if he missteps enough, so he nods to the guards at the door. They also step several feet back from me.

"Why are they acting scared?" I ask as we wait for the doors to open.

"Because you feel different to them, more powerful. They know you are not like them." Alwin grabs my hand, and Sailor steps behind us. The doors open, and my eyes go to Juniper and Evie immediately.

I don't even look at the two massive thrones that sit on top of the dais; I do not wait for them to announce us. I let go of Alwin's hand and blink right to where my siblings are pressed into the ground by guards. The guards' eyes widen slightly before I blow wind into them, shoving them away from my siblings.

"Evie." I drop down onto my knees and hug my sister. Her belly is so swollen I almost can't reach all the way around her.

"Serena. You're here," she whispers, tears streaming down her face.

"Of course, I am. I wouldn't leave you two here alone." I pull away, meeting Juniper's gaze. His eyes are blazing red and orange.

"You shouldn't have come." His voice is stern. He seems rigid in a way that tells me things might not have been so good for them. We will have time to catch up, but that time is not now. Alwin and Sailor are right at my back, as if following me to keep a safe distance from those who sit in their thrones.

"We will have time to catch up soon," I promise them both. Juniper stands since the guards aren't holding them down on the floor anymore. I help Evie up; she can barely stand because of her large belly. *"Where are Clara and Nolan?"*

Juniper answers me. *"The wolf pack kept them hidden. They are in Clove."* Relief floods my system.

"Good, I have Arlo and Millie going to retrieve them. They will be in safe hands," I promise him, knowing they are going to be in much better shape there than here. *"Have you been taken care of?"* I know eyes are pointed at me, so I ignore them for a few more moments. I hug my brother. The first hug in such a long time.

"No worse off than that time you forced us to go camping and it rained the entire time," Juniper says sarcastically. *"Oh, and I am married. Clara and I had a wolf pack wedding, and I am an official member of their pack."*

My eyes widen slightly. *"So, commander training is a no-go anymore?"*

A throat clears, and I turn to meet the very eyes I know I have seen before.

Chapter 62

Queen Serena Bloodworthy-Henry

I look to see a regal queen and king sitting on their thrones. Their son, the promised prince, stands beside his mother. They appear as though they are the perfect family. I walk a few steps away from my found family. Sailor stays with them, ready to attack anybody who would dare harm my siblings. Alwin trails beside me. I know whatever my next move may be, he will support it tenfold. Even if it gets us killed.

I grind my teeth down, unable to stop myself from saying something I might regret.

"Hello, daughter." My mother's voice sounds so sweet. I almost forget that she has caused a war in which thousands have died. So many have been stolen as well, as I have been before.

"Hello," I say softly.

"It is wonderful to finally meet you," my mother says sweetly.

"I thought you were dead," I answer back. My father's hands tighten on the armrests of his throne.

"I knew you were not," she responds back to me. I tilt my head and feel Alwin stiffen beside me.

"How would you know that? I thought you could just sense my powers. I didn't realize you could see me from other realms," I say harsher than I intend to.

"You think that I would send you there without a guard? Somebody to watch you closely?" Her voice gives nothing away.

My heart hammers in my chest. Then my pulse quickens when I see brown eyes I know far too well. "You had somebody watching me," I say while looking into the eyes I know have betrayed me.

"I did. I figured you were smart enough to know and figure it out. But you never did, did you? I sent clues for you. Then I thought surely you would kill Alwin Henry." She says the words with venom in her tone. My father's face turns red with anger. "When he called for those silly trials. I thought you would be smarter than that. Imagine my surprise when my spy told me you never figured it out. That you lived the life I gave you in hiding with that man I thought would be good for you. For you to see how weak humans truly are." Her youthful face furrows in discomfort. Juniper's rage heats my back, the room suddenly feeling far too small for us.

I cannot take my eyes from the man I have known my entire life.

"I thought you witnessing their weakness would be good for you when you came home and realized they deserve the lives we give them. They should bow to us. Instead, can you picture the disappointment when he came home to tell me you love them? Every time he would bring news to me, I just couldn't believe it. My daughter, my flesh and blood, loves humans? More than just in a pet way, like a dog. I couldn't believe it, Serena." I gulp down the large amount of betrayal I feel. "Don't fret, though, dear girl, I will show you our ways. We have a year together after all, and who knows, when you kill the weak links, I believe you will see our ways." Her venomous voice pierces through my mind.

I don't say anything back to the woman speaking, and I don't even look at her any longer. My hurt gaze lingers on the man standing at the base of the dais with his wife in tow. Fully alive.

"Hello, Mr. Benson." My voice is hollow and devoid of life. Because in what realm is he evil? "Mrs. Benson."

I nod my head and turn to leave the throne room. Alwin, Juniper, Evie, and Sailor all follow me to our prison.

About the Author

Abby Moore was born and raised in a small town in Oklahoma, the youngest of four siblings. From an early age, she learned how to find adventure in the world around her. It wasn't until twenty years later that she discovered books could hold adventures too, and that realization opened the door to a lifelong passion for storytelling.

As she began reading and writing, Abby found herself drawn to the kinds of stories she had once wished for as a child—stories where the characters didn't have to be perfect. Where they weren't always skinny or healthy. Where they went through real, often difficult experiences and still found strength, hope, and purpose.

Now, as a parent, Abby is inspired by her own children to create characters young readers can see themselves in. Her mission is to write books that not only entertain but offer a safe haven for those navigating a sometimes challenging world. Through her work, she hopes to show that while life isn't always easy, the pages of a story can be a place of healing, discovery, and belonging.